BANG GANG

International Bestselling Author

J A D E   W E S T

Cover design by Letitia Hasser of RBA Designs
http://designs.romanticbookaffairs.com/
Edited by John Hudspith www.johnhudspith.co.uk
All enquiries to jadewestauthor@gmail.com

First published 2016

For Maria

Maria, an incredible friend and a wonderful mother.
You're an inspiration – tireless, loyal, passionate...
awesome.
I see it all, everything you do, and I'm truly proud of the
woman you are.
This one's for you. Xx

PROLOGUE

Ten thirty a.m. and I was buried deep under the bonnet of Ken Farley's old Audi, sweating my bollocks off as I wrestled with the soon-to-blow cam belt he should've had replaced thirty thousand miles ago. Tight bastard. The sweet smell of Sunday night pussy was already lost under the stink of oil on my fingers, ears ringing with the same old chatter of local radio blaring through the garage, and the lads, full of banter as they recapped the Saturday darts win down the Dog and Drum.

Petey slapped a hand on the bonnet over my head. Tea delivery, nice and strong, just a splash of milk. The lad was learning.

I hardly know my own fucking name before at least three brews in the morning, especially on a Monday. The week ahead was already booked to the hilt, and then came the post-weekend breakdown calls. Three cars in our yard this morning before I'd even opened up.

Help us out, Darren, I've gotta get up Shrewsbury way on Wednesday. Help us out, Trent, I've got an airport run tomorrow. I've got to get the kids from school at three. I've got to get Aunt

Marjorie's shopping. Gotta get to the cinema. Got a hot date and no wheels, please squeeze me in, mate. You're a fucking lifesaver.

I downed tools and took a swig of tea, just in time to catch the conversation shift. Buck cranked down the volume on the radio, cleared his throat.

"Mandy fucking Taylor," he announced to Hugh and Jim, fresh back in from a Mazda pick-up out on the Abergavenny roundabout. "Last night. Me, Trent and little Petey boy." He ruffled the lad's hair as he dished out the rest of the mugs.

"Fuck off," Jimmy scoffed. "Talk about shitting on your doorstep. She's got a loose tongue, that one, you'll be the talk of the bloody village, man."

Mandy fucking Taylor had more than a loose tongue, but some things are best left unsaid.

"Told you," Buck continued. "She always wanted a piece of Big-Buck-loving, just a matter of time." He smoothed down his beard, struck up his bear pose. "Petey got right in there. Fucked her good, didn't you, lad?"

I watched the pink spring up on Petey's cheeks. It made me smirk. He was still wet behind the ears, still humping away on the ladies like a pup due to have his nuts off. He'd learn soon enough, and in the meantime having a youngster on the rounds was a thrill our clientele seemed to enjoy.

Mandy fucking Taylor had requested our little Petey boy by name, and she wasn't the first. The lad was turning out to be an apprentice on all fronts, not just on the car side.

Jimmy shook his head. "You've really gone and done it. Good old Mandy Taylor fucked Dave Dawson out the back of the Drum the summer before last. Whole village knew he had an extra bollock by nine sharp next morning."

Everyone knew Dave Dawson had an extra bollock. *Everyone.* A hernia apparently. The thought that that rumour came from Mandy's mouth gave me the shivers. I looked at Buck, and he shrugged at me.

"She said she'd keep it to herself," he offered, but it was limp. Hardly the steadfast declaration he'd pushed my way before we'd taken her on.

"*You* said she'd keep it to herself," I said. "Told me she was *one million percent* sound."

He shrugged again. "She's alright, is Mandy. She isn't gonna say anything... no way..."

Famous last fucking words. I chugged down the rest of my tea.

There's rarely such a thing as a secret in a village like ours. Pontrilas — a twee little place right on the Welsh border. It was amazing our little extra-curricular was still off the village radar. You can trace the family trees in this place back to when time began. Same old faces, same old news, same old cars.

Except the rumble of the one pulling onto the yard. We all turned to look at it, all five of us, conversation over. The engine was a fucking melody, the beautiful purr of a finely tuned Porsche 911. It came to a stop, at a graceful diagonal in prime position across our open shutters.

A cacophony of wolf whistles, and I wasn't sure whether the lads were complimenting the car or the huge pair of tits driving it. Probably a bit of both.

I turned back to Ken's engine, Monday morning wasn't the time for this shit, regardless of what tricks Eleanor Hartwell had up her sleeve. The Porsche belonged to her old man, a retired bigshot who'd been unable to get his dick up since turning sixty a few years back. This was their way to keep a happy marriage by all accounts. Him golfing, her getting a bit of rough from a group of sweaty mechanics, courtesy of cash advances on his Gold card. Different strokes for different folks.

I heard the clack of heels on concrete, the familiar husk of a woman used to getting her own way. "Hello, boys." She paused. "Hi Trent."

I waited until I could smell her perfume. She propped herself up on my tool trolley, her head tossed back.

"Eleanor," I grunted.

She raised an eyebrow. "I was... passing... I hoped you could..." Her eyes swept down my overalls, came to rest on my crotch. "Fit me in for a service..." My dick twitched under her stare, and I cursed myself. "I couldn't get hold of you yesterday afternoon... Ted was out on the course... we could've..."

"I was busy," I said. "I had the girls."

She nodded. "Of course, sorry." She fluffed her hair a little. "Sunday, yes, I should've known." She held up her keys. "I can go... if it's not convenient... I was just passing..."

I smirked, and no words were needed. Nobody just *passes* here from fifty fucking miles away. I grabbed a rag from the tray at the side of her, and her breath caught as I wiped the oil from my fingers. I could feel the tension, the four pairs of eyes fixed on me from across the room, waiting. Buck gave me a nod behind her back. Petey was all but fucking slavering. Hugh was still composed, sipping his tea, but Jimmy O was hip thrusting, his tongue pinched between his teeth. Dirty fucker.

I focused back on Eleanor, at the thick red lipstick on her lips and the tight little dress she was wearing. The diamonds around her neck were real and I knew it, her blonde curls bounced over her big tits, which weren't real in the slightest and I knew that, too. The woman must be approaching fifty, but you'd sure as fuck never know *that*. Botox and a personal trainer. She smelled of money. Money and hot, wet pussy.

I pointed at the Audi. "My good friend, Ken, needs this bastard fixed up by three o'clock." I tipped my head to the row of cars behind hers. "Mondays are never a good day for a drive-by. We've got breakdowns coming out of our ears."

She reached into her Gucci handbag, pulled out an envelope, crisp and white. "I'll be very generous, for the inconvenience."

The envelope looked thick, much thicker than usual. There was only the muffled sound of the radio and the silence of bated breath as I weighed it up. I took a step closer, until my mouth was at her ear.

"You have to be out of here by midday so I can get this shit done. Deal?"

I felt her nod, her breath tickling my ear. "Deal."

"What do you want?"

She knew exactly what I meant. "You..." she said. "And Buck..." She pointed over her shoulder. "I want to take the big guy. I want to take the both of you."

"Just the two of us?"

She nodded. "Unless you can spare me the afternoon, too. Maybe even the week." She laughed and licked her lips, and she looked like a cheap porno. It shouldn't have turned me on but it did. It turned me on a shit ton. "Hot and hard, Trent. I want it hot and hard." Her voice was just a whisper. "Oh fuck, Trent, I've been thinking about this all morning. I've been thinking about you."

My mouth was watering as I looked over to the guys. I pulled out my wallet, took out a couple of twenties. "Run to the shop, will you, Petey? Cigarettes and sandwiches, get a round in." I smiled. "Take your time about it."

The lad nodded, took the cash and made a dash for it. I tipped my head at Buck and he grinned. I flashed Hugh the look and he read my mind. He slapped Jimmy O on the back.

"Let's go to Brecon, pick up that old Clio."

Jimmy let out a sigh. "Some guys get all the pissing luck," he groaned, but he was already grabbing his jacket.

Eleanor smiled at me, handed over the envelope. I didn't open it, just slipped it in the rack on the wall behind me. Hugh pulled down the shutters as he went, leaving us bathed in the hard glow of strip lighting. I locked up behind them, and Buck turned off the radio.

Eleanor had hitched her ass onto the tool trolley and her legs were spread by the time I'd done with the lock, her skirt already high up her thighs, fancy-done nails rubbing her clit through a tiny pair of creamy lace knickers.

"I meant it," she said. "All morning, Trent. It's all I could think about. You guys drive me wild." Buck moved to the back of her, grabbed hold of the tool trolley and wheeled her in my direction as she squealed. She threw her arms back, grabbed hold of his shoulders and pulled him close. "Fuck me, big boy," she hissed. "I need to be fucked by real fucking men."

His hands found her big tits, gripped them through the slinky fabric of her dress, and she arched her back, her fingers darting back to the wet lace between her legs. I made for the sink to clean up, call it common courtesy, but she let out a groan.

"No," she said. "No, please don't wash it all off, Trent. I want you... dirty... I want you to leave filth all over me... I want to show it to Ted... I want him to see where you touched me..."

The shit some people pay for, but I didn't care. My dick was hard, and Eleanor was a classy piece of pussy. She was horny and experienced, a woman in her prime who could easily handle both me and Buck. She'd taken all five of us earlier that summer, a couple of mega splurges while Ted was at some US conference or some shit. She'd taken all five and ridden us like a fucking train the whole night through, and she was on form right now. A horny, wriggling slut, just fucking desperate to be fucked.

I shrugged my way out of the top half of my overalls, let them fall loose around my waist, and Eleanor's greedy hands tugged my t-shirt, helped me pull it over my head. She ran her palms over my bare chest, moaning as Buck slipped his dirty fingers inside her dress. He pinched her nipples and she let out a hiss.

I took her knees, shunted her further back on the trolley, unbalanced her enough that she wrapped her legs around my waist to hold herself steady. It felt good. *She* felt good.

"Fuck," she hissed. "Just fuck me, Trent."

Her fingers slipped inside my boxers and took hold of my cock. I watched the delight in her eyes as she worked it up and down.

"Hey," Buck grunted, and his overalls were hanging loose, too. He took out his dick and yanked her backwards, laying her flat on the trolley with her pretty blonde curls picking up grease from oily tools. He slapped his cock against her cheek and the dirty slut opened wide, gave a moan as she sucked him in. I rubbed my thumb along the slip of her knickers, left a dirty black smear. She squirmed, her head bobbing in rhythm as Buck fucked her slutty little mouth.

Her lips were wet, they smacked with every fucking thrust, eyes already tearing up as he pushed in deep.

"Swallow me down," Buck grunted. "All the fucking way!"

I circled her clit, nice and steady, pressing tight. She stared up at me, her hand still gripping my dick, working my shaft nice and firm. Her throat gurgled and Buck swore, told her how fucking dirty she was.

I pulled her dress down over her big ripe tits, watched them bounce. Her nipples were hard, dark and stiff as fuck. My mouth fucking watered for them. I lowered myself over her and sucked, fighting the urge to shoot my load as she picked up pace with my cock.

Buck pulled out of her mouth, left a big stream of spit dribbling from her lips. She raised her head and her dirty eyes met mine, my mouth full of her tit.

"Kiss me," she whispered.

Fuck.

"Please, Trent," she whimpered. "Kiss me."

Kiss me where Buck's dick has been.

I can't say tasting some other guy's dick gets me horny, but we were long past being creeped out by that shit. I took her face in my hands, held her tight in position while I kissed her. Her tongue was really fucking demanding.

I felt Buck press a wrapper into my hand, and I pulled away enough to watch him roll a johnny onto his cock. He was the biggest of the five of us; they don't call him Big Buck for nothing.

I took her hands from my cock, guided them between her legs while I tore the wrapper and slipped a johnny on mine, too. "Show me your cunt," I grunted. "Open it."

She moaned and spread herself open. It was a fucking delight.

I dropped to my knees and buried my face in her, licking that snatch like a man fucking possessed, and she grabbed at my hair, rubbed her sweet-tasting pussy all over my fucking mouth.

Her sighs almost blocked out the rattle of a fist against the shutters.

Someone coming for their car. Someone coming with a new one. Someone delivering some fucking part or other.

That someone would have to fucking wait.

Another rattle. That someone was persistent.

"Hurry," Buck growled. "Need to fuck her. I'm ready for it."

"Suck my clit!" she hissed, and her fingers were harsh, scratching at my scalp. "Suck my fucking clit, Trent! Make me come!"

She was so wet and hot. I closed my eyes and sucked on that hard little nub until she gasped, ignoring another round of rapping at the door.

"Yes!" she cried. "Fuck, yes!"

Eleanor's whole fucking body tensed up, her legs thrashing as she came. She flooded me, cut off my air until she was done, finally setting me free in order to take Buck's big dick inside her.

I watched him push his way in, and her pussy ate him right up.

"Hard!" she demanded. "Fuck me! Fuck me!"

The tools rattled as he rammed her, fucked her hard until his breath was short and his beard was glistening with spit from sloppy wet kisses. "Swap," he grunted.

My fucking pleasure.

Poised close, so fucking close, about to spear that sweet fucking snatch and pound her good, until the shutters shook again. Rattled fucking hard by the idiot outside, the impatient dick who wouldn't back the fuck off.

And then the dick's voice.

Only it wasn't a dick.

Not even close.

"Darren! What the hell?! I know you're in there! I need to talk to you!" Jodie's voice paused, and my mouth dried up. Guilt. Even though I had no reason to feel guilty and hadn't done for a long bastard time.

Buck stared at me, raised his eyebrows. Giving it all the *ignore her* shit he usually gives me. *She's just an ex, Trent. Leave her fucking be.*

But Buck hasn't loved Jodie Symmonds since he was a kid.

Buck didn't watch Jodie Symmonds bring two of his fucking kids into this world, hasn't loved her with every single fucking bone in his body and believed it'd last for fucking ever.

The shutters rattled again. "Darren! It's about the girls!"

Buck sighed.

Game over.

CHAPTER ONE

JODIE

Mere hours earlier.

World War Three didn't start over nuclear weapons, or oil, or violation of civil liberties. It didn't start over who pissed on someone else's prayer spot, either.

No. World War Three started at Number Two, Oak Crescent, Pontrilas.

World War Three started over standard-issue black school socks, and the eight-year-old diva who refused to wear them.

I gritted my teeth and prayed to the God of Monday mornings for a change in fortune.

"Ruby, please! Just. Put. The. Socks. On!"

"But Mummmmm! Black socks are the worst ever. I never ever *ever* wear black socks! I won't be Ruby Trent in boring socks! Urghhhhhh!"

I held up the offending items. Just socks. Just fucking socks.

"And who do you suppose you will be? Huh?" I tossed them over to her. "Ruby Trent doesn't *have* any other clean socks! Not since the washing machine went psycho-crazy last night!" My delightful daughter held up a truly heinous combination of odds. Green stripy and purple plain. Just no. *No.* The perfect-mother-brigade would never forgive such a crime against humanity. "*Matching* socks, Ruby. *Matching.*"

She let out a groan, threw herself on the bed, arms flailing. "Who *cares* about *matching*?!"

The entire snooty populous of the local village. Your teachers. My peers. Your peers. Cynthia Blackthorne and her pigtail-wearing twins. Georgie Graham and her child prodigy mathematics genius pre-schooler. I could give her the whole bloody directory.

Her cute little freckled face pouted up at me, and I almost let sock-gate slide in her favour. Almost.

Until she said the words. *The* words.

"*Dad* would let me wear them! *Dad* wouldn't make me wear disgusting boring socks!"

Oh yeah. She just shit right out of luck with that line.

I put on my serious-Mum voice. "Get dressed, Ruby. Black socks. Final answer." My *definitely-need-to-leave-the-house* phone alarm started up in my pocket. I pulled out my mobile to shut it up. "And now we're late. Again. Thanks very much."

The muffled voice of her elder sibling fog-horned from downstairs. "We're late! Mum! I'll miss the bus!"

Tell me something I don't already know. I stuck my head out onto the landing. "I know, Mia, dearest child of mine! Your sister is just putting her *black* socks on!"

I stared at Ruby until she sighed. "Fine! I'll wear boring-smoring socks to school!"

Praise the fucking Lord.

Monday morning is my morning. You wouldn't think it, not pre-nine a.m. while chaos reigns all around me. Not with two girls to get ready for school, suddenly remembering the homework they swore blind they didn't have over the weekend, and the sports shorts that they really, really need that afternoon but forgot to put in the laundry basket. You wouldn't think it was my morning as the cat tries to trip me up while I'm juggling breakfast plates, and Nanna is reminding me for the hundredth time to pick up her pills from the chemist, like I've done every single Monday in the past seven years we've been living with her.

You wouldn't think Monday morning belonged to me at all.

But it does.

It's my one single weekday morning without both work and kids, and I make the most of it. Or I try.

Ladies who lunch.

Only it's *ladies who grab coffee down the local coffee shop*. We are always well done by lunch.

I really needed it today. A couple of hours of just being me. Not Mum-Jodie, or Jodie-from-the-cafe, or Granddaughter-cum-Carer-Jodie, or Trent's-ex-Jodie. *Just* Jodie.

I could've air punched when I saw a cluster of kids still standing at the bus stop. I leaned across to kiss Mia as she gathered up her school bag, but she didn't smile. A few weeks into high school and it was still a tough routine to get accustomed to, I guess. She'd hardly say a peep about it without prompting.

"You sure you're alright? Got everything?" I asked.

She nodded. "Yeah. I'm good."

"Ok, good. Have fun, poppet, see you later."

I waved her off, beeped the horn and I finally got a lacklustre smile.

"I never want to go to high school," Ruby announced from the backseat. "High school stinks."

"How do you know?" I met her eyes in the rearview before I pulled away. "You might love high school."

"Mia doesn't."

My hackles prickled, mother-senses on high alert. "Mia does."

She shook her head. "Mia hates high school. She said so."

"She did?"

Ruby nodded emphatically. Then she pointed back through the window. "That kid with the glasses, Tyler Dean, he's mean to her."

"Mean to her?"

"Yeah, calls her Mia-stink-a-lot. Get it? *Me A Stink A Lot*." She sighed. "Other names, too. Names I'm not allowed to say."

"She told you this?"

Ruby pulled a face. "No! She never tells me *anything*! She told Daisy on Skype. I heard."

I drove down the hill and indicated into Pontrilas Primary School, pulling onto the verge since there were no spaces left. "How about you have a little think about what else you know, hey? You can tell me later."

"And be a snitch?"

I opened her car door, grabbed her sports kit. "And be someone who answers her mum when she's asked a question. That's not snitching, Ruby."

She shrugged. "Yeah, ok."

We trudged to the playground, and my curly-haired bundle of backchat was off like a shot to find her friends. I had to practically chase her to hand over her sports bag. I took my regular position at the leafy tree, with a big-arsed smile plastered on my face and sweet little waves for the other village mums. At least I'd successfully transitioned from PJs in time for the school run today, and you could hardly even see the butter smear on my top from breakfast. Adulting win.

I sometimes wondered if motherhood was like this for everyone. Constantly feeling like a hot mess, I mean. They say you can't judge what you see of other people and their *parenthood goals* statuses on Facebook. They say you're seeing everyone else's show reel while you're living through the uncut edition, but seeing some of the mothers in the playground around me, I wonder. They always seem to have this shit totally nailed, and still have time for Pinterest-worthy baking projects.

Jesus, I hate baking.

I soaked in the September morning sun, my mind already zooming ahead to a hot mug of cappuccino and the latest gossip. I'd been ingratiated into the ladies' club by my best friend, Tonya, whose friendship had been forged in steel back when we were kids, staying strong into adulthood through countless break-ups and job crises. She'd been my confidante and cheerleader through my two pregnancies and the epic break-up with Daddy Trent, too. That made us virtually blood sisters. *Closer* than blood sisters, since my real life one drove me insane through at least half the time I spent in her company.

The other ladies in our little coffee club were alright, not quite so close to my heart, but nice enough. Mandy, Steph, and Debbie. All local. All born and bred here.

Weren't we all.

The bell rang to signal the end of my parental responsibilities for the school day, and my heart soared. Thank fuck for that. I was already disappearing back towards my car when a voice rang out from the outdoor sandpit.

"Jodie! Jodie! You-hoo! Jodie! Can I have a quick word?"

I toyed with the opinion of fake-deafness, but Miss Davies, Ruby's teacher, was at my elbow before I could reach stage-exit.

"Hi," I said. "Sure, what's up?"

She did a little sigh, and pulled *that* face. The face that says your kid's been up to no good. Oh bollocks.

"I'm glad I caught you," she said. "It's just, Ruby..."

My heart dropped.

"...one of the other mums heard something worrying last week..."

"Worrying?"

She nodded, pulled an apologetic face and lowered her voice. "Bad words. She's been saying *bad* words."

I could feel the heat on my cheeks. "Bad words?"

I hoped for maybe a *bloody* or a *crap*. Maybe even a sneaky little *shit*. I mean, bad words have scale, right?

She leaned in. "*Very* bad words..."

Great. Just great.

I held out my hands. "I'm sorry... Ruby knows not to say bad words... we don't say bad words in our house..."

It wasn't really much of a lie, either. Ruby hears me swear, but not *at* her, not much, not unless I've really lost my shit. But you can't say that to her smiling teacher, can you?

No way, of course none of us swear. Not me. Never bloodied and shitted and fucked in my life. And Ruby *does* know, both girls know they can't get away with saying nasty shit, I wouldn't dream of letting that slip by on my watch.

I said as much to Miss Davies, and she nodded sweetly but she wasn't really listening.

"The C word," she said, just like that. "Ruby used the *C word*."

Oh the shame. The terrible shame. My parenting goals crawled into a hole and died right there in front of me. And I knew.

Trent.

King of the C word.

Otherwise known as God in Ruby's eyes — Daddy's girl doesn't even come close.

Miss Davies knew it, too. Her face said it all.

She shrugged. "Look, Jodie, for what it's worth it wasn't *at* anyone. She's not that kind of child. We have to act on it, but Ruby's a nice girl, she just has some challenges with managing her frustration. She kicked out at the netball hoop after she missed a shot... called it a stupid *C* and told it where it could shove itself."

I winced. I actually winced. "I'll talk to her," I said. "It won't happen again."

She patted my arm in sympathy. "Thanks, Jodie."

I pulled out my phone as soon as she left me.

King C Word himself could deal with this one.

By the time I'd shaken off Miss Davies, sent a text to Darren *C-word* Trent about our co-parenting issues, grabbed Nanna's prescription from the chemist and made the house look basically habitable, I was the last lady to arrive at the Velvet Bean coffee shop. Yes, that's actually its name, and I work there when I'm not on the customer side of the counter. That means, in real life terms, that from the very first day I stepped foot behind it and donned my Velvet Bean apron, I've been known as *Jodie-from-the-cafe* and my business is officially everyone else's business, and theirs is mine.

That's how it works around here.

I got a wave from Tonya as I stepped through the door, but the others were too deep in conversation to give me a second glance. They were a huddle of whispers and giggles, eyebrows raised as Mandy recounted some village happening or another. I grabbed a cappuccino from my boss Lorraine and made my way to the table, letting out a sigh of relief as I slipped into my seat, hoping beyond hope for a funny tale or two to take my mind off my own crap.

I'm sure I caught the end of a 'hung like a horse' comment, but then the gossip stopped. Entirely.

Not for an interlude of hellos and smiles, or to give me a chance to catch up with the flow of conversation. Nothing so innocuous as that. It just stopped. Dead.

Nobody said a word.

"What?" I said. "Have I got shit on my face or something?" I patted my cheeks, but couldn't feel anything out of the ordinary. I didn't even have any makeup to smudge.

Silence.

"So what's the news?" I settled into my chair, kept my smile bright.

Tonya cleared her throat. "Mandy was just, ergh... She was just saying how she had a..."

"It was nothing," Mandy interrupted.

"Nothing?" I asked. "It didn't sound like nothing..."

She shrugged. "Just a date. Nothing too much of note."

I'd have believed her if the whole lot of them weren't staring straight into their coffee cups and not at me.

"A date?" I prompted.

She wouldn't meet my eyes. "A date, yeah. A *kind* of date."

"Booty call," Steph said.

I smiled. "Someone got lucky, then. Tell me all, I'm desperate for a good giggle. Morning from hell." I sipped my drink and waited. Kept waiting.

Debbie started talking to Steph about her new blonde highlights, and they all jumped in, jabbering on about some boring hair crap that nobody really gave a shit about.

"Come on!" I laughed. "Don't hold out on me. What's going on?"

"It wasn't anything," Mandy said. "Just a... I had a..."

"An orgy," Debbie blurted. "Mandy had a gang bang last night. Three men to herself!" The others looked horrified, but Debbie shrugged. "It's all over Facebook, it's hardly a secret..."

I nearly spat out my coffee as I giggled, but they weren't joining in. I looked around the faces. "Seriously? For real? Three men at once?"

Mandy shrugged. "It was a... fantasy... of mine..."

Isn't it everyone's? Three hot guys at once. Ripped and well hung and well aware of what to do with it...

I stared at her, willing her to tell me everything. This kind of shit was like balm for my frazzled, chore-shackled soul. I could practically feel the restraints of Mum-Jodie slipping away at the thought of some decent sex-gossip.

I leaned in, elbows on the table. "So? Was it... *good?*"

Mandy nodded, and her face lit up like an arcade after dark. "It was absolutely. Fucking. Amazing."

Tonya coughed, shook her head at Mandy and my stomach did a weird little flip. "What?" I said. "Why the weirdness? What's going on?"

Debbie smiled straight at me. "So, how was your morning?"

I laughed. "My morning sucked, same as every other school morning. Only *this* morning I found the washing machine had decided to go all kamikaze overnight and take a load of school uniform down with it, Ruby had a tantrum over black socks, I found out Mia hates high school and *then* found out Ruby's been taking anger-management classes from her father." I sighed. "But none of this is even remotely as interesting as taking three guys at once, and you all know it, so what's the big deal?"

I waited, again. They said nothing — again.

And then Steph checked her phone. "Ooh, is that the time?" She downed her coffee and gathered her bag, and the others followed suit, except Tonya who stayed put.

"What?" I said, and then I saw it. The empty cake plates. The almost empty mugs. They'd been here before me, much before our regular time slot. I felt ridiculously hurt.

"We'll meet up again next week," Debbie said. "Catch up properly."

"But it's not even eleven..." I said.

I watched in silence as they all said their goodbyes, dumbstruck as they air-kissed me and told me to have a *great week*. I was watching them across the street when Tonya sighed.

"I'll get us another coffee," she said.

I grabbed her wrist. "I don't want another coffee, Tonya, I want to know what's going on. What time did you get here?"

She held up her hands. "This wasn't me. I didn't know you

weren't in on the earlier start time."

I folded my arms. "I'm hardly a prude, Tonya. Is that what they think? Do they think I'm a prude?" I shrugged. "I'd love to hear about a bloody orgy, same as everyone else around here."

She stared right at me. "I said they should just tell you, you're going to find out soon enough anyway. Mandy's vague Facebook status got over fifty likes last night, *PM me* comments all over the place."

I hadn't checked Facebook the evening before, I'd been too busy watching old films with Nanna. I pulled out my phone, typed in Mandy Taylor.

Best night ever, her status said. *Some fantasies are even better in real life!* Then a load of hashtags about bucket lists and being a bad girl.

It seemed the whole village knew about this shit already, but not me. Clearly this gossip wasn't for me.

I asked the obvious question. Spat it out like a rotten egg. "Who was it? Who did she fuck?"

"Buck," she said, and that made sense. Buck and Mandy had been flirting all summer. I'd seen it as well as heard it.

"And?"

"Little Petey..."

My stomach dropped. Petey was new, Trent's young apprentice mechanic. Cute and blonde and Polish. A nice guy.

She didn't need to continue, but she did.

"And Trent." She groaned. "Mandy fucked Trent last night."

I shrugged, pretended it didn't matter. "Trent's a free agent. He fucks loads of people, so I gather. That's his prerogative."

She shook her head. "Not like this, not three on one."

I thought it through, Trent, Buck, and Petey, with Mandy Taylor. Trent doesn't even like Mandy Taylor. Mandy's nice enough, but she isn't his type, not that I knew.

Maybe I didn't know.

"She paid them," Tonya said. "Trent's running a gigolo service down there. They call themselves the *bang gang*."

The thought made me snort-laugh. "The *bang gang*? That's the most ridiculous thing I've ever heard. Trent's no bloody gigolo, he struggles with people skills at the best of times."

"Not with *these* people skills, he doesn't. Not according to Mandy." Tonya looked so sorry. "It was him, Jo. She gave them three hundred, and that was a massive discount apparently."

"Three hundred quid?! For a fuck?" I still couldn't believe it. Couldn't imagine it.

She nodded. "Worth every penny, Mandy said. She's planning on a repeat performance when her wages come in." She sighed. "I don't imagine she'll be alone, either. Not when she's finished mouthing off about how brilliant it was."

I put another sugar in my coffee. "Everyone knows?"

"It's Mandy Taylor. I imagine it's reached the valleys by now..."

I looked around the coffee shop, the regular tables of regular people, and they were looking. Looking at me.

Everyone fucking knew.

"The kids," I said. "What am I going to tell the fucking kids when they start asking if their dad fucks for money?"

Tonya leaned in. "Maybe it'll go over their heads? Maybe they won't know anything about any of it? They're young... It could blow over without them knowing..."

I raised my eyebrows. "Mia is at high school now. She's fully aware of where babies come from. Somehow I doubt it's still the fluffy, biologically slanted version of the birds and the bees that I told her."

She stopped trying to make me feel better. "He probably didn't know," she said. "That Mandy would blab like this, I mean. He hardly knows her."

"I'd say he knows her pretty fucking well from the sounds of it."

"She's probably exaggerating... you know what she's like... you can't take her side of the story as gospel..."

"No," I said, and downed my coffee. "I can't take her word for it. Which is exactly why I'm going to hear it from the stud himself." I grabbed my bag. "Right now."

She grabbed hers, too.

◆

CHAPTER TWO

JODIE

Tonya let out a gasp as I swung my trusty little Ford into Trent's yard. The adrenaline had me on edge, over-steering enough that I nearly clipped Betty Baker's old Mini Cooper, but from the looks of the bumper on it, another little knock would be the least of her concerns. I pulled up with a screech beside Darren's hulking black beast of a truck, and Tonya opened the passenger door right next to it, swung her legs out to give her a clear view of the garage entrance, then lit up a cigarette.

"I'll wait here and block his exit," she said. "Holler if you need me."

"Enjoy the show," I snipped.

She blew out a long plume of smoke. "I'm here as your cheerleader, not for entertainment."

I rolled my eyes.

My legs felt weird and shaky as I crossed the tarmac to the garage office, mood veering between rage and this nasty little shard of hurt that wouldn't stop stabbing. Darren Trent, trusted local mechanic, father of two. Foul-mouthed, arrogant, loyal, hardworking, infuriatingly stubborn, brooding, blunt, honest, *hot*...

... *Gigolo*.

Gigolo.

A fucking man-whore.

I still couldn't quite believe it.

I tried the handle, but it was locked. Impossible. No way would Darren close up on a Monday. And his truck was here, bold as brass. You couldn't miss the fucking thing.

I tried the handle again and it rattled but wouldn't budge. I pressed my face to the dirty window and peered inside and there was nobody, just an empty counter. I knocked. Nothing.

What the fuck?

I walked around the side to the main shutters, and my heart did a flip as I saw the sports car there. A red Porsche, the kind of car that screams money. I checked out the badge and the licence plate — expensive and new and definitely not from these parts. I took a step towards it, checked out the scarlet paintwork, peered inside to see a woman's jacket there, her makeup bag still open on the passenger seat. The shutter doors were down and bolted, the whole place closed up tight.

But Buck's estate car was in its usual spot.

I rapped the shutters, then pressed my ear to the metal.

Nothing.

I rapped again until they rattled and shook.

Nothing.

I stepped back, looked around, scoped out my options as my heart thumped. *He was fucking. Of course he was. The woman from the Porsche.*

I shouldn't care. Didn't want to care. But the girls...

29

The village…

I hammered on the shutters again and this time there was rage in it.

"Darren! I know you're in there! I need to talk to you!" Nothing. Not one fucking sign of life. I hammered again. "Darren! It's about the girls!"

A clank from inside, and I knew he'd heard me. I folded my arms, waiting for the doors to open, not truly ready to believe he was fucking some posh Porsche-driving bitch in there on a Monday morning, but of course he fucking was.

She strolled out as soon as they cranked up, ducking a salon-blonde head under the door with a lipstick-smudged smirk on her face. Her dress was crumpled and her hair was greasy, and she had a black smear across her insanely huge cleavage.

Her diamonds caught the light and twinkled, and her toned legs looked so tanned. Her lips were plumped, and her eyes were glazed and cock-hungry.

She looked me up and down as she passed, and her snarky smile told me everything. She'd weighed me up in an instant and found me lacking, and suddenly I felt plain and awkward, my fingers brushing at the butter stain on my top even though she'd already seen it, already seen the circles under my eyes from a night up with Ruby's night terrors, already seen the limp mousy hair that hadn't seen a bottle of dye in years and the eyebrows that drastically needed shaping.

She'd seen me, and she'd judged me. Signed me off as a plain Jane battering down her ex's door.

She shot a glance back towards the garage before she got into her car, blew a kiss and gave a big smile. "Till next time, boys."

And then there was Darren, half-clad in the same pair of tatty old overalls he'd been wearing since he'd opened this place, yanking down the plain black t-shirt he'd certainly just pulled on over his head. His arms were as toned as they'd ever been, the dark lines of his tattoos twisting up around his elbows, smeared with oil.

He barely even nodded in Porsche Bitch's direction, gave her nothing but the faintest hint of a grunt in farewell. His eyes were fixed on me, heavy with questions and that bristle of brusque he's so fucking good at.

"What's up?" he said as he strolled over. His eyes were so light and his hair was so dark. His jawline solid; rugged with at least a weekend's worth of stubble. He lit up a cigarette, and his eyes didn't leave mine. "Well?" he prompted. "What's going on with the girls?"

The engine of the Porsche roared into life but he didn't look away.

I stared into the eyes of the man I'd known since he was just a kid with big dreams and a bad attitude. The man who'd claimed to not give a shit for anyone or anything, but had taken my hand and held it tight in his, who'd loved me like he'd never let go.

The man I thought I'd spend my life with.

I sighed. "Ruby's been swearing. Miss Davies grabbed me this morning. I sent you a message." I tried not to make the words barbed, but they came out that way anyway. He dug in his pocket for his phone. Took a drag on his cigarette as he scrolled through his messages.

"Didn't see it," he said. "Busy."

"I gathered." I folded my arms.

He let out a low laugh, his eyes glittering with a moment of amusement as he read my text. "Used the C word, did she?" He turned back to the open shutters, and I saw the bulk of Buck looming

31

inside. "You'd better stop teaching my daughter bad fucking words, Buck, you big fucking prick. She called her teacher a cunt."

Buck shot him the finger, and he was laughing, too. "Like *I* taught her to say cunt, you soft cunt."

I gritted my teeth until Darren's attention was back on me. "She didn't call her teacher a cunt, Darren. She got frustrated and called the netball hoop a cunt."

He shrugged. "Same fucking deal. Kids swear. All fucking kids, Jo. Some just hide it better."

I shook my head. "Don't. Just don't! She's only eight years old. She shouldn't even know the word exists."

Darren Trent has the most intense eyes of anyone I've ever met in my life. There's an aggression to his stare, even when he doesn't mean it. Just... something... it makes my skin prickle, but there's always this heat underneath. This burn.

He's straight and blunt and his eyes hit hard, and they hit me hard right then and there.

"I'll sort it," he said.

I couldn't temper my disgust. "How? What's your big plan? Hey? Are you going to be the one who assures Miss Davies that Ruby isn't going to spew obscenities again? Are you going to be the one who pulls Ruby up on her behaviour? You going to be the one who makes sure it doesn't happen again? Is that you? What the fuck are you going to do, Trent? Hmm? Have a chat with her? Play the big bloody disciplinarian for the day? You going to be the one who tells her off and teaches her that bad language has repercussions? Break the habit of a fucking lifetime?"

"I said I'll sort it," he grunted and his eyes were fiery. He shoved his phone back in his pocket. "Was that everything?"

I just stared at him.

"What?" he said. "What's with the big fucking chip on your shoulder today? I'd have got your message and you fucking know it."

My heart raced. "Who was that?" I pointed to the space the Porsche had left.

"Who was who?"

I rolled my eyes. "Miss Porsche. Who was she?"

"Customer," he said.

"A customer?" I scoffed. "Sure she was."

"In for a service. No big deal."

I stared him out. "And what kind of service was that? What kind of stuff are you offering down here?"

And he knew. His eyes said it all.

"Mandy fucking Taylor," he said, and there was humour in his tone.

I felt sick. So sick. Practically puked on the spot. "It's true then?"

He shrugged. "Depends what you've heard."

"How about that you're running some seedy gigolo outfit, charging people for gang bangs?"

He tipped his head to the side. "Maybe a bit of truth in it."

"It's all around the fucking village, Darren!" My hands were up and at him before I could stop them, gesturing madly. "Everyone fucking knows! Everyone!"

"Let them fucking know," he scoffed. "Who the fuck cares?"

"*I* care, Darren. *Me*." I saw him swallow, his eyes widen, just a little. "About the girls," I clarified. "About how they're going to fucking feel when their schoolmates tell them their dad's a man-whore who fucks for money." I put my head in my hands. "I can't believe you'd do this! Do this to the girls, to *us*, in this village! Why would you? How fucking could you?!" I was on a roll. "It's selfish, Darren! It's so fucking selfish! A quick scheme to get your dick wet, only you have to get paid for it as well, right? Like fucking for free isn't bad enough!"

His expression hardened. "I'm doing this *for* the fucking girls, Jo."

"Jesus, Darren," I snapped. "How the fuck can you be doing this for the fucking girls?"

I met his eyes, but he'd closed up again. His expression was hard and disengaged. "Forget it. I'll sort it."

"Forget it?!"

"Yeah," he snapped back. "Forget it."

I stared aghast. Just aghast. "You're really fucking for money, aren't you?"

He shrugged. "Way I see it, people need plenty of things. If I can give them what they want and charge them a fair price, I'll do it. This is no different, Jo, it's just a fucking gig, same as the others." He gestured at the cars around us. "Just like the motors, only I use a different fucking tool."

I shook my head. "I can't believe this... I just can't..."

He lit up another cigarette. "I've been keeping it away from here."

"By fucking that big-mouth Mandy Taylor?!"

"That was Buck," he said. "Likes her. Said she was sound."

"And now it's out! It's every-fucking-where! I have to face everyone in the village, and I *will*. But what about the girls?! What the hell do I tell them?!"

"Nothing," he said. "Tell them nothing, Jo." He scowled. "It'll blow over. Gossip will be chip paper next week."

I laughed a snarky laugh. "Sure it will." I shrugged. "Just like the broken washing machine will blow over, and Ruby's swearing, and every other thing that goes belly up around me." I had the most horrible, pitiful urge to cry, so I walked away. "It'll all just blow over, right, Darren? I'll just keep waiting, shall I? Pick Ruby up from school and pretend her dad isn't fucking half the locals?"

"I'm not fucking half the locals," he said.

"You think that's what they'll tell our girls?! *Your dad isn't fucking half the locals, just a few?!*"

"They can tell them what they fucking like, it's not true."

My phone bleeped in my pocket. I considered leaving it alone, but I never can. In case it's Nanna, or the school, or my parents from the coast whenever they get a quiet few minutes. It was Lorraine, my boss.

Can you cover Emma for a few hours this afternoon? You'd be a lifesaver.

I'm always a lifesaver, always running around after everyone else. And I'd had fucking enough of it.

"You can pick Ruby up, then," I said. "See how you like dealing with it."

He nodded, didn't flinch. "Fine. I'll pick her up."

"Half three," I said. "Don't be late."

"I never fucking am," he snapped.

"Good," I snapped back. "At least I can count on you for something."

I didn't give him another glance.

TRENT

I busted a fucking nut to get those cars done. Didn't even eat the sandwiches Petey came back from the shop with. We all worked hard, all knuckled down — even Hugh and Jimmy O — and at twenty-nine minutes past three I had my foot down in the truck as I sped across the village to get my little girl. The thought of her spouting *cunt* around the place shouldn't make me laugh, but it did. It really fucking did. Ruby's so pissing funny, you can't help yourself.

I didn't bother with the car park, just mounted the verge and pulled the truck to a stop. I could see the curtains twitching, people stopping midway about their village business to stop and gawk at me.

There he is. Trent. The gigolo. The whore.

The fucking dick.

Like I give a fuck what they think.

I don't know how Jodie manages to smile through this same old village playground shit every day of her life. The place was humming with people judging each other behind their fake-assed smiles, squawking on about what's what around here. They were all gossiping, all moaning about some shit or another, but every set of eyes in that school yard were on me. I kept my cool, lighting up a cigarette as I stood at the gate, right at the edge of the no smoking zone.

The snooty mum brigade always hated that, but there was a bit of a sizzle through them today. Their lingering glares in my direction were laced with something else.

It made me crack a grin to myself.

For all their whining and fucking moaning they all wanted a piece of Mandy Taylor's action. They'd be condemning with one hand while rubbing one off with the other, that's the way of the fucking world.

36

I'd just finished up my cigarette when Ruby's classroom door opened and kids came pouring out. She was one of the last, yapping on to Miss Davies, in a world of her own as she trailed her school bag after her. Her hair was a tangle, her freckles glowing in the afternoon sun, her toothy grin hitting me in the gut and making me so fucking proud.

When it was just Jodie and me, when things were good, I loved her more than I'd ever loved anything in the world. As much as it's possible to love anyone, that's what I thought. I'd have walked through fire for her, thrown myself under a truck for her, clawed through Hell just to make her happy.

And then Mia came, and Ruby after her, and then I knew I was wrong.

As much as I loved their mother — and fuck, I loved their mother — I'd have thrown us both to the fucking wolves if those girls needed it.

That's love.

I also didn't come up with that shit. Some celebrity guy came up with it and I read it in some crappy newspaper somewhere down the line, but that's beside the point. The guy who said it could have reached inside my heart and found exactly the same feeling. He just said it first, and said it better than I would have.

I'm not so good with words.

I waited, and waited, and Ruby kept jabbering on to her teacher, barely watching the path ahead. And then she saw me, and that toothy grin grew bigger.

"Daddddd!"

She was still a bit gangly, awkward feet pounding the tarmac until she launched herself right at me. I scooped her up, and she hung around my neck, hoisted herself up on my hip and started her school day monologue about dinosaurs and making a cup out of foil and how she'd fallen out with Sophie Green at lunchtime.

I dropped her at the truck and she shot round the other side, clambered up into the passenger seat, where her feet hung far above the footwell. She clipped her belt, pulled her pink sunglasses from the glovebox and grinned at me as I climbed into the driver's seat.

"Where's Mum?"

"Work," I said. "Extra shift."

"Cool," she said, just like that. "Can I come to the garage?"

"Sure," I said, and then I had to do the deed. I cleared my throat before I pulled away from the school. I gave her a look as I indicated out of the street. "You've been busted, Rubes."

She paused for just a second. "Busted?"

I sighed. Did my best to sound serious. "Did you use a garage word at school the other day?"

A pause and then a shrug. "Might have done."

"Remember what we said about garage talk?"

She nodded. "Yeah. Garage talk stays in the garage."

I tried my best not to smile. "And why does it stay in the garage?"

She sighed. "Because people get all butt-hurt if you say bad words in front of them."

I had to laugh at that. "Who's got butt-hurt now, do you think?"

"Miss Davies."

"And who else?"

"Mum."

"And what does your mum do when she gets all butt-hurt? Who does she come and moan at?"

She kicked her feet in the footwell. "You."

"Yeah, that's right. And then *I* have to moan at *you,* and we don't want to be dealing with this shit, do we?"

She shook her head.

"So, where's the place for butt-hurt words?"

"The garage," she answered in a beat.

"And when's the time for garage words?"

She looked right at me. "When Mum's not there."

"Right." I smiled. "We sorted here?"

She nodded. "Yeah."

I ruffled her hair. "Good girl." I headed over to the garage and Ruby stared out of the window. "When you're an adult you can butt-hurt whoever you like."

She grinned. "Like you do?!"

I grinned, too. "Yeah, like I do."

She sighed and folded her arms. "I can't wait until I'm a grown up and I can butt-hurt Sophie Green."

I pulled up at the bus stop to wait for Mia, and grabbed my mobile, scrolled until I found Jodie's text.

Mine to her was simple. Like always.

Sorted, it said.

I watched Ruby with Buck, passing him tools as he worked on Clare Evan's old Mercedes. I watched the concentration on her face as she stared at what he was doing, soaking it all in like a sharp little sponge. Usually I'd help out, tell her the extra details, answer her questions, but today I was sorting tyres with Mia, prompting her on the finer details of high school life.

She said pretty much fuck all, and that's not like Mia. She's quiet but she's not that quiet.

"What's going on?" I said. "Is it a pile of shit?"

She shrugged. "It's alright."

"Just alright?"

She nodded. "Just alright."

I met her eyes, but she looked away. "I hated high school. Hated all of it. You can tell me if something's shit for you, you know that, right? Maybe I'll get it."

"I'm alright," she said again, but she wasn't. She wasn't alright at all.

I let it go for now, gave her a smile.

"Let's get you home before your nanna sends out a search party."

Nanna has always been Nanna to me, too. Even now. Her eyes lit up for me as she opened the door to let the girls in, and I had that fucking sadness again, that horrible pang that rears up in my gut no matter how many times it happens.

"Kids!" she said, giving them a smile as they raced on by. "There's cake on the rack! Don't gobble it all at once!"

"Alright, Nanna?" I said.

"Oh, Darren," she said, and that was it. Two simple words with one simple smile. I'd normally have made myself scarce, hopped back into the truck and taken off before I could think about it too hard, but not today.

"Alright if I come in?" I said, and she pulled the door wider.

"Yes, yes," she said. "To see Jodie? She's not back yet…"

I shook my head, held up my tool bag. "No," I said. "I'm not here to see Jodie. I'm here to see your washing machine."

CHAPTER THREE

JODIE

Afternoon one of gigolo-gate, and I already felt like a zoo exhibit. The cafe had been busier than it had all summer — streams of villagers heading in for coffee, cake and a gawk.

Does she know? Is it true? Is he really whoring his cock out?

I may as well have put a sign up on the counter. One giant YES.

Yes, it's all true. Yes, I fucking know about it. Now eat your bloody Victoria sponge and stop with the whispering. I'd never say it, of course. That would never do. Not in my job. Not with two girls to bring up here. I kept quiet, kept smiling, serving those coffees like this was just a day like any other day.

And then I went home with a scowl on my face, cursing Darren Trent and his easy fucking dick.

The front door opened with a creak, and I stepped into the ambient sound of the girls bickering over whose turn it was on the laptop. Same old shit, different day.

Nanna was in the kitchen clearing up crumby plates. My heart softened as I saw the rack of sultana cupcakes, my favourite since I was a kid.

"You looked tired this morning, love," she said, and squeezed my arm. "Thought I'd make your favourite."

I watched her potter about the kitchen, and she was so much smaller than she used to be, her slippers shuffling across the tiles. She used to be so big and strong.

"Aww. Thanks, Nanna." I put her pills on the table and grabbed a seat. I'd managed two bites by the time the girls were upon me, not with *hellos* or questions about my cruddy day. No. I was simply a referee in their escalating laptop war.

They both set their case out at the same time, competing for volume.

"Ruby's watched YouTube for half an hour already! I want to check my farm!"

"Mia doesn't even have any crops ready yet! She's just being greedy!"

I held my hands up. "How about you give it a rest and come and sit at the table?"

Silence.

"Sit down, please," I said. "Both of you." They pulled up their chairs and their morose expressions summed up my day completely. "Ruby," I began. "Did your dad speak to you today?"

She kicked her heels against the chair legs and nodded.

I folded my arms. "And what did he say? Hmm? About your swearing?"

She sighed. "He said don't say bad words because people get all butt... *upset*... People get all *upset* if you say bad words." She paused. "And then they all moan."

Not quite how I'd have put it, but I nodded anyway. "They all *moan* because it's not nice language, Ruby. You wouldn't see me or Nanna going into your school, or the cafe, or the shop and saying bad words, would you? That's not what people do, sweetheart, it's not how people behave."

Contrary blue eyes met mine. "*Dad* would. *Dad* went into the shop and told Mr Evans to shut his stupid *bleeping* mouth, remember?" She smiled triumphantly.

Lord help me.

"Yeah, and then your dad had to buy his cigarettes from Allensmore for a month, remember? Who was butt-upset then, hey?" I brushed cake crumbs from my top. "I'll tell you who. It was your dad."

She was quiet for a while before she offered out her little finger. "I won't say bad words at school again, Mum. Pinky promise."

It melted my heart as I linked my finger with hers.

I turned to Mia, but she was staring at the table top. "How was your day, poppet?"

She barely shrugged her shoulders. "Alright."

"Just alright?"

"Yeah."

"Want to talk about it?" Ruby's morning revelation was twisting in my belly. "You can talk about it, Mia, if something's bothering you. You know that, right?"

"Yeah, I know," she said.

"Are you having problems?"

She shook her head. "The boys on the bus are idiots, that's all." She sighed. "It doesn't matter."

"It *does* matter. If they're upsetting you then it definitely matters."

"Nah," she insisted. "It's just Tyler Dean and he's a jerk. Everyone knows it." She met my eyes. "I'm alright."

"If you're sure." I finished up my cupcake and reached for a second, noting with amusement that the stash had already been decimated. Nanna always cooks twelve, but there were only two left and a smattering of crumbs for good measure. "You two have done quite a number on Nanna's cakes." I laughed. "I'd better eat quick before they're all gone."

Nanna came to my side, and her eyes were twinkling. "Oh no, it wasn't the girls, not this time," she said. She nudged me with her elbow. "It was Darren. He polished off quite a few of them."

My stomach did a lurch as I stared up at her. "Darren was *here*? Actually in here?"

The anger from earlier bubbled up again. Selfish prick, not giving a toss for anything, causing so much shit for us all.

She nodded. "Brought the girls home nice and early with some chips for tea." She smiled. "He fixed the washing machine for you."

For me. She always adds pointed little extras like that.

I looked over at the pile of washing I'd abandoned on the kitchen floor, and the stack of whites was definitely smaller. Sure enough, the little green light was flashing on the machine, load finished. My cheeks burned at the thought of him going through the underwear pile. I'd had my tatty grey-white apple-catchers piled up in there, probably even some period-bloody ones...

The blonde bitch from the garage came into my mind. Her stupid tanned legs, so fucking *perfect*.

Nanna's smile was sly. "Took him an age, it did. Had the whole thing apart. He cleaned up after, though." I waited for it. "He's a good one, your Darren."

44

"He's not *my* Darren," I said for the millionth time. *And he's not a good one. He's a fucking arsehole.* I bit my tongue.

She put a hand on my shoulder. "You know what I mean, love. Figure of speech."

I sighed. "I only mentioned the washing machine to him in passing." *Right before I told him I couldn't count on him.*

I got up and pulled the washing from the drum, and it was perfect, not a chewed-up sock in sight. Sure enough, there were my granny pants. The sight made me cringe.

"He must have come straight round, then. As soon as he could," Nanna pointed out. Like it was needed.

Yes. Yes, he must have.

Our altercation came back into my mind. The way Porsche-bitch had looked at me, the way *he'd* looked at me, worried about the girls and without a toss to give for her or her goodbye.

The way he'd opened the shutters and turfed her out.

And I had so many questions. Not least *why?* Besides the obvious, of course. Why gangbangs? Why for money?

And how? How the fuck did this even start? How long has it been going on for?

My brain fizzed.

Who with? Who else?

Nanna knew me well. She winked and smiled. "Why don't you pop out for a bit, love? Get some fresh air? I'll watch *Question King* with the girls... they can keep me company awhile..."

I got my coat.

45

Darren's place is right in the middle of the village — a stuffy little two-bedroom flat above the fish and chip shop. It used to be our place, back in the day, before things went tits up and I moved me and the girls in with Nanna.

I always thought he'd leave when the garage started doing well. Get somewhere bigger, somewhere where everything wouldn't stink of fish and chip fat... But no.

I walked over slowly, my mind whirring with questions and how I'd phrase them. Maybe he'd tell me to fuck off and mind my own business before I'd even asked.

Maybe it would be easier if he did.

I took a breath before I climbed the stone staircase to his front door. It was littered with cigarette butts, and as usual the bucket ashtray at the top was filled to the brim.

The door was open. I rapped my knuckles on the glass before I stepped inside and into the sound of the TV playing loud in the living room. *Question King*, Nanna's favourite, but it wasn't Darren watching it, it was Buck.

And Buck was wearing a tuxedo.

I stared in shock, and he was oblivious at first, a beer in his hand as he called out answers to an empty room. He started when he saw me, his huge frame jolting in the armchair.

"Jesus, Jo! I nearly shit myself!"

Buck looked totally different away from the garage. His beard was tame, his hair slick and styled, and the tux highlighted just how toned he was underneath it. He was ripped, biceps like tree trunks. I'd known Buck a long time, as long as I'd known Darren, and yet I'd never noticed him like this before.

"Where is he?" I asked, and he gestured behind me as a door-handle sounded.

I stepped back into the hallway — and practically stepped into Trent — only to realise

the world had gone crazy — stark-raving mad, in fact — because the guy standing before me wasn't the one I remembered like the back of my hand, and sure didn't look like the one I'd shared a bed with for six years straight. This Trent was a different animal altogether.

He was wearing nothing but a towel, and that towel hung precariously low on his hips. Far too low for decency, and precarious enough that my heart thumped at the thought of it falling. That towel highlighted a deep muscular V that was definitely more prominent than it had ever been when we were together. His abs were like a washboard, rippling under his skin, and his chest looked sculpted from steel. He was dripping wet and smoking hot, and I couldn't stop my jaw from dropping as I checked him out. My eyes shamelessly roved him, powerless to look away, checking out the similarities and the differences. Mainly the differences.

His tattoos had grown somewhat since I'd last seen him naked, the work on his arm reaching up to his shoulder and snaking round to the back. There were more, too. More tribal pieces on his side. One on his hip that disappeared under the towel and away from my prying eyes.

He stared at me staring at him, and I was burning, trapped.

"Jo," he grunted.

"I, um... wanted to talk..."

He tipped his head for me to follow him, and my mouth turned dry as he headed to the end of the corridor and the room that was once ours. I followed in silence, propping myself against the doorframe as he rooted for clothes. He pulled out a tux I'd never seen before. It wasn't the stiff old one he'd worn to Aunt Beth's wedding, that was for sure.

"Girls alright?"

I nodded. "With Nanna."

He laid the tux on the bed. "I'm off out. Got a gig."

My stomach lurched at his words. "Yeah, sorry. I won't be long. I was just…"

He met my stare and my nerves caved. I turned away to save his modesty, but he let out a low laugh.

"Christ, Jo. Don't be a fucking prude. You've seen it all before."

But I hadn't. Not like this.

I looked back just in time to see him tug the towel from his hips, and I was stuck there, gawping at the thickness of his thighs… of his toned calves… of his… his…

"Fucking hell, Jodie. You've gone redder than a baboon's arse." He took his cock in his hand, and he was smirking. "Dunno why. You've definitely seen *this* before."

I made myself blink, and cleared my throat as he dried himself down.

"I wanted to say thanks," I said. "For the washing machine… I really appreciate it…"

He shrugged. "Text would've done." It was his turn to check me out, and I could've shrivelled into nothing. Whereas *he'd* turned into some kind of muscular Adonis since we'd last fucked, all those years ago, *I'd* turned into a village mum. My hair was crap, and I knew it. My skin was pasty and plain without even a dab of mascara. My clothes were practical and… well, they were dull… my nails were short and bitten to shit. Let's not even get started on what was under my clothes, either. "Spit it out," he said. "What are you doing here?"

I shrugged. "I don't know really. I just wanted to... talk."

He pointed to his alarm clock. "I've got ten minutes."

I nodded.

"Go on, then," he said. "What's up?"

I took a breath. "This... this gigolo stuff..." I paused. "Why do you do it? Besides the obvious, I mean..."

He tossed the towel aside and sprayed some deodorant under his arms. "Does it fucking matter why?"

I held his stare. "It matters."

He groaned, and dipped down, reached under the bed. I could feel my heartbeat in my temples. He pulled out a box, a big wooden thing with a clasp and a lock. "Want the fucking truth?"

"Please."

"Righto." He dropped the box on the bed and tossed me the key, let out a sigh. "See for your fucking self if it matters so much."

My fingers were shaking as they turned the key in the lock. I opened it slowly, carefully, and inside was a picture of our girls taped to the lid. It was a couple of years old, and they were at the beach, smiling proudly at a monster of a sandcastle he'd helped them build. The tide was coming in, but the girls were unaware, still believing their castle would last forever.

I hadn't been there, but I'd heard them tell the sandcastle tale many times. *Many* times.

Trent's box was stuffed full of cash — tens and twenties, some fifties, too.

"For the kids, like I said," he grunted.

I was taken aback. "But you support the kids already... they don't need..."

He shook his head, and his expression was heavy. "University."

My heart dropped, and I knew exactly where his head was at. "Darren, you don't have to..."

He held up a hand. "I want to. For Mia." A soft smile flashed across his lips. "She's smart... Clever, like her mother. She should go to university." He paused. "Like *you* should've gone..." The thought smarted, and he saw it. "If we'd done things by the book... if we'd..."

I nodded, but didn't say the words aloud. I'd been just sixteen when I'd fallen in love with Darren. Seventeen when I gave birth to his first baby. An accident, but the most beautiful accident in all creation. Mia changed everything for both of us.

He sighed, and pulled on a pair of boxers. "I'm not saying we're... that we... I wouldn't change anything. I just want the girls to do what we didn't." He paused. "If that's what they want."

"A university fund? From gangbang sex?"

He scowled. "Doesn't fucking matter where it's from. Point is it's fucking there."

"But the garage already does well..." I ran my fingers over the cash and it felt so weird, so dirty.

"Yeah, it does, but you gotta make hay when the sun shines, Jo. That latest rig cost me forty fucking grand. The truck cost thirty. With Petey and Jimmy O learning the trade... well, it all costs. Bang Gang money's not tied to anything... and the only overheads are condoms." He laughed and slipped on a crisp white shirt. I fought the urge to help him with his collar.

"So you take it while it's there? Put it in a box for Mia's university fund?" I could barely believe it. My voice felt heavy in my throat.

He shrugged. "And for Rubes. But she'll probably end up with me, in the yard. Can't keep her away." He fastened up his bow tie.

"So, now you know, alright?"

I met the gaze of the man I'd known better than anyone. "How, Darren? When?"

He pulled on his trousers and smiled. "Charity calendar three summers back, remember it?"

Of course I remembered it. It was to fund the local hospice, and workmen around the county had signed up for it. Trent's team had been June — a glossy picture of them half naked, straddling tyres in a field full of hay bales. "Yeah, I remember."

"Got a call after that. Got several actually. Women with a lot of money, looking for more." He shrugged. "Word spread."

"Three years, that's how long you've been doing this?"

He nodded. "Right after I stopped seeing Stacey... When you were hooking up with Brian..."

I cringed at the memory. A couple of years with Brian was enough to make anyone cringe.

He checked the clock. "I gotta go, Jo."

I stacked the money back in the box and handed it to him. His fingers felt so hot when they touched mine. "You could stop," I said. "There's a lot of money there, Darren."

He didn't answer, just slid the box back under the bed.

I continued. "I mean, enough to pay for tuition fees, surely... that's enough, no?"

"I'm not stopping, Jo," he said. "It's too good a thing."

My heart dropped and it wasn't just the village rumours. I didn't even know what it was anymore.

"I'll leave you to it," I said. I turned away, but he reached me in the doorway, his fingers on my wrist.

He spun me around and his face was in mine, his breath hot. "I fucked up with Mandy Taylor. I fucked up and now it's round the whole fucking village, but I'll sort it, alright?"

A knock at the front door and a trample of feet and wolf-calls. I didn't need to look to know it was Hugh, Jimmy O and Petey come to join the gathering.

"Just sort the rumours, Darren," I said. "For the girls."

He nodded.

I adjusted his bow tie, smoothed down his shirt and let out a sigh. "This is so fucked up," I said.

"Life's fucked up, Jo."

I sighed. "Then you'd better just go nail the shit you've got to nail, hadn't you?"

He gave me a nod, and stepped away. And I missed him. I missed his body as hard as I'd missed him in the beginning, when I could barely fucking breathe because it hurt so bad. It was crazy, and ridiculous, and so fucking over, but it hurt like a bastard, right in my gut.

His eyes caught mine. "You alright?"

I smiled. "I'm good." I let the feeling pass, pushed through it. "Just do what you've got to do, Darren."

"Righto," he said.

I followed the guys outside when they went, and they looked a picture. Five suited studs, all set to service some rich cow or other.

Seeing them together made my tummy tickle.

They'd been working out, all of them. Seeing them all suited up made it so obvious.

Hugh smiled at me and gave me his best. He was a silver fox, in his late forties, but still quite the dish. I wondered how his wife felt about this shit, but didn't ask, just smiled and gave him mine back.

Jimmy O still looked like a wiley coyote, even in a tux. His curly dark hair blew loose over his eyes, and made them even darker, more mysterious. His eyes ate me up, his smile dirty. I felt it between my legs.

And Petey. Cute little Petey. His cheeks were glowing and his smile was bright. I could already see the tent of his cock in his trousers. The whole thing must be a bit much for a youngster like him.

They climbed into the back of the truck, and Buck climbed up front, leaving me with Trent to say my goodbyes.

"So, this is it?" I smiled. "This is your *bang gang*?"

He smirked. "One face of it. The rest is mainly sweat and oil."

"Where you off to?" I quizzed.

"Cotswolds."

I sighed. "Then you'd better go. I'll head back home." I met his eyes. "Just be careful, Darren. Don't..."

"Don't what?"

"I dunno," I said. "Just don't do anything stupid."

"Bit past that now, Jo."

He climbed up into his seat, lit a cigarette and turned the key in the ignition. I listened to the roar of the engine as it started up — a beast you could hear through the village. It suited him.

"I'll be seeing you," he said, and put his foot down.

I watched him out of sight, watched that truck until it left the village straight and disappeared from view. I watched until there was only the cool autumn evening left to watch.

And then I sat on his steps to catch my breath, wishing I had a cigarette of my own to smoke.

CHAPTER FOUR

TRENT

Moreton-in-Marsh. A classy little place at the heart of the Cotswolds, with quaint stone buildings and posh signage and Hayley Friar's latest menswear boutique.

That's why we were dressed up like prize pissing poodles — her big opening night bash. That and the fact Hayley loves her bit of rough trussed up in pretty packaging. We'd been doing this gig since last summer, once a month without fail. Her *downtime* she called it. Her little break from the prissy little store owner she made herself out to be.

The shop was still full, people going gaga over fancy silk ties and her other high-end shit. She was at the back, fawning over some couple who'd whipped out the gold card. The guy had a toupee like a squashed hamster. His girlfriend was a fucking model, legs up to her neck. That about sums up this place, and sums up the circles Hayley Friar schmoozes in.

I gave her a nod and kept my distance, pointing the others over to a quiet space by the window. Jimmy O held up some swanky shirt with ruffles, twirling around with it like a daft fucking prick. He was still doing it when she made her way over.

She took the hanger from him, placed it back on the rack with nothing more than a shake of the head.

"You polish up well," she said, and her eyes were all over us. All over me. "Suits you, Trent. You too, guys."

Did it fuck.

I gestured to the crowd. "This shit wrapping up soon?"

"Very soon," she said.

Hayley Friar's *very soon* was over two pissing hours long, but I forgot all about that once she turned the open sign to closed and lowered the shutters. Her sparkly white dress was fitted and fine — and on the floor at her feet in two seconds flat.

She stepped out of her knickers and flashed a grin.

Hayley was mid-thirties, tops. Perky little tits with pointy nipples. A thin line of hair between her legs that didn't match the auburn on her head. Makeup that runs like a fucking dream when she's gagging on dick.

"Where do you want it?" I said, my hand already on the swell in my pants.

She beckoned us over with a laugh, hitching her ass up onto a low display table in the middle of the store. She cleared her pretty little tie rack in one swoop and kicked a pile of shirts onto the floor along with them. Then she laughed.

"Fuck me," she said. "And make it hard. I'm so sick of all this pretentious shit. I'm sick of being a good girl!"

My dick twitched as she gathered her heels up onto the edge. Her fingers were at her pussy, her head lolled back as we closed in. Her cunt was sopping, nipples like bullets, mouth nice and wide as she sucked Jimmy's dick into her mouth — he always gets straight fucking in there. Hugh was latched onto one tit and enjoying the fuck out of it, so I nudged Petey to the other. He was still nervy, still on edge, still needing direction every five fucking seconds. Like any of us were there to hold his fucking hand.

I took my cock out and dropped to my knees between Hayley's thighs. Her cunt was so fucking ready, knees falling open like the wanton whore she loved to be. She moaned around Jimmy's cock, squirming on the table as I lowered my mouth to her pretty wet slit. Her pussy was like a fucking peach. I tongued her with tight little flicks, nice and steady until her legs were twitching. I pushed two fingers inside and she bucked her hips, reached for my hair and held me there.

She sucked in a breath as Jimmy's dick plopped from her mouth.

"Fuck yes!" she hissed. "Fuck me, Trent! Fuck me!" She tugged at my hair, her fingers raking my scalp. "Fucking fuck me!"

Dirty bitch.

Buck took her fingers and wrapped them around his thick dick, held them tight as he thrust away in her hand. I pulled my fingers from her cunt and moved them to her asshole instead. She tensed and wriggled like a fish on a line, that tight little hole opening up nicely.

Hayley likes to take two at once. One in the pink, one in the fucking brown. She's used to this shit — takes two dildos at home, so she tells us.

I slipped a johnny on and went for the pink. She felt good. Really fucking good. Her legs wrapped around my waist and demanded more, demanded harder, demanded every fucking thing. She choked and spluttered on Jimmy's cock and the dirty bitch in her turned feral.

"Give it to me!" she ordered. "All of it! Make me fucking take it!"

Jimmy did make her take it, pinching her nose and ramming her throat deep and hard. Her cheeks billowed and she squirmed, her legs gripping tight as I rammed that sweet cunt and spit-roasted the shit out of her. Her hand was still on Buck's dick, and she reached out for Hugh's with the other.

Jimmy gave Petey a tap. Offered him turns. Between them they fucked Hayley's dirty mouth until her mascara was a train wreck, and I gritted my teeth, pulled out of her pussy before I shot my load.

I rubbed her clit off again — rough and fast this time, in the way I'd come to know she craves. She came for me with a retch and a groan, her legs kicking out as I worked her on through it.

"My turn," Buck grunted when she'd tipped over the peak. I moved to one side and he pushed into her in one thrust. Fuck, how he pounded her.

I squeezed at her tits until she arched her back, flicked at those stiff nipples with my tongue. Jimmy changed position, fucked her throat until she quacked. And then I made my move.

I took her by the waist and lifted her up, and the guys moved without being told.

Buck took her place on the table, and I dropped her sopping pussy right back onto his cock.

She moaned and groaned and rode him like a fucking pro until I pushed her forwards and jammed my thumb in her asshole. She stilled, panting ragged breaths.

I smiled at Petey. "Get up here, lad, and get a fucking johnny on it."

He scurried over. His hands were shaking as he ripped into the foil.

"Fuck her ass," I said. "That's what she fucking wants. Hey, Hayley?"

"God yes! Fuck me!" She squealed as he pressed his cock to her hole. "Do it!"

The lad fucked her, and fucked her good. His balls slapped against Buck's underneath and he didn't give a fuck, just kept fucking ploughing her. He fucked hard, and so did Buck, stretching that dirty bitch wide open between them as she cried out for more.

Petey didn't last all that long. He came with a groan, his cheeks flushed, and Jimmy O was straight in to take his place.

I took Jimmy O's spot after him, and her ass was well and truly fucking ready by that point. I barely had to push inside, but being in there was fucking bliss. I circled my hips to spread her wider, and she rolled her hips with me.

"Yes..." she hissed. "Oh God, oh fucking God..."

I wrapped her hair around my fingers, pulled it until her back arched. "Is this fucking dirty enough?"

She nodded. "Fuck yes!"

I breathed into her ear. "Gonna fuck you until we're all fucking done. That what you want?"

"Yes!"

The pressure built in my balls, the urge to shoot my load threatening to take me. Buck was feeling it, too. His thrusts were frantic.

"Fuck!" he groaned. "I'm fucking done!"

He shot his load and bellowed like a beast, and the jerks sent me over the edge, too, sent me coming hard inside Hayley's hungry fucking asshole as Hugh emptied himself in her mouth.

End of round fucking one, and we switched it up.

Fingers on her clit as she took us one by one, and the bitch came over and over, her pussy so fucking pink and raw. Her asshole was a fucking pleasure, slack and hot and hungry for cock. Her mouth was fucking insatiable, her dirty moans egging us on.

Fuck, how we took that dirty bitch, and she loved it, she fucking loved it.

We held off on the final load until she'd had her fill — we knew her game by now.

When she'd flailed through one final climax she held up her hand for time out, a big dirty grin on her sweaty face. When she was ready she dropped to her knees in the middle of the store and opened wide as we pressed into a circle around her.

I focused on her gaping mouth, all smudged and dripping with spit, working my cock hard until my balls were tight enough to blow all over again.

I shot my load right onto her filthy tongue and she ate it all up, then smacked her lips for more.

There was plenty more.

Four fucking loads more.

I left the foray before they were done. I gathered up my used johnnys and tossed them in the bin. I'd straightened up my clothes before the others had even finished up.

I was done. Job complete. Balls empty.

Customer satisfied.

JODIE

Don't think about Trent. Don't think about Trent. Don't think about Trent.

I herded the kids through bath and bedtime, and made sure Nanna had taken her tablets before I sat with her to finish up her evening TV.

"Well?" she said during the advert break. "Did you sort things out with your Darren?"

I shrugged. "Nothing to sort, Nanna. We just... I said thanks for the washing machine." I gave her my *don't-be-ridiculous* eyes. "He's not mine to sort."

She chuckled to herself. "So I keep hearing..."

I held my breath — half expecting to field gigolo questions raised by over-the-fence gossip — but she let out a sigh at the end of her crime-drama and made her way to bed. Maybe she didn't know... I could hope.

Once Nanna was tucked up for the night, I resumed my regular schedule. I wiped down the kitchen worktops, fed the cat for the twentieth time, sorted school lunchboxes and cleared the scrubbed-out baking pans away. It was late when I finally dragged myself to the machine to sort out the Trent-washed laundry. I did this while totally not thinking about him and his five man gigolo outfit, of course.

I sorted the kids' blouses, then the socks, then the miscellaneous whites before I faced the inevitable, embarrassing confrontation of my underwear pile. *Oh Lord.* I cringed afresh as the full horror of the granny pants hit home, and it seemed so much worse now, now that I'd seen *him* — the one I was definitely not thinking about. Definitely not thinking about *at all*.

I definitely *wasn't* thinking about how kind the years had been to the man I was definitely, definitely over.

Definitely.

Totally over.

Anyhow, it wasn't just the passage of time that had served Trent well. No. It was the gym — sweat and time and effort. That and a fat wedge of cash from a string of loaded women like Porsche-bitch, no doubt. I bet *she* had nice knickers. I bet she had nice *everything*.

I looked through my pitiful pants collection. Some had holes. In at least one pair the elastic had snapped. One pair was still vaguely blood-stained. All of them were grey and tatty and thoroughly unattractive. That's when it occurred to me that I might be too...

Ouch.

Super ouch.

Was I grey and tatty and thoroughly unattractive?

I scoffed the thought aside. Porsche-bitch has *time* to look great. Porsche-bitch probably has nothing better to worry about *than* looking great.

I could look great, too. If I really wanted to. I had makeup, I could put a face on any time I felt like it...

I fished my cosmetics bag from the odds-and-sods drawer. My heart dropped to find the situation was worse than expected...

One cruddy foundation — congealed around the top. Lid missing.

One blunt eyeliner pencil.

One *neutral glow* palette of eyeshadow — half of the colours missing, the other half broken and crumbly having been stabbed with an applicator. *Thanks, Ruby.*

Two lipsticks. One was just a paltry stub left in the bottom. One was so red I'd never even tried it.

Had it really been that long..?

Yes. It had been that long. The occasional night out down the local with Tonya had turned into a Christmas-only event. Ladies-who-lunch had become a makeup-less affair, hair scooped up in a pony after the school run.

Brian hadn't cared a toss about my makeup through the two piss-poor years of our relationship... Hadn't cared about my hair, either... or sex, in fact...

Or me...

Big pants had become a thing of comfort — bumper packs of five with standard white bras were easy-peasy. They covered my baby podge nicely. And who was there to worry about now, anyway? Who would ever see them? Not even Brian... not since I'd ditched the loser last winter.

Trent. He'd seen them.

And it smarted. The embarrassment prickled my chest. Shit.

He'd seen my ugly, stained knickers and now he was off fucking some rich bitch who probably had stylists to choose her panty-stash for her.

In a moment of madness I crumpled up those gross knickers and tossed them straight into the outside bin. My makeup bag followed soon afterwards.

I slammed the lid with a satisfying thump.

Good fucking riddance.

Late night shopping at the 24-hour supermarket was surprisingly calming. The aisles were empty and the music was loud, and I wandered freely through the clothes and makeup section without hindrance. A strange sense of guilt washed over me as I contemplated my purchases — some irrational mantra that said if I wasn't buying it for the kids it wasn't worth buying at all. But *I* was worth it. Surely I had to be worth it?

I picked up a handful of frilly knickers and a couple of matching bras. I grabbed a tight little teal V-neck that showed off the dip of my waist and a smaller pair of jeans to go along with them. A pair of low heels that wouldn't totally destroy my feet through the day at the cafe. Some foundation, and an eyeliner that worked. A decent lipstick, too. A new eyeshadow palette, with green and gold and blue. It was a start.

My heart was thumping as I went through the self-scan checkout, shoving my card in the reader before I could change my mind.

It felt exhilarating, and indulgent and strangely naughty. It felt *good*.

I sang along to the radio on the way home, hoping that everyone had slept through my late night disappearance. They had. Of course they had. They weren't babies anymore, weren't glued to me 24/7. They had Nanna, and Mia was almost old enough to babysit herself. It was only me who worried about leaving them, worried about going out for five minutes and not being there.

Only me who worried about *everything* all the time.

Back at home, I tried on my new undies and scoped myself out in my wardrobe mirror. Sure, I had a belly podge, but show me a mother of two kids who doesn't. The rest of me looked pretty alright. I'd lost weight without realising it, and admittedly I didn't have the ass I'd had a decade earlier at sweet nineteen — but it was still fairly pert and curved in the right places. My waist dipped in enough to give me a half-decent shape. My thighs were a little wobbly but who really cares? And my tits... well... they looked so much better in a decent push-up bra.

I'd pass. Whatever passing even means. It wasn't hideous… it was certainly a lot better than the shape I'd been presenting in plain, comfortable — yeah, ok, over-sized — clothes.

By the time I went to bed I'd managed to turn a full 180, convincing myself I'd wasted a pile of money for nothing, and nobody would even notice the difference. Convincing myself I was running a fool's errand just because some salon-perfect woman had crossed my path down the garage. But despite all the self-talk, I couldn't shake off this little pang of something. Excitement? Relief?

Hope?

I don't know what it was, but it sure felt good. Underneath the resignation and the embarrassment and the fear, there was something alive and kicking. It was so alien I could hardly fathom it.

I wondered when I'd written myself off. From being a woman, I mean — because that's what it felt like, ultimately. Like somehow, somewhere along the path, I'd traded in my female identity for some all-encompassing idea of motherhood and a minimum wage job down the cafe. It had happened so slowly, I guess. Losing myself just a tiny little piece at a time; a busy schedule, not enough sleep, a lousy boring boyfriend like Brian…

He'd never fucked me like he wanted me. Not like Darren used to.

With Darren it was raw, and tempestuous, and exciting. In the early days, when we were still good together, he'd fuck me like I was the only woman in the world, the only woman he'd ever want. He'd fuck me with a wildness that I'd never found since — something so real… so unapologetic…

Figures — unapologetic could be Darren Trent's middle name.

Sleep didn't come easy. The early hours came and went and I was still wide awake, just thinking — stewing life around in my head. So many questions, so few answers...

Had I really lost myself with Brian? Was that when my life went stale?

No. It wasn't, and I knew it.

It had started long before that. Long before Darren and I called time out. Long before we even *considered* calling time out.

It had started when I first had Mia and realised the whole universe had shifted on its axis. That I was no longer just Jodie, Trent's girlfriend, but Mum, too.

Somewhere along the line I stopped being me and Darren stopped being Darren. We were just... I dunno... two people stuck in a rut together. One long, painful, sour rut.

Oh how it had fucking hurt to let it go.

But we were good with the time out now, had been for years. So many years. It was the right decision for both of us, *all* of us... we knew that... we both knew that... of course we did...

It was *still* the right decision. Definitely.

Absolutely one million percent definitely.

I didn't want him at all, no way. Not even in a tux. Never. Not even a consideration... Not even a fleeting thought in my mind...

I definitely didn't want Darren Trent...

Especially not in a tux...

And definitely, definitely not enough to reach under my bed for my bodywand...

CHAPTER FIVE

JODIE

"You look like a princess, Mum!"

"That lipstick looks super cool!"

"Oh, Jodie, that colour really does suit you. What a lovely top!"

Seeing the shock on their faces cemented the fact that my late night shopping splurge had been the right call. Oh the wonder of a top that actually fitted properly and a splash of *Autumn Berry* lippy. My choices hadn't even been that extreme, not really. I could have picked *Mystic Plum* or *Scarlet Harlot*. Maybe I would one day. Never say never.

I made the school run with more confidence than I'd felt in a long time, head high as I stood amongst the other mothers – despite all the whispers that were clearly circulating post gigolo-gate. Today I felt strangely immune, my own entity of just Jodie, separate from Trent and his *bang-ganging* ways. My hair was freshly washed and straightened, my skin glowing through the wonderful illusion of decent foundation. I looked better and I knew it, and maybe it was a far cry away from the glitz and glamour of Porsche-bitch and her ilk, but it was good enough for me.

It was good enough.

Lorraine gave me a *twit-twoo* as I stepped into the cafe for the beginning of my shift.

"Get you!" she said. "You look fantastic. Have you dyed your hair?" She ran a section of my straightened hair through her fingers, held it up to the light.

"Not yet," I said with a smile.

I was so concerned with how good I felt that I barely noticed the change in demeanour of those around me. Yesterday's scorn had turned into curiosity, and further still into this strange ripple of interest that was whispering through the female village populous.

Hannah Bowen never usually gives me the time of day. She comes into the cafe at least three mornings a week, and besides a polite smile she gives me nothing. Not even a half-arsed *how are you?* Hannah Bowen has a reputation for being stand-offish, but it seemed that today was the day that all changed.

She leaned over the counter as I prepped her coffee, and she had bright pink lipstick on, foundation so thick she looked slightly orange.

"Hi, Jodie. Wow. Nice top." Her smile was fake and bright, but I appreciated the compliment all the same. "How are you?" she said. "How are the girls?"

You could have knocked me down with a feather.

I spooned out the milk froth for her cappuccino and gave her a paper smile. "I'm good, thanks. We're all good. And yourself?"

She flashed a look around the cafe, and then her smile grew brighter. "I'm great, yeah. Really great."

"Pleased to hear it." I placed her cup on the side, put a biscuit on her plate.

She didn't even pick it up, made no effort to leave at all. She cleared her throat, and smiled some more, then she twisted a stray wisp of blonde hair around her fingers. "Say, Jodie, have you, um... have you seen Trent lately? I mean... is he, um..."

"Is he, um...?" I met her eyes and held her stare.

"Is he, um... you know..." Her eyes widened. "Is he really a... *gigolo*?"

I felt my cheeks warming beneath the foundation. "You'll have to ask him yourself," I said.

She laughed, just a little. "Well, I would, but..." She leaned in further. "We don't really know each other..." Her eyes twinkled. "I just heard he was offering... *group activities*. If you know what I mean."

"Like I said, you'll really have to ask him."

Another clear of the throat. "Is that his thing? *Gangbangs*?"

Not that I ever knew.

"I'm really not the person to ask." I pushed her cup in her direction. "We were together a long time ago. I'm really not qualified to give you the lowdown on Trent's current sexual preferences."

I watched her deflate in front of me, huffing out at least a little disappointment. "Let me know, if you hear anything. I mean, if he has a website..."

Like he has a fucking website. Bang Gang - orgies on demand.

I forced a smile. "I'll be sure to let you know."

Hannah Bowen may have been the first to ask directly about Trent's little moonlighting project, but she sure as hell wasn't the last. Women who'd seemed as impartial to a full face of makeup as I'd been were suddenly rocking up with beautician-perfect smoky eyes and glossy lipstick. Must be something in the air.

Sweet little Amy Tanner from Elm Grove stuttered her way through questions about *Trent's services*. Rita Powell laughed her way through a monologue on how she fancied *living wild* and did I know anything about five hot mechanics out for a good time? Sarah Kelly came right out with it and asked if she could book Trent and Buck through me, and that really did make me blush, foundation or no.

Lorraine handed me an espresso as a break in the queue came around. Her eyes were sympathetic, like they always are when it's shit about Trent. She gestured to the packed out cafe and raised her eyebrows.

"I'm guessing the horny females of our lovely village haven't all just taken a sudden liking to Tuesday morning coffee," she whispered.

"Sorry," I said.

"Don't be, all business is good business, I just hope this isn't too hard on you." Her look was so pointed. That *Trent's-an-asshole-and-you're-better-off-without-him* look I'd come to know so well. She put a hand on my shoulder. "Best thing you ever did splitting up. He's so..." She groaned. "Troublesome."

And really hot in a tux. I forced the thought from my mind, pissed to find the same flutters in my belly that I'd felt the night before. A bodywand session should have sorted it. *Did* sort it. Or so I thought. It hadn't meant anything, just fantasy gone mad. The shock of seeing Darren so... toned... the thought of some rich bitch being fucked by him and Buck, the others, too. I mean, that could never be me... I'd never take five guys... even if I'd had the orgasm of the century at the thought of it. It meant nothing.

Totally nothing.

I definitely wouldn't want that.

That's for women like Mandy Taylor and Hannah Bowen. Women who are... brash.

Confident.

Horny.

Sexy.

I checked out my reflection in the side of the coffee machine. Was *I* horny and sexy? The thought made me laugh out loud. A couple of dabs of eyeliner did not make a sex kitten, that's for sure.

Not yet, anyway.

Tonya came in at the end of lunch, puffing and sweaty and midway through an apparent jog around the village.

She gripped a section of belly and wiggled it at me over the counter. "Keeping fit, need to tone up a little. Then I might hit the online dating. Again."

"You look great as you are," I said. She did, too.

Her eyes met mine and widened. "Not as fine as you! Jesus, Jodie, what the hell happened? Did someone break in and commit *armed makeover*? If they did then please send them my way, I'll leave the window open and won't call the cops."

"It's just a bit of foundation..." I mumbled, but I was smiling.

"Like fuck it is! That top's new." She pointed straight at my chest. "Those babies are definitely in a decent push-up, and..." She leaned over the counter to check out the rest of me. "New jeans. Definitely new. So, what's going on, pussycat?"

"Just thought I could smarten myself up a little." I handed her a mug of tea. "Seems I'm not the only one around here. World's gone crazy."

"The Trent effect." She rolled her eyes. "Mention a five-mechanic gangbang and the whole village goes makeup crazy, go figure."

I leaned over the counter. "That's not why I'm doing this."

"Oh, I know," she said. "You're doing this because it's about time you put some effort into being *you* again."

"It is?"

"Oh yes," she smirked. "It really is. Which is exactly why you're taking a day off to come shopping with me. Girls' day. Don't say no."

"But..."

Lorraine's hands appeared on my shoulders. Her voice was loud in my ear. "Yes, you *are* having a shopping day. You haven't taken time off since Easter."

"Exactly!" Tonya exclaimed.

"Definitely," Lorraine insisted. "This Friday. I'll get Emma to cover."

"Friday," Tonya confirmed. "Spa, lunch and shopping."

Spa, lunch and shopping sounded expensive. I said as much.

Tonya just scoffed at me. "Get Trent to help out, now you know about his lucrative little side-line, I'm sure he won't mind dishing out a bit so you can have some downtime."

I shook my head. "This has nothing to do with Darren. He does enough. We do alright."

I could feel Lorraine's scorn at the back of me, but she didn't say a word. That was something she'd never been right on, truth be told. You can say a lot of things about Darren Trent, but the accusation that he doesn't do his bit to look after the girls was way off the mark.

Tonya didn't even try to argue with me, she knew as much, too.

I let out a sigh. "I could come, maybe get my nails done, just the cheap ones..."

Tonya clapped her hands. "Get in!"

"But!" I added. "I'm not going to be going shopping crazy, I'll just be there for the company. I'll be your personal shopper."

"It's a start." She downed her tea in one and started jogging on the spot. "In that case I better keep up with the keep fit, see if I can drop a dress size in the next few days. Laters."

I watched Lorraine chalk my day off on the rota and couldn't help but smile.

TRENT

Petey shrugged at me, hung up the phone. "Another service to book in," he began, but I waved him quiet.

We'd had ten new service bookings today already. Ten.

None of them due, all of them female.

Mandy fucking Taylor had a lot to answer for.

Buck grinned at me, tugged at his beard. "Think we should open the books up? Take on some new clients?"

I shook my head. "Fuck that. Not locals. Got enough shit going on already."

I dived back in to the air-con job I'd been working on and only surfaced again when a chorus of wolf whistles started up. My gut dropped at the prospect of another Eleanor Hartley drive-by, but the figure approaching our shutter doors wasn't anyone after a Bang Gang special.

I've known Tonya since we were kids. She was already Jodie's best mate by the time we started up. I don't think they ever weren't. She was jogging today, in some pale grey leggings that showed enough to get the guys whooping.

"Knock it off, lads," I grunted, tossing a roll of tape in Jimmy's direction to get him to quit with the hip thrusting.

Tonya came bounding straight up, her dark ponytail bouncing around her shoulders as she jogged on the spot, her tits bobbing up and down. I smiled, but it wasn't in *that* way. I'd never seen Tonya in *that* way, pretty though she was. Her cheeks were flushed pink and her breath was heavy. I knew exactly what the guys were thinking, but she seemed oblivious. Oblivious or totally disinterested. It made a change around here lately.

I raised an eyebrow. "Come to chew me out about Mandy Taylor?" I asked. "If so, you needn't bother. I already know what a fuck up that was."

"Jesus, Trent, would I?" She gave me a healthy tut. "I don't need to tell you when you've been a wanker. Pretty sure you can work that out for yourself."

I made my way outside and she followed, stopped jogging to do some stretches. I lit up a cigarette. "So?"

She rolled her eyes at me. "I'm on a route, you know, keep fit. Maybe I was just passing."

"Never kept fit past my door before."

"Never kept fit before," she laughed. "Ah, fuck it." She stopped with the exercises and pulled a pack of cigarettes from her bra. I smirked as she lit one up. "Jodie," she said. "I'm here about Jodie."

"So *she* sent you to chew me out?"

"Has Jodie ever once sent me to say her piece for her?" She took a long drag. "She's no idea I'm here."

"Oh?"

She smiled. "I guess you haven't seen her today."

"Why would I have?"

"No reason. She's just... found herself a little." I didn't have time to ask questions before she changed topic. "I'm taking her out for the day on Friday. She totally deserves the break. I wanted to make sure you'll have the girls, don't want her racing back for the school run before we're done."

I nodded. "Righto."

"So you will?" Big dark eyes sparkled at me.

"Goes without saying, Tonya."

She clapped her hands together. "Excellent!"

Her enthusiasm was infectious, I found myself smiling. "Where you taking her?"

"Hereford," she said. "Spa, beauty shit, shopping."

I pulled a face. "She's up for that, is she?" I couldn't remember the last time Jodie went in for all that girly pampering crap.

"Yes. She's up for it."

I felt a niggle in my gut. I puffed away on my cigarette, tried to play down the unease. "What's this in aid of? She got a hot date or something?"

She shook her head. "No, no. She's just... you'll see for yourself when you run into her." She tapped my arm. "She's finding herself again. New clothes, makeup... she looks fucking amazing. I just want to give her a helping hand along the way. It's time she lived for herself again. It's been too long. Work and the girls." She flashed me a look of scorn. "And Brian."

"No argument from this end," I said.

"Good." She grinned. "So, it's set. You have the girls, I'll take Jo out for some hardcore girly time. I can't fucking wait." She stubbed her cigarette out. "I'd better get going, this belly fat isn't gonna burn off by itself, Darren."

I scoffed at her. "You don't need to lose any of that, you look fine enough as you are."

"Thanks," she said. "You can tell Jimmy O he isn't getting a piece, dirty bastard. I saw him thrusting."

"Will do."

She slapped my arm. "Seems I'm the only woman in the village who's not going gaga for a gangbang." She met my eyes. "Don't fuck local, Darren. Plenty of rich bitches out there without crapping on your own doorstep. It isn't on."

"Wasn't intending on it." I sighed. "Mandy Taylor was a one off. For Buck."

"Ah," she said.

"Ah fucking right. I knew it was trouble."

She shrugged. "Just be more careful who you stick it in from now on." She grinned. "Lecture over." She groaned as she looked back at the road. "I fucking hate keep fit, it stinks."

I laughed. "Want a lift?"

"Nah," she said. "No pain, no gain." She let out a sigh and resumed her jogging on the spot. "Laters."

I grabbed her elbow before she could escape. Her eyes were wide as I pulled her close, stepped to the side of the shutters. They grew wider still when I unbuttoned my overalls and reached inside.

I smirked. "Fucking hell, Tonya. I'm not about to give you the pissing gigolo act." I pulled out my wallet, counted out three hundred in twenties. She raised her eyebrows as I shoved it into her hand. "For Jo," I explained. "Make sure she has a nice day, yeah?"

She flicked through the notes. "She'll never take this, and you know it."

I shrugged. "Make something up. Say you won it at bingo or some crap. Whatever you want."

She smiled and slipped it in her pocket. "I'll work something out."

"Just don't say it was from me. It's not a... I just want to..." I sighed. "Just make sure she has a good time."

She winked. "I will. You can count on it."

Yes, I could.

The guys were wolf whistling again before she was clear of the yard. I'd have given them another roasting if she hadn't spun on her own sweaty heels and given them the finger herself.

I got back to that air-con.

CHAPTER SIX

JODIE

"I'm nervous," I admitted, eyes still closed tight. "Maybe I shouldn't have..."

"You really should have," Tonya insisted.

I finally dared to look. The sight in the mirror took me aback.

"You like?" the hairdresser asked, her smile wide.

I ran my fingers through my shorter hair, and it felt so soft. So stylish. I hadn't had a long bob since I'd had Mia, having neither had the time nor the inclination to maintain it. Or the money, for that matter, not in the beginning.

I hadn't had the time, inclination or money to keep up with the deep-cherry hair dye, either, but it was another thing I'd opted to revisit with a little encouragement from Tonya. I shook my head, and the longer lengths shimmied, just about grazed my shoulders.

I grabbed a deep breath and couldn't stop smiling. "I love it. I really love it." I turned to Tonya. "I feel like me again! Oh my God, I really feel like me!"

"You *look* like you, as well," she said. She still had foils in her hair from her highlights, but came over anyway, wrapped her arms around my neck. "It's just like old times. Ahhh, can you remember? You and me, singing along to the top-forty pop chart in your bedroom. You had this hair then."

I laughed. "With Nanna singing along on the landing in her opera voice. How could I ever forget? Happy days."

They were indeed happy days, when Pops was still alive, too. He and Nanna used to be at ours all the time. The thought hit me in the belly. I'd been so close to Pops. Darren, too. He'd been close to both of them.

But now wasn't the time to be thinking about any of that.

The hairdresser held up a second mirror and I was pleasantly surprised to find how much of a difference my new cut made to the back of me. I looked cared for. No more straggly limp pony, no more freshly-raked mess of split ends. The style changed my face, too. Made me appear younger. Fresher. *Sexier*.

I felt my eyes welling and it was so ridiculous I had to laugh.

"Daft old goat," Tonya said, but she was teary-eyed as well. I laughed harder at the realisation and she pulled a face. "This is from the ammonia!" she protested. "Don't for a second think it isn't, missy!"

I stared at myself with a strange mix of elation and sorrow. Sorrow for the me I'd abandoned all that time ago. Sorrow for the self-esteem I'd buried with Brian and only just started to rediscover. Sorrow for the years going through the motions. For the years when I didn't matter to myself.

Sorrow for the years I'd written myself off as a woman.

"I can't believe how emotional a silly little haircut is making me." I met Tonya's eyes. "Never again," I said. My voice was low and steely. "Not ever. I'm never giving myself up again."

She nodded. "Not ever. You're back now. Forever."

Yes.

Yes, I was.

I had a spring in my step as we hit the shops, and suddenly the racks of clothes held promise – a little excitement, too. I picked up items I'd never have considered before, cute little tops that showed a bit of cleavage, some dresses in brighter colours, fitted at the bust and flared enough to skim my hips. I tried everything, and put it all back, committing to *maybe I'll come back for it* every time Tonya tutted at me.

I held my breath as she stopped outside *Jaunt* – a trendy but uber tasteful boutique that I'd admired from outside but never ventured in.

"Come on!" she said. "We're on a roll."

I looked at the price tags in the window. "This is a bit... extravagant..."

She took my arm. "No harm *trying*, Jo. No harm at all."

As soon as I was inside I wished I'd held my ground. The place was teeming with beautiful clothes that made my heart stutter. Tonya picked up a scarlet tunic top with a handkerchief hem and the fabric billowed and rippled like a dream.

"Try it," she said and shoved it in my direction. I held it up to my torso in front of the mirror.

"I can't..."

She found some fitted black jeans from the rack and forced them into my arms. "And these."

I didn't hand them back, because in truth I didn't want to. My soul had already taken ownership of them, my fingers gripping tight. I added a cold-shoulder turquoise number to the mix, a slightly boho blouse that screamed at me from the mannequin, a cherry blossom bodycon dress that I'd have to wear with shaping underwear, and a couple of decent camis with lace trimmings.

I daren't imagine how much the little bundle would come to, convincing myself that most of it would look totally shit on me.

But it didn't. It didn't at all.

"Oh my fucking God!" Tonya squealed as I stepped from the fitting room in the bodycon dress. "That was made for you!"

Even without the shaper knickers I was inclined to agree with her. It wrapped me in its beautiful contours, highlighting the slopes and curves that should be there, and somehow managing to skim over the ones that shouldn't. Fuck knows how.

The other items followed suit. Teamed with the new hair and a splash of makeup it was like another woman staring back at me, and I liked her. I really liked her.

Every item ended up on the yes pile. Every single one.

I sighed as I re-examined the selection. "Which one shall I take?"

Tonya waggled a finger at me. "Uh uh, no fucking way, girlfriend." She laughed. "These babies were made for you."

I totted up the total. "There's nearly four hundred quid's worth of clothes in this haul," I groaned. "I'll take the bodycon dress, and that's pushing it. A hundred quid for a bloody dress, I must have lost my mind."

I pulled the dress from the pile and made to hang the others on the *no* rack before my heart could break, but she stopped me, tugged the clothes from my fingers.

"I'll get these," she said.

I grabbed her by the elbow before she was even a foot away. "Sorry?"

She sighed, looked pretty shifty. "I was going to tell you, but I wanted it to be a surprise." She put her hand on her hip, like she meant business. "I won six hundred quid on a scratch card. I want to share it with you." She looked at herself in the mirror, checked out her highlights. "Spent my bit already, got some good shit coming in the post. Quite an eBay haul..." She pulled a face, looked a little embarrassed.

"Well, congratulations!" I said. "And I'm touched by the gesture, but that money's yours. You should spend it on you." I gestured to her own pile of maybes back in the changing room.

"Don't like them," she lied. "I think I'll probably need to lose a couple of inches first."

"Whatever, Tonya." I laughed. "I know you're trying to save me and all that, and I appreciate it, I really do. I appreciate it more than you could ever know, truly, but I'm not taking that money from you. No way." I yanked back the clothes before she could protest. "I'll get the bodycon dress, as a one-off ridiculous splurge, and I'll wear it on a night out. You can buy me a drink or two with your winnings, deal?"

"Not really," she said. She fumbled in her handbag pulled out a handful of notes. A big handful. "I already got the cash out. I wanted to give it to you."

I felt a strange tickle of gratitude in my chest, but I forced it aside. I took her hand, pushed that cash back in her purse. "No," I said. "Thank you, but no. Spend it on you, please. You deserve it more than I do." I smiled. "My lucky day will come. Maybe I should get a scratch card myself, eh? Maybe we're onto a winning streak?"

She looked thoroughly fucking mortified. "Please don't do this," she said. "Those clothes look amazing on you. I know you want them. I know you feel good in them, I can see it written all over you."

"They're only clothes!" I said. I ignored my pained heart. "It doesn't matter, Tonya. I got my hair done. That's a start, right?"

"Please, Jodie." She stared right at me. "I want to do this."

I closed my eyes, shook my head. By the time I opened them again I was as strong as steel. "And *I* really want you to spend the money on *you*."

I hung the rejected items on the *no* rack and made an exit, but every step towards the register and the inevitable exit beyond grew harder. My mind went to the forbidden zone, to that extra card in my purse, the one I never use. The one I've never even considered using, not since Darren and I nearly came to blows over my plans to use it for Disneyland for the kids.

No, he'd said. *No fucking way, Jodie. We'll find a way to pay for Disney ourselves. This isn't what that money's for. This isn't what Pops meant it to be for!*

I checked in my purse and there it was, the pristine plastic tucked cosily behind my standard dog-eared debit card. I pulled it out and rubbed it between my fingers, got a feel for it.

Tonya saw me and sucked in breath. "Pop Pop's money?!" She nodded. "Oh yes. Yes! This definitely counts! One hundred percent!" She tugged me back to the changing rooms and I had to dig my heels in to slow down.

"I don't know," I said. "The will said it was for me only. For *experiences of a lifetime*." I gestured to the clothes. "I'm really not sure this counts. It's just some clothes. Pops worked hard for that money... I don't want to waste it..." Tears pricked at the thought, at the memory of having the five grand transferred to my savings account and knowing it was his final gift. His instructions had been clear.

This is for Jodie, and Jodie only. It is to be spent on life. On living the dream. On the experiences of a lifetime, just for her, courtesy of old Pop Pop.

Tonya squeezed my arm, squeezed it hard. "Pops would count this as living," she said. "Pops would know how hard you've worked, how hard you've tried, know everything you've sacrificed to bring those girls up." She smiled, and she was sad, too. "It's your time," she said. "The time you find yourself again. This *is* an experience of a lifetime." She sighed. "Please, Jo, if you're not going to let me buy these clothes for you, then at least let Pops do it. I know he'd want to."

I looked at the clothes again, and she was right. He would want to. I know he would.

"I feel good in them," I mumbled to myself. "It's so nice to feel good again." I looked at the scarlet top, remembered how amazing I'd felt in it. "Maybe this really *is* the experience of a lifetime – finding myself again after all this time. Maybe it's the start of a whole new world."

Tonya nodded. "Definitely."

Could I do this?

I weighed it up, back and forth. I mean, once I'd started spending it, would I be able to stop? It's a slippery slope, right? This *living*. I'd got used to scrimping and saving, used to making do and putting the kids first, putting Nanna first, putting the essentials first. The non-essentials, too, just so long as they weren't for me.

Moment of truth and I let my heart make the call. I walked quickly, quickly enough that my frugal, responsible self couldn't step in and trash the whole thing for me. I handed the clothes over at the register and presented the card with a flourish.

I keyed in the numbers I'd memorised by heart and waited for the transaction to go through.

It went through just fine.

Tonya said very little as we exited the store. I don't think she could quite believe it.

She was even more surprised when I walked a circuit back through our previous locations for the rest of the *maybe-I'll-come-back-for-thems* too.

Living sure felt good.

"I didn't spend much of it, not really," I justified as Tonya and I piled through my front door.

She dropped her bags in the hallway next to mine. "*I* know that. It's *you* who's having the problem with it."

Not a problem enough to take any of the items back, nor the cute little owl tunics I'd picked up for the girls, either. Or the plum silk headscarf I'd grabbed for Nanna. We could all *live* a little today, push the boat out.

"Wine?" I asked. "Just the one. A girly end to our girly day." I checked the clock, Darren would be bringing the girls back any time now. My stomach flipped at the thought. Ridiculous. Like he hadn't brought them home a million times before in the past seven years.

But not when I've had a freshly chopped, dark-cherry bob and a full face of makeup.

I grabbed a couple of glasses and asked Nanna if she was joining us. *No,* she said after gushing about my hair awhile. *She only drinks on special occasions. Christmas and birthdays and Sundays. Sometimes a Saturday too.* She was about to watch *Question King* anyway. She'd leave us girls to it.

Girls. I loved the way she still called us that.

Tonya let out a sigh, dropped into a seat at the dining table and held up her glass. "To new beginnings."

I laughed. "To cherry-red haircuts, and gangbanging mechanics." I paused. "And to Pops."

"To Pops," Tonya agreed.

We clinked glasses and took a healthy swig. I kicked back in the chair opposite, cast aside my heels and let my aching feet breathe.

"So," Tonya said, and she had that mischievous look I'd come to know so well over the years. "Since every other horny bitch in the village is chomping at the clit for some *Bang Gang* servicing, where do you sit on it?"

I almost spat my wine out. "Sorry?!"

She scoffed at me. "Jodie Symmonds, like I don't know you. Don't even try and tell me you haven't thought about it, no matter how pissed off you are."

"I don't know what you're talking about," I said, but my cheeks were scorching.

She laughed. "I knew it." Her grin was wide. "Bodywand? Many times over, right? Was it about Trent? He featured, right?"

"Shh!" I chided. "Nanna!" But Nanna was well out of earshot and I knew it.

Tonya's eyes twinkled. "If it's good enough for Mandy big-gob Taylor and the rest of the village, why not?"

"Because..." I began. "Because... Darren... because the girls..." I lowered my voice. "Because it's been ages, I might have forgotten what the fuck I'm supposed to do." I let out a giggle. "It's probably bloody healed up by now. I'm a reborn virgin." I smirked to myself. "Brian wasn't exactly... adventurous."

She groaned. "Brian was such a boring douchebag. Fuck knows how you even ended up with that loser."

"You know how I ended up with him."

"Yeah, yeah. I know the version you told me at the time."

I smiled. "Internet dating, like I said."

"Boring Dudes dot com?"

Oh my poor cheeks at the thought of the real story. Me looking for some casual hook-ups to finally get me over Darren, looking for guys who could fuck me senseless and make me feel like a woman again. Risky guys. Wild guys. Guys who'd make me bow-legged and exhausted for days to come. Only I'd found the safe option. Mr Thirty-grand Salary. Mr Respectable. Mr Safe As Fucking Houses.

Mr Fucking Dull.

Tonya leaned in. "The thing I never quite got," she said. "And I can ask you this now, since you're..."

"Since I'm..?"

She looked me up and down. "Since you're... *you* again. I just never got the move from someone like Darren to someone like Brian. I mean, you and Darren were... *intense.*"

"Humping like fucking rabbits, you mean?" I laughed.

"Like rabbits on Viagra." She downed some more of her wine. "I remember the shit you two used to get up to. Getting it on in Mary Hart's garden, while her parents were manning the barbeque... that time you disappeared in the Drum's loo and the whole fucking pool team could hear you... Sucking his dick in the back of Buck's car on the way to Jenna Ward's birthday bash..."

I couldn't help but smile at the memories. "A *long* time ago."

"Maybe not *so* long ago." She tipped her glass in my direction. "You'd have loved this Bang Gang crap then, just for the wildness of it. I know you would've."

I kept it coy. "*Maybe.*"

"So, what's different? Like I said, if it's good enough for Mandy bloody Taylor, it's more than good enough for you."

I waved her suggestion aside. "Why don't *you* have a go, if you're so sure it's a good idea?"

"Yeah, right." She rolled her eyes. "Like I have either the cash or the inclination. Trent and Buck are like fucking brothers to me. One million percent friend-zoned."

"And Petey, and Hugh and Jimmy O?"

She grinned. "Maybe Hugh and Jimmy O. I hear Petey's not up to all that much."

"How would you..." I questioned, but the answer was obvious. I smirked, and so did she, and we said it in unison.

"Mandy. Fucking. Taylor."

We were still laughing when the front door thumped its trademark thump into the wall. The regular Ruby entrance. She'd bang it off its hinges one of these days.

I composed myself as she came bounding through, a caked-on oil smear across her cheek. Standard. Mia followed a lot more meekly, dropped herself into the seat beside me. They pulled and prodded my hair, full of giddy compliments.

"Did you girls have fun?" I asked, grabbing them both in for a kiss. I rubbed at Ruby's cheek and she pulled a face.

"They've eaten," a voice called from the kitchen doorway, and the moment I'd been anticipating was upon me. Darren dropped their schoolbags on the floor by the fridge, and then his eyes met mine, and widened.

"Granny T cooked us stew," Ruby told me. "She put carrots in it and made me eat them. Urgh."

"That's lovely," I said. "Granny T makes a lovely stew, even if it does have carrots in it. I hope you said thank you."

She nodded, but I wasn't convinced, and right then I didn't have the resolve to push it. My parenting goals had frittered away to nothing and I was burning under Darren's stare, that low simmer behind his eyes scorching me alive. I couldn't tell what he was thinking, not even close, not even after all this time, but my heart was racing, my skin prickling.

"Thanks," I said to him. "For having the girls."

"No bother at all," he said.

I wanted him to say something, *anything*. Nice hair, or nice lippy, or *that colour really suits you*, but he said nothing, just stared.

It was Tonya who broke the tension, shrugged at Darren and gave a loud sigh. "Well?" she asked. "What do you think of Jodie's epic new do?"

He swallowed before he answered and it made my tummy flutter. I couldn't look at him. Couldn't bear it.

"It's not new," he said.

Tonya rolled her eyes. "Ok then, her new-*old* do. Do you like it?"

Ruby and Mia giggled and I half-wished the ground would swallow me.

"I *always* liked it," he said, and the way he said always made me feel so weird, so exposed. "You look great, Jodie. Really great. You look amazing."

He ran his fingers across his stubble, his mouth closed tight, as though he'd said too much. He shifted from foot to foot and cleared his throat.

"Thanks," I said, and my eyes found his again. "I feel really great. Thanks for helping to make it happen."

He nodded. "Right you are."

"Don't you want to see Jo's sexy new outfits?" Tonya prompted, and it was too far, much too far. I cringed at the embarrassment in his eyes, the absolute discomfort, hovering in the half-light of our old life together, staring at the reincarnation of the girl he fell in love with when we were just kids.

I felt it, too.

He gestured a thumb towards the front door. "Better be off. Shit to do."

Ruby groaned. "But Dad! You could stay! See Mum's new stuff! She'll look like a queen!"

"Your dad's probably very busy," I said.

"Work stuff," he said. "Another time, Rubes."

It broke my heart to see the deflation in her eyes.

"Go see your dad out," I said, and he didn't hang around a second longer. He raised a hand in goodbye to Tonya and gave me a nod, and then he was off, with the girls close behind him.

I listened to him call goodbye to Nanna, listened to the girl's goodbyes afterwards, Ruby's loud chatter and Mia's quieter *please don't go just yet, Dad*, and it hurt.

I don't know why it hurt so fucking bad, but it felt like I'd been stabbed right in the pit of me.

I exhaled a loud breath when I heard the door click shut, and Tonya breathed one of her own.

She picked up the bottle of wine, poured us both another big one.

"I think you need this," she said.

She wasn't bloody wrong.

TRENT

I could have been anywhere. It wouldn't have mattered shit to me. Balls deep in some slutty bitch's pussy in a posh hotel on the outskirts of Cheltenham, rutting away on her with other guy's dicks all around me. It took me a second to remember her name.

Melissa.

Melissa with the hairy pussy.

I ran my thumb over it and she jerked, offered an appreciative grunt as she choked on Buck's dick.

That's when it first fucking hit me.

I didn't want to be here. Didn't give a shit about the cash waiting at the end of this shitty fucking romp.

Jimmy O shot me a glare and I realised I'd stopped thrusting, standing like a fucking moron with my dick still half inside her.

"Get up here," I grunted, stepping aside to give him a turn. He shrugged and grinned, took up the spot with gusto, and Melissa didn't give a shit, not really. She squirmed under him and groaned for more. Like they always do.

I took a step back and watched, strangely vacant, like I was watching a shitty porn film after too many beers.

This fucking craziness was all Tonya's fault, dragging Jodie into her girly makeover crap and dragging me along with it. I felt a smile as I recalled Jodie's happiness, the easy grin on her face before she realised I was watching her. I'd stepped into a time warp and right there on the other side was the girl I'd loved so fucking hard I

91

thought it would kill me.

Only she wasn't mine to love anymore.

Hadn't been mine to love for a fucking long time.

I'd loved Jodie Symmonds when she was a slip of a girl with a dirty smile and a slick, sharp bob of dark-red hair. I'd loved Jodie Symmonds when she was so swollen with pregnancy that she could hardly walk, when her hair was greasy as fuck and she was moaning about under-boob sweat, pushing her fingers between her tits and smearing it under my nose as a demonstration. I'd loved her when she'd sat and eaten a whole bumper bucket of KFC and then farted like a stinky bitch all night long. I'd loved her when she was angry, when she was sad, when she stared at me as though she was unsure whether to fuck me or kill me. Maybe both at the same time.

I'd loved Jodie Symmonds when she'd forgotten how to love herself.

I thought I'd loved her enough for both of us. But no.

Life fucking sucks like that.

I pulled on my jeans, resigned to sitting this one out. Hopefully Melissa wouldn't notice with four other dicks to keep her attention.

My phone was in my back pocket, I pulled it out to check the time, only it was flashing with messages. I pressed Unlock.

The icon flashed with photo messages from Tonya, and my heart pumped as though I'd shot my load into Melissa's hairy pussy after all.

I scrolled through them, screenshot after screenshot of sexy underwear. Lacy bras and knickers, a cute red suspender belt with matching stockings. A corset, and one of those flouncy white babydolls that make your balls tighten.

Jodie wouldn't take the three hundred, her message said. *I tried my fucking hardest, too. I ordered these instead for her, next day delivery.*

My mouth was watering, fingers fucking shaking as I scrolled down to the final message.

Big grinning smileys, a load of them, all in a row.

You're welcome, the text said.

CHAPTER SEVEN

JODIE

I always make *me time* plans during Darren's weekends with the girls, but it rarely happens. Not with the unavoidable mega-clean that I'm obligated to perform to keep the house barely liveable. If there *is* any additional time, it's usually spent making sure Nanna gets her weekly trip to the supermarket, and cramming in any extra hours on offer at the cafe. There's always something that needs doing.

But this weekend started off quite differently.

I woke with a muggy head after a bit more wine than I'm accustomed to, then had the usual panic getting the girls ready to leave for their dad's. *Socks? Check. Clean underwear? Check. No, Ruby, you can't take the entire contents of your toy cupboard. You're going for one night, Ruby. One night! Yes, I know Mia's taking her phone, yes, I know that probably feels like the injustice of the century, but please, for the love of God, just put the monster trucks back in your bedroom! One. Alright, you can take one. ONE!*

The rumble of Trent's truck sounded outside at 9 a.m. sharp, and the girls piled outside before he was even out of the driver's seat. I waved them off with a happy smile, determined that this weekend would really be it, one for me. I had a playlist of YouTube makeup tutorials lined up, because seriously, makeup is a whole other level of skill than it was when I used to stick on eyeshadow with a bog-standard applicator and wear lippy without a lip liner. Heaven forbid.

Tonya told me so.

I'm learning.

When there was a knock on the door less than five minutes later, I figured one of the girls had forgotten something. My stomach did the dropping-from-a-great-height lurch as I swung it open, but it wasn't Trent standing there, it was a courier. He held out one of those touch-screen dooberrys for my signature and under his arm was a massive parcel. Surely not?

I was about to say he was at the wrong address when I saw *Symmonds* and *2 Oak Crescent* bold as brass on the screen. I looked at the parcel in shock. It was taped up tight, Priority Next Day all over it.

"Sign please," the driver said, and I realised I'd been gawping.

I scribbled something barely legible and took the bundle from him. Plain packaging, felt soft, like clothes.

Clothes.

Urgh, Tonya.

I called her up and she answered with a voice that made it clear she was still in bed.

"I'm here staring at a priority next day parcel that feels suspiciously like your doing. Am I right?" I asked.

She grunted and yawned a bit. "Might be..."

I couldn't stop smiling. "You're a very good very bad friend, you know that?"

She laughed. "Tell me how bad I am when you've opened it. The girls are away, right?"

"Right..."

"Then enjoy. Send me selfies. Later though, I was a-fucking-sleep before you called. You early risers piss me right off."

"This?! This isn't early, this is mid-bloody-day for us parents." I turned the parcel over in my hands, enjoying the rush of excitement that was replacing my muggy head. "I'll send you selfies," I said. "Thank you, honestly. I'm really touched."

"Open it before you say that, and no, I'm not sending them back. No matter what."

She was gone before I could argue.

I tore open the parcel with less care than I should've considering my recent investment in false nails, and let out a gasp as the items tumbled free. Underwear. Raunchy underwear. I held up the suspenders, looked at the posing woman on the front and tried to imagine me in her place. It made me laugh out loud.

I sent Tonya a text. *I love you, but you are a very bad influence.*

Use them! She sent back. *Book yourself in for a bloody Bang Gang before Mandy poxy Taylor takes all the slots!! Live a little!!*

Live a little... I'm not sure a five-man fuck-fest counted as living *a little*, even if it was on my bucket list.

I pulled myself up. *Since when has it been on my bucket list?*

But I knew since when. Since bloody tuxedo night. My bloody bodywand hadn't known the meaning of overworked until I saw those guys dressed in their finest. *And Trent out of it.*

I called to Nanna that I was heading upstairs for a bit, and it mattered little to her since she was busy reading the Saturday

Fashion pull-out. I crept away with the raunchy haul in my arms and examined the stash on the bed.

Some of it was elegant and tasteful. Some of it was drop-dead gorgeous – all lace and rich colour and fine styling. Some of it made me burn up at the thought – stockings, suspenders and… oh my life, a pair of crotchless red knickers to go with them. I held up a babydoll in floaty white – beautiful but so… *sexy*.

I took down my jeans and pulled my top off over my head, my underwear went next, and I took a breath as I looked at myself in the mirror. My flabby bits looked a lot less glorious in the morning sun than they did under lamplight. But so what?

I tried on the babydoll and pulled up the matching thong and my mind was made up.

I could actually get away with this…

I may be no supermodel, but the drape of the fabric hid my wobbly tummy, and the push-up bra did what it was supposed to. The thong was high on my hips and made my legs look longer than they were. I put my hand on my waist and turned, shot myself my sexiest look.

Fucking hell, maybe… just maybe…

I did another twirl and imagined Trent in the room. Would he look at me the way he used to? The way he did when I was still young and firm and desperate for his dick at every opportunity?

What about Buck? Hugh? Jimmy O? Would they want a piece of this? Would this be up to standard? Standard enough for young Petey, who's probably more used to girls his own age..?

I shuddered at the thought.

And should've stopped thinking about it altogether, but I couldn't.

I tried on the suspender belt and the crotchless knickers – *Sweet Jesus!* – then slipped on the racy little bra that went along with them. They complimented my new hair perfectly. One for the win. *I just needed...*

I reached into the wardrobe and tugged out a dusty box from the back. The cardboard was all battered but the shoes inside weren't. I stepped into the ridiculously high black heels and did another twirl and it looked awesome, like I'd never stopped wearing them.

Shit. Maybe I could really do this...

Maybe I really could be sexy again...

Maybe, just maybe...

I snapped a crazy impromptu selfie, complete with pout, and sent it off to Tonya before I could change my mind. She called in a heartbeat.

"You look fucking incredible, Jo! Oh my God, you look amazing!"

I laughed. "Maybe I'm not quite past it yet."

"Like hell you're past it!" She paused. "So... you going to go in for the Mandy Taylor special? Since the rest of the village is doing it, why not?"

The thought of the school-mums getting down and dirty in Darren's garage gave me weird shivers.

"Will you ever let it up?" I sighed. "I couldn't..."

"Why?"

"Because... Darren... because of what we were... because I'm..."

"Scared?" she finished. "Christ, Jo, everyone is going to have the shits before they do something like this, and Trent's Trent. It was a long fucking time ago. He does this shit for a living, he's not going to get all fucking freaked out, is he? He'd probably do Nanna and not even break a sweat."

I cringed. "Jeez, Tonya. Too much."

She laughed. "Sorry. You know what I mean."

Maybe she had a point. Not about Nanna, but about Trent being so mercenary about all this. I sighed, sat on the edge of the bed.

I heard her rustle about, flick the kettle on. "Answer me this. Is it over, really? Between you and Darren, I mean?"

My answer was instant. "Yes. Totally yes." And it *was* over. We'd tried and tried before we called time, and that was years ago. Neither of us had made a move since, neither of us even hinted at it. Once upon a time I'd secretly hoped he'd turn all Casanova and howl at the moon outside my window, profess his undying devotion and climb up my hair to my bed, but of course he hadn't.

He was with Stacey long before I ever contemplated getting with Brian, and they got pretty serious pretty damn quick. She'd even earned an engagement ring by all accounts, she'd gushed right the way around the village about it – and he'd never got that far with us, not even in all those years, which says a lot.

He was definitely over it. Long over me.

He wouldn't even break a sweat.

"So?" Tonya prompted. "You need to get laid, and there's a fantasy right there on offer. You're over Trent, yes? Talk about kicking off your new lease of life in style. Back in the game with a boom!"

Was I over Trent? Yes. Yes, I was. Definitely.

"I'm going now," I said. "Before you talk me into something I shouldn't even be thinking about."

"So you *are* thinking about it?" Her laugh was infectious. "Go. Get the bodywand out, weigh it up a little."

I did just that.

The weather was a piece of shit, so I took the girls back to mine. Mia was on usual form, disappearing off into their room to catch up with Daisy on Skype. She was never off the thing. There was only one thing Ruby was rooting for, I could read her a mile off. She sat herself on the sofa and stared at the blank TV with a grin on her face.

"Top Gear?" I said, and she punched the air.

I fired up the re-runs and put the kettle on, delivered Mia a cup of tea to her room before I settled down on the sofa with Ruby. She sat like I did, a foot casually tossed over her knee, her mug in one hand, fingers splayed just like mine. It made me smile.

We made the same scoffing sounds in the same places, ridiculed the driving in the same places, and nodded in appreciation in the exact same places. Genetics, or learned, I didn't know and didn't care. I ruffled her hair and she smiled her toothy grin up at me and it gave me that warm feeling inside.

"I'll be nipping to the yard later, thought maybe I'd let you and Mia have a practice in the truck."

Ruby's eyes were like saucers. "Driving?! Really?!"

"*Half* driving, nothing crazy. Don't want your mum freaking out, do we?"

She shook her head, smiling from ear to ear.

I gestured to the rain outside the window. "Just wait until this crap passes, it's supposed to brighten up later."

We turned our attention back to the TV, and Clarkson took a flash Audi convertible for a spin through some mountain tracks. I watched Ruby's face as he took the winding roads at speed, the starkness of the landscape looking really fucking awesome. She was absolutely transfixed.

"What do you make of that?" I asked.

"Cool," she said. "Epic cool."

They did the round-up of the car, bigging up its awesome handling, the flashiness of the optional extras. Then they called it *a chick magnet. A sure-fire way to land the ladies.*

Ruby pulled a face, stared up at me with eyes full of questions.

"What?" I said.

She paused, just stared. "Is that what your truck is?" she said. "A *chick magnet*? Is that why all the ladies want to..."

I raised an eyebrow. "Want to what?" She shook her head, but I called her on it. "Come on, Rubes. Spit it out."

She shrugged. "Mia told me not to say anything."

"And I'm telling you to spit it out."

"It's the kids at school," she began. "They say you like... they say you're a *gigolo.* What's a *gigolo,* Dad? Are you really one?"

Shit. My stomach dropped.

"What do you think a gigolo is, Rubes?"

She shrugged again. "I think it means kissing, like kissing lots of people..." She stared at her mug. "And the other stuff... the icky stuff... more than kissing..."

I didn't know whether to laugh or cry.

She sipped her tea. "They say you're doing the icky stuff with all the ladies in the village." Finally, she looked at me. "Are you doing that, Dad? Are you doing the icky stuff with all the ladies in the village?"

I opted for honesty. I find it's usually the best way. Well, honesty within reason – she's eight-years old.

"No," I said. "I'm not doing the icky stuff with all the ladies in the village. I made a mistake and may have done some icky stuff with one of them, because I'm a stupid prick sometimes. I'm sorry about that, Rubes."

She pulled a face. "Mandy Taylor."

Shit. Playground gossip knew no fucking bounds.

"I'm not doing any icky stuff with ladies in the village, Rubes, especially not Mandy Taylor. Not even any kissing."

"Pinky promise?" she asked, and held up her little finger. "I don't like Mandy Taylor. She smiles funny and I don't like the way she laughs. I don't want her to be my step-mum."

Jesus! I hooked her finger with mine. "Pinky promise, Ruby. No women in the village, and Mandy Taylor will *never ever* be your step-mum."

I thought that might be the end of it, but blue eyes stared into mine, her smile dulling just a little. "If you want to kiss people and all that other stuff, why don't you kiss Mum? She looks really pretty now with her new hair and everything, *and* she has nice clothes! She looks like a princess!"

Awkward question of the year award goes to Ruby Trent.

"Your mum is very beautiful, Rubes, whether she's got new hair and nice clothes or not. She always looks like a princess. But we're just friends."

Her face dropped and I felt it, it fucking hurt.

"But just-friends could kiss each other couldn't they? If they both wanted to? If she looks like a princess then why don't you want to kiss her?"

I sighed. "Oh, Rubes, it's not that simple. Adult stuff isn't ever that simple."

She looked away from me, back at the TV.

I tried to make light of it. "Your mum wouldn't even want to kiss me, Rubes. Princesses only kiss frogs in fairy tales, not in real life."

She laughed at that. "You're not a frog!"

"I am so a frog," I said, and did a slurpy face, made a frog croak. "Anyway, what's your issue with frogs, hey? Are you some kind of bloody froggist? You know what happens to froggists around here?" I took her mug from her and put it on the floor, and then I grabbed her, tickled her until she squealed and giggled and squirmed in my arms. I let her go, gave her a few seconds head start before I chased her, and Mia appeared in the hallway, grumpy-faced at the noise interruption until she dropped her *cool* front enough to laugh. She looked so old these days, all grown up at high school. Too old for this kind of shit, and that was sad, I missed it.

"Dad's a frog!" Ruby squealed. "And he's coming to get us! Run! Run, Mia!"

And to my surprise Mia did run, squealing and laughing and pulling her sister along with her as I ribbited down the hallway after them.

JODIE

I'd stashed all my new undies safely at the back of the drawer long before Darren dropped the kids back on Sunday. They arrived after teatime, and as usual they looked bloody exhausted, Ruby's hair all fluffed up like she'd been dragged through a hedge backwards. Still, as long as they were happy.

They gave me a quick kiss before they went to dump their things upstairs, leaving me standing in the doorway with Darren, feeling more than slightly uncomfortable given the amount of the weekend I'd spent imagining getting down and dirty with him and four of his filthy friends.

He didn't seem to pick up on it, and if he did, he certainly didn't say anything.

Part of me wanted to just to blurt it out and get it over with, drop in a casual *how do I book in?* before the girls were even back down the stairs. But I didn't. Of course I didn't.

Darren leaned in and looked beyond me. My skin prickled while he made sure the coast was clear. I wondered what he was about to say, my heart soaring with ridiculous notions.

It was none of them, of course.

"There's been gossip, at school," he told me, his voice low. I'd feared it would crop up at some point, and let out a sigh. "It's alright," he said. "I've talked through things with the girls."

"What did they know?"

He took his cigarettes from his pocket, stepped back on the porch to light one up. I stepped out after him, pulled the door closed behind.

"Ruby asked me what a gigolo was, then asked me how come I was *doing the icky stuff* with everyone in the village."

"Oh my God, Darren," I groaned. "What did you say?"

He shrugged. "I told her the truth, that I'd done the icky stuff with Mandy Taylor but it was a mistake. Told her I wasn't going to be kissing anyone else in the village."

"But you..." I pulled a face, completely unsure where this kind of stuff landed amongst best parenting practice. "I mean, I know you can't tell the truth, but to lie..."

His eyes narrowed. "Who's fucking lying?"

"Well, aren't you..?" I shook my head. "Never mind, sorry. I don't know. It's none of my business. Just as long as the girls are ok."

He took a drag. "Ruby didn't know about the money, neither of the girls did. That's a saving grace, at least."

"Let's hope it stays that way."

"Should do, I've made it pretty clear around the village where people need to be coming if they've got anything to say. They can say it to me, not whisper about the pissing place."

I nodded. "Good. Hopefully that's the end of it, then."

He grunted at me, and then the kids were back, already arguing whose turn it was on the laptop.

They took a break in negotiations to say goodbye to their dad, then disappeared into the living room to get Nanna's take on their dilemma.

"I'd best be going," Darren said.

"Thanks for having them," I said.

"Pleasure," he said.

"Ok, then," I smiled.

"Right, then," he smiled back.

"I'll see you... around."

"Be seeing you."

He didn't look back, but my heart raced like a fucking horse until his truck was out of sight.

Disappointed. I was so fucking disappointed.

In myself.

Because I hadn't asked him, and I'd wanted to. Shit, I'd really wanted to.

I should have just dropped it in, should have said...

I took a deep breath, pulled myself together.

Tomorrow, I thought. No dicking about, just a straight question. Where could possibly be the harm in that? Just a customer, like any other customer... why shouldn't I be?

I went back inside to referee laptop-wars before they drove poor Nanna to the brandy.

CHAPTER EIGHT

JODIE

I toyed with doing it by text, but that seemed so chicken-shit, and the thought of giving Darren the chance to formulate a rejection was more than I could bear. Maybe I should have opted for a quick call, called him at the garage and booked it in just like a car repair. I mean, that's what everyone else was probably doing, right?

I didn't fucking know.

Urgh.

I gave *ladies-who-lunch* a miss this week, opting for the extra hours. It appears nobody else much fancied it either, as there was no sign of Mandy, Debbie or Steph at our usual allotted time. I served our other Monday morning customers with my usual smile, and slowly but surely the string of compliments and impressed grins worked their magic on me. My confidence grew, little by little, and by lunchtime I was determined. Now or never, make or break. No big deal.

It's not as if I didn't know him. Of course I knew him. And this was just a business transaction. How wrong could it possibly go?

A text message came in from Tonya.

Is it done yet? All booked in?

On my way to the booking office, I replied, *wish me luck. This is your fault if it all goes wrong.*

You'll be thanking me later, she said.

I bloody hoped so.

I'd thought about it at length over the weekend. Hell, truth be told I'd hardly thought about anything else. I can't say that the thought of spending Pop Pop's inheritance money on a five-man orgy filled me with a massive amount of pride, but it was true to the sentiment in his instructions. It would surely be an experience of a lifetime, for good or for bad.

I just hoped Darren would appreciate my perspective on that.

There was no Porsche outside the garage when I pulled up — thank fuck for that. The garage itself was relatively quiet, the usual jam of cars stacked up waiting for their turn, but no customers in sight. I pulled up in front of the shutters, and felt eyes on me, all five pairs of them. *Shit.*

Darren stepped outside, armed with his usual intense stare, and I nearly crapped my new frilly knickers and reversed the car straight out of there. I took a breath, plastered on a big smile as I turned off the ignition. He'd lit up a cigarette by the time I'd made my way over. He puffed away with his eyes on me.

I heard a chorus of wolf whistles behind him, and he shot a godawful glare over his shoulder, slapped his palm against the shutters.

"Knock it off," he barked, then he turned back to me. "Something up?"

My smile was too big, much too big. "No. Well, maybe..."

"What?" he said, and he looked worried. "Is it the girls?"

I felt like a tit. "No!" I said. "No, nothing like that. It's about me."

"What about you? Something wrong?"

I took a breath. *Jesus.* This had seemed so much easier in my head. "I'm fine," I said. "I have a... question... it's nothing major, no big deal..."

"Too big a deal for a text, it seems."

"It's more..." I stepped closer. "Personal..."

He raised his eyebrows. "Personal?"

I closed my eyes. Now or never. "I want to book in for a *service*," I said. "A *special* service. I mean, if it's good enough for Mandy Taylor and that blonde woman in the Porsche it's good enough for me." I was in flow and I couldn't stop. "I'm a woman, Darren, the same as them. I have *fantasies*. I have... *needs*. I may not be as... *obvious* as they are, but I'm as up for this shit as anyone else in the village, and if they're all doing it then why can't I?" I paused. "I mean, I can, can't I? You don't need to be... some kind of..."

"Slut?" he said.

I held up a finger. "I was going to say supermodel, but slut will do." I smiled. "So, how about it? Do you have a diary... or...."

His expression was like thunder, his jaw hard. My bravado deflated, drooped like a saggy tit.

"No," he said. Just like that. "No fucking way."

I'm sure I gulped like a fish, and then I asked the most basic question in the whole universe, delivered without any finesse whatsoever. "Why not?"

"You're not signing up for a fucking gangbang, Jo, no fucking way." His voice was raised, and I caught Buck turn his head from the corner of my eye. I felt the heat rising up, not just the burn of my cheeks, this heat was all over me, prickling my arms, my chest, as though every part of me was glowing beetroot.

"But I..." I started. "I've thought this through. It's what I want. Why can't I?" My confidence dissipated and I felt small and pathetic. I remembered Porsche-bitch's dismissive glance, Mandy Taylor's glee as she told me how *fucking amazing* it was. I held my ground regardless of how shitty it felt. "Mandy Taylor isn't all that, Trent, and neither was that blonde you had here. If they're bloody *acceptable* then why aren't I?"

He shook his head. "It's got nothing to do with being fuckable, Jodie. That's what you fucking mean, isn't it? Like we pick out the fucking hot ones. Like there's some fucking merit system, *nice fucking tits, let's give her a go*. We don't give a fuck about that. *I* don't give a fuck about that."

"Then what?" I felt the beginnings of anger. "What *has* it got to do with?"

He stubbed out his cigarette. "Just no."

The little plume of anger was blooming, shooting right up my spine. "*Just no?!*"

"*Just* no!" he snapped, and turned tail. "I'm not booking you in for a fucking gangbang, end of fucking story."

I folded my arms. "But you *will* book Mandy Taylor in for one? What's so special about Mandy fucking Taylor, Trent? Why can she pay for a good fucking time but I can't? My money's as good as hers!"

He stopped in his tracks, and he was simmering, absolutely seething. I knew this look well. We'd argued like this more times than I cared to remember, when things were going tits up all around us and we couldn't agree on any-fucking-thing anymore. "What money?" he said. "How do you think you're going to pay for this shit, Jo? It's not like a bastard TV subscription, we're talking hundreds of fucking pounds, you saw that fucking box of mine."

I felt my resolve faltering. I couldn't even say the words, and he knew, he fucking knew.

I think I preferred his angry face to this one. This one was horrible. Shock, disappointment. Maybe a bit of disgust. He had some fucking cheek, but I didn't feel that, I just felt the shame.

"Don't say it, don't even fucking think it," he said. "That's *not* for *this*. He wouldn't have wanted this. Fucking hell, Jo, what the fuck?"

"He would have wanted me to *live*, Darren. How *I* choose to live is up to me."

"Fine, *live*. But I won't be a fucking part of this shit. You won't be getting your kicks here."

Be damned if I was going to back down now. I willed myself to stay calm, to stay cool, to stay anything but the embarrassed little Jodie whose confidence was taking a battering when it was just getting started. "And you speak for everyone, do you?"

He stared right at me. "Yes. I fucking do."

I took a step forward, cleared my throat. "How about it, guys?" I shouted. "If it's good enough for Mandy, how about letting me have a go? I can pay!"

I waited. And waited. My eyes wandered from face to face, and yet none of them would meet my stare. They were all looking at Trent, every single one of them.

I smiled a bitter smile, mainly to hide my upset. "Oh, I get it," I said. "It's like that." I turned back to Darren. "You really are the head honcho. Guess it feels good to be the big I am, casting judgement on who's *good* enough to have a go."

"It's not like that," he said, but he was still angry, and so was I.

"Fine," I said, and I was already on my way back to the car. "I'll find some other guys who'll give me a good time. You can't be the only fucking gigolos around. The internet's a fucking wonderful thing."

I slammed the car door behind me, and got the hell out of there.

TRENT

I got back to the Land Rover on the ramp, launching a kick at pile of tyres as I went. *Fucking hell. Just what the fucking hell?*

My temples were pounding, jaw so tight I had an annoying twitch flickering away. My anger was low and hard, bubbling under the surface like a fucking volcano about to blow.

The guys left me well alone for an hour or so, and it was Buck who brought me a cup of tea over. I guess Petey was too fucking scared.

"Wanna talk about it?" he said, propping himself against the rig.

"No," I snapped. "Not fucking really."

Buck didn't give a shit. "That was well fucking off, mate. She had a point."

"And what fucking point would that be?"

He shrugged. "We're normally not so fucking picky. She knows it. We know it. She wants a go and why shouldn't she? Everyone else in this poxy village is after some."

"She's different."

He nodded. "Alright, but how so? You've been split a long fucking time, mate."

"She just is," I barked. "Leave it, Buck. Just fucking leave it."

He slapped a hand on my shoulder before he left me to it. "I think you're making a mistake. You ain't gonna want to hear this shit, but I'm going to say it anyway. I've known Jodie a long time, we all have.

You tore her a new asshole out there for wanting what everyone else wants, for wanting to live a fucking fantasy. And why shouldn't she? Why the fuck shouldn't she, Trent? We've taken enough money from women in her shoes, why not offer her the same fucking courtesy?"

"As if it's about fucking courtesy. Are you that fucking greedy for the money?" I stormed away, practically swung the office door from its hinges. I grabbed a wedge of notes from the till. Buck didn't even flinch as I threw them in his direction. "If you're that desperate for the fucking cash, Buck, then take it and get the fuck out of my face for the rest of the fucking day."

Buck gathered up the notes with a sigh. He tapped them on the side, lined them all up, then left them there. He held up his hands. "Alright, I'll leave it. Just forget I said anything."

As if I'd be able to forget about this fucking mess anytime soon.

He got back to work without another word, and so did I.

JODIE

I heard nothing from Darren for three days. I dropped the girls at the yard after school and he dropped them outside the house when they were ready to come home. That was it, no texts, no polite conversation on the front doorstep, nothing.

I saw him through the cafe window on Thursday lunchtime, making his way to the village shop for cigarettes no doubt, but he didn't even glance in my direction, and I made damned sure I wouldn't have been looking his way if he had.

Tonya said he was jealous. I told her that was ridiculous. It wasn't *me* who'd wanted to marry the next person I hooked up with in his wake. It wasn't *me* who was fucking the whole fucking village without a care in the world.

Darren Trent wasn't jealous.

He was an asshole.

And he didn't see me as a woman, not anymore. That was the bottom line. I was just *Mum. That's* how he saw me, and in that deep dark place in my heart that's how I'd feared he'd seen me for a long, long time. Since I'd had the girls, in fact. It never felt quite the same after.

Maybe that's what killed us, ultimately.

Maybe I'd stopped being a woman in his eyes before I'd stopped being a woman in my own.

But I was a woman again now, even if he refused to see it. I kept hold of myself, kept putting that makeup on every morning, kept making the effort to feel like *me*.

And it worked. It really worked.

Maybe I didn't care so much what Darren Trent thought after all.

I realised that was a lie when I found his truck next to mine in the cafe car park at closing. I walked quickly, straight to my door, ignoring him until he was out of his and close enough to my side that he could put an arm across the door handle. I ignored him like he didn't matter, but my heart was racing and my mouth was dry, my whole body thrumming with anger and upset and something else.

"What?" I said, then looked around him, stared back at his empty truck. I'd asked Tonya to drop Mia and Ruby down at the garage, since I was working late, and yet there was no sign of them.

"They're at Mum and Dad's," he said. "I'm here to see you."

"Well, you've seen me now." I went to push his arm away. He wouldn't budge.

"I want to talk," he said just as the sky opened up and started pissing itself down. *Great.* "Please, Jo," he said. "Just get in the truck a minute."

I made a big old sigh out of it before I relented. I hauled myself into the passenger seat, stared straight through the windscreen at the rain outside.

It took him a while to speak.

"Why do you want to do it?"

I shot him a look of surprise. "What?"

"The sex," he said. "Why? I didn't have you down as the orgy type."

I shrugged. "Maybe you had me down wrong then."

He smirked. "Thought I knew you pretty well, Jodie. You never fucking mentioned having a fucking gangbang. I'd have remembered, believe me."

I relaxed into the seat, tried to work out the right words. "I didn't think about it back then. We were... everything. And then we weren't." I paused but didn't look at him. "Since then I've been... Brian wasn't..." I sighed. "I didn't feel like *me*. I haven't felt like *me* in a long fucking time."

"And now you do?"

I smiled, kept staring at the rain. "I'm getting there."

"And banging four fucking guys will get you further *there*, will it?"

Four. He said four.

"I dunno, Darren. I just want to live again. Mandy Taylor shot her mouth off and it sounded good. It sounded really good. I couldn't stop thinking about it, couldn't stop thinking about how good it would feel to live that kind of fantasy. I want to feel like that." I took a breath. "I miss sex. I miss crazy, intense, fantastical, amazingly hot, fuck-me-harder sex. I'm still a woman, Trent. I still watch porn, I still get off every night to the thought of some crazy wild night where I get lost in the fantasy. I'm still..."

"I get it," he said. "You want the big bang, the explosion. You want the same primal shit they all go on about. I hear it all the time."

I closed my eyes. "I guess you do."

"Why the guys? Why not some randoms from online dating?"

"Because I *know* the guys. I *know* I'd be safe. I know I could let myself go and enjoy it for what it is, and not be freaking out that I've made some godawful mistake and landed myself in a load of shit I can't get myself out of."

"But you'll do it anyway, if I say no? You'll find some randoms and do it anyway?"

"I don't know," I said, honestly. "Maybe." I risked a laugh. "Christ, Darren, I've been virtually celibate for more years than I care to remember. I don't want to end up in a nunnery, I want to get laid, just as much as every other woman around here. Just as much as the other women you... *service*."

"But you're different," he said. "*This* would be different."

Would be.

"Why so?"

"Just because," he said, then held up his hands. "I wouldn't have to be involved, that's not what I'm saying, but you know these guys. *We* know these guys. Our girls know these guys."

The thought of the girls made my stomach lurch. "And I *trust* these guys. Hell, Darren, I trust our girls with these guys. I know they'll give me what I'm looking for without any nasty repercussions. It's a one-off, just a crazy, ridiculous, horny one-off." I sighed, wished he'd offer me one of his bloody cigarettes. "I'm not going to beg you, I get that your word goes and no means no. I just wish you'd give me the same courtesy you give every other woman who wants a go."

"Courtesy, that's an interesting way of looking at it." He rested his head on the headrest. "Everyone's banging on about fucking courtesy. This isn't about courtesy, Jo, it's about sex for money. A cold, hard dirty fuck for money. Is that really what you want? You really, truly want to fucking do this? Bang the guys and hand over the cash afterwards? Wham-bam fucking thank you, ma'am?"

I mustered all the confidence I could.

"Yes," I said. "I really, truly want to fucking do this."

He sighed, rubbed his temples. "Fine," he said. "If that's what you really fucking want, then I'll set it up."

I couldn't hide the shock. I must have been gawping, mouth open, staring like a fucking moron. "You will?"

"I don't want you scraping up the dregs of online fucking dating for a cheap thrill, Jo. No fucking way."

"Thanks, I think." I was smiling. The grin crept up slowly, my heart thumping.

He put the key in the ignition. "Four guys," he said. "Four hundred quid. That's a good rate."

I nodded. "Ok."

"You can use my place, if you want. Somewhere familiar."

I nodded some more. "Please. That would be good."

"Alright," he said. "I'll set it up, and then I'll stay out of it. Just a one-off, though." He held out his hand. "Deal?"

I shook it. "Deal."

Four guys and me, for real. This is really fucking real.

I didn't want to be disappointed, but I was. I pushed it aside, told myself four would do. Probably better Darren wasn't there. He didn't even *want* to be there.

I definitely didn't want him to be there, either. That's what I told myself.

No way.

But I *did*. I *did* want him to be there. I just couldn't bring myself to tell him.

"I'll drop you a text with some dates, we'll book it in," he added, just like this was some random car repair.

"Thanks, Darren."

He nodded. "I'd best be off. Mum's doing a mid-week roast."

"Nice," I said. "Give her my best. Your dad, too."

"Will do."

I let myself out of the truck, and he didn't even give me a second look as he drove away.

He definitely, definitely, definitely didn't want to be there.

But that was ok.

I'd make it ok.

It would be hot. Intense. Crazy. Wild.

It would be the ultimate fantasy. One big tick on my bucket list.

So why did it feel so goddamn bad?

JODIE

I was watching a late-night crime with Nanna when Trent's text came through.

Wednesday week. Or maybe the Friday.

I checked my ovulation calendar app.

Friday, I text back. *I'll make sure I'm not working the day after.*

Ok, he said. *I'll book it in.*

Thanks, I sent back.

My belly was full of flutters, a tight ball of excitement with just a hint of disappointment underneath. That was good enough.

I was surprised when another text came through.

Just a thought, but I could be there, if you like. Just for the intro. Just to make sure it kicks off smoothly.

My fingers were a blur. *Yes, please. That would be nice. Help with the nerves.*

I sent it off and kept typing. *I'll be crapping myself, I'm sure. It would be nice if you were there.*

A few minutes went by and I could hardly keep focused on the TV. Nanna was going on about the killer, and I could only smile and nod, pretend I knew what the hell she was talking about.

I was shaking as the next message bleeped.

I could stay if you like, just to watch. Keep an eye on things. If you're nervous, like.

I forced myself to count to ten, slowly, the thought of Darren watching me getting fucked made my pussy squirm. *If you could that would be great. I'd feel more comfortable.*

Would I really feel more comfortable? My fingers were jittery just at the thought, but there was a thrill there, too. A weird kinky thrill and a strange sense of relief.

That thrill pulsed at my clit.

Bodywand calling.

Shit.

I could barely bring myself to open the following message. My nerves were shot.

I'll be there, then. No problem.

I typed and re-typed a reply. Words bloody failed me. I forced myself to get a grip, just spit it out and get it out there.

I'll pay you. Just for watching, if that's what you want. Whatever you want. Unless you don't want to.

I sent it and realised what a rambling mess it was. I typed out another before I could change my mind.

I'm trying to say you could be there. Be there be there. Just like any other job. I'll pay. If that's what you want. If you don't, then it's cool. Just thought I'd say it's cool with me.

Oh shit. Shit. Shit. Shit.

Nanna pulled a face at me.

"Are you even watching this, Jodie? They're going to arrest the killer any minute! You'll miss it!"

"Sorry, Nanna," I said, and tried my best to be interested.

That went to hell as soon as my phone bleeped again.

I looked at it through splayed fingers.

If it's cool with you it's cool with me. No big deal.

I couldn't hold back the grin.

"Jodie!" Nanna groaned. "You aren't even watching!"

"Sorry, Nanna," I said again. "I'm just talking to Darren."

Her face lit up. "Oh," she said. She patted my hand. "Then you keep talking to him, love. I'll tell you who the killer was after."

"Thanks, Nanna."

No big deal, I replied. *We're adults. It's just… sex. No biggy.*

Just sex, he sent back. My phone bleeped again a couple of seconds later. *You don't need to pay me, though. I don't want the money.*

How do you even reply to that? I tried not to laugh.

Thanks.

120

What a ridiculous message. What a ridiculous conversation.

The whole thing was crazy ridiculous.

I didn't get any other messages, not before Nanna put the TV on standby and announced that the killer was the little old lady with the rose garden the whole time. Her smile was bright.

"It's always the sweet little oldies," she said. "You never know what goes on behind closed doors, do you?"

I smiled. "It's not based on a true story, Nanna."

"No," she said. "But still, nowt so queer as folk. It could be old Mary Brown from number ten. She's a strange one. She has a rose garden, too. She's always been shifty, that one."

She had a point. Mary Brown was a strange old bat with a creepy son. Their house was like something from *Psycho*, only more tea and roses than showers and stabbings.

That's village life for you. Got to love it.

I waved Nanna goodnight and handled my chores with a spring in my step.

Five men. I'd be having the Bang Gang special.

I'd be having Trent.

Oh crap. Oh crapping crap. I tried my best to stop smiling, but even the cat sick on the kitchen floor couldn't dampen my mood.

That's really saying something.

I'd crawled into bed by the time I checked my phone for the last time. It bleeped in my hand the second I'd tapped the Unlock screen, and there it was, another message from Darren.

Been thinking. Maybe we should break the ice, it said. *Just so it's not awkward. Don't want it to be all weird, like.*

The butterflies in my stomach swarmed.

You think we should have sex first? Just us?

My face was burning. My pussy was burning. My heart was . . .

A bleep: *Thought it might help. With the nerves.* Another bleep. *No pressure, just thought I'd put it out there.*

I took a deep breath, willed my fingers to calm down and tap the right bloody keys.

Makes sense, I said. *Breaking the ice sounds sensible.*

Sensible? Like anything about this crazy shit sounded bloody sensible.

I waited for the bleep. *Saturday night? Can Nanna have the girls?*

I thought through the practicalities. I could happily leave Nanna with the girls after bedtime, when they were already asleep and wouldn't overload her with laptop squabbles.

Late? About eleven? I'll get the kids to bed first. Shall I come to yours?

A booty call. I had an *actual* booty call. With Trent.

Oh my life.

My whole body was on fire.

Another bleep. *Eleven at mine works for me.*

I hugged my pillow, fought the urge to let out a squeal.

See you then, I replied.

I'll be seeing you, he said.

Yes, he would. He'd be seeing me, alright, lumpy-bumpy bits and all.

I pulled the bodywand box from under the bed.

CHAPTER NINE

JODIE

The girls' bedtime seemed to take forever.

I'm not tired! Mia whinged. *Daisy doesn't even* have *a bedtime on the weekend! It's so unfairrrr!*

You can read a book in bed if you're not tired. No phone though, Mia, I bloody mean it! Give it here, please. Give it here! Yes, I'm a horrible, mean parent, whatever, just give me the bloody phone and brush your teeth!

Lord Almighty.

It was all quiet by the time I'd finished in the bathroom. A smoother shave than I'd had in years made my legs feel tingly and naked – the other parts, too. The soft fabric of the babydoll felt risqué and luxurious against my skin, hidden from view under my new scarlet tunic. I slipped on my black jeans, and my ridiculous heels after them, then did a full 360 in the mirror to make sure there was none of the negligee poking out.

I crossed Nanna on the stairs on my way out. My makeup was heavy and my hair was slick and styled, my steps only slightly unsteady as they adjusted to the killer heels.

"Oooh!" she said. "You look lovely, Jo! Really lovely!"

"Just popping out with Tonya," I said. "Is that ok?"

She waved me off with a smile. "You go on, love. Have a good time."

"It's just for a few hours," I said. "I'll be back long before morning."

"I'm sure I've still got my wits about me enough to tip some cereal in a bowl, my girl." She gave me a wink. "Go, have fun. Meet yourself a nice man."

If only she knew.

"Nanna!" I said. "You're a bad influence."

She waggled a finger at me. "I was quite a dish before your Pop Pop, I'll have you know. Oh, to be young again. I've met many a nice man in my time." She laughed to herself as she climbed the rest of the stairs.

At least now I knew where I got it from.

I was grinning as I eased the door closed behind me.

I should have brought wine. Why didn't I bring wine? Or even vodka. I should definitely have brought vodka.

It was too late for that now. My nerves were jangling as I skirted the river towards the fish and chip shop. I prayed that for once Trent wouldn't be smoking outside his front door. That spot would put him in prime position to observe my less than sterling negotiation of the bumpy path in stupid heels.

I should never have worn these heels.

I should have worn bloody flip flops or something instead.

Anything rather than risk jabbing a heel in a rut and toppling ass over tit. There's nothing sexy about a twisted ankle, that's for sure.

Sexy. Oh my life.

I was going to have sex.

Real, proper open your legs sex.

I paused for a moment before Trent's place came into view. Was I ready? I smoothed my hair. As ready as I'd ever be.

My mouth was so bloody dry, my knees weak and pathetic as I walked the final strait. I kept my eyes away from the steps up to his, making out I was busy rooting in my bag, just to avoid any eye contact that might be lurking if he was outside waiting for me.

As it turns out, he wasn't.

My heels clacked against the stone as I ascended the steps, and I noted with interest that there wasn't a cigarette butt in sight, not a single one. The bucket at the top was empty, too.

I'd never known it empty.

I breathed deeply outside the closed front door, leaning back against the railings and trying to reach my *Zen state.*

Yeah, right. Like my life was ever Zen-like.

I gave myself a pep talk, told myself this was no biggie. Just sex, just like we'd said. We'd done it enough times before.

I tapped the door like a little mouse, then chided myself, gave it a decent knock.

I aimed for bright and casual with my smile, but I'm not so sure it held when he opened the door. An outsider would say Darren was dressed casually at best, but I'm no outsider. His jeans were faded but clean, and his t-shirt had an actual collar. We were hardly in tuxedo territory, but there was no doubt about it – Darren Trent had made an effort.

He stepped aside to let me pass, and he smelled shower fresh – that same cool blue stuff he'd been using forever.

"Hey," he said.

"Hey," I said.

He stepped into the kitchen and I followed, backing myself against the sink to give him space enough to pull a bottle of wine from the fridge. *Thank fuck.*

"I got this," he said. "Or I can put the kettle on? I'm not out to get you wasted."

I smiled. "It's alright, I could do with a glass." *Or ten.* "Thank you."

He made light work of the cork, pouring me a large one into a glass that used to be ours. He grabbed a beer, and there we stood, smiling polite smiles as though this wasn't awkward in the slightest.

It was really fucking awkward.

I had prickles on the back of my neck, burning up so hot that I'm sure I was sweating. The room seemed airless and the wine didn't do shit for my dry mouth.

"We should go through," he said, and my eyes widened. "To the living room," he added. He pointed to my feet. "They can't be bloody comfortable, Jo."

They weren't. They weren't at all.

Darren flopped into his usual seat at the far end of the sofa, and I perched on the opposite side. I kicked off my heels and rubbed my feet, not sure exactly what I should be doing. All my intentions of throwing him against the wall and ripping his clothes off had well and truly been demoted to fantasy.

I felt like a bloody virgin again.

His stare was on me, his eyes not letting up as he downed his beer. "Girls alright?"

"Girls are fine," I said. "Mia showed off a bit, wanted to Skype Daisy all night long, you know what she's like. Ruby not so bad, think she was tired to be honest, it's the only time she isn't full of backchat."

He smiled. "Yeah, she's full of it."

"Yeah, she is."

Cue another awkward polite smile-athon.

My heart lurched as he rested his beer can on the floor and moved a little closer. "Look, Jodie, if this is weird for you, we don't have to do this..."

"It's not weird," I bluffed. "Not at all."

Please don't stop this. Please don't. I felt the beginnings of panic, my heartrate kicking up a hefty notch.

"Don't feel... pressured, like."

"I don't!" I said. "Christ, Darren, I'm totally down for this." I flicked my hair but it felt ridiculous. "I feel great."

He gestured to my white knuckles as they death-gripped my wine glass stem. "You're gonna fucking break that if you squeeze any tighter." He sniggered to himself. "Doubt I'll be moaning about that later, mind."

I seized the moment, mustering every scrap of bravado for an epic sex-kitten move.

I downed my wine and placed the glass at my feet, then – in the most sexy way I knew how – I wiggled my way out of my tunic to reveal the lacy brilliance of the babydoll underneath. I still had my jeans on, but the babydoll showed enough – the swell of my tits in the push-up cups, the pale of my tummy under the gauzy fabric.

My tummy. I was sitting down. Shit, did my belly look flabby? I looked down in panic, sucked my breath in.

When my eyes met his again all I registered there was shock. He stared at me, eyes wide, and didn't say a word.

I guessed my stripper act fell quite short. Seriously fucking short. Embarrassment burned like a bitch.

"Wow," he said, but he was still gawping, still totally taken aback. "That's..."

Stupid. Ridiculous.

Totally non-sexy.

"That's..." he attempted again, but I was done.

This was a terrible idea poorly executed.

"Forget it," I said, grateful for the warmth of the wine in my belly. I pulled on my top in a jiffy and yanked it down over my jeans. I reached for my bag and shoved my feet back in those stupid heels. "I'll go." I got to my feet. "This was silly. *I'm* silly." I headed for the door. "Sorry, Darren, this was... I was stupid... as if I could ever be like them."

"Wait," he said, but I carried on regardless.

I unlocked the catch and yanked the door open. "I'll drop you a text tomorrow, about the girls... I think Ruby wants to head over, I think she wants to..."

I stopped dead as I felt the heat of him at my back. He reached an arm over my head, pushed the door closed again. The click of the latch was loud.

"Wait," he said, and his voice was low. The sound gave me shivers, made my clit tingle. He brushed the hair from my neck. "You're not stupid, Jo," he said. "You've never been fucking stupid."

"I'm..."

"Nervous," he finished. "Yeah, well, I guess I am too."

The thought seemed absurd. Darren doesn't do nervous.

His hands on my shoulders turned me slowly. I could hardly breathe as I came to face him. He was so close.

He didn't speak, didn't utter a sound as his hands came up and tangled in my hair. I knew this move. Oh fuck, I knew it so well. His thumbs moved to brush my cheeks and rested there. He held my face in the exact same way he used to do, his palms rough against my skin. So familiar, yet not. They were much rougher than they used to be.

I looked at him, truly looked at him for the first time in years, and his eyes were older, his skin more rugged, more lined. Seven years had aged him. Seven years had turned him from a lean youngster into a man. A proper man.

Seven years really suited him.

My lips were already parted when his landed. My tongue ready for his as he pushed his way inside. My hands gripped at his shoulders, and he was broader, firmer. He backed me into the door, his kiss hot and heavy, so deep that I felt consumed.

I always felt like that with Darren.

His body pressed against mine, his crotch to my belly, and I felt him there, the thick ridge of his cock straining in his jeans. My fingers sought out his belt, dithery as they fumbled with the buckle. His hands didn't leave my face, didn't let me go, not until he broke the kiss long enough to tug my top up over my head and throw it aside.

He made lighter work of my jeans than I had with his. I stepped out of my heels and kicked them aside with the tangle of denim, and I felt so exposed, smaller without my heels and so much less sure of myself than I'd been in front of the mirror at home.

I felt the blush on my cheeks as he stepped away, those heavy blue eyes eating me up, taking in everything – every curve, every wobble, every imperfection.

"I like this," he said. His fingers trailed up the floaty fabric, his thumbs seeking my nipples through the frilly cups.

I let out a breath and his touch became rougher, fiercer, squeezing at my tits as he pressed his thigh between mine. I gasped as he came in for another kiss, and this time the endorphins rescued me, made me brave enough to wrap my arms around his neck and hold him tight. His thigh ground against my pussy and made me shudder and moan.

Oh fuck, how I wanted him.

I'd forgot how it felt to want him this fucking bad.

He tugged my babydoll down and my tits spilled over the top. He flicked my nipples with his thumbs and they sparked so hard I felt it in my clit. My pussy clenched and he responded, grinding his thigh just that little bit harder, enough that I couldn't stop my hips moving, grinding right back at him. I felt the waves building, my clit buzzing against the coarseness of denim through flimsy lace. My breaths turned shallow, my hands snaking down his back until they landed on his ass. I urged him on, rubbing against his leg like a bitch on heat, so fucking needy that my legs were wobbly and weak.

"Easy, tiger," he breathed. "We're not even in the fucking bedroom yet."

He stepped away and my whole body sagged, bereft at the abandonment. He took my hand and led me down the hallway, and it suddenly seemed so funny, so surreal. I giggled, and he flashed me a smile over his shoulder. He pushed the bedroom door open and flicked on the light.

I soaked it in, all of it – the obviously clean sheets on the bed, the way the covers were so tidy. His dirty clothes were piled up in the laundry basket, not scattered all over the floor, and there was an absence of dirty mugs on his bedside cabinet.

He pulled his t-shirt over his head and my appreciation of the room lost its gusto. We could have been in a hotel from Hell and I wouldn't have given a damn with that fucking body in front of me.

"What?" he said. "What's the grin for?"

I shook my head. "I'm just... you look so different."

He pulled a face. "Not that fucking different, Jo." He dropped his jeans and took hold of his cock. "See? Some things haven't changed a fucking jot."

My heart was fucking hammering.

God no. His cock hadn't changed a jot, and I was glad of it. His cock was still as thick and dark as it always had been, the same veiny pattern creeping from his balls to the swollen head of him. Fuck!

His thighs were thicker and his abs were way more defined, but his balls still hung heavy in exactly the same way they always had. I knew how they'd feel in my hands, knew how the nest of wiry hair would tickle my nose as I sucked them into my mouth.

I felt myself relax, let my clammy thighs drift apart as I stood before him.

"It's been a while," I said.

"Like riding a fucking bike," he said.

"Well thanks."

"You know what I mean. It'll be great. You'll be great."

"I hope so."

He smiled. "I'll show you." He held out his hand and I took it, let him guide me to the bed and push me backwards. I landed with a bounce and a giggle, my hand across my eyes as he dropped to his knees and eased my legs open.

He lowered his head, and my belly tightened, my pussy tingling with expectation. I could feel his breath against the lace of my knickers, his mouth so fucking close.

"Fuck," he grunted. "I've fucking missed this."

My whole body tensed as his tongue found my clit through the fabric. My hands gripped his head, his hair spiky against my fingers.

"*Shit,*" I hissed. "*Oh fuck, Darren.*"

He sucked at my pussy through my knickers, driving me fucking crazy before his teeth nipped the lace and pulled it away. He hooked his fingers inside and ran them across my slit, spread my lips wide until I felt the heat of his breath against my needy little clit.

The touch of his tongue was electric.

"*Yes!*" I squealed, all reservations out the window. "Oh dear fucking God, please!"

Two fingers pushed inside me, his tongue working fucking magic. My legs started jerking and I gripped the bedcovers as his mouth drove me insane. I could hear my own wet pussy, the noises his fingers made as they fucked me nice and hard. He pushed in a third and twisted, and his knuckles pressed something, pressed something inside that felt really fucking good.

This. This was new.

This was really new.

"Relax," he said. "Let it happen."

I cried out as worked his fingers, his knuckles grinding a spot that made me want to pee.

"That's it," he said. "That's so fucking good, Jo."

He took my clit between his lips and it set me on fire. My thighs clamped around his head and my back arched, a string of expletives hissing from my mouth as I lost myself to the sensation.

"Darren... Darren, I'm going to..."

He twisted his fingers again and I went off like a rocket, bucking and hissing and thrashing my legs as he worked that fucking spot. The pressure inside exploded, sensations so intense they took my breath, waves of pleasure riding through my whole fucking body.

I collapsed in a saggy mess of limbs, breath jagged and loud, a big fat smile on my face as he kissed his way up.

He pressed his lips to my flabby belly and I didn't even care.

He pulled the ribbon loose on my babydoll as he passed, and the fabric fell open, leaving my tits in all their deflated glory. I watched his eyes as he soaked them in, and all I saw was hunger.

It made my clit flutter all over again.

His cock thumped against my thigh, and I shifted myself, squirming until he was positioned at my pussy. I reached between us and took his dick in my hand, worked the thick shaft of him up and down. His face was over mine, his eyes glazed.

"Fuck me," I whispered. "Please fuck me."

He thrust into my hand and I squeezed him tighter. I kept squeezing as he lowered his mouth to my tit and gobbled me up. He sucked hard, my nipple between his teeth, his tongue flicking as I moaned for more.

And then he kissed me.

He kissed me like he wanted me.

He kissed me like I was the only woman in the world, and I kissed him right back.

I guided his cock to me, and he pushed in just a little, stretching me enough that I groaned against his mouth.

He rocked his hips, just enough to tease, and I wrapped my ankles around his calves, encouraged him on.

"Wait," he said. He reached into the bedside drawer and pulled out a rubber. "Better to be safe than sorry."

Who'd be fucking sorry?

I fought my own insanity, casting aside the crazy part of me that wanted Darren's dick inside me raw, wanted to feel him come inside me and fill me up with another beautiful baby like the two he'd given me already.

I was officially losing my fucking mind.

Batshit fucking crazy.

I nodded. "Better to be safe."

He tore the foil and pulled out to slip the thing on, and this time he didn't hold back. He braced himself above me and pushed in deep. It felt so fucking good that I grunted, squirming like a needy whore as he slammed that big dick all the way inside.

This. This is what I wanted.

This is what I fucking needed.

He propped himself on his forearms, his face in mine, and I wrapped my legs around his waist as he slammed me over and over.

It was hard.

It was deep.

It was brutal.

It was absolutely fucking amazing.

I dug my nails into his shoulders and demanded more, demanded he fuck me, fuck me so fucking hard. *Fuck me, Darren, fucking fuck me! Oh fucking God, just fucking fuck me!*

He repositioned himself, rocking me backwards and hooking my knees over his shoulders, and he was so deep there, so fucking into me.

I gritted my teeth and took him, loving the way it ached as he slammed all the way home. His balls slapped my skin, his breath coming in fast grunts, his forehead clammy against mine as he took me with everything he had.

I touched his face, my palms against his cheeks in just the way he usually held mine. I dared to look into his eyes and I found him there, the same Darren I'd loved all those years ago.

The same Darren who'd loved me so fucking hard it hurt.

I loved the way it hurt.

He was like a fucking hurricane, and this was dangerous. So fucking dangerous.

"Gonna come," he said. "Fuck, Jo... fuck."

I held his face firm, wanting to see it, wanting to see every moment of pleasure on his face. He closed his eyes and held his breath, the slap of skin on skin so fucking loud as he emptied his balls inside me.

Only it wasn't inside me.

Fuck, how I loved to watch him come. I loved every second of rapture on his face as he rode the climax right the way to the end.

I smiled as he collapsed onto me, his skin hot and sweaty, his heart beating fast. I wrapped my arms around him and I could feel it. I could feel everything.

He stayed inside me, just breathing, his cheek to my cheek until he calmed.

When he raised his head again he was smiling, eyes warm as they fixed on mine.

"Just like riding a fucking bike," he said.

CHAPTER TEN

JODIE

"I don't feel well," Mia said. "I'm sick."

I pressed a hand to her forehead. "You don't feel hot."

"But I am!"

"You seemed fine last night." I put my hand on her shoulder and she was tense. "Are you really sick, or is this Monday-morning-itis?"

She shook her head, pulled away from me and grabbed her school bag. "I dunno," she said.

At least she was honest about it.

I looked at the clock – almost time to go.

"Mia, if there's a reason you don't want to go to school today…"

"I'm fine," she said. "I want to go to school. It's nothing."

I'd been keeping an eye on her for days, any sign of school problems and I'd have been on it like a shot, but I'd seen nothing. Heard nothing.

She'd seemed happy. She'd seemed totally herself, laughing away to Daisy on Skype like life was roses.

"Do you want to stay home with Nanna?" I asked. "I've got extra hours this morning, but I can be home by lunchtime if you're not well. I'm sure Lorraine would call in cover if I asked her."

She sighed. "No, Mum, it's cool. I've got an English test, anyway."
I stared at her until she met my eyes. "I'm good, Mum, I don't even
feel sick now."

The time was ticking. Even Ruby was ready to go, which meant
we were certainly cutting it fine.

"I'll go to school," she said. "Really, I'm good. Me and Daisy are
doing maths revision at lunch."

"Ok," I said. "But if you feel ill at all you make sure you head up
to medical and I'll come and pick you up. Deal?"

"Deal," she said.

We piled out to the car and I felt uneasy, but Mia busied herself
on her phone and gave no indication that anything was really off
with her. I dropped her at the bus stop and watched her join the
crowd, making sure I hovered in the pull-in long enough to keep an
eye out.

She seemed fine, still tapping away on her phone without any
sign of stress or illness. Maybe it was a five-minute blip. Maybe she
was old enough to be getting her period. Maybe she slept funny.

Who could possibly know?

It appeared big-eared Ruby Trent could know.

"It's Tyler Dean," she announced when we were on our way. "He
had tonsillitis. He's back today. *Probably*."

My stomach dropped. The kid with the glasses, the kid I'd been
keeping an eye out at the bus stop for and hadn't seen hide nor hair
of. The kid I'd asked Mia about time after time and got nothing back
from her but bravado and *he's just a stupid idiot who calls me stupid
names* and shrugs.

"You heard this from Skype, did you?"

Ruby nodded, her smile smug. She leaned forward from the backseat until her belt strained. "Don't worry, Mum. I've been keeping an eye on things."

"Oh, you have, have you?" I said. "And this is the first you thought to share the details of your covert operation?"

She shrugged. "Mia's already mad at me for telling Dad he's a gigolo. She said if I say anything else I'm banned from her bedroom, and she has a better TV than me."

Priorities.

"Mia can be mad at you all she wants," I said. "We don't have secrets in our house, understand? If something's going on we talk about it."

Unless it's me booty-calling your father. We definitely won't be talking about that little secret.

My tummy was a fluttery mess again, ridiculous.

I considered turning the car around and driving Mia right up to the school gates, but the bus would likely have been already. I marked it down for an urgent after-school chat and left it at that.

There were no awkward little chats to be had with Miss Davies today, which was something at least. The real awkwardness still loomed ahead in the form of the *ladies who lunch* brigade, minus me since I was working instead.

I'd seen the invite in the group chat. *Meeting as usual.*

Oh the joy.

The thought of seeing Mandy Taylor's conceited grin made me cringe, but at least I was in line for the same privileges, and I'd got my first decent fucking in years on the back of her big running mouth, which had to be a good thing, even if it was a crazy one-off.

It was definitely a one-off. An awkward farewell outside mine had been the last I'd seen of Darren. No calls, no texts, no Casanova howling outside my bedroom window. But why would there be?

Of course there wouldn't be.

We'd said sex, no biggie. I guess he'd meant it.

I'd meant it, too.

I'd totally meant it.

He'd probably banged half the village since then – maybe even Mandy Taylor herself, who fucking knows?

I guessed I'd find out with the rest of the Velvet Bean soon enough.

TRENT

"Aye aye, here she comes." Buck slapped the car bonnet over my head.

My stomach did a sappy flip at the thought he might mean Jodie, but of course he didn't.

Jimmy O let out a piss-poor catcall and it told me all I needed to know.

There it was. The rumble of the fucking Porsche grew louder. Bollocks.

No fucking way. Not today.

I'd told Eleanor Hartwell no Mondays. I'd told Eleanor Hartwell to call ahead first.

The problem with Eleanor Hartwell is that she's too fucking used to flashing the old man's gold card and getting her own way.

"I want a go on her today," Jimmy leered. "I'm gagging for a ride on blondie. Hugh can do the next pick-up on his fucking own, I'm staying here and getting a look in."

I jabbed a finger in his direction. "You'll be doing whatever I fucking tell you to do. Don't like it, you can take your wages owed and get the fuck out of here."

He raised his hands. "Take a bastard chill-pill, *boss*. Just setting my pissing stall out."

Petey was grinning at the Porsche like a dope, dick already tenting his fucking pants. The lad needed to cut his teeth a little and calm it down. His pump and go technique was alright for so long, but the novelty of being young and fit wouldn't last forever. Especially not for women like this one.

Eleanor was wearing pink today, one of those celebrity style tracksuits and shades. To be honest, I thought she looked like a prize-fucking tit, but what would I know?

"Boys," she said, that big dirty smile on her face. She lowered her shades as she looked in my direction. "Trent."

I didn't have time for this shit.

"We're busy," I told her. "Monday mornings are busy, Eleanor, like I fucking said last week. Was I talking to myself, or what?"

She shrugged, flicked her hair. "And, like *I* said, I don't mind paying for a priority service." She pulled out another fat envelope. "Ted was out all weekend, didn't even call. Turned up last night drunk on vintage champers and pissed in the laundry hamper. I think I deserve a good time on the back of all his shit, paying for it is the *least* he can do." She sidled up to me, ran a manicured fingernail up my arm. "Please, Trent. I promise I'll be good."

I sighed. "What do you want?"

"You," she said, like fucking always. "You and the big guy, unless you can give me the afternoon?"

Déjà fucking *vu*. I shook my head. "No can do, Eleanor. Got too much shit on already." I stepped away from her and grabbed my keys from the side. "I'm off out," I said. "Got some parts to collect." I gestured to the guys, all of them standing around like a bunch of horny cunts. "Take your pick of the others, but you'll have to be done and gone by the time I'm back. Got customers here at lunch."

Her face dropped, pouty lips pursing like a puckered asshole. "But Trent... I was hoping..."

"Noon at the latest," I said to the lads. "And we'll be staying late tonight on the back of it." I turned back to Eleanor. "Gotta go," I said. "I'll be seeing you."

I pulled down the shutters on the way out.

The Dog and Drum doesn't open til late on a Monday, so no chance for a sneaky pint while the lads were rutting Eleanor. I went home first, checked out cruddy daytime TV before I decided to ditch the overalls and head back out.

I had an hour or so to play it safe, I could have fired up my crappy old laptop and tackled some of my invoicing backlog from home, but I fancied a coffee, a decent one, not that instant shit I have at home.

That's how come I ended up face-to-face with Jodie over the Velvet Bean counter, and that's how come I ended up sharing the same fucking airspace as Mandy pissing Taylor and her gaggle of cock-starved cronies.

Tonya shot me a pained look as I walked in through the door, but I was already committed. I stared Mandy out on my way past, made it as clear that her gossipy shit wasn't welcome. She paid no pissing attention.

Whispers and giggles and a wave from Debbie Gibson. She'd been trying to book in for a week now, tried every bloody trick in the book, including a slow puncture that wasn't a bloody puncture at all.

Jodie felt awkward, I could see it in the blush on her neck. She was polite, too polite. Flashing me a quick smile before taking my order.

"Just a coffee," I said.

"Americano?"

"Whatever."

She met my eyes for just a second. "Not working?"

"Popped out."

"I see," she said. But she didn't, she didn't see at all.

Mandy's laugh roared through the place, some comment about going *all night long*. I shot the bitch a glare.

When I turned back to Jodie she was cringing, I could see it written all over her.

"Shall I tell her where to go?" I asked. "I don't mind telling her."

She shook her head. "Leave it," she said. "It's a cafe, she can laugh about whatever she likes as long as she's paying."

"She's not paying *me*," I said.

"That's not what *she* thinks," she replied. "Nor the others, since apparently they're in the *queue*."

I sighed, lowered my voice. "There is no fucking queue, Jo. They're full of shit."

"Whatever, Darren," she said. "It's really none of my business if they're in your *bang gang* club or not."

Her tone felt like a slap. "Fair enough."

She placed a take-out mug on the counter, one of those crappy polystyrene things. "Three pound twenty, please."

I guess I was having coffee to go.

I handed over the cash and she gave me a smile. Just another fucking customer, like she hadn't come on my face the night before last.

I guess it meant nothing to her, just a prelude to the main fucking event.

She busied herself with the coffee machine and I didn't budge. She looked nervous as she registered I was still waiting.

"What?" she said. "Did you want something else?"

"Sugar would be a start," I said.

She blushed. "Sorry. Shit. I didn't think you took sugar."

"Only for the past fifteen years."

She looked flummoxed as the coven at Mandy's table started laughing again. "Guess I must have forgotten, sorry. My bad." She handed over some sugar sachets and I emptied them into the cup. "I serve a lot of people a lot of coffees, Darren."

"I'm hardly a lot of people," I said. "You should know how I like my bloody coffee, Jodie, you made enough of them over the years."

She smiled. "I guess I did."

"I guess you did." I took my cup. "And I guess I'm taking this out."

Her face dropped. "Did you want to drink in? I didn't think..."

"No bother," I said, and stepped away.

She sighed. "Sorry, Darren... I should know this kind of crap."

I raised the cup to her. "Another time."

I'd taken a few steps toward the door by the time she spoke again. Her low laugh made my stomach lurch.

"Except I shouldn't know this kind of crap, should I?" She paused. "When did I last make you a coffee, Darren? Six, seven years ago? You always have tea, and you never have it here, not once in all the years I've been working here."

I turned back to her, played it cool. "I come here…"

She shook her head. "No. You don't."

I took a sip of coffee and gave her a nod. "It's good."

She gave me the first proper smile since I'd walked in, despite another uproar from Mandy's table.

"I'll make sure I give you your sugar next time."

So much I wanted to say, and none of it was about pissing sugar.

I don't want your sugar sachets, Jodie, I want your pussy on my fucking face. I want you to ride my dick until you squirt all over me. I want to take your asshole until you moan like the dirty little bitch I used to love.

Used to. What a fucking joke.

I said nothing.

JODIE

Tonya stayed later than the other ladies. She hovered until there was a lull, checking out her phone for an age with just the dregs of a cappuccino in her cup. She waited until the coast was clear and Lorraine was out the back before she came to the counter.

"She was talking shit," she announced. I stared blankly. "Mandy," she said. "All bluster. All her *a lady never tells* bullshit is just a cover up for the fact she hasn't had another go yet. If she had we'd be hearing all about it by now. It would have been plastered all over her Facebook. Lady my bloody arse."

"What's your point?" I asked. "That Mandy's far enough down the queue not to have banged Trent and co again yet? I'm sure it's just a matter of time."

"I don't think Mandy's in the bloody queue at all, Jo, nor Debbie for that matter."

I laughed a little. "Nice try."

"What?"

"Trying to make me feel better about the fact the father of my children is fucking every pussy who'll pay him within a fifty mile radius."

"Including yours," she said, then poked her tongue out. "So, how was the gigolo? I know it was a freebie, but I don't imagine the service was substandard." Her eyes sparkled. "Was he a good reintroduction to the land of the sexually active?"

I looked around for Lorraine but she was still out the back, there was nobody in earshot.

"I told you on the phone," I began.

"You told me fuck all on the phone," she laughed.

"It was good." I smiled. "It was really good. It was great."

She punched the air. "Trent shoots, he scores."

I grabbed her a fresh mug. "It was *different*. I mean, it was Darren. I know Darren. But some stuff was new. Very new."

She grinned. "I guess some of his more refined clients have taught him a thing or two, hey?"

The thought of Porsche-bitch or Mandy Taylor teaching him anything turned my stomach, but Tonya was right. He'd learned his shit from somewhere, and it wasn't from a Haynes manual.

I added milk to her coffee. "He's definitely had some pointers."

"You owe someone a drink then," she said. "I doubt it's Mandy. That silly cow doesn't even own a decent vibe. I doubt she even knows what a multiple orgasm is. It's all talk."

I love the way Tonya bands that crap around like it's standard.

145

She tells me she's the poster girl for multiple orgasms. Three towels doubled over before she'll even risk getting the vibe out.

That's one of the reasons we'd forged the friendship of a lifetime – a shared appreciation of a decent fuck.

Only I'd left that crap at the roadside at about the same place I'd left myself all those years back.

She took her coffee. "So, you still going for the big bang? T-minus four days, right?"

The thought made my clit tingle, and I could still feel Darren there, still feel where I'd been fucked.

I let myself smile a proper smile. Fuck Mandy and Debbie and all those other bitches in the queue. I was going to get mine, and it was going to be worth every penny, the *experience of a lifetime* alright. Darren's new tricks had made it crystal clear this wasn't some half-rate service, these guys were serious.

Maybe *I'd* be the poster girl for multiple orgasms come Friday.

"Four days," I said. "And I can't fucking wait!"

TRENT

I went through the motions, told myself this was just another mid-week gig that meant nothing more than a fresh wedge of notes for the university fund.

I pulled up her Facebook profile as I got myself dressed. Janie Ryan. Daughter of some rich banker from London, on a break at their country pad over Brecon way.

She'd heard of us through a friend of a friend by all accounts, and she was no stranger to paid-for sex. She'd rattled off a load of escort services over the telephone, told me she knew *exactly* what she was buying into.

This time she was after a bit of countryside rough, and she expected the best our neck of the woods had to offer.

New clients make me twitchy, but not twitchy like this. I showered and shaved and told myself to pull my shit together, told myself to stop being such a soft fucking idiot.

This gig was casual dress, nothing fancy. I pulled on some jeans and a nice enough t-shirt, put some gel in my hair and I was ready to roll. I smoked a cigarette before I got in the truck, having the strangest hope that the bastard wouldn't start.

It did start.

Of course it fucking did.

I did the rounds and picked up the guys, and the atmosphere was the same usual lairy banter we go through every fucking time. I kept quiet, chain smoked out of the window all the way, kept thinking about Janie Ryan and hoping her pretty little snatch would be enough to get me off.

She'd sent pictures and they were good ones. Janie Ryan was quite a fucking looker.

Her Brecon pad was little short of a mansion, a big stone barn conversion amongst the hills. I pulled up next to a sporty little BMW and we piled out, game on. The banter stopped and we were ready to roll, charged with testosterone and stiff fucking dicks.

Only my dick wasn't all that fucking stiff.

Fucking hell.

Janie was nicer in real life than she was in her pics. A tall natural blonde with legs up to her pits and a nice perky rack on her. She was dressed in nothing but a silk robe, her lounge set out with candles and this weird scented shit that hit me right in the temples.

It was like she thought she was getting a massage, not a fucking gangbang.

She set herself up in a lounge chair with no time for niceties, beckoned us over like we were fucking lapdogs.

The others didn't seem to give two shits, just went where she instructed, performing like sea lions with every fucking click of her fingers. She had Buck and Jimmy O double-teaming to eat out her pussy, Hugh giving her a fucking shoulder massage and Petey groping at her tits with his eyes like saucers. And there was me, still fucking hovering, still not feeling this shit – not feeling it at all.

Hugh shot me a look of confusion, beckoned me over to join him on the masseur shit, but I'm no pissing masseur. I watched her spread those swanky pins of hers, saw her tight little cunt well enough as Buck and Jimmy worked her up, and still it did nothing for me. Not one fucking thing.

She didn't come, stopping them just as they started getting somewhere.

"I want to orgasm through penetration," she snapped. "Now!" She looked around the guys, not even seeming to notice I wasn't playing along, and her eyes landed on Petey and the jut in his pants. "You!" she said. "Fuck me!"

The lad was straight fucking in there. He dropped his jeans in a flash, rolled a johnny on his prick with shaky fingers, and the lad was already half-gone. Buck looked at me in horror as Petey mounted the blonde under him, but there was nothing I could do. He was quick, desperate, his pasty ass bobbing as he humped her like a virgin at a strip club. Her expression was one of disgust, nothing better than a grimace as he hit well short of the mark.

She went to shove him away but it was too late, Petey was already grunting, already shooting his fucking load. The rest was like a car crash, unfolding in slow motion.

Janie's groan of revulsion was enough to shrivel every dick in a five mile radius, the look she gave Petey as he plopped his still-jizzing dick from her cunt could wilt fucking flowers. He was still out of breath, a goofy grin plastered on his face until he realised he'd fucked up bad. He backed away too quickly, a clumsy hand on his cock that managed to pull that pissing johnny straight off. It landed with a slimy plop on Janie's belly, splattering spunk all over her snatch. She leapt up and made a right hoo-hah out of it, acted like someone just pissed in her Pimm's.

"What the fuck?!" she bleated. "For fuck's sake! What the fuck is this?!"

"Jizz," I said, venturing forward for the first time in this whole sorry spectacle. "A standard by-product from a fucking gangbang last time I checked."

Petey looked mortified, poor sod. I slapped him on the shoulder, gestured he should get his bloody pants back on.

"This is... unacceptable!" she carried on. "What kind of cheap shit outfit is this?"

"Lad got carried away," I said. "Shit happens. We'll call it a night, sorry for the trouble."

"Oh, no!" she said. "We won't fucking call it a night! I haven't had a single fucking orgasm!" She stared at me, and I stared right back. "Trent, right?" she said.

"That's right."

She flashed a vicious smile. "Well, Mr Boss-man, you can be the one to rectify this fucking disaster." She wiped herself off and sat herself back down and splayed those fucking legs again, offered up her pretty pussy like a fucking raffle prize. "You," she said. "Now!"

The guys looked at me, all of them. Buck gave me a nod, told me to get right in there. Jimmy O was grinning, expecting me to whip it out and get the job done.

"Come on," she said. "Show me what I'm paying for!"

I felt the simmer of anger, that primitive urge to fuck that bitch so hard she learned some fucking manners, see how smart her mouth was when she was coming all over my fucking cock. I stepped up and pulled off my t-shirt, and she managed a smile.

"Nice," she said. "I do like my men with a bit of ink. Show me what else you've got."

Just a job, it was just a fucking job.

I dropped my jeans and was relieved as fuck to find my dick was getting with the agenda. I took a rubber from Buck and rolled it on, hitching Janie's perfect Barbie legs over my shoulders and lining up to hit the perfect spot. I closed my eyes, told myself this was nothing, just the same old shit, different day. That this meant fucking nothing. Nothing at all.

Told myself I could get the job done and get out of there.

But my body wouldn't fucking move.

"Come on," she said. "Fuck me! I'm fucking ready for it!"

But I wasn't.

I looked at Janie Ryan's pretty face and all I saw was a big fucking mistake.

My dick backtracked and bailed on me, and my jeans were up before I'd even pulled the rubber off. I fished it out and stomped off to find a bin.

Janie really was pissed off then. Her face turned beetroot, her squeals of annoyance betraying her for the spoiled little brat she really was.

I didn't even look at the guys, just dumped my johnny in the trash where it belonged and picked up my t-shirt.

"Sorry for the inconvenience," I said. "But we're not anyone's fucking sissy-boys. I think it's best you find yourself another outfit." I pulled some notes from my back pocket, left them on the side for her trouble. I gestured to the guys, told them we were done, and they made a sharp fucking exit as I listened to Janie rattle on about our piss-poor service.

I don't think she'll be booking in her BMW anytime soon, that's for fucking sure.

Nobody said a word as I climbed back into the truck. Hugh put an arm around Petey's shoulders in the back, ruffled the lad's hair. Poor kid looked like he was going to cry, can't say I blamed him. Buck knows me well enough to know when to mind his tongue, he gave me a nod as we pulled away from her gates and that was the end of it.

I stopped at the yard on the way back through the village, opened up the office and unlocked the safe. I dished out the earnings – just as they should have been, but by the time I'd locked back up there were a pile of notes on the dashboard.

"Don't be soft," I said. "This was my call, just take the cash and stop being so fucking sappy about it."

But none of them would take a thing.

CHAPTER ELEVEN

TRENT

Hugh was in early next morning. He got us both a cup of tea and hovered in the office while I organised the job cards.

"You know what the lad needs," he said. "Either that or he's off the squad. He's too inexperienced, doesn't know what the hell he's doing. You know it as well as I do." He took a swig of tea. "Take him to her. She's the one to sort him out, we all know that. Especially you."

I'd been avoiding *her* for weeks, months probably.

"No," I said. "It's a barrel of shit, Hugh. I'm out of that."

"Then you'll have to drop him from the side. He's not up to it. Lad was practically a virgin when he started, he's got no idea."

"He'll pick it up," I said, but I was lying. Lad wasn't picking up shit.

Hugh slapped my back as Jimmy O's bike roared onto the yard. "Take him to her. You can stay out of it."

Like hell I could.

I took out my mobile and fired off a text despite my better judgement, rather that than see the lad's confidence shrivel to shit.

I'd had a reply by the time I'd finished up dishing out the jobs for the day. The guys hadn't even started up by the time I took Petey off to the side.

"Afternoon off," I said. "On-site training." He looked at me, trying to work out what the hell I was on about, but I didn't offer him much more than that. "Just be ready," I said. "We go after lunch." I smirked and gestured to the toilet. "Make sure your dick's sparkly fucking clean, standards are high where we're going."

JODIE

I'll be getting fucked by five men. Tomorrow. To-fucking-morrow. Oh my fucking God.

Nerves and excitement, and this weird achy feeling whenever I thought about Trent being there. I just hoped I'd be up to it when push came to shove.

Tonya insisted I should wear the red crotchless. *Make a statement*, she said. Like signing up for a five-man orgy wasn't statement enough.

The cafe was busy for a Thursday, but finally the Bang Gang whispering seemed to be dying down.

Fred Crocker had stumbled from the Drum the night before, managed to tumble into the river when he was taking a piss over the railings. They'd had to throw him one of those bright orange life rings and fish him out. Apparently his trousers were still round his ankles when they pulled him clear, nothing bruised but his ego.

That was the talk of the day. Darren's little sex business had taken a backseat for the time being.

Thanks, Fred.

We were in the middle of the lunchtime rush when Lorraine ditched her apron and put her coat on.

"I'm out for the afternoon," she said. "Going to the cash and carry."

"Now?!" I said, looking out on the sea of people cramming in for the toasted teacake special.

She didn't even pause. "I've asked Sharon to come and give you a hand, she should be here any minute."

Sharon doesn't know her ass from her elbow. She put cabbage in a ham salad sandwich a few shifts back, and forgot to debone the salmon. Mrs Hartley nearly choked on it, threatened to call *Law4You* and make a claim for a new set of dentures.

"Fine," I said. "See you later."

"Tomorrow," she said. "I'll be awhile."

"But I put in an order already, we just need..." I called after her but she was already gone. "Napkins," I finished, to myself.

I plastered on a smile and made the best of it. I'd always make the best of it, for Lorraine's sake if nothing else.

Lorraine was much more than a boss to me. She was a friend, too.

She'd taken me under her wing after Pops passed away, listened to my crap as things fell apart for me, and listened some more when things fell apart for me and Darren soon afterwards. She'd been so supportive; so strong when I was weak. So sure when I was so indecisive. She'd helped me make the best of things, taught me to keep a practical head on my shoulders.

To make the right choices, for me and the girls.

Choices like Brian.

Alright, so sometimes even Lorraine gets shit wrong, but that isn't the point.

I'd been keeping the Darren icebreaker right under her radar, which felt kind of shitty, but I cared about what she thought, and she wouldn't think much of it.

Lorraine's never had any time for Darren.

I felt like a shit friend for keeping things from her, at least I could hold the bloody cafe together while she nipped out for essentials.

But we didn't need any essentials.

Still, it was the least I could do.

Tonya arrived before Sharon, fresh from her lunch shift at the fish and chip shop.

"I stink," she said, then looked around at the tables still waiting to be cleared. "Where's Lorraine?"

"Cash and carry," I said. "I'm expecting Sharon."

"Sharon doesn't know her ass from her elbow," Tonya said. Great minds. She stepped behind the counter and grabbed a Velvet Bean apron. "Needs must," she said. "Let me sort those bloody tables."

TRENT

I can't say I felt easy about pulling onto Lorraine Marchant's driveway, but Petey was oblivious, grinning away in the passenger seat like a dippy spaniel.

If only he knew.

I didn't need to knock on the front door, she was already in the doorway by the time we were at the front step. I cast a glance around the street, checking for neighbours.

As if they wouldn't have seen the fucking truck already. Luckily Allensmore seemed to be far enough out to stay off the village radar.

"Well well," she said. "Look what the cat dragged in. I was

wondering when you'd darken my doorstep."

"Been busy," I said.

"So I heard." She raised an eyebrow. "Mandy Taylor and Debbie Gibson?" she scoffed. "I thought you'd have more class than to entertain those cheap skanky bitches."

Her condescending tone got my hackles up. "Business is business, Lorraine, as you well fucking know."

She let out a snide laugh. "So you *have* done Debbie Gibson. I thought that was a mindless rumour."

Petey flashed me a look of confusion, I willed the fool to keep his mouth shut. Lorraine is the last one I want knowing my fucking business.

I shoved the lad forward. "Present for you," I said to Lorraine. "Enjoy."

I'd stepped away from the door before she tutted at me. "No no no," she said. "You know the rules, Mr Trent, you scratch my back, I'll scratch yours."

She'd scratched my back plenty of fucking times, crazy bitch.

I gestured to her flashy red Mini Cooper. "Next service is on me, I'll throw you in a new set of tyres, too."

She laughed. "Oh come on, Darren. We're a bit past all that, don't you think?"

Petey was still staring at me, still trying to wrap his head round what the fuck was going on.

"What do you want?" I said.

"You know what I want," she replied. "You've been avoiding me, why?"

I shrugged. "Haven't been avoiding you, Lorraine, just had shit to do."

"Shit like chasing after Jodie by any chance?" She smiled a sly smile as my mood dropped. "Oh dear. You didn't think I knew? Poor you, so naive."

"What goes on with Jodie and me is none of your business," I said. "You'd do well to remember that." I lit up a cigarette.

"That's not how she sees it," Lorraine said. "You really shouldn't try so hard with her, you know, it's embarrassing."

I felt my cheeks fucking burning. "Like I'm running around after her like some fucking idiot. Fuck off, Lorraine."

She shrugged. "She's better off without you, and she knows it. Who do you think this hot new image of hers is for?" She laughed. "You can't honestly think she doesn't have irons in the fire. She's a beautiful woman with a good head on her shoulders, two beautiful girls... Christ, Darren, she's long over you. Let it go, have some dignity."

My gut fucking pained.

Petey looked fucking horrified.

She changed the subject. "Next week," she said. "You and me. Don't pretend you don't want it, I know how to make it feel better, don't you worry."

I sighed to myself. "Just do a good job with the fucking lad."

"You know it," she said.

"I'll pick him up later."

"Don't worry about that," she said. "I'll drop him back when I'm done with him." She looked him up and down, weighed up the rabbit-in-the-headlights expression on his face. "This may take some time."

"Take as long as you want, just get him up to fucking speed."

I didn't even say goodbye.

"Call me," she shouted after me. "Soon, Darren. I'm looking forward to it."

Shame I couldn't say the fucking same.

CHAPTER TWELVE

JODIE

No babysitting duties for Nanna this evening, Tonya insisted she stay at mine to make sure my Bang Gang special risked no disruptions. I think she was really there to make sure I wore the slutty red.

It worked.

Darren dropped me a text as I finished up my makeup. I could barely contain my nerves, belly churning as I clicked to read it.

Ready when you are.

Shit. Shit shit shit.

"I can't believe I'm really doing this," I said to Tonya, spritzing myself with a second round of perfume.

"Go get 'em," she said. "Enjoy it. Experience of a lifetime, remember?"

I checked the envelope of cash was still in my handbag. I'd felt like such a slut as I took four hundred in twenties from the bank that lunchtime, but it would be worth it.

At least, I hoped so.

Experience of a lifetime.

I hoped my pussy would take it. Darren had been a good intro, and a vibrator had picked up where he left off. I'd been practicing.

As much as you can possibly practice for something like this.

I'd set out my fantasy to Darren by text, worked through the technicalities, too – how to call it off, how it would take just a simple statement of *I'm done* if I'd had enough. What was acceptable and what was not. Pussy, *yes*. Mouth, *of course*. Ass, one big *maybe*.

I didn't want to admit it to him, but Darren was the only man who'd been in the backdoor, and that was a long time ago. Brian tried it once, in a moment of drunken madness completely at odds with his regular modus operandi, and it was terrible. Just terrible.

Darren's cock and my ass seemed to form a mutual alliance from the get go, it just worked. Nothing else seemed to fit like he did, no vibrator and certainly not Brian.

So, yeah, I'd put a big *maybe* and said I'd see how I felt on the night.

Righto, he'd said.

Positions, I'd said *whatever works*. Spunk in the face, I'd said *yes, please*.

Condoms were an absolute. He assured me they always were.

Any particular kinks? he'd asked. I'd said *No. Not this time, anyway*.

He hadn't replied to that.

I had a quick glass of wine with Tonya to still my nerves, and another for the road which I chugged down before I set off.

The journey seemed to take no time.

This time Darren *was* outside smoking. He watched me totter along the road, and I think his scrutiny was the only thing that kept me moving forwards, kept me putting one foot ahead of the other and not caving to last minute nerves.

He met me on the stairs and his eyes were every bit as intense as usual.

"You sure this is what you want?" he said.

No. Yes. Maybe.

I want you.

"Yes," I said. "This is definitely what I want." I smiled. "I'm looking forward to it."

"Good," he said, and it was so clipped, so professional.

Hold my hand, I wanted to say. *I'm scared, and worried I'll be rubbish, I'm worried this will be the shittest gangbang you guys have ever had.*

I followed him upstairs and he didn't even look back at me, just finished up his cigarette at the top and held the door open as I stepped inside.

I took the opportunity to pull the envelope from my bag, handed it over without a word. He took it without looking at it, dropped it on the key shelf like it was toxic.

"Don't you want to count that? Make sure it's all there?"

"No," he said.

I shrugged. "Ok, cool."

I heard the guys in the living room, and they were so loud, laughing and joking just like any other day. I would have stalled if Darren hadn't been right at the back of me, but his presence kept me moving, made me paste that big smile on my face and remind myself why I was here.

I want this.

I want to be wild again. I want to be a woman again.

I want the kind of crazy experience that will last me a lifetime.

The guys abandoned their conversation the moment I came into view. They smiled, and Buck and Hugh shifted apart on the sofa enough to offer me a seat. I felt myself relax a little.

I knew these guys, I *liked* these guys. Even Jimmy O who had a reputation for being a filthy dirty bastard down the pub had always been so nice when it came to me, when it came to my girls, too.

Buck leaned in, gave my arm a squeeze, nothing dodgy. "You alright, Jo?" he asked, and I nodded.

"Yeah, I'm good. Just nervous."

He smiled. "No need to be nervous, whatever you want, however you want it. This is your gig, Jodie, we're just here when you want us."

I looked around for Darren but he wasn't in the room. I heard him banging about in the kitchen, and it seemed to take him an age. He came out with a glass of chilled white and I could have kissed him.

The others were drinking beer, but he had nothing. He sat himself on Ruby's tatty beanbag in the corner and hardly said a word.

I slumped back in my seat and drank my wine quickly, the heady warmth of it loosening up my inhibitions. I could feel them slipping away, becoming muggy and distant. I liked it. It felt really nice.

Suddenly the red knickers seemed absolutely the right call. *I could do this.*

Jimmy took my empty glass from my hand and offered me a refill. I saw Darren shoot him a glare.

"Steady," he said. "She's had enough."

"Chill out," Jim said. "Christ, man, she's fucking fine."

Darren followed him into the kitchen and I heard raised voices that the other guys tried to drown out with chit-chat. When Darren came back it was with a glass of water, and Jimmy was quiet. Jimmy offered me a shrug, tipped his head at Trent and pulled a face.

I took the water from Darren's hand. "Drink up," he said. "This shit goes down sober or not at all."

He seemed so fucking mean tonight.

I rolled my eyes before I knocked it back, "I'm not drunk, Trent. I've had three bloody glasses."

"Yeah, and you won't be having three more."

I saluted him with a stupid hand gesture once he'd turned away and Jimmy let out a snigger, took the empty glass from me and put it on the side. I tried to forget about it, all of it, just let it all wash over me.

I relaxed back into the sofa and closed my eyes, listened to my thumping heart and tried to prepare myself for what was to come.

The wine made it easier. It definitely made it easier.

Then something changed. The guys stopped chattering and the room became quiet and heavy. Thick with anticipation.

I was going to fuck these guys. All of them.

And I was going to remember it forever.

I flinched as a hand landed on my knee, giggling as I realised it was just Buck.

"Alright?" he said.

I nodded. "Yeah, I'm good."

His fingers tickled and crept up, tracing gentle patterns up my thigh, slowly. So fucking slowly. I took a deep breath. *Here we go.*

I chanced one final glance at Darren but he wasn't even looking in my direction. He was so cold, so business-like it hurt, but I didn't have time to worry about that. This was *my* experience. *My* night.

I just wished he'd have wanted me, too. Even if it was just a little bit. That would be enough.

I guess it's hard to get excited about something you do every single night, especially when it's a freebie.

I was just a freebie.

Fuck him, then. Mandy Taylor wasn't a freebie. I bet he made sure she had a damn good time.

Buck's fingers moved so slowly as they climbed, ending up so close to my pussy that my clit pulsed, and it was now or never, make or break. In a moment of crazy wine-induced confidence – mixed with a tiny little bit of *fuck you* – I wrapped an arm around his shoulders and pulled him in.

His beard tickled my chin as his lips landed.

Fuck, I was kissing Buck. Oh my fucking God.

Buck was a good kisser, too. He wasn't wild and possessive like Darren. There was nothing all-consuming in the way his tongue danced with mine. It was good. It was nice.

I could really fucking do this.

I was really doing this.

Another hand landed on my leg and gripped my knee, and together two guys spread them wide. I went with it, letting my thighs fall open. I only flinched for a heartbeat as someone dropped to the floor between them. *Shit.*

Strong fingers grabbed at my tits through my fancy new boho blouse, and my nipples were already hard, poking through the flimsy red lace underneath. I kept on kissing Buck, letting the sensations take over as a strong thumb rubbed my clit through my jeans.

I came alive as my pussy did, fantasies bubbling up and over, and when Buck broke the kiss and pulled away, Hugh was already waiting. I smiled before my lips touched his, and that silver fox was an old hat at this. He kissed like he spoke – considered, with the wisdom of age. I liked kissing Hugh very much.

I think it was *his* hand that first slipped inside my blouse, but I wouldn't swear on it. It wasn't his fingers that popped the button on my jeans, though, and definitely wasn't his hands that lifted me from the sofa enough to shimmy me out of them.

Darren, I want Darren.

I couldn't bear to see his nonchalance, so I didn't look for him. There was just the dullest pain, hiding deep, under all the excitement and wine and endorphins. Hiding deep behind the rush of my throbbing clit as someone took advantage of my crotchless knickers to slip their fingers inside the lace.

I heard a grunt of approval, and it wasn't Darren. Several more, and they weren't from Darren, either.

I felt someone's breath between my legs, and it wasn't him. None of it was him.

Hugh broke the kiss and guided my arms through my sleeves, casting my blouse aside. Just me and the sexy undies remained, and I was glad I'd worn them. My bra was tugged down, my tits flopping free, but I was past caring, the tongue against my clit felt too fucking good.

I reached down, took the pleasurer's hair in my hands, glad I had the aesthetics of stockings to show me in the best light. *Curls.* Jimmy O. Definitely Jimmy O.

Jimmy O was good. He pushed two fingers inside my pussy and made me moan.

Buck's beard tickled my ribs as he sucked my tit into his mouth,

I arched my back. *Oh God. Oh fucking God.*

Little Petey appeared from behind. He leaned over the back of the sofa and came in for a kiss, fingers reaching for the nipple Buck wasn't sucking.

I clamped Jimmy's head between my thighs, let out a choked moan as he sucked hard on my clit. He twisted his fingers, just like Darren had done, and it made me feel so strange, so feral.

Slurping and sucking noises, all around me, all *on* me. The sound of a zipper as someone dropped their pants, and the others followed suit. I heard clothes dropping to the floor, well-orchestrated enough that I barely felt an interruption to the fingers and mouths. Jimmy was working wonders with my pussy. Buck's mouth sending sparks from my nipple to my clit. Petey's mouth was wet and keen. I could hear him playing with his dick as his tongue whirred its way around mine. What he lacked in finesse he made up for in appreciation. I knew he wanted me, he was practically jerking off in my face.

Murmured compliments gave me confidence, the awareness of hard horny dicks egging me on.

My thighs lolled open, hips rocking into Jimmy's hot mouth. A third finger opened me up, and it felt so good I let out a cry, muffled by Petey's mouth. A hand on mine guided my fingers to a hot hard shaft. Someone else followed suit, and that someone must have been Buck, because that dick was fucking huge, and everyone knows that's why they call him Big Buck. It felt so fucking weird, stroking two cocks at once, my fingers straining to keep a grip on Buck's massive girth. I knew what was coming even before Petey pulled away and clambered over the back of the sofa. My mouth was already open wide for his dick when it arrived in my face. He pushed it all the way to the back of my throat, too fast, too soon. It made me gag, and that made me giggle, and the whole thing felt so much better then, ice broken.

I sucked on Petey's dick, and he had quite some length on him, if not quite the girth. Buck licked at my nipple and thrust his fat cock into my hand, gripped my fingers with his. I heard Hugh groan, another hand gripping mine around a dick, working my fingers up and down.

My head bobbed back and forth, the sound of wet cock loud in the room. I never knew it would be so fucking loud.

Jimmy spread my pussy lips, blew hot breath onto my clit. *Oh please.*

Jimmy O was going to make me come. Jimmy O was going to make me come really fucking hard.

Jimmy O knew it, too.

He grunted and flicked my clit with his tongue, ran it back and forth as I wriggled under him. His fingers were right on point, the build-up of pressure making my feet twitch.

Darren. Where the fuck was Darren?

I wanted to see him, wanted to touch him, wanted *his* cock in my mouth, *his* tongue on my clit. With Petey blocking my view, I couldn't have seen Darren if I'd wanted to. I tried to forget about him, focused on nothing but the moment, on the sensations in my body as it rushed towards climax. I couldn't keep a steady rhythm with my hands, my mouth neither, but it didn't matter. The guys did the work for me, shifted me into position, moved my body for me. I loved it like that. I loved feeling so... taken.

I pulled my mouth from Petey's dick as I reached the point of no return, and Hugh and Buck let go of my fingers, giving me free rein. My hands fell to Jimmy's head, tangled in his hair and I asked for *more, more, more. Don't fucking stop, please God, don't fucking stop!*

Fingers pinched my nipples at the perfect moment, and my pussy unravelled, sending shockwaves right through my legs. *Yes, oh fucking yes!*

I wriggled and squirmed and moaned like a filthy whore, and in that moment I recognised myself from years gone by. Recognised the dirty girl who'd ridden Darren like fucking bronco in the pub toilets, turned on by the thumps and raps on the wall as everyone heard what was going down.

That dirty girl was me.

More, I moaned. *Fuck, please, more!*

Jimmy stretched my pussy a little further, slamming in his fingers to the knuckles. It felt fucking divine.

That's it, I hissed, *that's fucking it! I'm coming, oh fuck, I'm fucking coming!*

My legs were splayed wide, my tits hanging free, the squelch of my own wet pussy so fucking loud as four men watched me explode.

Five men.

At that final moment my eyes landed on Darren, still perched on the bean bag in the corner. Our eyes locked as I came, and his were wild and wide.

I couldn't look away. I didn't look away.

There was nothing in the world that would have made me break that stare.

He was all I wanted. Everything I fucking wanted.

Jimmy O's mouth felt so fucking good between my legs, but Jimmy O meant shit to me. Jimmy O could have been anyone. These guys could have been anyone.

My mouth was open and my eyes were fluttery, riding the high as Jimmy triggered the perfect spot over and over again.

Darren swallowed.

I gasped.

His hand moved between his legs, gripped his dick through his jeans.

Please want this. Please fucking want this.

Please fucking want me.

Buck pressed his cock to my cheek as the waves subsided. I turned my head to suck him in, but my eyes were still on Darren, on his hand as he palmed his dick.

I felt like a slut, a filthy slut, but it felt so good I couldn't fucking stop.

I heard the tear of foil, the unmistakably wet noise of a rubber being rolled onto cock.

It was Hugh who positioned himself first, took my thighs and shunted me onto my back. I let my head loll to the side, Buck's dick still pressing inside my cheek, making me dribble and gag.

Hugh rubbed the head of his cock against my slit.

Darren swallowed again.

I pressed a hand to Hugh's naked chest, but I needn't have. He paused of his own accord, looked back at Trent over his shoulder.

Time stopped, Hugh's dick pressed to my throbbing clit. Waiting. Just waiting.

And then Darren nodded. One simple tip of the head said everything.

Hugh slammed to the balls in one thrust, fucking me like a doll as my tits jiggled and bounced over my slutty little bra. My suspenders were straining, crotchless knickers spread wide, my cunt on display to anyone who cared to look.

I wondered what Darren could see. Wondered if he could see Hugh's cock slamming inside my greedy pussy.

I begged for harder, my voice quacking and broken around Buck's dick as I jerked back and forth on Hugh's. Petey held my bouncing tits together, pushed his dick between them and rode the waves. Jimmy O had his dick in one hand, sniffing his pussy-stained fingers with the other.

"My go next," he grunted. "I need that sweet fucking cunt."

Oh God, I wanted him to take it.

I wanted all of them to take it.

Nearly as much as I wanted Darren to watch.

Please want this. Please enjoy this. Please let this turn you on.

"Shit," Hugh groaned. "I'm close, I'm really close."

I could feel it, feel the pulse of his dick inside me, my pussy clenching and fluttering as he ploughed the right spot.

Darren let out one word, the only word I'd heard him speak since Buck first reached out and touched my knee.

"Jimmy," he said, and gave him a nod.

Hugh stopped, just like that. He closed his eyes and gripped the base of his dick, shuddering for just a moment before he pulled his cock from me. He stepped away, and I watched him with wide eyes as he turned his back and finished himself off with his hand. He let out a groan and his thighs tensed, his ass, too, spurting his load into the rubber before he caught his breath and disappeared into the hallway.

I just stared.

Jimmy didn't waste any time. He took me by the wrists and pulled me up and onto him, spinning me around until my back was to his chest. He gripped hold of my hips and forced me onto his cock in one thrust, and it felt so fucking good that I pressed my fingers to my clit, brought myself off through the slit in my own wet slutty knickers.

Jimmy grabbed at my tits, squeezed them hard, and little Petey surprised me by grabbing my hair and yanking my head back, slapping his dick against my lips.

I let him ease his cock down my throat, taking him deeper with every dirty fucking bounce.

Buck pushed my fingers from my clit and his took their place. He pinched the tender little nub between his thumb and forefinger, and rolled it until I squealed, thrashing about as I reached the peak for the second time.

Please. Yes. Oh yes!

Darren's palm moved slowly, up and down the bulge in his jeans. His eyes were fixed between my legs, at Jimmy's cock stretching me open, at Buck's rough fingers working my clit. Buck lifted me from Jimmy's lap the second I was finished, no regard for Jimmy's frantic thrusts as he rushed towards the finish line.

He reclined against the arm of the sofa and pulled me down onto him, my tits pressing into the fabric underneath. His cock thumped against the back of my throat and I retched, gagging harder at the shock of another cock spearing me from behind.

Petey. I could hear his grunts.

My pussy was swollen and so fucking raw, stretched by more dick than I'd taken in my life. Petey reached around my thighs to flick at my clit, and it was enough to stoke the fire, lacking finesse enough to drive me to orgasm. That didn't matter, though.

My tummy was a floaty mess of endorphins and lust, my

inhibitions all spent.

Petey didn't last long. He pulled out of me to come, but barely made it. I heard the wet slap of his dick in his hand, his grunts as he came right above me.

I caught my breath, pushed my fingers inside my pussy to find it puffy and slick.

My stomach lurched as Buck took the next position.

He rolled on a rubber as I watched him, and his cock looked bigger than ever.

He rolled me onto my side and lifted my leg. *Deep. This is going to be fucking deep.*

I was ready for it. I rubbed at my clit and held my breath, feeling the stretch as Buck's massive cock pressed up against my slit.

Do it! Fucking do it!

But Buck didn't do it. Buck stayed statue still.

I looked around at the other guys, dicks still hard and ready to go again, but they weren't making any moves, weren't attempting to come in for seconds.

I might have been offended if I hadn't seen the want in their eyes. It made me feel so tingly – tingly and dirty all at once – being wanted by so many.

And they did want me. I could see it. I could feel it.

My mouth dropped open as Darren got to his feet.

My stomach did this pitiful lurch as he pulled his shirt off over his head.

He dropped his jeans and his dick was hard, glistening at the tip.

Hugh handed him a packet, and he had the rubber on before he'd even reached me. Buck moved aside in a beat, I barely felt him go.

There was only Darren. His eyes were fierce and they stalked me, his jaw tight and twitching with that little tick he gets when he's really angry.

He was angry.

He flipped me onto my back, yanked my stockings down until the suspenders pinged loose. He tugged down my suspender belt and my slutty knickers with them, tossed it all aside and practically ripped off my bra.

I was nervous. Really fucking nervous.

Hornier than I'd ever been in my whole fucking life but nervous.

He gripped my jaw in his hand, held me firm, eyes burning mine. I didn't even try and struggle, didn't want to go anywhere.

"Kiss me," I begged. "Please, Darren, kiss me."

He dropped his body to mine, his face in my face, his chest to my chest.

"Please, Darren..."

He was so angry. His eyes flashed with hurt.

Jealousy.

Was he jealous?

Fuck.

Holy fuck.

Holy fucking fuck.

Surely not?

There's just no way...

His mouth was savage when it met mine, his tongue on a mission to wrestle me into submission. I took it. I wanted it.

He kept his grip on my chin as he rammed his cock inside, and I let out a yelp, gripped him tight with my legs.

It was such a beautiful fuck. Deep and angry and full of sorrow.

I felt sad. I felt so fucking sad I could hardly breathe, and there was liberation there. There was bliss there.

"Take me," I whispered. "Please, take me..." He breathed against my mouth, hard and deep, his forehead pressed to mine. "All of me..." I said. "Please..." I held his face, and he let go of my jaw.

I felt the urge to cry. Crazy, unhinged tears.

I felt free.

Absolutely totally free.

"You're the only one..." I whispered. "The only one who's ever... been there..."

He stopped. His eyes softened. Just enough.

"Do it," I said. "The maybe just became a yes. It's a big yes, Darren. Please..."

I wriggled under him, and he pulled his cock from my pussy. It was so tender I sucked in breath, but I was smiling.

I twisted underneath him, and he pulled me up onto all fours, spread my knees with his. His thumb sank into my pussy before he moved it to my asshole, circling around to make me wet. I gasped as he pushed in to the knuckle.

"Yes!" I hissed. "Fuck me! Please!"

He folded himself, his chest to my back, and we both doubled up, my face pressed flat against the sofa cushion. His fingers curled around my throat. Squeezed. *Oh my God.*

I felt the head of his cock against my asshole. I held up a hand as he began to push inside.

I turned my head to meet his eyes. "No," I said. "No rubber. I want *you*. Just you."

He breathed against my ear. "Fuck," he said. I heard him tug the johnny away. Felt the heat of his dick against my ass. Just him.

"Now!" I said. "Oh God, Darren, fuck me!"

It was such a beautiful pain. It burned like white heat. A couple of short brutal thrusts and my ass let him in, just like it used to do. He groaned in my ear, a guttural noise that sounded like a primitive battle cry.

That's what it felt like.

A war and a baptism all at once.

Jesus, how he fucked me.

Jesus, how I wanted it.

I was barely aware of the clothes being gathered from the floor. Barely aware of the guys making their way out of the room.

I didn't care. Not about any of it.

Darren took me so hard my eyes watered. It felt good enough that I screamed.

"Don't stop!" I hissed. "Whatever you do, don't fucking stop! Don't you dare fucking stop, Darren!"

We were young again. Crazy again. Dirty again.

We were everything.

"I'm not gonna stop," he barked. "...All fucking night, Jodie. I'm gonna fuck you til you beg me to fucking stop."

He twisted my face until he could look me in the eye.

I smiled. Oh how I fucking smiled. "All night," I whispered.

"Until you fucking beg," he said and pushed his cock in to the hilt.

CHAPTER THIRTEEN

JODIE

I opened my front door tentatively, ears pricked for signs of life. All quiet.

I breathed a sigh of relief and tiptoed inside. The sun wasn't up yet, but the dog walkers were. Three villagers to greet with smiles and *good mornings* as I made the walk of shame back from Trent's. Insisting I make my own way home had been a good call. That gossip would have been across the village faster than I was.

The light was bright enough to make out Tonya in her full snoring glory. She was star-fishing in my bed, mouth open wide, an empty wine glass on the bedside table. It made me smile.

Everything made me smile this morning.

I threw off my clothes and pulled my comfy old PJs on, then slipped into bed beside her. I lay awake with a grin on my face, staring up at the ceiling, my stomach still fluttering. Sore. I was sore.

Good sore, though. Really good sore.

Tonya rolled over with a grunt, and her arm flopped onto mine. She pulled it back instinctively, and her eyes blinked open. Once, twice, three times before she looked at me with a squint.

"Fuck, Jo. What time is it?"

"Early," I said, then giggled. "Or late. Depends which way you want to look at it."

She propped herself up on an elbow. "Come on, then," she said. "I'm all ears. Was it everything Mandy Taylor cracked it up to be?"

I sighed. Grinned. Giggled. Covered my face with my hand.

Tonya giggled right back. "I think that answers my question."

"To quote Mandy big-mouth Taylor, it was absolutely. Fucking. Amazing."

"Shit," she said. "My God, Jodie Symmonds, you just had the Bang Gang special. For real."

I nodded. "Yes. Yes I did."

"Was Buck as big as they say he is?"

My tits prickled at the memory. His thick cock in my hand, the length of him thumping the back of my throat. "Oh yes."

"And Jimmy O? Was he as dirty as they say?"

I shook my head. "Not that I saw, but I didn't see that much."

She pulled a face. "No?"

"Darren," I said. "I think I got the pre-watershed version of the Bang Gang special." I laughed. "I mean, comparatively. I got fucked plenty good enough, just I think..."

"You think what?"

I shrugged. "I think they were holding back."

"Because of Trent?"

"Oh hell, Tonya, I don't know." I smiled again. "I'm not moaning. It was brilliant."

"You think he put the brakes on?"

"Maybe I'm reading too much into it. I probably am."

"I doubt that somehow."

I rolled over with a grimace, looked her in the eye. "I spent the night with him. The others were long gone."

She laughed. "You say that like I should be surprised."

I groaned. "This is playing with fire. I mean, the girls... *me*..."

"Anything to do with Darren Trent is playing with fire. The guy's explosive."

"Hot-headed."

"*Pig*-headed."

I smiled. "Short-tempered. Blunt."

"And you're totally in love with him."

My eyes flew wide. "What?"

She shook her head. "Jesus Christ, Jodie. How long have I known you? You can try this denial crap with yourself all you want, but it isn't gonna wash with me."

"That's not what this is," I said, but my tummy was tickling. "Not for me, and certainly not for him. He fucks for money, Tonya. This was a job."

"You're delusional."

"No," I said. "I'm not. This *thing* is... *was*... sex. Just sex."

"Just sex?"

"*Just* sex."

"If you say so."

"I do." I grinned all over again. "Good sex. *Great* sex. Amazing, mind-blowing, crazy, dirty sex."

I grabbed her hands under the covers, squeezed hard, and we were teenagers again, sleeping over and drinking too much wine.

"So, when are you booking back in?" she asked. "Don't even try and pretend it was a one-off."

My heart was pounding at the thought. I had thought about it, too. Couldn't keep my mind off it all the way home.

"I can't," I said. "I can't blow Pop's money on getting laid, no matter how incredible it was."

"Like hell you can't."

"No," I said. "I can't. I just can't. I'm four hundred down and an *experience of a lifetime* up. It's done, that's me out."

"And Trent? What about Trent?"

I shrugged. "I guess that's done, too. Why wouldn't it be?" I heard footsteps on the landing, the familiar sound of a half-asleep Ruby clomping her way down the stairs. The TV sounded up through the floor.

"I can get up with the girls," Tonya said. "You get yourself some sleep."

I shook my head. "You've done enough. Time to put my *mum* hat back on and get with the schedule." I slipped my legs out of the covers, hissed out breath as I got to my feet. "There'll be more milk on the kitchen floor than there will be on her cereals if I don't get my ass downstairs."

Tonya sat up in bed, stretched her arms with a groan. "Fuck cereals," she said. "Let's go get a proper breakfast, you can sit on the other side of the counter for once."

The rumble in my stomach answered for me.

Lorraine took our order with a smile. Four full English breakfasts coming up.

"How come Mia gets a grown-up breakfast?" Ruby moaned.

"Because Mia's a lot bigger than you are, even if her mouth is smaller." I ruffled her hair.

"A young woman now," Tonya said. "Practically a teenager."

Mia smiled an *Autumn Berry* smile. A full face of makeup courtesy of my new cosmetics stash and Tonya's makeover skills. She looked so much older with a bit of eyeshadow, my little girl growing up so fast. A felt a pang of sadness. It only seemed five minutes ago she was a little tot starting primary school.

"Why didn't Nanna come?" Ruby said. I took the salt shaker from her fiddling fingers before she tipped it everywhere.

"Because Nanna says fried food gives her wind."

Ruby pulled a face. "Nanna's farts stink like eggs."

"*Your* farts stink like eggs," Mia said. "Rotten ones."

"Do not!"

"They so do."

"I don't even fart!" Ruby protested.

"You're always farting! Stinky bum! Nanna's bum's got nothing on yours!"

"Shut your face, Mia-stink-a-lot!"

Mia's expression changed in a heartbeat, her smile shrivelling to nothing. Her shoulders slumped, her eyes down. I felt it right in the pit of my stomach.

"Ruby!" I snapped. "That's enough. Apologise to your sister."

"Sorry," Ruby mumbled. "It's true, though! They *do* call her Mia-stink-a-lot!"

"And *they* are stupid little twerps who should know better, Ruby. *You* should know better."

"Sorry," she said again, and this time she meant it.

Mia shrugged but didn't smile. I could feel her sadness in my heart.

"Mia…" I began, but the first of the plates arrived. I grabbed a knife and fork, cut up Ruby's sausage before she sent bits flying in all directions.

Tonya put a hand on Mia's shoulder. "Don't listen to idiots, Mia. There are plenty of them around. You're beautiful, and you smell lovely." She dipped her bread in her egg.

"It's Tyler Dean and his stupid friends," Mia said. "He's a moron."

"I think Tyler Dean should watch his mouth," Tonya said. "He'll regret ever opening it if your dad finds out."

Mia's eyes widened for just a moment. She spooned up some baked beans and didn't say another word.

Ruby was grinning as she speared a piece of sausage. "Dad would punch Tyler Dean right in his stupid mouth! Pow, pow, pow!"

"Your father won't be punching *anyone* in the mouth," I said. I shot Tonya a look.

She took my cue. "Oh no," she said. "Your dad isn't gonna be punching anyone, Ruby."

Ruby actually looked disappointed. I worry about her sometimes.

"I wish he would," Mia said, and it was so out of character I dropped my cutlery. She caught my expression and tried to laugh off her comment, but it was too late. So much for the *it's no big deal, Mum* line she'd been giving me for weeks.

I opted to let it slide until we were back at home. I met Tonya's eyes and she read my intention, made a couple of *yum* noises and said how good the bacon was.

Lorraine delivered another rack of toast. She looked me over with a smile.

"You look tired. Late night?"

Tonya answered for me. "We went out," she said. "Girls' night.

Late. Just for a couple."

Lorraine let out an exaggerated groan. "Girls' night?! And where was my invite? I haven't been out for ages."

I felt like such a fraud. A dirty stop out. "It was only a last minute thing," I said. "Nothing major."

"Some other time," Lorraine said. "Don't go having all the fun without me!"

I saw Tonya's eyes light up. "Next weekend!" she said. "Let's hit the town, all three of us."

I tried to protest but Lorraine was straight on it. "That works for me," she said.

"Jodie?" Tonya asked. "Come on! It'll be fun. Trent's having the girls, no?"

Well, he was... but...

"It'll be fun!" Lorraine said. "Nothing like a few drinks and bit of dancing to let your hair down."

They both stared at me, smiles too big to ignore.

"Alright," I said. "I'll drive, though."

"Oh no you won't!" Tonya said. "We'll get a taxi, do it properly."

"A taxi," Lorraine said. "Definitely! You have to drink with us, Jodie."

I sighed, smiled back at them. I hadn't hit the town in years, couldn't even imagine it. Then again, I wouldn't have imagined myself paying for a five-man gangbang a few weeks back, either. "Alright. You've twisted my arm."

"We're on!" Lorraine said. "Saturday night, dress to impress."

At least these days I had something vaguely impressive to dress in. Maybe it wasn't such a bad idea after all.

The village was busy when we piled out of the cafe. Tonya lit up a cigarette and I rubbed my bloated tummy, and together we stood at the roadside contemplating our next move.

Mia stepped away from us as a Skype call came in from Daisy, and Ruby was a few metres away checking out a posh silver Audi parked next to the kerb. Neither were in earshot. Not if we were quiet.

"You gonna tell him?" Tonya said. "About this Mia stuff?"

I'd been waiting for it. "No," I said. "The last thing we need is Darren blowing a fuse and going after some high school kid."

"Tyler Dean's hardly a kid, Jo. He turned sixteen a few weeks back, saw the announcement in the paper. His mum's the redhead from Abbey Dore tearooms. You know the one I mean. Annoying laugh." She gave an impression.

"Vaguely."

"His dad lives over your way, Elmcroft. The house on the corner. Only has the lad at weekends."

"You seem to know enough about them."

She smiled. "You're not the only one with the village A to Z committed to memory. I do work in the chippy, you know." Tonya shrugged. "You should tell Trent. Might put an end to it. Kid's upset, you can see it."

I felt guilty. I should have seen it, should have seen through all Mia's bravado. "I'll go to the school," I said. "Sort it out with the teachers. They'll know what to do."

"They'll probably give him some counselling, ask him nicely not to be such a naughty boy."

"They'll have policies, *procedures*," I insisted. "They'll know what they're doing, they probably deal with this kind of shit all the time."

Tonya wasn't convinced. "He's a local lad with local parents, doesn't need the school to sort this crap out, Jo. Trent would sort it in five minutes flat. You know he would."

"Yes," I snapped. "And how, exactly? By kicking off? Giving the kid a slap? Mouthing off in front of the whole village?" I lowered my voice. "I've dealt with enough Darren Trent gossip these past few weeks without another fresh load on top. I could do without it. So could the girls."

She held up her hands. "Fair enough. It was just a thought."

"I know," I said. "Thanks. I appreciate the concern, I just…"

"It's alright," she said. "Handle it your way. I'm sure the school will sort it."

I hoped so. The idea of more drama filled me with dread.

"A bit of peace would be nice," I laughed. "Just a bit. A quiet life for a while."

But there was no chance of that.

I heard a gruff voice barking out some choice words about a *rotten little vandal*. I turned on instinct, and sure enough the *vandal* was my freckle-faced daughter. She was facing up to the owner of the Audi – a skinny old posh guy in a suit. I didn't know him.

I groaned and dashed over with Tonya behind me, grabbing Ruby by the arm before she could antagonise him any further.

"I'm sorry," I said. "What's going on?"

He was flummoxed, exasperated. Pissed off. "Your daughter kicked my car!" he snapped. "It's disgraceful! You should keep her under control! Do you have any idea how much this car's worth?!"

I looked at my *out of control* daughter. "Did you kick this man's car, Ruby?"

"No!" she said. "I kicked his *tyres*!" She stared up at him with defiant eyes, then pointed to the back wheels. "Those tyres are balder than you are, mate."

Oh Lord.

At least she didn't use the C word.

I looked at him in horror, at his wispy excuse for a comb over. His eyes were piggy and too small for his face, and it really didn't look like he was seeing the humour in it.

"I'm sorry," I said again. "Her dad's a mechanic. She likes to help."

"By kicking people's cars?" the man snapped. "Maybe her *dad* should teach her some manners then, ignorant little hooligan. No respect. No respect at all."

I saw Tonya's eyes widen, saw her stare behind me with an expression of horror.

"*I'm* her fucking dad," Trent's voice barked. "What's going on here?"

Oh no.

I turned on my heel, all ready to play pacifier. *No big deal, just a misunderstanding.* But Audi-man answered before I could.

"Your daughter kicked my car," he snapped. "This is an *expensive* car, as you should well know, I don't need *hooligans* kicking it."

Tonya made an exit and I can't say I blamed her. She headed over to Mia who was still yapping on to Daisy on Skype.

Trent opened a fresh pack of cigarettes. He stuck another in his pocket. Shop run. Of course.

Godawful timing.

He looked at me, then looked at Ruby.

"What's going on, Rubes?"

"His tyres are bald," she said. "Tried to warn him. Guess he got butt-hurt." I heard her pathetic excuse for a whisper. "I didn't say any garage words, Dad, I promise."

Garage words. Brilliant. Just brilliant.

He ruffled her hair, then lit up a cigarette while Audi-man gawped. My stomach dropped as Trent took a step back onto the road, eyed up the car's back tyres.

And then he kicked them.

"Those tyres are balder than you are, mate," he said. I would have laughed if I hadn't been so horrified. "She's done you a favour. Got wire showing on the rear driver's. It's fucked."

Ruby folded her arms, gave the man a smug nod. "Told you," she said. "Balder than you are."

I wished the ground would open up and swallow me.

Audi-man didn't even look at his tyres. "Your daughter shouldn't go around kicking cars," he said.

"You shouldn't be driving on those tyres," Trent said.

"Stay away from my car," the man said.

"Stay away from my fucking daughter," Trent said. "Raise your voice to her again and it's not going to end well."

The man sneered. "No wonder she has no manners."

I put a hand on Trent's arm. *Please stay calm.*

"I think you should get in your fancy fucking car and drive away," he said.

"I was planning on it," Audi-man said. "I should never have parked up in this backwater shithole. Full of halfwits."

"Roll on, mate," Trent said.

Audi-man bleeped his central locking, slipped into the driver's seat. I took a deep breath as he drove away.

Darren put his hands on Ruby's shoulders. "Good spot," he said. "You were doing him a favour, ungrateful prick."

It wasn't exactly how I would have put it, but it *was* exactly the moment I decided to handle the Tyler Dean situation with the school and definitely not with Darren.

I watched Ruby watch the car down the street, a quizzical expression on her face.

She turned to look at her dad when the car was out of sight.

"Can I ask you a question?" she said. "A garage question?"

He smiled. "Go for it."

I nearly smiled along as he dropped to her level to hear her out, my skin prickling at the memory of his body against mine.

Ruby folded her arms, and scowled. She jabbed a finger at the spot the car had vacated and let out a sigh.

"How come a cunt like that gets to drive such a nice bloody Audi?"

TRENT

I sent Ruby over to Tonya with a tenner for ice creams. She took the girls over to the shop and I tackled this Audi shit with Jodie.

"He was a prick," I said. "She was right about his fucking tyres, arrogant cunt."

"That's not the point," Jodie said. "She kicked someone's car, Darren, and she was rude."

"She kicked his tyres, it's totally different."

"She's eight years old," she said. "She shouldn't be kicking anyone's anything."

She looked tired. Really tired. I pictured her under me, squirming as I fucked her tight ass.

"You should be in bed."

You should be in my *bed.*

"I came out for breakfast with Tonya. The girls were up early."

I looked her in the eye. "You alright, Jo. About everything?"

She nodded, gave me a crappy smile. "I'm good, yeah. You?"

"Alright."

"Good," she said. "Then we're alright. That's good."

So fucking awkward. She played with her fancy fake nails. I watched her, just watched her.

I sighed. "You should get some sleep this afternoon. I'll take the girls."

"But it's not your weekend..." she said.

"Fuck that, Jo. When have I ever cared if it's my fucking weekend or not?"

She looked at the floor. "I thought you might be... busy..."

Busy *Bang Ganging.* That's what she thought. That's what she meant.

Ruby came charging down the road, her face covered in whippy ice cream and chocolate sauce. She had the ice cream clenched in her fingers, trying her best to lick it and run at the same time. Even Mia had hung up Skype for the sake of a whippy cone, but she was more demure about it, walking slowly at Tonya's side.

Once again I noticed the makeup on her, and it made me feel weird. Made *me* feel old. She was too young for all that shit, but then again, what did I know? All her friends were probably doing it.

"Wanna come with me, girls?" I said. "We'll take the truck over to Sam's place. Get some practice on the track. How about it?"

They didn't need much convincing.

I sent them ahead to the truck with the keys and Jodie said her thanks.

Tonya took her by the arm. "Better get this one back to bed," she said. "I'll stay on call for Nanna."

I smiled at her, gave her a nod.

"I'll be seeing you," I said.

CHAPTER FOURTEEN

TRENT

I took the truck up to Sam Brown's. He's got an off road set-up up there, perfect for letting the girls loose.

Sam was working on an old Honda Civic when we pulled up. He raised a hand as I lowered the window, gave the girls a wave.

"Alright," I said.

He headed over. "Good day for it."

"Hoping to take the girls up the track, let them have a go behind the wheel."

"Be my guest," he said.

I shook his hand. "Cheers, Sam."

He kept an elbow on the window. "Big event at the Brecon track end of this month. Gary Finch can't make it, family wedding up north. Think you'd be game? Nothing major, would just appreciate an extra pair of hands if we need it."

"I'm game for that," I said.

I didn't need to see Ruby's face to know she was busting a gut to get in on it. "Rally cars?" she said. "Can I come?"

Sam smiled. "It's an open event," he said. "Plenty of people gonna be camping. Bring a tent, make a weekend of it."

"Might just do that," I said.

Ruby wouldn't let it go as I took the truck on up to the ridge. "Please!" she said. "Please, Dad! Pleeeeease! I'll be good, I promise! I won't kick any tyres or anything! Not even one!"

"I'll have to think about it," I said. "I'll be busy, it's work for me, Rubes."

"Mum could come!" she said. "She could get a tent, she wouldn't mind!"

I laughed. "Not so sure about that. You'll have to ask her." I looked back at Mia in the rearview. "What about you, Mia, you up for a weekend's camping?"

She shrugged. "Will I get phone signal?"

"I dunno," I said. "Maybe Daisy could come, too. Talk to her in real life for a change, how about that?"

She smiled. "Cool, Dad."

I pulled up on the flat, nothing but open fields ahead of us. "You're up, Rubes," I said. I patted my lap and she clambered over the gearstick, sat between my legs and strained to reach the pedals. Her feet kicked short. "Not quite," I said. "You'll have to grow a bit."

She groaned. "Sucks."

"You can steer," I said. "Steady, remember?"

She pulled a face. "*Yeah*, of course I *remember*."

She giggled as I put the truck into first, her cute little fingers so small on the wheel. She was a natural, cranking that wheel and setting us right on the track lines. I pushed us up through the gears and she handled it like a champ, skirting the edge comfortably in third. She bounced as the truck did, shrieking in delight at the bumpy ground.

She'd done three laps by the time Mia came up front for her turn. Mia could reach the pedals. Ruby huffed in the backseat at the revelation.

I took the passenger seat, told Mia to buckle up and take it slow.

She knew the drill. She put us in first and crawled around awhile before she got brave enough to notch it up to second.

"That's the way," I said. "Give it a bit of welly now."

She was grinning her head off by the time we'd done for the afternoon. "I did it," she said. "I can practically drive already!"

"You're on your way, sure enough."

Ruby was sulking when she climbed back up front. She folded her arms in the passenger seat and glared out of the window. "She wasn't *that* good," she said. "*She* hardly even went in third."

"You were both great," I said. "*Both* of you. It's not a competition, Rubes."

She didn't look convinced.

"I mean it," I said. "You're sisters. You should be supporting each other, not squabbling over stupid shit." I shot them both a look. "There's only two of you, make it count."

Ruby was quiet for a minute. "Why does there have to be only two of us? Violet Harvey's got two sisters *and* a brother, and Kelly May has three brothers all to herself. Why can't *we* have a brother?" She sighed. "It's not fair. I'd like a brother, *he'd* like cars too. Violet doesn't even like *her* brother, she says he's a pig."

Mia laughed from the backseat. "Don't be such a sausage, Ruby. We're not going to have a brother, Mum hasn't even got a boyfriend, and even if she did we'd have a *half*-brother. You're such a baby sometimes."

"Steady," I said. "She's not a baby, she's just a lot younger than you."

Mia shrugged. "Yeah, I guess."

Ruby grimaced. "I don't want a *half*-brother, I want a *proper* brother, and I don't want Mum to get a boyfriend. Not if he's like boring Brian."

The thought punched me in the gut.

I should have done the right thing and told her of course a half-brother was a proper brother, of course it would be just as good, but the words stuck in my throat. They stuck and they stayed there. I couldn't speak a fucking word of it.

I changed the subject back to the rally and thanked my stars when they took the bait.

I took the girls to the Drum for their dinner, had a nice cold pint with my steak and ale pie. They chattered and bickered and chattered some more, conversation never straying far from the rally weekend and Daisy coming camping. Ruby was still a messy monster with her food, tomato sauce and peas all over the table when she'd finished. It made Mia seem all the older, holding her knife and fork so properly now, patting her lips with a napkin.

Where the hell was my little girl going? She was turning into a bloody teenager right in front of my eyes.

It was approaching eight by the time we set off back to theirs. I stopped off at mine on the way, dashed upstairs while they stayed in the truck. Might as well get this out of the way now, while it was fresh. I shoved the envelope in my pocket and headed back out.

Jodie was up and about by the time we arrived, and Tonya had already made a move. Just as well.

I waited on the porch as the girls told their driving stories, watching Jodie's expression like a hawk as talk of the rally weekend sprung up.

"We'll see," she said.

"But Mum!" Ruby wailed.

"I said we'll see. That's not a no, Ruby. It's a we'll see."

They shot off to watch TV with Nanna and I gave Jo their dinnertime lowdown.

"Thanks for today," she said. "I appreciated the sleep."

"No bother."

I gave her a nod when I was sure the girls were settled, and beckoned her further onto the porch. Her eyes widened as she pulled the door closed behind her.

I took the envelope from my pocket. It was still unopened.

She turned it over in her fingers. "What's this?"

"Your cash," I said, like it wasn't obvious.

Her eyes were like saucers. "But why?"

"Lads didn't want to take it."

"I'm not a charity case," she said. "I can pay."

I stared at her. "That isn't what they think. They just didn't want to take it, last night was on the house."

"Shit, Darren, I wanted to pay my way."

I shrugged. "What difference does it make?"

"A lot," she said.

I tried not to think about it, tried not to remember her pretty mouth gagging on Buck's thick dick. Tried not to remember the way she moaned for them, the way she rode Jimmy O's cock like he was a fucking stallion.

"Put it back in the bank," I said. "Forget about it."

"Or not," she said, and her eyes were twinkling. She could hardly hold back the smile.

"What?" I said.

She tried to hand me back the envelope. "Keep it," she said. "For next time."

I raised an eyebrow. "Next time?"

She nodded. "I mean, I wasn't going to... not using any more of Pop's money... but if last night was a freebie, and I still have the money I thought I'd spent already, then it makes sense to do it again..." She smiled. "I'd like to do it again, Darren." She paused. "All of it. It was amazing, thank you. If that's alright?"

No. It's not fucking alright.

The words were on the tip of my fucking tongue, a fire in my belly that wouldn't quit burning. The thought of them touching her again made me want to retch, anger so fucking black I had to fight the urge to punch the wall.

Her eyes were right on me. "Unless... unless they wouldn't want to... unless it was shit... I'm out of practice, it's been a while..." Her cheeks turned pink as I watched, her shoulders sagging.

Fucking hell.

I couldn't do it to her.

"It wasn't shit," I said. "Christ, Jo, of course it wasn't."

"Then what? What is it?"

She had no fucking idea.

I took the envelope back and slipped it in my pocket. She looked so relieved. "I booked you in early last time as a favour," I lied. "We've usually got a backlog. It might take some time."

She nodded. "I see."

No. No, you don't fucking see.

"A couple of weeks," I said. "That'll be the absolute earliest.

Diary's pretty rammed."

She smiled but it was awkward. She wouldn't look at me. "I guess you can thank Mandy Taylor for that."

I wouldn't be thanking Mandy Taylor for fucking anything. "I'll have to let you know when."

"Thanks," she said. "I get you're busy. I don't expect to jump the queue."

The thought turned my fucking stomach. I lit up a cigarette. "Righto."

She nodded. "Good."

Was it hell.

"I'd best be going," I said. "Shit to do."

She laughed a weak laugh. "Guess you've got to get that backlog down."

"I'll be seeing you," I said.

I called goodbye to the girls and Nanna and got the hell out of there.

JODIE

Ladies who lunch was off for me this week. Instead I was sitting outside Mrs Webber's office, waiting for an audience about Mia's Tyler Dean problem.

It had taken a real effort to get to the bottom of what the hell was going on. Mia had been determined to play it down, right to the bitter end. She'd cried when it finally came out, the whole sorry story of him and his dickhead friends taunting her all the way through the bus journey. It had broken my heart.

Please don't tell the school, Mum! Please don't! It'll only make it worse!

I'd assured her it wouldn't. Assured her that Mrs Webber would get this crap sorted out in a heartbeat. That's what head teachers are for, I'd said.

Eventually she'd listened, but she'd gone to sleep hugging Mr Fluff, her tatty old teddy, and I hadn't seen her do that in years.

"Miss Symmonds?" Mrs Webber appeared from the staffroom, she shook my hand before opening her office door for me. I took a seat on the chair in front of her desk, took a breath.

She sat herself down opposite, smile polite and professional. "I understand you have concerns about bullying?"

"On the bus," I said. "Tyler Dean and some of his friends."

"Go on..." she encouraged, and I did go on. I told her everything, every taunt, every sneer, every horrible name those assholes had called my daughter when she was supposed to be in a safe environment.

Mrs Webber nodded, jotted down notes. "We take this kind of accusation very seriously," she said. "We have a zero tolerance bullying policy here." She pointed to a poster on the wall, a big smiley face with *Say no to bullies* in bold font.

"What happens now?" I asked. "Mia's very worried, she doesn't want any repercussions from this."

"I'll call him in," she said. "And then I'll be calling his mother, I've already looked her details up from his file."

I smiled. "Thank you," I said. "I appreciate it."

"Anytime," she said, and got to her feet. I shook her hand. "I'll keep you informed."

She'd better do.

I pulled out my phone to text Darren, thinking it probably best to give him the lowdown on what was going on. I typed out a message, just the essentials, but my stomach churned at the thought of the angry questions, the very idea of him charging on in like a bull in a china shop and causing a right bloody hoo-hah.

I deleted the message before I sent it.

I'd handle it myself first, then give him the details later. It's not like I couldn't deal with this, and things with Darren were already... complicated.

My heart pounded.

Darren.

The way he'd felt inside me. The way his body felt against mine. The way I'd wanted him so much I couldn't even bear it.

The thought that he was probably humping some skanky posh bitch at that very minute sobered up my desires enough to put that phone back in my handbag and get with the plot.

I picked up Nanna's pills from the chemist and tried my best not to give him another bloody thought.

TRENT

I could hardly bear to fucking look at them. Not any of them.

I holed myself up in the office with the radio on, kept myself focused on invoicing and nothing else. I didn't even greet customers, just kept my head down and hoped this nasty shit feeling in my gut would clear the fuck off.

I handled the calls when they came in, some car related, some not. They all got the same gruff treatment; I didn't give two shits who they were today.

I opened up the black book and scribbled out anything Bang

Gang related in the coming few weeks. There wasn't all that much to scrub, I'd already been holding back most of it. *Mid-November earliest*, I told the callers. *That's when we're looking at.*

There were some grumbles, but most of them took it just fine. It's not as if they had a choice.

I'd have my shit together by then, I *had* to have my shit together by then.

I ventured out for a cigarette just before lunch, walked into a load of banter that would normally have amused the fuck out of me, but not today.

Today's humour was at Petey's expense. Some fucking idiot had loosened the lid on a big can of lubricant then sent the lad over to pick it up. Cue the inevitable fucking mess of spilled lubricant all over the fucking floor.

The lads were in hysterics, cracking all the pissing jokes about Petey spurting it everywhere, Petey dropping his load everywhere, flooding the place before he'd even got the fucking lid off.

Poor kid was beetroot, looked like he was gonna fucking cry.

I lit my cigarette and told them to knock it off. It only made them laugh all the harder.

"What's up with you, boss?" Jimmy goaded. "On your fucking monthlies or something?"

"Just sick of your shit," I said. "It's fucking tiring, Jimmy. Someone better get a mop and bucket and clean that fucking mess up quick sharp."

He pulled a scowl, never knowing quite when to shut his fucking mouth. "This little hissy fit ain't got nothing to do with us fucking your missus by any chance?"

"Leave it, Jimmy," Buck said. "Just fucking leave it."

"I won't fucking leave it," Jimmy said. "He told us to fucking do it, now he's got his frilly fucking knickers in a twist. Do the crime, take the time. Don't like what went down, suck it up and get fucking on with it."

I glared at him. "Are you quite fucking finished?"

He nodded, gave me the usual Jimmy O swagger. "Yeah, I'm finished," he said. "Just telling it like it is."

I took a drag on my cigarette then stubbed it out, made my way back over to them. "*This* is how it fucking is," I said. "We're taking a break for a few weeks, I'm booking in nothing til mid-November."

"Why?" Hugh asked. "Christmas is coming, was counting on the cash for that."

I shrugged. "You'll have plenty of backlog to catch up on before Christmas, Hugh. Overtime here, too. The diary's rammed full of car shit."

"This is bullshit," Jimmy snapped. "Putting the dampeners on everything just because you can't get your dick in fucking line."

"What the fuck are you talking about?" I barked. "Got no fucking problem with my dick, Jimmy."

He laughed. "Yeah right, mate. Don't think we didn't fucking notice your little *erectile dysfunction* issues last week."

"You're talking fucking shit," I said. "Did I look like I had *erectile dysfunction* issues this fucking weekend, Jimmy?"

He shrugged. "You sat on the reserves bench for most of it, how would we fucking know?" Buck shook his head, told Jimmy to leave it, but Jimmy was on a roll. "Why don't you pop some little blue pills and get over yourself? Save us all the fucking bullshit."

"Why don't you just shut your fucking mouth before I shut it for you?" I said.

"You want a piece?" Jimmy said. He dropped his spanner, slapped his hands on his chest. "It's not my fucking fault your missus wanted my fucking dick, Trent. You just gotta deal with that shit."

I pictured Jodie riding Jimmy's cock, his grubby hands on her waist. His face between her legs. I was up and at him before he'd really prepared for it, but Buck pre-empted me, pushed his way between us while Hugh grabbed hold of Jimmy. I swung for him but I was too far back, too many fucking bodies in the way to get a punch in.

"What the fuck?!" Buck yelled. "Jesus Christ, guys, just chill the fuck out! Leave it! Just fucking leave it!"

He shunted me backwards once, twice, three times until I'd calmed down enough to shake off the red mist, but even then I was seething, on the edge of blowing my fucking fuse all over again.

I held my hands up. "Alright," I said. "I'm fucking calm!"

Buck wrapped his arm around my shoulders to be sure, steered me back outside. "Fucking hell, Trent," he said. "What the fuck's wrong with you?"

I said nothing.

"Is this about the shit with Jodie? Christ, mate, nobody was out to cross any lines. You said it was fine. You said you'd be cool with it."

"I am," I lied. "This is just about Jimmy and his running fucking mouth."

"If you say so," he said.

"I do fucking say so."

He sighed. Patted my back. "Look, Trent, you want to hold off until mid-November, we'll hold off until mid-November. It's your fucking gig."

I had nothing to say, so I said nothing at all, just pulled out another cigarette and lit up like I hadn't just launched myself at one of my employees.

The prick was fucking asking for it.

"Kiss and make up," Buck said. "It's not worth falling out over this kind of shit, Trent. Jimmy's alright, he's just got a dirty fucking mouth on him."

"Jimmy can kiss my fucking ass," I said. "I'll make it up when I'm good and ready."

Buck slapped my shoulder. "Ain't none of us after your fucking missus, Trent, it was just a fucking gig."

"Jodie's not my missus."

He sighed. "Yeah, right. Keep telling yourself that." He gave me a jab in the arm. "Gotta get back to it, that bloody Rover isn't gonna fix itself."

I nodded.

Maybe I'd have calmed it down enough to make it up with Jimmy. Maybe I'd even have calmed it down enough to laugh at Petey's little lube accident, too.

Maybe I'd have put the whole fucking situation behind me and got on with business as usual.

If only Eleanor Hartley's fucking Porsche hadn't pulled onto the yard.

Fuck it. Fuck all of it.

This time I was in my fucking truck and out of there before she'd even turned off the ignition.

CHAPTER FIFTEEN

JODIE

I played it cool, even to myself, pretended that I wasn't hoping for a text or a phone call, wasn't hoping for him to pop in for another coffee or be waiting outside for me in his truck.

Of course he wouldn't. It was a job and now it was done.

But it'd felt so real. *He'd* felt so real. So... *there*.

Maybe he felt like that with all of his *clients*. The thought made me nauseous.

Oh well, fuck it. Fuck all of it.

Same customers, same gossipy school mums every morning, same people to wave at and shout good morning to. Same old same old.

I got on with it with a smile on my face, same as every other week of my life. There are worse things in life than a bit of routine.

I heard from Mrs Webber that she'd had Tyler Dean's mum in for a meeting the very same day, assuring me that she'd made it clear that bullying was not to be tolerated on the school bus. I breathed a sigh of relief at the news, thanking her for her prompt action. I relayed it to Mia with a smile, telling her it was all done now and she wouldn't be getting any more trouble. *Always the best way*, I said. *Speak up about your troubles and they'll get sorted.*

I just wish she'd have told me sooner, to save herself all the upset.

I still kept my eye on things, hanging on that few minutes longer at the bus stop to make sure the situation looked calm, but Tyler Dean and his friends never went within two metres of her, not while I was watching. They kept a seriously wide berth, and that brought a puff of self-righteousness to my chest – Mamma Bear at my finest. I hoped Mrs Webber had given those little dipshits quite a roasting.

In fact, I hoped they'd be in detention until the end of time. Serve the little assholes right.

"All's well that ends well," Tonya said. "Poor Mia, this should make those little bastards think twice before they open their mouths in future."

"Definitely," I said. "Mrs Webber takes this kind of thing *very* seriously. She told me so."

We clinked coffee mugs, and life felt good again. The kids were all smiles, Ruby talking non-stop about this upcoming rally weekend, determined to drive me insane with her begging that we all go, *all* of us – even Nanna and Tonya. *Like Nanna is going to cope on a bloody airbed*, I said. Mia didn't seem nearly so bothered about camping, knuckling down to her school test revision with the kind of dedication that made me proud. She didn't even watch *Question King* with Nanna, just ate her dinner and went straight up to hit the revision.

I'd have to plan a celebratory meal out when she was done, maybe even get a cake. Maybe get Darren along, make a proper family thing out of it. *A proper family thing.* I laughed when I caught myself.

There *was* no proper family thing between me and Darren. A

family thing between him and the girls, and me and the girls, but between us, no. Separated. We were separated. Long-time separated – even if the thought of being with him was still getting me off every night. Maybe sometimes in the morning, too.

So what if I was thinking about him sometimes during lulls at the cafe? So what if my tummy would tickle every time I thought about his face in mine?

So what about the other tickles... the dirty thoughts... the dirty thoughts that wouldn't let up... not ever... not even knowing that he was probably fucking half the women in the village and barely giving me a second thought...

Luckily I had my girls' night out to keep me occupied.

One epic night of drinks, dancing and good girly chatter, topped off nicely by the opportunity to wear my flash new bodycon dress.

I could hardly wait.

TRENT

I made up with Jimmy O over drinks at the Drum. We shook hands and grunted apologies and bought each other pints in the usual way of it. No hard fucking feelings and all that shit.

Rutting Eleanor Hartwell always seemed to put the guys in good spirits. Talk of Jodie was off the menu and I kept it that way. No point dwelling on it now. It was already done.

I put a lid on it, but the whole fucking thing was a barrel of shit. I'd be raging one minute, wanting to face off to every single one of them for going anywhere near her, and the next I'd be in the garage toilet, jerking one off to the thought of her face as she came with her eyes on me and another guy's dick in her pussy.

Just as well I was taking a break from the Bang Gang business, I couldn't trust my dick to play ball if I'd wanted to. It had a mind of its fucking own these days.

I handed Buck the black book and he stared at me, raised his eyebrows.

"What's this for?"

"What do you think?" I said. "Knock yourself out, book in whatever you fucking like. This week, next week, sometime never. I don't give a shit."

He didn't look convinced. "And you? You planning on joining in or what?"

No.

I shrugged. "I'll play it by ear. Might be there, might not be."

"Fair enough," he said. "I'll let the guys know. If you're sure?"

Not really. I pictured the piles of notes I'd be adding to the university box if I could sort my pissing head out.

"I'm sure."

"Alright," he said.

"Alright," I said.

And it was done.

I contemplated just texting her. A *did that mean shit to you?* text that would set my mind at rest one way or the other, but every time I pulled my phone out Lorraine's stupid smug face put me off again. *It's embarrassing. Christ, Darren, she's long over you. Let it go, have some dignity.* I thought about them laughing over me at the cafe, Jodie brushing it aside and hoping I didn't get the wrong fucking idea about her little Bang Gang splurge.

No fear, I wouldn't be getting the wrong fucking idea. I'm not that much of a soft fucking twat.

At least Lorraine was sorting Petey out. The guy had the permanent balls-emptied kind of grin that we'd all had at some point or other while she was on the scene. Me first, right in the beginning, before we were even a group act. Even the thought of it now gave me the shivers.

"Mum's getting a tent," Ruby announced one night after school. She was sitting on a pile of tyres, sucking on a cherry pop while her sister caught up on Facebook in the office.

I stuck my head out from the Citroen's engine. "That right?"

She nodded, a big toothy grin on her face. "And Tonya might be coming. Not Nanna, though, Mum says if we put her on an airbed she'd never get back up again."

I smiled at the image of Nanna slumming it in a sleeping bag. "Your mum might well have a point there," I said.

"Will I be able to help? With the cars?"

I let out a sigh. "Not sure, Rubes. It's not like round here, it's pretty fast, all hectic like while the racing's going on."

"But I can help! I can be fast!"

"I know you can," I smiled. "I'll make sure you get to see enough of it, don't you worry."

"Can I sleep in your tent?"

I thought of the lads along with me, the fact that Buck was already planning to throw a sleeping bag in my tent to save setting up his own. "Probably best you stay with your mum," I said. "She'll be worried otherwise."

She didn't argue.

I wondered if it meant anything, Jodie coming. Jodie's never been interested in Rally in her life.

But Ruby was.

Ruby wasn't interested in a whole lot else.

It was almost certainly for Ruby's sake and not for mine.

I picked up the girls on Saturday morning, and Jodie seemed shifty, nervous even.

"Good week?" she asked.

I nodded. "Alright. You?"

"Yeah, average," she said. The girls piled into the truck and I went to follow them but she called me back. "I'm out tonight," she said. "First time in ages. Just a night in town with Lorraine and Tonya."

Lorraine. The thought hit me in the gut.

"Have fun," I said.

She sighed. "It's just... I haven't been out before... not for so long... not so far away..."

"Girls will be fine," I said.

"It's not that," she said. "It's Nanna. You couldn't... if she called, I mean. Could you keep an ear out, in case the club's too loud for me to hear my phone?"

I smiled. "I'll always keep an ear out for Nanna, Jo, you know that. Any problems she can call me, I'd be straight round."

"Thanks." She smiled. "I mean, she's fine, it's just sometimes she gets a bit dithery. Her pills are above the sink, the green bottle. Mia's got a spare key."

"I know," I said. Ruby beeped the horn, let out quite a racket. "I promised them a drive out," I said. "Told them we'd get some lunch up on the Beacons."

"Nice," she said. "You'd better go."

You could come, if you wanted. You and Nanna. The words were on the tip of my tongue, but I didn't say them.

"I'll be seeing you," I said. "Have a good night."

"You, too," she said.

JODIE

I was glad I'd had a couple of glasses before we'd hit the town. The place was so much louder than I remembered. Girls that didn't look much older than Mia drifted about the streets in miniskirts and no sleeves without a care – even in October. I was absolutely freezing in my bodycon dress, my legs goose-pimpled to hell, even though I was wearing a coat.

Lorraine laughed at me. "You feeling your age?"

"I'm feeling something," I said.

"Get another drink down your neck, you're still in your twenties, still young enough pull off young, free and single with authentic flair."

"I have mere months left of my twenties," I said. "It barely counts."

She leaned in, wrapped an arm around my shoulders as we crossed the road towards *Club Crystal*. "I'm forty-nine years old," she said. "Forty-fucking-nine. What I'd give to be thirty all over again. I sure wouldn't waste it being married to a dickhead like I did last time round."

Tonya laughed, flashed a grin over her shoulder. "You should go on the pull, Lorraine, plenty of guys love a cougar. You'll be hot property in here."

I looked at Lorraine, checking her out as cougar material. She'd definitely pass. Her dress was tighter fitting than mine, her heels higher than mine, too. Her hair had thick blonde highlights over shades of mahogany – a posh salon job, for sure. Her makeup was dramatic but not over the top.

Yes, Lorraine was definitely cougar material.

"I might well pull me a hot young stud," she laughed. "Or two." She nudged me. "How about you, Jodie, are you out to meet yourself a fine young man?"

"No, I don't think so," I said in a beat.

"No?" she raised her eyebrows. "Why ever not?"

Tonya smirked back at me. "She's already taken, mentally if not physically."

I wished she hadn't had that extra vodka on the way in. I shot her a glare to stop her running her mouth off.

We arrived in the queue, and Lorraine wouldn't let it go. "You can't surely mean Trent?" she said. "Please tell me you're not still pining over that useless imbecile."

"I'm not pining," I said. "I'm over it."

She stared at me. "You're sure about that?"

I nodded. "Yes." *No.* "I have the girls to think about, we're all good as we are. No point rocking the boat with any of that."

"And that's putting aside the fact the guy's a man-whore. For heaven's sake, Jodie, he's fucking every paying woman within driving distance. He's hardly *daddy* material, is he?"

I met her eyes. "Darren's a great dad. He's a lot of things, but a crappy father isn't one of them."

"If you say so." She laughed. "I admire your loyalty, but the guy's nothing more than a filthy waster. Those girls would be better off without him."

I stepped away from her. "Those girls would never be better off without him, Lorraine, that's too far." *And neither would I.*

She held up her hands. "Jesus, Jodie, I'm only half serious. You know how I feel about Darren Trent. You know how I feel about what's best for you."

Yes. Yes, I did know.

"Trent's alright," Tonya chipped in. I could have hugged her. "Got his issues but show me someone who hasn't. Ain't not one of us angels, Lorraine, you included. I'm sure your shit stinks just the same as the rest of us."

"Point taken," she said, but she didn't look like she'd taken any point on board. She lit up a cigarette and flashed Tonya a smile that was clearly false. "You must have been there when it all fell apart, Tonya, as I was. You must have seen how much better things were for Jodie and the girls when it was all over."

"I saw two people breaking their hearts over losing each other. Two people breaking their hearts that their girls wouldn't have their daddy at home. *That's* what *I* saw, Lorraine." She lit up a cigarette herself. "No winners in a situation like that, only losers."

I wished I smoked. I could have happily puffed away on a whole bloody pack.

"It's all over now." I smiled. "Let's just get dancing, shall we? Forget about Darren and the bloody village for one night, at least."

I didn't even wait for a consensus, just hit the bar as soon as we'd checked in our coats.

Tonya leaned in when Lorraine nipped off to the toilets. "I don't like it," she said. "There's something off with her."

I shook my head. "She's just looking out for me, that's all. She only got one side of it when I split up with Darren, she hardly knows him." I squeezed her arm. "She's just on team Jodie."

"*I'm* just on team Jodie," she said. "But that doesn't mean I think

Trent's a total fucking tool."

"You *know* Darren," I said. "She doesn't."

"Not convinced," Tonya said. "I think she's acting sketchy, there's something about her I don't like."

"You don't like anyone," I laughed. "You think everyone's got an agenda."

She winked. "Everyone *has* got an agenda, I just like to know what it is before I decide I want to bosom buddy it up with them. Lorraine's cagey with hers. We don't know shit about her, not even after all these years."

I scoffed. "I do."

She shrugged. "Do you? About her home life? Has she had a boyfriend? Got a boyfriend? Wants a boyfriend? Why did she get divorced? What's she been doing since? Do you know any of this stuff?"

"She *sees* people," I said. "Just casual. She doesn't really talk about it."

"Exactly," she said. "Cagey."

"Dating websites probably. She's probably embarrassed."

"Embarrassed or cagey," she said.

I rolled my eyes. "You liked Lorraine last week. *You* invited her out."

"*She* invited *us* out." She did a twirl. "And she hadn't launched an anti-Trent offensive off the cuff back then. Hadn't said his kids would be better off rid of him."

I groaned. "She just doesn't like him, Tonya."

"She doesn't *know* him, like you said."

"Seems I don't either. I had no idea he was whoring himself out to the whole village, Tonya. How do you expect her to feel after that revelation?"

She shrugged. "Still, I think there's something off with her."

I kissed her cheek. "I love you, Tonya, I love how loyal you are, even to those people you half-think are douches."

"He's a good dad," she said. "And he thinks a lot of you, too."

I wish I was as convinced as she was.

I downed a glass of Bacardi and Coke and disappeared further into the crowd.

Fuck Darren Trent, tonight was all about the music.

Alright, so dancing wasn't as easy as I remembered. I managed less than an hour before my feet were blistered and killing me. Bloody heels.

We sat in a booth, a fresh bottle of white in an ice bucket on our table, wetting ourselves as Lorraine recounted her *weirdest ever customer* stories. These always made me laugh, but the drink made them all the funnier.

I was giggling like an idiot when I felt my handbag vibrate. I pulled my phone out in a flash, hoping beyond hope it wasn't Nanna.

It wasn't, it was Darren.

My heart did a weird jump.

You alright? Club good?

I smiled. This was as conversational as it ever got from Darren.

Alright, thanks. Girls ok?

I held my phone under the table and turned my attention back to the conversation. They were both laughing too hard to notice. It vibrated again.

Girls are asleep. Just be careful out there.

I smiled. *Be careful? I'm alright, Darren. I have Tonya and Lorraine with me.*

I pressed send and took another swig of wine. Lorraine was well away, into the one with the woman who claimed one of the waiters had put poop in her stew.

Another message.

Just be careful. Don't go home with any assholes, Jo.

I fired off a response. *I wasn't planning on it.*

Another buzz. *I'm sure you'll be taking your pick. Just make sure it's a good one.*

I stared at the phone, wishing I could ask the Tonya and Lorraine what they thought. I couldn't. They'd probably come to blows.

My reply took some typing with clumsy fingers. *You're telling me to go fuck a stranger, but just make sure they're nice? Shall I get a copy of their current CV, take some references?*

I waited for it. *No. That's not it. Forget it.*

I'd pissed him off. The wine made me giggle. *Sorry. I'm being silly. Wine.*

Have fun, he replied.

My fingers kept typing. *I'm not going to be fucking any strangers, Darren. I'm not going to be going home with anyone.*

Your business, he said. *Just be careful.*

I was flummoxed. *Why bring it up then?*

It took a few minutes to get a reply to that one. *Just bothered.*

Bothered I might fuck someone or bothered they might be an asshole? Shit. I can't believe I actually sent that.

I tried to focus on the conversation. Tonya was talking fish and chip shop horror stories now.

I could hardly bring myself to look at the next message. *What do you think?*

I don't know what I think, I said.

A buzz almost straight back. *Makes fucking two of us, Jo.*

My heart was thumping. Wine made me brave. *If I fucked another man tonight would it bother you? Yes or no?*

His reply made me want to pull my hair out. *Would you want it to?*

I was done with this. I fired off one final message before I shoved my phone back in my bag. *I don't have time for this, Darren. I'll catch you later.* x

A kiss. I added a kiss.

Oh well, fuck it.

I downed my wine and dragged the others back to the dance floor. Those blisters would just have to go fuck themselves.

I was so ready to go home. Sober enough to feel the pain in my heels, drunk enough to limp on regardless, I was sick to death of Lorraine pointing out every hot young guy who was after some and nudging me to go make a slut of myself.

I'm no slut.

Even if I did bang five men at once last weekend.

I didn't admit to that, of course.

Go get them yourself! I'd insisted, but she'd laughed me off.

Tonya kept shooting me looks, but said nothing. Maybe she thought Lorraine was alright again now they'd bonded some over food and beverage stories.

I let out a sigh of relief as we piled into a taxi.

"Allensmore first," I said to the driver. "Then onto Pontrilas."

"No, no," Lorraine said from the backseat. "I'll come to Pontrilas, too, get out at Allensmore on the way back."

I pulled a face at her between the seats. "Why?"

She sighed. "I think I might have left the cafe unlocked. The door around the back. My bad."

Tonya laughed. "I think it'll probably either be robbed by now, or safe until morning."

"I'll just check anyway," Lorraine insisted. "Wouldn't be able to sleep otherwise."

I shrugged. "Pontrilas then, please," I said.

We made drunken small talk all the way back and the village was upon us in no time. I began directions to mine as we passed Trent's yard, telling the driver to drive on through the village and up the hill the other side. I rooted in my bag for my keys, and that's when I noticed my phone flashing.

One message. Darren.

I clicked Open.

Yes, it would bother me if you fucked another man tonight. It would bother me a lot.

My heart leapt, legs all wobbly in the footwell.

We pulled into the village, passing the shop and then the cafe.

Then Trent's.

The light was still on. I could see the glow through the living room curtains.

"Stop here," I said, my thumping heart making me feel dizzy. "I'll walk the rest."

The driver looked at me. "Here?"

216

I nodded. "Just here." I pointed to the pull-in by the fish and chip shop. He stopped next to Darren's truck.

Lorraine leaned forward and I shoved a tenner into her hand. "My share," I said.

"What are you doing?" she said. "We'll take you home."

Tonya laughed, patted her shoulder. "I think this is where she wants to be."

I watched Lorraine figure out what was going down. I felt strangely guilty.

"Oh," she said. "I see."

I opened the door, gave a load of goodnights.

"Don't do this, Jodie," Lorraine said. "It's a mistake."

Tonya unclipped her seatbelt, clambered forwards enough to pull the passenger door closed. It left me out in the cold. I smiled as she flashed me a smile. "Go!" she mouthed.

I watched the car pull away with a grin.

Shit.

Oh shit.

What the hell was I doing?

My throat was dry and my legs were all wimpy and useless as I clacked along the pavement up to Trent's.

He was already outside. Standing at the top of the stairs looking down on me.

I gripped hold of the railing, trying to think what the hell I should say.

He took a few steps down. "I saw the taxi," he said. He was smoking, of course he was smoking.

"I was..." I began. "I just... your message... I got it in the car..."

A few more steps down, and I could smell his cigarette. I could smell him.

I could feel his stare, even in the shadows, feel those eyes right on mine. "What are you doing here, Jo?"

I sighed. "I've had a little wine. I got your message."

"Are you drunk?"

I sighed again. "A little bit."

Another step and I could feel the heat from him. He flicked his cigarette away. "The girls are asleep. If you come up... we'll have to be quiet..."

I nodded. "Yes, yes. I know."

"Is that what you want? To come up?"

I laughed, this whole thing was so fucking stupid. Back and forth, back and forth, back and forth. "Do you want me to come up?" I swung myself on the railings, let myself laugh.

I stopped laughing when he grabbed me, his palms on my cheeks like they'd been so many times. His thumbs were rough on my cheekbones, his palms pressed tight. I put my hand on his, took a breath. A drunken breath.

And then he kissed me.

He kissed me so hard I toppled back into the chip shop wall, and he pinned me there. His body pressed to mine, his mouth so hot and so fucking needy. I wrapped my arms around his neck, and he took my weight.

"My feet," I hissed. I smiled, giggled. Stared into his eyes so close to mine. "They're sore. I can hardly walk in these shoes."

"Righto," he said. He lifted me out of them, and the heels went toppling onto the tarmac.

Thank fuck for that.

He turned his back to me and crouched. I giggled harder as I leapt

218

up and wrapped my arms around his neck.

"I'm heavy," I whispered. "Too heavy for a piggyback."

"Nah," he said. "You're not."

I laughed as he scooped down low for my shoes, trying to smother my amusement as he climbed the stairs to his front door. He made light work of it.

It felt so good to be carried by Darren Trent.

He dropped me at the top and pressed his lips to mine. "Quiet," he said. "The girls..."

I nodded.

We went inside, and I held my breath all the way to his bedroom.

CHAPTER SIXTEEN

JODIE

I felt so young. Tipsy drunk with messy hair and sore feet, that same intoxicating thrum of nerves I'd always had when Darren looked at me the way he was looking at me now. I tried to keep my steps light, tiptoeing through the strewn clothes over his bedroom floor. He hadn't been expecting me this time and it showed. But I liked that. I liked all of it. The crumpled sheets on his bed, the messy pillows, still misshapen from the last time he'd slept. I sat on the edge of the mattress, ran a hand idly along the place I knew he'd been sleeping the night before.

I knew exactly how he slept – it was emblazoned into my memory for all time. I could picture him like it was yesterday. Lying on his front, his head on the side facing my direction, one arm under him, bunching up the pillow. The other would be over me, once upon a time. I missed that, the warmth of his arm over me through the night, knowing he was there, knowing he would always be there.

But I'd been wrong.

Darren pulled the bedroom door closed so slowly, eased the door handle up until the latch clicked. He placed my shoes on the floor and I pushed some of the dirty mugs on his bedside table aside to clear space for my handbag. I shrugged my coat from my shoulders as he stared, his eyes like white heat on my skin, giving me prickles. My legs were crossed, and my foot tapped in the air, nervous.

Shit, I was so fucking nervous. Third time in and the nerves were worse than ever.

Because I'm not a client, not tonight. Because this isn't a job for him. Because this is just about us.

He was still staring, looking at me like he'd never seen me before. His jaw was tight, his eyes not letting up, taking in every little thing and I knew it. I smoothed my hair and attempted a smile, but he didn't smile back.

He took a step towards the bed and lifted his shirt over his head. He tossed it in a ball towards the laundry basket and loosened his belt. His cock was hard when he dropped his jeans, springing free from his boxers as he pulled those down too.

Yes. Oh, yes.

The corner of his mouth curved into a half-grin. He ran his fingers across day-old stubble and closed the distance between us. He stood before me, his belly level with my face, and I took a breath, kept my eyes on his as my fingers wrapped around his cock and gripped him tight.

He thrust his hips, moving against my hand, his dick so close to my mouth that it was the most natural thing in the world to take the head of him between my lips. His hand landed on the back of my head, his fingers curling in my hair and holding me tight.

I sucked him deep and he hissed out a breath, tipped his head back and closed his eyes. I cupped his balls just like I used to do, ran my thumb across the wiry hair I knew so well. Just a little bit of pressure, just how he liked it, and his grip on my hair tightened, his hips thrusting harder.

Yes. Oh fuck yes.

I loved to see him like this. Loved to see the bliss on his face as I ran my tongue along the underside of his shaft, the way his eyes closed that little bit tighter as I swirled my tongue around the head of him. I'd so missed this.

He swallowed, and arched his back. I wrapped my arms around his thighs, stroked my fingers up his legs until I gripped his ass, and he had free movement. Another hand in my hair and he was moving forward for a deeper angle.

Oh fuck.

He pushed in deep, slowly, inching his dick to the back of my throat as I stared up at him with wide eyes. I squeezed his ass and pulled him closer, relaxed my throat to let him in. A bit of a splutter and my nose was to his belly, the wiry hair at the base of him tickling my chin.

"*Fuck,*" he breathed. "*Oh fuck, Jodie.*"

He still smelled of oil and sweat. He smelled of him, too. He smelled perfect.

He pulled out and I sucked in a breath, eyes watering almost as much as my mouth. He thumbed up the spit from my chin and smiled, then came in for seconds. This time he was rougher – thrusting right from his thighs, a strong grip under my jaw to keep the position right.

I felt so *taken*. So *secured*.

I felt amazing.

I blinked and my watery eyes spilled over. I smiled around his cock and he smiled back, brushed my cheek with this thumb.

Sweeping thrusts, his cock thumping the back of my throat until my cheeks billowed and my mouth made low gurgles. I felt his ass clench, his thighs, too, his movements more urgent, his breath quickening.

I stared up at him and encouraged his thrusts, kept my hands tight on his ass and my mouth wide. I wanted this, wanted him to peak, wanted him to unload all over my tongue and let me swallow him down like a hungry little bitch, but he stopped without warning and pulled his dick from my mouth.

He pushed me backwards until I flopped onto the bed, and dropped to his knees on the floor between my legs. His palms were rough against my calves, warm against my goose-pimpled skin. Calloused fingers climbed up my thighs, hitched my dress to my hips and tugged down my tiny little knickers. He took my feet in his hands and kneaded the soles until I squirmed. It was bliss.

I gripped the bedsheets as he worked, his touch magic on sore toes. I gasped as his lips landed on my ankle and grazed their way up. I was too squirmy to stay still by the time he reached my knee, and my the time he reached my thigh I was a breathless wreck, legs lolling apart in desperation for the touch of his mouth against my pussy.

He paused, his breath on my wet pussy lips, and I couldn't look, I was already too far gone. I reached for him, my hands on his head, his hair spiking my palms as I urged him closer. He pushed one leg up onto the bed and hitched the other over his shoulder, and I was spread wide, exposed so totally that the nerves in my belly spluttered and fizzed.

Oh God.

When his mouth clamped onto my pussy it clamped hard, his

tongue hungry and horny as he sought out my clit with hard, flat strokes. He eased my dress up further and rested his hand on my belly, his thumb moving back and forth across my flabbiest parts like they were beautiful. He made me feel beautiful.

I rested my head to the side and smiled, let myself rock into him, grinding my pussy against his mouth as he licked at me. I expected him to fuck me with his fingers, but he didn't, just kept on working that magic with his tongue until my clit was pulsing and wired, my movements becoming jerky as my breath grew ragged.

I'm going to...

I gripped his hair and bucked, letting out a single solitary groan before I caught myself. *The girls.* I bit my lip and thrashed, arching my back as he sent me over the edge, lapping at my pussy like a hungry fucking dog. *Fuck!* An explosion of white behind my eyes and my ears started ringing with the strain of silence. I grabbed for one of the pillows and brought it to my face, biting down on it and shuddering out my orgasm as he flicked that heavenly tongue.

He didn't stop until I was long spent – a mushy, limp bag of limbs flopped uselessly on his bed.

He didn't waste any time. His body was so warm, his chest so hard against mine as he pressed his full weight onto me. Oh God I wanted to take him.

"Shh," he breathed into my ear. His lips were soft against my cheek, peppering their way to my mouth. I kissed him deep, kissed him hard, and he was right back at me, crushing my head into the covers underneath.

Yes...

I wrapped my legs around his hips, my arms around his shoulders.

Yes...

His cock pressed to my slit, teasing.

Yes...

My legs squeezed, coaxed him, but he held back. I stared into his eyes and they were so hungry, so feral.

Please... Please fucking fuck me...

He broke the kiss. "I need to grab a johnny," he whispered. "To be safe."

But I didn't want to be safe. I didn't want to be safe at all. I wanted to be reckless, and crazy, and free. I shook my head.

"I've got an app," I whispered. "With dates..."

He stroked my cheek, his eyes serious. "I'm clean..."

I nodded. "I want you... I want to feel you..." He kissed me as he pushed inside and it was the most incredible feeling, his dick filling me up, filling me raw. "Please," I hissed. "Oh God, Darren, please..."

"What?" he whispered, his voice ragged. "What do you need?"

I pressed my palms to his cheeks. "Take me," I said. "Take me like I'm yours, take me like you mean it."

"Oh I fucking mean it." His voice was raspy, that caveman edge to it I loved so fucking much.

He pulled out and flipped me onto my front, practically tore my dress off over my head. He unclipped my bra and pulled it free, then shunted me further onto the bed and stretched my arms out over my head. He grabbed my wrists and held them in position, his weight keeping me still. He pinned my legs together with his and slammed his cock in my tightened pussy in one thrust.

Oh fuck.

His full weight was behind him, his dick thumping all the way inside me. I could feel his balls against my ass, tight between us, his hips rolling for leverage, deeper and deeper.

He didn't pull out, just stayed there, circling his hips wider and wider, his cock straining to loosen my pussy but achieving nothing, my legs were pinned shut too tightly.

The pressure built, his hips thrusting and rolling as I moaned into the bedcovers, praying I didn't wake the girls. It ached, a glorious ache, the urge to pee becoming too much to bear.

"I need to..." I began, but he shook his head at my shoulder. "Darren... I need to..."

"Take it," he breathed. "Fucking take it, Jodie."

He thrust hard, and I whimpered. A good whimper.

"Shh," he hissed. "Take it..."

I nodded, breathed into the bedcovers. "Fuck me, Darren... hard..." I could hardly hear myself, but he could. He adjusted, braced himself on his spread knees and took a breath. He took both of my wrists in one hand and used the other to gag me. His palm pressed tight to my lips, fingers gripping my cheeks and holding firm.

And then he fucked me.

He fucked me so hard the bed shook and creaked under us. He fucked me so hard I was sure the girls would hear us. His skin slapped against mine, and my pussy took all of him. He slammed and then he circled, alternating over and over until I was a squirming wreck underneath him. My pussy felt weird, achy, desperate to piss, but there was another feeling, something deep and crazy and threatening to blow.

"Let it go," he breathed. "Let it happen, Jo..."

Let what happen?

Oh... Oh, that...

My pussy exploded with crazy sensation. My body turned tense and thrashed under him, my head flying back and pressing against his shoulder. He kept his hand tight to my mouth, wouldn't let me escape. Just a hiss of breath and a couple of muted squeaks as I came, and that made it all the more intense.

I strained. Strained against his palm. Strained for breath, strained for the freedom to squeal out my pleasure and ride the waves, but he didn't let go. He kept fucking me, driving me higher, ploughing that spot inside that was driving me to insanity. I thrashed all over again as the next wave ripped through me, and this time I felt wetness, a splash of heat between my clamped thighs.

"That's it," he hissed. "Fuck, Jo, yes..."

My breath was raspy through my nostrils, my face hot against his hand. Damp hair stuck to my forehead.

I was rigid as he circled his hips all over again, my body spasming and shaking under him.

"Fucking beautiful," he said, "Just fucking beautiful."

Another gush of heat between my legs and my pussy had taken on a life of its own. He slammed hard, his breath in grunts, so fucking deep that my pussy was squelching with every thrust.

And it felt so good, so horny, so fucking dirty.

Again, and I flailed. Again, and I kicked my legs out, my whole body trembling with uncontrollable sensations.

"Gonna come," he hissed. "Oh fuck, I'm gonna come..."

Yes. Yes, Yes, Yes!

Come inside me...

I'd have said it if I could. I'd have said the crazy stupid words on my tongue without a second thought.

Come inside me, Darren... come inside me...

"Fuck, Jo, this feels too good…"

I felt him come – his mouth to my neck, his breath hot and wild. His thrusts were desperate, his skin sweaty as it pressed against mine.

Yes! Oh fuck, yes!

I felt his balls tightening against my ass, his thighs clenched and solid.

Yes!

We jerked and writhed and quivered on the bed, bodies pinned together as we rode the wave. He slammed all the way inside to shoot his load – hissing out expletives as he filled me up.

Oh God. Oh God yes!

He collapsed onto my back, his skin warm, heart thumping against my ribs. His breath was loud in my ear and mine was loud against his palm. He took his hand from my mouth and wrapped it around my waist and pulled me onto my side and into his arms.

He held me. He held me in our old bed like it was old times, smoothing the hair from my sweaty face like he'd done a thousand times. I rolled into him and pressed my cheek to his chest, listened to his racing heart.

And then I felt the dampness under my ass. I squirmed away enough to pat the sheets and they were soaked, ridiculously soaked. Embarrassment flooded worse than I had, but he brushed all that away when he pulled me back into his arms.

"I made a mess," I whispered.

"A hot mess," he whispered back. "It's a good mess, Jo, believe me."

He tugged the bedcovers from under us and shifted us into a sleeping position.

"I'll take the wet patch," he said.

I grinned.

He left me long enough to grab a glass of water from the kitchen, then settled back into bed and pulled me against him like he always used to do.

"We'll have to be up in the morning," I said. "Before the girls… before they…" I lowered my voice. "Can you set your alarm?"

He nodded. "Already done."

I smiled. "Goodnight then," I whispered.

"Goodnight then," he said.

Only it wasn't.

We were kissing again before he'd even got the lamp.

CHAPTER SEVENTEEN

TRENT

I watched her all night. Well, what was left of it. She rolled over in her sleep and wriggled herself against me, just like old times. She stole most of the duvet and it ended up piled up on her side, just like old times. She'd stick her feet out of the covers, then press them to my calves to warm them back up, just like old times.

That soft grunty snore she does, then swears blind she doesn't. Her hair in my face, the smell of her, the bliss of her skin next to mine.

The smell of sex hanging in the air.

I hadn't had a woman in my bed since Stacey, not all night. Twelve months that lasted, limping on another couple as she got the message that it was really fucking done, that *I* was really fucking done.

Lucky man, they said. *Wouldn't mind waking up to that every morning. She's a fucking catch, mate.*

Hard to feel that lucky when you're saying goodbye to your kids at dinner time every fucking night and wishing you weren't. Hard to feel lucky when you're seeing your forever every fucking day as you hand your girls over and knowing you fucking blew it.

Stacey made the right move at the right time, that was all. Rocked up in the Drum for a hen party, made a play at closing and didn't let it go after. It seems that silence is all the affirmation some people need. *Drinks in the Drum tonight, babe? I'll call in at the yard at lunch, babe, I'm passing anyway. I'll be over on Friday night, babe. I've bought you some beers in, babe.*

Fuck me, babe. Fuck me harder, babe. You make me so fucking horny, babe.

And then the L word. Jesus.

I let it slide, and why wouldn't I? A hot, horny body next to mine every night, a pussy that wanted me every fucking night. A pair of eyes looking into mine that didn't see a long list of every fucking mistake I'd ever made.

It was fun for six months. Drink, laugh, fuck. Repeat. And then the questions came, questions that didn't require just silence as an affirmative.

Shall we get a place together, babe? How do you feel about more kids, babe? I'm thinking of going part-time at the salon, babe, maybe I could work part-time at yours, in the office? Make it more ours...

I've seen just the dress I'd like, babe. Ivory satin, beautiful train, babe. Do you want to see a picture, babe? What do you think, babe?

I pulled Jodie tighter to my chest and she sighed in her sleep.

The kids liked Stacey. Said she was fun. My parents liked Stacey. Said she was a nice girl. The lads liked Stacey. Said she was a hot piece of snatch.

I liked Stacey, too. Just not enough. Not nearly enough.

I thought maybe it *could* be enough, maybe if I just gave it a bit of time. Maybe if I stuck with it I'd grow to care, even grow to love her.

But then the temper tantrums started, spoiled little blow ups with a healthy side of silent treatment. *I don't think you're even planning to propose, babe. Have you even looked at rings? Have you even thought about a venue? Are you even bothered, babe?*

No. No, I fucking wasn't.

I said it, too.

Give it a rest, Stace. Just chill the fuck out a bit, Stace. Drink your wine and stop with the fucking sulking, Stace.

I'm not about to walk up the fucking aisle, Stace. I'm happy living here, Stace. I don't need any help in the office, Stace.

Thanks but fucking no thanks, Stace.

Maybe not the words I should've said, but I've never been good at that.

I don't love you, Stace. I'm in love with Jodie. I'll always be in love with Jodie.

She started snooping. Started getting paranoid, checking my phone, calling me at work ten times a day. Started pulling a face when I said I was dropping the kids back to Jodie, that I'd probably stay and have a cuppa with Nanna.

She's not your fucking nanna, Darren!

Darren. That's when I became Darren. That's when I thought it was over. I was fucking glad of it.

But then she found the fucking ring.

The light was shining through the gaps in the curtains when I heard the girls. Some argument or other. The thump as Ruby dropped down from the top bunk, the creak of the door handle, the sound of the fridge door opening and closing. The TV.

It was the TV that woke Jodie. She started, rolled onto her back with wide eyes as she acclimatised to where she was. My lips were on hers before she could make a sound, my finger taking their place when I pulled away.

"Shh," I whispered. "Girls are live and kicking."

I braced myself for the regret in her eyes, the *oh shit, we shouldn't have* noises coming from her pretty mouth, but they didn't come. She stared up at me with streaky makeup, her hair a right fucking tangle on the pillow, and she smiled. It was a quiet smile, not one of those that bloom quick and fade, this one crept up slowly. This one was real and raw and came with nervous eyes.

This one hit me right in the gut and grabbed tight. My arm snaked around her waist and pulled her close, her wine breath in my face as I smoothed her messy hair from her forehead.

A clatter in the kitchen. Ruby-induced – I'd have put money on it.

Daddddd! Dad are you awake?! Mum gets me frosty hoops now! I don't like crunchy crispies anymore!

I raised an eyebrow at Jodie.

"Last Wednesday," she whispered. "She changed her allegiance to frosty hoops last Wednesday." She was still smiling. "It's a new thing. I'd still buy the crispies if I were you, I don't think it'll last."

Daddddd!

A groan from Mia. *He's asleep, Ruby, shhhh! Just have crispies!*

Who died and made you queen of everything, Mia? Daddddd! Mia's being mean to me!

Jodie put her hand across her mouth to stop herself laughing, and I felt it, too. I pressed my forehead to hers. "I'd better get out

233

there before they come to blows."

She nodded. "I'll have to hide. Just in case."

"Hide? Righto."

I pulled the duvet over her head and buried her, squeezing her tight before I got to my feet, loving the way her body moved as she fought the giggles. She peeped out from under the covers as I pulled my jeans on, didn't stop looking at me as I crept to the bedroom door and checked the coast was clear.

I winked at her as I stepped into the hallway.

She blew me a kiss right back.

Ruby was glaring at the crispies box. She let out one of her most dramatic sighs. "I *hate* crispies, Dad! I haven't liked crispies in ages!"

"She's being a baby," Mia said, rolling her eyes like we were two adults together. It made me smile.

I ruffled her hair, then Ruby's after her. "Why don't you girls get dressed? We'll see if Granny T can rustle up some egg on toast, how about that?"

They didn't need much encouragement.

I slipped back in the bedroom and Jodie was right where I'd left her. I'd have given anything to climb back in there after her, but I pulled a t-shirt on and went about keeping this thing under the girls' radar.

Whatever the fuck *this thing* was.

I looked at Jodie's crazy-killer heels by the hamper. "How are your feet?" I whispered.

She gave the so-so gesture with her hand.

"You should stop wearing the bloody things," I said. I reached into the top of the wardrobe, past a load of old paperwork and boxes of random old shit until I came to a bag at the back. I pulled it out and gave it to Jodie. She looked inside with a puzzled grin.

"Meant to give it back to you," I said.

Sure I did.

She pulled out an old pair of sandals, the ones she'd worn when we first went to the coast with her parents and Nanna. I still remembered her tapping them on the wall to get the sand out.

"Lifesaver," she whispered. Next she tugged out the satin robe she used to hang behind the bedroom door, followed by the sparkly bracelet I'd bought her from a market stall down Bristol one Christmas. She covered her mouth as she pulled out the pair of knickers she'd left in the laundry when she moved out.

"They were in the hamper," I whispered.

"They were?"

I smiled. "Yes, Jodie, they were. Do you take me for some kind of panty sniffer or something?"

Her eyes were so warm. "Nothing would surprise me, Darren Trent. I know you too well, remember?"

Ready, Dadddd!

I chanced a final kiss, nothing more than a peck on the lips before I joined the girls. "Door's on the catch," I said. "Let yourself out when you're ready. No rush."

I brushed my teeth quickly, grabbed a jacket and my keys from the side.

"Let's go," I said. "Last one to the truck gets the hardest yolk."

JODIE

It was so surreal. I lay back in Darren Trent's bed, which used to be mine too. Only now it smelled just of him. Of musk, and shower gel, and cigarettes, and sweat and oil, and sex...

I pulled the covers to my face and breathed him in.

We had sex again last night. I couldn't stop grinning.

I would have stayed there all morning if I didn't have to get back to Nanna. I dragged myself up with wobbly legs, aching with that just fucked feeling that felt divine. I used Darren's toothbrush, plucked it from the holder where it rested by the two girls'. I knew whose was whose. Ruby's would be the funky green one, Mia's would be the glitter purple. I took a pee and I couldn't stop staring at them, those three toothbrushes, a small token of the life they lived together here. A life without me.

I wandered into the girls' room, my heart racing even though it was stupid. I was hardly an intruder.

The bottom bunk was freshly made, the bright heart pattern all lined up neatly. The top bunk was a disaster area. I raised myself on tiptoes and cleared a monster truck from up there, managed to find a couple of Haynes manuals and a plastic beaker, too. I put the beaker in the sink, then thought better of it and washed it up, along with the dirty mugs from Darren's bedside table.

There were another couple in the living room, a couple of empty beer cans stashed down the side of the sofa that I threw in the recycling.

I made Darren's bed and my tummy was tickly.

I don't want to leave.

I put his dirty clothes in the hamper then figured I'd return his washing machine favour – loaded up a load of whites and set it going.

I found a pack of wipes and dusted down the bedside table,

cleaning off the mug stains.

I shouldn't have opened the drawers, but I did.

The top drawer was the usual shit. Some of it had probably been there since before I'd moved out. A couple of old watches, some membership cards, his passport. Condoms, lots of condoms. More condoms...

Lube...

I closed the drawer, reminding myself that this was him now, this was his new thing. Just a job.

He said it was just a job.

The drawer handle polished up nicely. The one on the drawer below it, too.

I took a quick nose inside, since I'd already snooped my way through the first. Paperwork. Cheque books. A little black book. My heart pounded as I looked inside, laughing when it turned out to be car events listed not women's phone numbers.

Stupid, this was stupid.

I'd nearly closed the drawer when I spotted the little blue box at the back. The kind you can't mistake. A little velvet number with a flip lid.

My God.

Surely he wouldn't have kept it. Surely Stacey would have kept it? Maybe she gave it back to him.

Maybe he kept it in case she changed her mind.

I took a breath as I opened the box.

It was beautiful. A single diamond on a white gold band, delicate and classy and not too in your face. I tried to imagine Stacey wearing it. She'd been so larger than life, so blonde and bubbly and... not white gold.

I guess I was wrong.

The box listed a jeweller in Carmarthen. My skin prickled, and it wasn't in a good way. We'd always stopped in Carmarthen on the way to the coast. We went every year, sometimes twice. My parents ended up moving that way, their guesthouse wasn't far away from there – Saundersfoot.

I imagined Stacey and Darren there, walking those same streets that we walked, holding hands like we did. I pictured them on the same beach we'd sat on, grabbing ice creams like we did. Playing with the girls like we did.

I wondered if she played with my girls on the same beach we went to.

Of course she did.

I told myself to stop being an idiot. Everyone has a past. My relationship with Brian lasted way longer than Darren's had with Stacey.

But I hadn't loved Brian. Hadn't proposed to Brian. Hadn't bought a ring with Brian.

Hadn't kept it in my bedside drawer for years after.

So what if he had her engagement ring in his bedroom? Who cares about that anyway?

It's not like we were together. Not like this was a thing. How could it be?

We had the girls to think about, and I had Nanna and a job and a whole life that was already packed to the rafters without him.

He had the yard, and the pub, and a thousand women to keep serviced for the sake of a boxful of cash under his bed.

And I love him.

This was sex. Just sex. Of course it was.

I put the ring back where I'd found it and walked home in my old sandals.

CHAPTER EIGHTEEN

TRENT

I was all smiles at breakfast, helping Mum with the pans while Dad played dominoes with the girls. I wanted to say something, wished I could have said something, but there wasn't really much to say anyway.

I fucked Jodie last night, Mum. It meant everything.

"You alright, Darren?" Mum's eyes were fixed on mine, her eyebrows raised.

"Alright, Mum, yeah."

"Anything happened? You seem... bright..."

"Just the usual."

She nodded, like that even fucking meant anything. The usual what?

Ruby tipped over the domino tower in time for eggs. I watched the girls eat, listened to the way they laughed, soaked up all the stories they told my mum and dad.

Today all I saw in them was Jodie, even in Ruby. Her eyes, her laugh, the way she flicked her hair.

"Dad's taking us rallying," Ruby said. "And Mum and Tonya and

Daisy are coming too."

Mum smiled at me. "They are, are they? Is that right, Darren? Is Jodie going?"

I shrugged. "Think she's getting a tent."

"She *is* getting a tent," Ruby said. "A big one with three rooms, I've seen the picture on the internet."

"How lovely," Mum said.

"Lovely," Dad said.

I ate my eggs.

I took the girls to the cinema for the afternoon, some magical crap film that bored the shit out of me. I ate popcorn and stared at my phone, waiting for a text from Jo that never came. I don't know what I was expecting.

Ruby was in high spirits as we left, but Mia was quiet.

"What's up?" I asked as we drove back to the village, but she shrugged and claimed it was nothing.

I had a paranoia that she knew Jodie had stayed over, that it would be weird for them. The kind of weird that no kid should have to deal with, at least not until her parents were with the fucking plot. I wondered if I should text Jodie, scope out whether I should push it with Mia and what I should say if she did know, but I held back.

I made them a cruddy sandwich at mine and they didn't seem to mind. Ruby watched TV while Mia played around on her phone. I smiled at the flashing washing machine, load completed, couldn't help but notice that there a lot more clean mugs in the cupboard.

We were getting ready to leave for Jodie's when Mia headed off into her bedroom. I found her on her bed, scrunched into a little ball with her hands over her face.

"Mia's sad," Ruby said, like I couldn't work that out for myself.

"Why don't you go watch some Top Gear, Rubes?" I said. "I'll be right out."

I closed the door when I heard the theme tune ring out, sat on the edge of Mia's bed and asked her if she wanted to talk. My heart was pounding, guilty, like I'd been caught out doing something I shouldn't, but the truth of it was nothing like I imagined.

She twisted around and grabbed my waist, buried her face in my t-shirt. I could hardly make out her words.

"Please don't make me go to school tomorrow, Dad. I don't want to go to school tomorrow! Please, Dad, please say I don't have to go!"

"Hey," I said. "What's wrong with school tomorrow?"

I thought about homework, some shitty teacher, some cruddy sports day she didn't want to get involved in, all the usual.

"It's Tyler..." she cried. "Tyler Dean. He's really mean to me on the bus, calls me names... Says I'm ugly and stinky and makes all the other kids laugh at me. Mum told Mrs Webber and Mrs Webber told Tyler's mum, but now he's even more mean! He sits by me and pretends to smile, rubs my hair and uses his knuckles..." She let out a sob. "He says we're *friends* now. That he'll be friends with a slimy stinky ugly snitch like me, but I owe him now, and if I tell anyone..." She was crying too hard to make the rest out.

I could feel the twitch in my jaw.

"And what did the little fucker say will happen if you tell anyone, Mia?"

"He said he'll make life horrible! So horrible I'll kill myself and he'll laugh about it! He's been getting people to block me on Facebook. I've seen horrible things about me on other people's timelines." She gulped in a breath. "He says he'll make sure nobody likes me, that every single person on the internet knows what a stinky little snitch I am!"

"Tyler Dean?" I said. "Lanky little shit with glasses?"

She nodded. "He's so horrible, Dad. He's really horrible. His knuckles hurt my head so bad, and I can't cry because he'll get mad at me."

"And your mum knew about this, did she?"

She shook her head. "Only about the names, she went to Mrs Webber, said Mrs Webber would sort it out." It broke my heart to see the tears on her cheeks. "I couldn't tell her, Dad! Because she'll only go to Mrs Webber again and Tyler Dean will be even worse! He'll be even worse, Dad!"

"He won't be fucking worse, Mia," I said. "Don't you worry about that."

Her eyes were glassy. "You promise?"

"I fucking swear it." I brushed the tears from her cheeks. "Chin up, now. Get your things together, we're going out." I gave her a hug, kissed her head.

"Are you going to say something to Mum? I don't want her to be mad at me."

"She won't be mad at you," I said. "And I'm not going to be saying anything to your mum. Not yet."

I turned off the TV, told Ruby to get a move on through her huff at having Clarkson cut short. I smoked a cigarette while the girls got belted up in the truck. Paced up and down the street while the twitch twitched in my jaw.

Roger Dean lived up Elmgrove. The house with the green painted fence. He drives a Rover, I did his tyres the month previous.

I didn't say a word as I drove up the hill and past Jodie's turn off. Didn't say a word as I took the road up to Elmgrove. I parked the truck right outside Roger Dean's house, left the engine running and told the girls to stay put.

Roger was in his yard by the time I reached his gate.

"Trent," he said, and he was smiling. "What brings you up here?"

I spotted the dipshit in the doorway, his arms folded, face white as a fucking ghost. I jabbed a finger in his direction and the red mist exploded.

"Your cunt of a son," I barked. "That little fucking wanker of yours has been bullying my Mia." Dipshit went to dash into the house, but his dad called after him, stopped him in his tracks.

"Tyler! What the fuck is this? Is this fucking true?"

The kid looked like he was going to crap his pants.

"We're friends now..." he said. "After Mrs Webber said..."

His dad took a step towards him. "What do you mean after Mrs fucking Webber said? Have you been bullying Mia Trent?"

"Mrs Webber called his mother," I grunted. "He knows just what the fuck I'm talking about."

"Christ," Roger said. "That fucking woman. Dawn's too fucking soft with him, lets him get away with fucking murder. I knew nothing about this shit, Trent, I swear."

That made fucking two of us.

"Little cunt knuckles her hair, says she should kill herself." I lit up a cigarette. "She's been crying her fucking eyes out this afternoon."

He rubbed his eyes. "Fuck, Trent, I'm so fucking sorry. She ok?"

"She will be now." I shot him a glare. "You gonna sort this shit out, Roger, or do I have to?"

He gave me a nod. "I'll sort this shit out, Trent, don't you worry about that."

"If I catch wind of any more of it..."

He slapped my arm, tipped his head. "Understood, mate. I'll sort it. I'm not like his fucking mother."

I shot Tyler a glare, flicked my cigarette away. "Stay away from my fucking daughter," I snapped.

The girls were watching through the truck windows, eyes like saucers. I climbed up into the driver's seat, watched Roger go storming down his garden path after his dickhead son.

"Thanks, Dad," Mia said.

"Should have punched him in the mouth," Ruby said. She showed me her fist. "POW!"

"No need," I grunted. "Not yet anyway. Lad's got his old man to answer to now."

The girls were quiet as I drove back to Jodie's. They piled out of the truck and gave her a hug in the doorway. She smiled at me but I didn't smile back.

Then she saw Mia's face, her puffy eyes. She wiped her cheeks, and I could see the fear in her eyes. "What the hell happened?"

Mia started crying all over again. "Sorry, Mum," she said.

"Go inside," I said to the girls. "Watch TV with Nanna."

Jodie stepped out, closed the door after her. "Darren? What..?"

I lit up a cigarette. "Tyler fucking Dean!" I snapped. "That's what!"

Her face turned pale. "But that's sorted... Mrs Webber..."

"Mrs Webber didn't sort shit, Jodie. Mrs Webber told the lad's fucking mother who lets him lord it around like little lord fucking muck."

She stared at me. "What did you do?"

"What fucking needed doing! I went to his fucking father, sorted this shit out man to man!"

"Did you hit him?!"

I stared right back at her. "No, I didn't fucking hit him. I didn't need to fucking hit him, Jodie, he just needed telling like it fucking is."

She let out a breath. "Good," she said. "Is Mia alright?"

"No," I snapped. "She's not fucking alright. Hasn't been fucking alright for weeks from what I can fucking make of it."

She held up her hands. "I thought it was sorted. I sorted it, Darren. With the school. Mrs Webber said they have a zero tolerance policy on bullying. I told her everything! She said she'd sort it!"

"Yeah, well, what about telling me, Jodie? What about what I'd have to fucking say on it?" I took a drag. "I guess that didn't mean shit to you, did it? Keep fucking Trent out of it, he'll only cause fucking trouble."

She shook her head. "It wasn't like that. I didn't mean it like that."

But that's exactly how she meant it.

I felt the twitch again.

I stared at her but she wasn't looking at me. Couldn't look at me.

"Don't ever keep anything like this from me again, Jodie, I fucking mean it. I'm their fucking dad. They're my fucking girls, too. You've no fucking right to cut me out like that."

"I know," she said. "Darren, I'm sorry. I should have said... I just didn't think..."

"No," I said. "You fucking didn't."

I turned my back on her and went to the truck. Stubbed my cigarette on the pavement and climbed in. My jaw was gritted, my

246

temper at red, that horrible feeling in my gut that said I wasn't a part of this family anymore, not when it mattered. Jodie was at the door before I pulled away. She yanked it open and stood with her arms folded.

"What are you doing?" she said.

"Need some space," I said. "Let me go."

She sighed. "Pub? A pint or ten down the Drum? Get yourself wasted and pick a fight with Buck? Or Jimmy? Take it out on little Petey?"

I didn't say a thing.

"That'll make you feel better, will it, Darren?" Her voice was strained. "I said I'm sorry. I said I should've told you."

My fingers tapped on the wheel.

"What else do you want me to say?" she said. "I didn't tell you because I thought I could handle it. I thought the school would deal with it. I didn't want to *bother* you with it. *Yes*, because I was worried you'd fly off the handle and go causing a massive fucking scene, Darren, *just* when everyone's *stopped* talking about us and all our shit."

I stared ahead, my insides fucking knotted up.

"You think I don't *know* that you're their dad? That I don't see it every day, that I don't hear it from them every day? You really think I believe you're too unimportant to care about?"

"Don't you?" I met her eyes. "Good for nothing but my temper, isn't that right, Jo? Too fucking bull-headed, too blunt. Better get them a new fucking daddy. A *nice* daddy who doesn't swear and plays golf and wears tweed and likes opera and fucking *quinoa* and lavender. *That* kind of daddy, eh?"

"He was never their dad, Darren, not even close," she said.

"Yeah, well, not for the want of trying, eh?"

"Brian was a mistake."

"A long fucking mistake, Jo. Would you have told *him* about Tyler fucking Dean? Bet he could have went to Mrs Webber's office and pulled a stern face along with you. Called the cunt a *naughty little hooligan*."

"I would never have taken Brian to Mrs Webber's office! It was never that serious. It's not like I was *engaged* to the guy!"

It knocked me in the gut. "What's that supposed to mean?"

She took a step back, and her expression was full of pain. "Nine months, Darren, maybe slightly less. Nine months to propose to Stacey, to introduce a new *mum* to our girls. She had them picking out fucking bridesmaid dresses before Ruby even knew what a bridesmaid was!"

"Like I had anything to do with that, Jo." I shook my head. "Fuck this shit, I need to get out of here, got shit to do."

"Client waiting?"

"No!" I snapped. "I just need some fucking space!" I was too loud, too harsh. I closed my eyes, took a breath. "I'm not going to a client, Jo. I just need to get out of here."

"Fine," she said, and her voice was weak and broken. I turned to her and her eyes were glassy, just like Mia's had been, her lip shaky.

It'd been a long fucking time since I'd seen her like this.

"I said sorry," she said, but it was just a breath.

I swallowed, and the pub was calling me, the thought of a cold pint, a load of mindless chatter. Shit. It was all shit.

"Don't be upset," I said.

"Go," she said. "Leave, like you always leave when you get pissed off, when things get too fucking hard for you, when I get *upset*, when

I get *angry*." Her breath was ragged. "Go!" she snapped. "Leave me, leave us! I'll just sort it out, like I sort everything. Come back when you feel like it, when you've drunk yourself stupid and punched someone, when you feel all-fucking-right again."

"It's not like that," I said.

"It's *always* like that!" she said, and the tears came. "I'd wait for you all fucking day, Darren. All day! Running around after a little girl with a baby in my arms, holed up in that flat just waiting for you, looking forward to you coming home. Did you know that?"

"Stop," I said.

"And then what? You'd come home. Tired and sore and pissed fucking off, sweaty and grubby and worked half to fucking death! You'd come home and you'd hardly even look at me! Just stare at the fucking TV like I wasn't even there!"

"I was still new to it," I said. "I had to get the hours in, Jo. What did you expect me to do? I was fucking knackered, Jo! I was exhausted!"

"Love me," she said. "Love *us*. That's all I expected from you."

I felt a pain in my chest. An actual fucking pain. *I did fucking love you. I did it fucking for you, all of it. Every poxy fucking shift. Every fucking hour of overtime. Every fucking thing.*

"I was tired," I said. "I didn't think you were happy. You didn't seem happy."

"*We* weren't happy," she said. "Jesus, Darren, when you were an apprentice we had nothing but each other, nothing and a hundred poxy quid a week. We got a bit of money and I lost *you*. Don't you see that? You weren't there! I only wanted *you*! Not you when you were tired from working, not when you'd gone drinking with the others after work, not when you wanted a quick fuck after I'd just got Ruby off to sleep."

"What's the point in this?" I said. "We already know all this, Jo. We've already said it a thousand fucking times."

Her voice broke as she said the words, and I felt it. I felt it all the way inside. "Because I *still* only want you! Because I still hope you'll stay! Because I hope that one time, even now, even when you're pissed off, you'll grit your teeth and stand firm and see it out, with *me!*" She turned away from me. "I never wanted to do this on my own. But I *did*. I *did* do it on my own." She turned back. "I make decisions all day every day about our girls, every single day, Darren. *Yes,* I should have told you about Tyler Dean. *Yes,* I should have told you about going to see Mrs Webber. *Yes,* I should have told you everything, before I even did anything, before I even thought about doing anything. But I didn't. Maybe it's because I've got so used to doing everything for myself that I don't even think about it anymore! That's my bad, Darren! I'm sorry for it!"

Or maybe it's because you think I'm a fucking loser who only knows how to fix cars and fight.

Fight and fuck.

"Jesus, Jo."

"Go," she said. "Just drive away."

I put truck car in gear. "Say bye to the girls. Nanna too."

She nodded, slammed the driver's door shut.

I watched her walk up the path, saw Ruby's face in the window, staring.

I fought the urge to cry like a fucking baby.

Shit.

I slapped the steering wheel, slammed my head against the headrest.

Shit.

A cold pint. A cold pint and mindless fucking banter.

But no. I didn't want it. I'd never fucking wanted it.

I was out of the truck before Jodie had reached the door.

"Wait," I said. "Jo, just wait a fucking minute."

There was surprise in her eyes, so much surprise. It hurt to see how fucking surprised she was.

I lit up a cigarette as she stared at me. "I'm not going to the fucking pub," I said. "I'll just... I'll stay here. If you'll have me in."

She brushed the tears from her cheeks, took a breath. "I'm cooking sausage and beans," she said. "Do you want some?"

I smiled, breathed a sigh of fucking relief that lightened my fucking soul.

"Yeah," I said. "Sausage and beans sounds really fucking good."

CHAPTER NINETEEN

JODIE

I composed myself in the doorway.

He didn't leave. He didn't leave. He didn't leave.

I smiled at Ruby and Nanna in the living room, but Ruby stared back horrified, eyes big and scared. *Shit.* The fucking window. It was open at the top. Bloody Nanna and her fresh air. I wondered what they'd heard.

"Alright, Jodie love?" Nanna said, and she was worried too, I could see it in her face.

Darren appeared behind me. "She's alright, Nanna, aren't you, Jo?"

I nodded. Smiled. "We're good, Nanna. Darren's staying for dinner."

"Ohhh, that's nice," she said. "Sausages and beans, you like that, don't you, Darren?"

"Everyone loves sausages and beans, Nanna," he said. He smiled at Ruby. "You alright, Rubes? Nothing to worry about, don't look so scared."

She nodded. "You really staying for dinner, Dad?"

He took his jacket off, dumped it on the back of the armchair. He sat down, made himself comfortable, like he'd always been there. "Wouldn't miss sausages and beans, Rubes. Not with you and Mia and Nanna." He looked at me. "Or your mum. Wouldn't turn down an invite like that for the world."

My poor nerves, they were shot. Up and down and up again. The Darren Trent effect.

"Where's Mia?" I said. "Skype?"

Ruby shook her head. "Mia's sad."

"She doesn't need to be sad now," Darren said. "Tyler Dean's not going to be bothering her again, that's a sure fact."

I stepped into the hallway, called up the stairs. "Mia? You alright up there? Your dad's staying for dinner."

No reply. I leaned over the bannister. Her bedroom door was shut.

"I'll go up," I said. "Make sure she's ok."

Darren got to his feet, joined me in the hallway. He watched me as I climbed the stairs, his eyes burning my back as I tapped Mia's door. "Mia? Can I come in?"

No reply.

I eased the door handle down. "I'm coming in, love, ready or not."

My heart smashed like glass, my little girl on her bed, crying into Mr Fluff like the world was ending. I rushed to her side, pulled her close. "It's over now," I said. "Your dad's sorted it, that little shit won't be bothering you again, Mia, I promise. I'm so sorry, I really thought Mrs Webber had sorted this out." I heard footsteps on the landing, the door creak open. I turned to find Darren there, face ashen as he took in the scene. "It's sorted now, isn't it, Darren? No more Tyler Dean, he won't say a word."

"It's done, Mia," he said. "I'll pick you up in the morning, take you to the bus stop myself, see what Tyler Dean's got to say for himself then, eh?"

Mia shook her head, but she couldn't speak. Her words were just sobs, I could have cried myself.

"Don't argue... don't argue over me!" she cried. "Please don't! I'm sorry, I shouldn't have said anything! I shouldn't have said anything about Tyler! Just please don't be mad..."

"Hey," Darren said, he came over, knelt at the side of the bed. "Nobody's arguing, Mia. You've got nothing to be sorry for."

"I heard you..." she cried. "Arguing over me... and I'm sorry! Please don't be angry with each other! Please don't!"

"We're not," I said. "It was just a conversation, Mia, sometimes people get a bit upset, it doesn't mean they can't sort it out, does it, Darren?"

I met his eyes, willed him to say something, anything.

His answer melted my shattered heart.

"You know what I'm like, Mia. My mouth runs away with me sometimes. Bit of a hot head." He squeezed her arm. "I can be a bit of a prick, getting butt-hurt all over the place. You can forgive your dad for being a bit of an idiot, can't you? I hope you can, I was looking forward to having sausages and beans with you."

I felt the tears coming. I smiled at him, and he smiled back, but there was such pain there, such pain in all of us.

Mia let go of Mr Fluff and rolled over, faced her dad with puffy eyes. "Don't go, Dad, I won't make you argue again, not if you stay, not ever again. Not like last time." Her face crumpled. "Not like when I was little, I'm big now, I can be better, I won't make you argue ever again, I promise!"

My jaw dropped and so did his. We stared at each other, sharing that one moment of horrified parenthood.

"What are you talking about?" I said. "We never argued over you, Mia, never. You never made us argue, not once."

"You did!" she said. "You'd argue and Dad would leave and then you'd cry, Mum. You'd cry and pretend that you weren't!"

I stared in disbelief. I thought she was too young to remember this, too young to have seen it.

Guilt hit hard. It made me feel sick.

"It was me!" she said. "I know it was me! And I won't do it again, I promise! I promise! Just stay! Just stay with us, Dad!"

Darren put his hands on her cheeks, brushed her tears away. My heart lurched.

He stared her straight in the eye. "Not once," he said. "Not once that we argued was it ever *ever* your fault, Mia, I promise you that. It was mine. All mine."

"And mine," I said. "It was *our* fault, me and your dad's. Not yours, not ever yours." I looked at Darren then back at my poor daughter. She looked so young again. Too young for this, too young for any of this. "Never ever think that was your fault, it wasn't. None of it was your fault."

She took a horrible gulpy breath. Then she nodded.

Darren's voice was thick when he next spoke. "I'm your dad, Mia. I'll never leave you, no matter what happens, no matter how much me and your mum argue. No matter how butt-hurt I get, no matter how much of an idiot I am, I'll never leave. I'll always be right here, just down the road, whenever you need me. That's a promise, alright?"

I let out a breath as she smiled. She held out a finger, Ruby style.

"Pinky promise?"

"Pinky promise," he said and linked her finger.

I pulled her up and held her tight, her arms around my waist, her head on my shoulder. I rocked her like she was little again, too little to be embarrassed by her mother. My eyes were closed when the bed dipped next to us, my heart skipped a beat as I felt his arms around me, around both of us. His head pressed to mine as he kissed Mia's hair, and I wished he'd never leave, not ever again.

Another creak of the door, and there was Ruby.

He beckoned her over. "Come on, Rubes, group hug, room for another small one."

She smiled her brightest smile, and came over, flung her arms around all three of us, and there we stayed, four broken people who hadn't realised they were broken, not until they were put back together again.

I hugged Ruby and Mia, and Darren hugged all of us.

I felt safer than I'd felt in years. More complete than I'd felt in years.

"I'd better get the sausages on," I said, before they saw me crying.

TRENT

I sat at the kitchen table, the same one Nanna had had since forever, laughing with the girls and making Nanna giggle so hard she gave herself hiccups, but inside I was fucking dying.

The thought of walking out that front door again was more than I could bear. The thought of driving home to the flat without the girls, without Jodie, without Nanna. Alone. I was so alone.

I'd never felt grief like it, so close and yet so fucking far.

Jodie's foot touched mine under the table, and I know she was feeling it too. I could see it behind her smile, behind the way she dished up dinner and cut up Ruby's sausages and acted like everything was normal.

I thought of all the things I wanted to say. Thought about dropping my knife and fork and taking Jodie's hand and begging her to take me back, take me home. Begging for another chance, a proper chance. Begging for another shot to stay with her rather than hit the pub in a foul temper. Begging for another shot to hold her tight as I watched the TV in dirty clothes, knackered from a long day at the garage.

As usual, I said fucking nothing, just ate my dinner and made sure the girls kept smiling.

I helped Jodie clear the plates. We didn't speak much, but she passed me plates to dry with the kind of lingering glances that made me fall in love with her all over again, just like the very first time. Fall in love with the girl with the dark red bob, asking me for a cigarette every morning as she waited for the school bus. The girl whose laugh made my heart beat so fucking fast as I walked past her on the way to work.

The girl who'd asked for my name and told me hers.

"I'm Jodie," she'd said. "Thought you might want to know the name of the person robbing you of cigarettes every morning."

"No bother," I'd said. "I'm Trent." I'd caught myself. "Darren. Darren Trent." I'd pointed down the hill. "I'm training, fixing up cars. Just down there."

She'd looked me up and down, like she needed to. I was wearing fucking overalls streaked with oil. She giggled, and I still remember how that sounded. "Kinda gathered," she said. "It's really nice to meet you, Darren Trent."

"I'll be seeing you, Jodie," I'd said.

And I did see her. Every fucking day from that point onwards. Slowly but surely, bit by bit we got to know each other.

I stopped seeing her at the bus stop and just started seeing her. I'd talk to her, laugh with her, walk along the river with her.

Then one day she'd reached for my hand.

I remembered the first time I'd kissed her, round the corner from the fish and chip shop as we finished up our supper. I remembered the first time I'd taken her, in bed at her parents' house, listening out for footsteps on the stairs. She'd been so nervous, all giggly and breathless, the most beautiful thing I'd ever seen.

"We can wait," I'd said. "Whenever you want, Jo."

"Now," she'd said, and she'd kissed me, so hard. Kissed me hard enough to make me sure she was sure. "I'm ready," she'd said, and I knew she was.

I'd been with her when she did the pregnancy test, as shocked as she was when the blue line appeared.

I'd been with her when she told her parents we were having a baby.

I'd been with her when she gave birth to our little girl, held her tight as our Mia cried for the first time.

I'd always been with her, even when she couldn't see it. Even when she didn't believe it.

"Darren?" She smiled, and the plate was dripping, hovering between us as I gawped at her.

I took it from her. "Sorry, was a million miles away."

"Kinda gathered," she said and smiled.

It made my heart ache.

"You staying for Question King?" she asked. "Celebrity special on a Sunday. I think that guy from the jungle is on. Should be good."

I nodded. "Righto."

Nanna took the armchair and I took the sofa with Jodie and the girls. Ruby was on my lap, squirming around the place as she tried to answer all the questions, Mia snuggled in tight to my side. Jodie kept her distance, her legs folded under her, her head on the backrest, trying to pretend she was looking at the TV and not at me.

I know that, because I spent the whole show doing the same.

I had a cup of tea before I went home. I'd have had ten in a row just to prolong that awful fucking moment.

It came too soon, much too soon. Bedtime for the girls, and I'd said goodnight, said I'd be round to pick them up in the morning and take Mia to the bus stop.

It'd been Ruby that had stared at me with glassy eyes, Ruby whose lip started trembling this time around.

"But Dad..." she said. "Can't you stay? You can stay now, right? Now you and mum are proper friends again..." She turned to Jodie. "Mum, tell Dad he can stay! He can stay with us now, can't he?"

Jodie looked as fucking gutted as I did.

"Your dad has to get home," she said. "He's got work in the morning, things to do."

"Yeah," I said, ignoring the lump in my throat. "Got things to do, Rubes. I'll see you in the morning though, bright and early."

"But you're gonna stay with us! You said so! I heard you tell Mia!" Her cheeks were so pink, her eyes so wide. "We can be a proper family now! Like Sophie Pickton's family! Her dad still lives with her. Selena Murphy's dad still lives with her, too!"

Fuck how it hurt.

"I gotta go, Rubes," I said. "We are a proper family, I just got my own place, that's all."

"Tell him, Mum!" she begged. "Tell him!"

I wished she fucking would. How I fucking wished.

But she didn't.

"We've all got to get to bed," she said. "Come on now, Ruby, clean your teeth and get your PJs on. Your dad stayed for Question King, he's only going home to sleep."

"He can stay in my room!" Ruby told her. "I don't mind! I'll sleep in with Mia!"

"Bedtime," I said. "Your mum's tired, Rubes, be a good girl now."

And she'd cried. She'd cried really fucking hard.

"I thought you were staying..." she said. "I thought... I thought..."

It was the worst fucking feeling. The most soul-destroying fucking feeling.

I needed a cigarette, needed a cigarette so fucking bad I could hardly hold my shit together, but I stayed put, kept breathing.

"A bedtime story," Jodie said. "Maybe your dad can read you one, if he's got time?" She looked at me and I nodded.

"I've got time."

"There you go," Jodie said. "You won't even notice he's not staying, Ruby, you'll be asleep by the time he's gone, and he'll be right back round in the morning, won't you, Darren?"

"Yeah," I said. "Right back round in the morning."

Ruby gave a nod and accepted defeat. She went up the stairs with her sister, cleaned her teeth and put her PJs on like a good kid.

"Day from hell," Jodie said when they were out of earshot. "Talk about an emotional wringer. I could drink a whole bottle of Nanna's brandy and my nerves would still be shot."

"It'll be alright," I said, but I wasn't so sure.

Rubes was asleep by the time I'd finished up her Rally Car Racers story, flaked clean out with her mouth open, catching flies. I sat and watched her sleep, just a little while. Flicked on her nightlight before I left.

I said goodbye to Mia, who was back on her phone. She handed it over as I kissed her goodnight. "Mum always takes it," she said. "Ask her to put it on charge, will you, please?"

I did just that.

Jodie plugged it in, then put the kettle on. I hovered, just in case there was one for me.

There was.

"We need to talk," she said. "But Nanna..."

I nodded. "I'll wait."

We sat at the kitchen table, drinking tea while Nanna watched her programmes next door. I'd smoke out by the back door, come in again and drink another cuppa, on and on until Nanna said her goodnights and climbed the stairs.

We went into the living room, sat at opposite ends of the sofa, and Jodie looked as drained as I felt.

"This is all fucked up," she said, and I agreed with her.

"The poor girls," she said, and I agreed with her.

"Whatever this is, we can't... we can't let it affect them, we just can't... it would be..."

I agreed with her.

"So what?" she asked. "What do we do now?"

"I've got no fucking idea," I said.

"Last night was good," she said. "Great," she added.

I agreed with her.

"But... we can't just... jump in... we have to be..."

"Sure," I said. "We'd have to be sure."

She nodded. "Really sure. One million percent sure. Forever sure."

I already am.

"Sounds right," I said. "For the girls."

"For the girls."

Please don't make me go home.

I cleared my throat. "The sex, Jo. Is that what you want? The bang gang stuff? Is that still what you want?"

She sighed. "I don't know, Darren. Christ, last night was amazing. The whole thing's been amazing. But today was... tough."

"Tell me about it," I said.

You're not the one who has to go home alone.

"Maybe we should play it by ear," she said. "Just for a while. See where things go."

"Righto," I said.

"That's what you want, too?"

No. I don't want to play it by ear. I know what I want.

I shrugged. "Sounds fair, Jo. For the girls."

She smiled. "For the girls, yeah. We'll do that, then. We'll play it by ear. Be careful. Until we're sure."

I nodded.

"I'd better get some sleep," she said. "Monday mornings are always crazy."

I wish I knew.

"Right," I said. "I'll be seeing you."

I finished up my drink and put the mug on the table. I grabbed my jacket and fished the truck keys from my pocket.

She walked me to the door. "Goodnight, Darren."

I smiled at her, but I couldn't bring myself to say it back.

I'd never have got the words out.

CHAPTER TWENTY

JODIE

I couldn't sleep. Even though I was exhausted and emotionally frazzled and maybe even still a bit hungover, I couldn't sleep.

I fired off a message to Tonya, and she was awake, too. She replied with a big smiley.

☺ *How did it go?*

Great, I replied. *Really great.* I wanted to tell her I loved Darren Trent, that I'd always loved him, that I would love him until the day I died and I was sure of it, but the little niggle in my heart wouldn't let me do it. I was too scared, too scared to put that out into the open.

Not with everything at stake.

Not with the girls breaking their hearts.

Not with the whole village booked in for a Bang Gang special.

Not with Stacey's engagement ring still in his bedside drawer.

And?? she prompted.

I don't know, I replied honestly. *We're playing it by ear, just for now.*

I waited for the response. *What the hell does that mean?*

I didn't know. I told her as much.

Shit, she replied. *I think you two need to lock yourselves in a room for a week and fuck out the details.*

It made me laugh. *I'd be game for that.*

But would I be? Would I really? Knowing he was dipping his wick in anyone who was paying for it?

Hell, half the women in the playground might be riding his cock all night for all I knew.

Could I live with that?

No. No I couldn't. Not even if I wanted to. Not even if I thought I could at first, that kind of crap eats away at you, eats away at everything.

I'd never do that to the girls.

You want him, the next message said. *He wants you. Jesus Christ, Jodie, you two are fucking crazy about each other, you'd have to be blind not to see that.*

Maybe I was blind, because I wasn't nearly so sure.

Not with his box of cash under his bed and another woman's engagement ring in his bedside drawer.

I sighed, went to type out goodnight, but another message came through before I could. I hoped it was Darren, but of course it was Tonya.

Ladies who lunch tomorrow. You coming?

I typed *yes* on instinct, then thought about it. Deleted it.

No. I wasn't going to ladies who lunch. If I was honest with myself I couldn't stand Mandy Taylor's smug face ever since she'd blabbed that she'd been fucking Darren. The thought of it made me feel sick. The thought of it made me feel like a jealous bitch, a crazy, the kind of woman who wanted to pull Mandy Taylor's hair out and tell her to *stay the hell away from my man, you skanky fucking hoe.*

I'd never admitted to myself I'd felt like that before, but there it was, lurking beneath the surface, the undeniable vitriol.

No, I typed. *I'll give it a miss tomorrow.*

Working? she asked.

No.

She sent a line of smileys that took up two rows, and it made me smile. She knew me so well.

Go get your man, she said. *Fuck him senseless. Figure out the details later. You know you want to. xx*

I put my phone on the nightstand and smiled to myself, daring myself to live, just a little. To be reckless, just a little.

A safe amount.

An amount of reckless that wouldn't hurt anyone.

I picked up my phone for the last time before I went to sleep. One final message to Tonya.

I think I might just do that. xx

TRENT

I was outside Jodie's well in time to take the girls to school. They seemed to be in their usual spirits, just like any other school day. Ruby screamed blue fucking murder when I told her it was Mia's turn to sit up front.

It's not fairrrr! I wanna go up front! That's my seat!

Not today it wasn't.

She sulked in the backseat, but that would have to do. I wanted to keep an eye on Mia.

I parked up by the bus stop, and today I cut the engine and got out with her. I stood with her while we waited, scoping out the kids around.

None of them put a foot wrong, full of smiles and hellos like butter wouldn't fucking melt.

Tyler Dean saw me from up the road. He stopped, looked unsure of himself, like the little weasel he was.

Come on, dipshit.

He walked so fucking slowly. Dawdling like a prick, pretending to check out his phone.

I waited. I'd gladly wait all fucking day.

He stayed well away from us, huddled with a few of his dickhead mates, but they were all quiet as mice. They wouldn't even look at Mia.

"Alright, lads," I called. I lit up a cigarette. "I'd best not be hearing about any bullshit going down on the bus today, or the shit's gonna fly. Do you fucking hear me?"

A load of nods, a load of mumbles.

"Tyler," I snapped. I waited until he met my eye. "I'm gonna be here tomorrow, and the next day, and the day after, and every fucking day after that, so I'd think very fucking carefully about the seat you choose on that bus, understand?"

He nodded. "Yes, Mr Trent."

Pussy assed prick.

The bus pulled up and Mia smiled at me. I kissed her head, ruffled her hair. She smoothed it back down again, gave me a tut.

"See you later, Dad." She looked back at me from the doorway. "Thanks."

I slapped the side of the bus as it pulled away, gave her a wave as she looked out the window.

Ruby was up front when I got back in the truck. "Still should have punched him in the mouth," she said. "He's a prick."

I smiled. "Yes, Rubes, he's a fucking prick alright."

We were late for school, I pulled up on the verge just as the kids were filing in to class. The mums all stared at me, whispering like usual – probably commenting on my sack of shit parenting skills – but none of that mattered. None of their bullshit ideals had ever meant shit to me.

"Be good," I said as I waved her off. "No garage words, alright? Try your hardest not to butt-hurt anyone."

She rolled her eyes. "I'll try," she leaned in close, put her hands around her mouth. "But butt-hurting stupid idiots is so fun."

She gave me the thumbs-up, and I couldn't stop laughing all the way to the fucking yard.

That girl was my fucking daughter, alright.

The lads were already at work when I got there. The banter eased up as I stepped through the shutters, just the sound of the radio blaring out the same old shit.

"Alright?" I said.

"Yeah," Buck said. "Opened up early. Just getting our heads down, got shit-loads on."

I counted the breakdowns lined up outside. "Good call."

He cleared his throat. "We were hoping for a bit of time, if Eleanor..."

I nodded. "Get this backlog down, then."

Petey dished out the drinks, then got down to it, checked out the diagnostics set up with Buck. He was learning, I could see it. Good lad.

I wondered how he was going with Lorraine, then checked myself. It was none of my business how he was getting on with Lorraine, none of my business how he was getting on with any of it.

I didn't want it to be my business.

Not anymore.

I checked out Cheryl Neath's old blue Fiesta outside. The thing was fucked. Head gasket. Poor cow. I slammed the bonnet closed as an engine purred onto our yard. Nice, but no Porsche, thank fuck.

Lee Pullen was behind the wheel of a big silver Audi convertible. He pulled up next to me, wearing shades in fucking October, daft prick.

"What do you think?" he said.

I can't stand convertibles. Wouldn't have one if someone fucking paid me, but I gave him a nod.

"She's alright, yeah. My Ruby would go mad for her, she loves Audis."

"A girl with taste," he said.

I gave it a look, thing must have set him back a small fucking fortune, the car was only just past warranty, judging by the plates.

"Was hoping you'd check her over for me. Got a month's no quibble guarantee from the dealer."

"Can do," I said. I tipped my head towards the empty spot in the garage. "Pull her in there." He parked her up and handed me the keys. "Pick her up end of day," I said. "I'll get on it after lunch."

He slapped my arm. "Cheers, Trent."

The lads were impressed, I could tell. I was more interested in making sure Ruby got to see it, maybe even give her a spin with the roof down. Needed to test drive the thing anyway. She'd love that.

The next job was a fucking nightmare, had to get Petey to give me a hand with the hoist, taking the whole bastard engine out of a Mercedes. I was covered in oil in no time, black with the fucking stuff before Petey had made the next round of tea.

I heard another car pull onto the yard, turned my head in recognition. No fucking way. My heart beat faster, my stomach doing this daft sappy flip.

Jodie looked great. Her hair was glossy and straight, her smile bright. She was wearing tight black jeans with her old sandals, a floaty blouse with a beaded necklace that made her look like she was from one of those holiday brochures.

She got a box from the backseat and I met her by the doors.

I'd never have known she was nervous if I didn't know her so well, hadn't noticed the flush on her neck.

The lads gave her a wave but laid off the whistling. Just as well.

"You alright?" I said. "Girls alright?"

She nodded. "I was just..." She didn't look at me. "Nanna wanted a bacon and egg sandwich, so I went to the shop, on a mission..." Her eyes crept up. "I was going to go to ladies who lunch, but Nanna hasn't asked for breakfast in ages... and I thought... I thought I may as well..." The smell hit me as she lifted the top of the box. Five sandwiches, wrapped up nice in foil. "For you, and the guys."

"Thanks," I said. "That's really nice, Jo."

I took the box from her and handed it to Buck to dish out, and she smiled as the guys called thanks. Then she hovered.

"...It was no trouble, I was cooking anyway. I mean I have Monday mornings off... usually... it's my free time..." She cleared her throat. Looked really shifty. "Are you... busy?"

"Mondays always are," I said.

She nodded. "Sorry, yeah... of course... I'd, um... I'd better leave you to it."

She wouldn't look at me.

I noticed her lipstick, the way she was so made up. I caught a whiff of perfume, the expensive shit she gets from her mum every Christmas. She had her best earrings in, the set Nanna bought for her 21st birthday, I could see them sparkling through her hair. Her nails were the same bronze colour as the beads around her neck.

She pointed to the Audi. "Ruby would go crazy for that."

"I'll take her out for a spin in it later."

"She'll love you forever."

I gave her a nod, a smile. Still she didn't move. She brushed her hair behind her ear, jangled her car keys in her hand, but didn't move.

"What you really doing here?" I asked, my voice low. "This isn't just about bacon sandwiches, Jo, is it?"

She sighed, and her cheeks were pink. She smiled to herself and shook her head, then stepped away, heading back to her car with quick little steps. "I'd better leave you to it," she said.

I headed her off before she could get in, and I felt as awkward as she looked, my mouth dry at the thought of reading this shit wrong.

But no. There's plenty of shit I get wrong, but knowing when a woman's after my dick isn't ever on that list.

"Jo..." I began. "Let's call a spanner a fucking spanner a second, shall we?" I looked her up and down. "If I didn't know better, I'd almost think you were trying to bag yourself a bit of rough on a Monday morning." My eyes met hers and locked there. Her pupils were big and dark, her breath shallow. "There wouldn't be any truth in that, would there?"

She looked so fucking embarrassed, and so fucking pretty for it.

"Enjoy your breakfast, Darren," she said. She made to sidestep me, but there was no fucking way.

I moved between her and the car door, and we collided. She recoiled with a smile, but I leaned into her. I could smell her perfume so strong, her shampoo too. Her hair was soft against my cheek.

Uneasiness in my gut. A sense of sadness as the prospect dawned.

I whispered, right into her ear. "What's this about, Jo? You wanting to jump the queue or what?" I felt her stiffen, shoulders tense. "If this is about a Bang Gang special..."

She was shaking her head before I finished. She pulled away enough to meet my eyes. "Jesus, Darren. No! This isn't about a bloody gangbang! I didn't even..." She sighed. "This was stupid. Sorry." She reached for the handle. "I don't know what's come over me this morning. Ridiculous."

Me. I'll come over you this morning.

My voice was just a growl in her ear. "I'm less than ten seconds from hauling your pretty ass over to that Audi and fucking you on the bonnet." I felt her take a breath. "Tell me that's not why you're here. Tell me I've got it wrong."

Her heart was racing. I could feel it. "I wanted... I want..."

"Go on," I prompted. "Just fucking say it, Jo."

I wrapped my arm around her waist, grabbed her ass and hitched her against me. My cock pressed to her belly and she gasped.

"I came here for you," she whispered. "I wanted..."

I tangled my oily fingers in her hair, and it felt so fucking good. "Say it."

"I wanted..." Her eyes were wide, her lips just a breath from mine.

"Oh God, please just fuck me, Darren."

I smirked, and then I kissed her, hard.

The guys roared out a cheer. I gave them the finger, and Jodie giggled against my mouth. I took her hand in mine, led her over to the shutters.

"It's break time," I said to the lads. "Go eat your bacon in the truck."

They downed tools and bailed, slapping me on the back as they went.

I made a move as soon as Buck pulled down the shutters on his way out. Jodie squealed as I grabbed her, laughed as I lifted her clean up and dropped her pretty ass onto the Audi's bonnet.

She didn't laugh long.

I kissed her as I unbuttoned her blouse, hands grubby and frantic as she moaned into my mouth. I yanked down the floaty fabric and threw it aside, lowered my head and bit and nipped at her nipples through the lace of her bra. She tipped her head back, her fingers in my hair.

"*Darren...*"

I unbuttoned her jeans, tugged them down, and she wriggled to help them on their way. She kicked her sandals off, and the jeans followed them. She wrapped her legs around my waist, picking up oil from my clothes. I ran my fingers over the smears, then up to her pussy, left darker smears on her white lace knickers.

"*Fuck! Yes... Yes!*"

I'd forgotten this.

I'd forgotten how dirty Jodie could be.

I fucking loved how dirty Jodie could be.

I ditched the top half of my overalls, loosened my jeans, and her hands were waiting for my cock.

"*Fuck me,*" she hissed. "*Hard, Darren. Really fucking hard...*"

No fucking fear.

I tugged her knickers aside and she groaned as I sank my dick into her. I pushed her backwards onto the bonnet, thrust in real fucking deep as she squirmed against the paintwork.

"*Fuck... oh fuck, Darren!*"

How I fucking slammed that pussy. Jesus Christ, I fucked her so fucking hard. She jerked with every thrust, her tits bobbing in those lacy cups, her bottom lip pinched between her teeth as she took it.

I flipped her long before I came, rolled her right onto her front and flattened her to the metal. Her feet touched the ground but didn't last long there. My first thrust took her balance and she jolted forwards, her cheek pressed to the bonnet. I took a handful of hair and pulled, forcing her right back onto my cock, and she loved it, she fucking loved it.

I reached round for her clit, strummed that wet little bud until her legs were shaking. The sound of my skin slapping hers was fucking bliss.

I folded over until she took my weight, kept hold of her hair as my body pinned hers.

"Is this what you wanted?" I hissed. "Nice hard fucking dick?"

She moaned for me. Shuddered under me.

"*You!*" she said. "I wanted *you!*"

"And four other cocks along with me?"

She shook her head. "No." Her teeth were gritted. "Just you. That's what I want! That's what I fucking want, Darren!"

"Just as well," I snarled. "Because no other man's cock is going near your tight little cunt again, Jodie."

She twisted her head.

"I mean it," I said. "You'll have another fucking gangbang over my dead fucking body, I fucking swear it."

I pressed my lips to her ear, breathing hard, like she was breathing under me.

"I'm... I'm not on the list?" she hissed.

My balls tightened, threatened to shoot my fucking load all the way inside her.

There is no fucking list, Jodie, not for me.

"No. You're not on the fucking list, Jodie. You'll never be on the fucking list."

She cried out as I changed position, hands braced against the windscreen, leaving sweaty palm smears.

I was hitting my home stride now, thighs tight as fucking wire. I wrapped my hand around her throat, held her there, held her tight. The beads around her neck made a lovely rattle as I pounded her.

My fingers kept teasing her clit, quick little flicks until she moaned, flailing under me as the waves of climax ripped through her.

And then I came.

Deep.

All the way inside that perfect pussy.

Mine.

I claimed her, pumped her full of me, made sure that sweet little slit ate me up.

We lay panting, my clammy chest against her back. We lay panting until she giggled, and I laughed, too.

She rolled under me, wrapped her arms around my neck and pulled me in for a kiss.

"I'll take this over ladies who lunch any bloody day," she said.

I kissed her over and over, all the way through getting dressed and making our way back to the shutters.

I was grinning like a fucking lunatic, couldn't fucking stop myself, didn't ever want to stop myself, until I heard the engine.

I'd already committed myself, already engaged the catch.

Oh shit.

Eleanor slipped out of the driver's seat, shot me a smile that dried up as soon as Jodie stepped out from the garage.

I could have fucking died when the women clocked each other. They stared for a couple of seconds, neither saying a word, not to each other and not to me either.

Jodie fastened up the last of my overalls, then leaned in and kissed my dirty cheek. I wrapped my arm around her and gave her a squeeze.

"I'll be seeing you soon, Darren Trent," she said.

She stared at Eleanor Hartwell all the way to her car, a strange little smile on her face, and Eleanor looked like a slapped arse, her lips pursed and her cheeks bright pink.

She watched Jodie slip into the driver's seat. Glared as Jodie did her lipstick in the rearview.

"Another client?" she said. "I thought Mondays were busy, Trent? You told me Mondays were a no go!"

I smirked at her.

"That's not a fucking client, Eleanor," I said. "That's my fucking missus."

I let her pick her own jaw up from the floor.

CHAPTER TWENTY ONE

JODIE

I dashed into town to grab Nanna's pills with a big 'ole smile on my face.

Porsche-bitch had seen a different woman staring back at her today. Not the dowdy, defeated, meek little shell of myself she'd dismissed as nothing, oh no. Today she'd seen *me*, and she'd balked. I'd seen it in her eyes, in the purse of her fake pout. No amount of money, no posh car or Botox or expensive makeup could bring me down, not anymore.

I knew he wouldn't fuck her. Not right then, not there, not with his balls freshly emptied and my sweaty hand prints all over that Audi. Not even for the sake of the money. Maybe I was naive. Maybe I was being stupidly optimistic. But, no. I just knew it.

Porsche-bitch wouldn't be getting anything from Darren Trent. Not today.

A small victory, but I enjoyed it. Bigger battles were on the horizon, a whole assault course of issues with our names written all over them, but I pushed those aside and sang along to the radio, enjoying the knowledge that I'd put myself out there and he'd wanted me right back. Enjoying the sensation of my well-fucked pussy, too. I was still full of him.

Shit.

Probably nothing to worry about. I tried to remember the purple shaded ovulation dates on my period app – I'm sure I was safe enough.

The traffic was godawful and the queue for Nanna's pills was long – the woman behind the counter was busy for an age, yapping on about athlete's foot to some old guy who wouldn't stop asking questions.

I checked the time.

Late.

Shit.

I raced back to work and Lorraine pulled a sour face at me.

"Nice of you to show," she said.

"Sorry," I said. "Nanna's pills took ages. I'll make up the time."

Ten minutes, it was only ten minutes.

She took it out on me all afternoon, and it was unlike her. The whole thing was off.

I grabbed her by the arm when there was a lull in customers.

"Have I done something?" I said. "I mean, I know I was late, but you seem..."

She stared at me for ages and then she sighed. "Sorry, Jodie, it's just... I'm concerned."

"Concerned?"

She put a hand on her hip. "I thought you were past all this running around after Darren Trent. I thought you'd moved on. I *hoped* you'd moved on, for your sake."

My cheeks burned, the memory of bailing from the taxi, drunk, ignoring Lorraine's efforts to deliver me back to mine.

"I'm not *running around* after Darren, we're just... exploring our options."

She slapped her hand on the counter, and it took me aback. "Exploring your options?! With that fucking loser? He's nothing but a player! He's a fucking disgrace!" She caught herself, shook her head. "Sorry, Jo, I just... I didn't want to say anything..."

My heart dropped. The expression on her face said it all.

"What?" I said.

She let out a sigh. "I tried to book my car in for some tyres last week, and do you know how long it would have taken him to fit me in?"

I shrugged. "I have no idea."

"Three weeks," she said. "Three weeks for some poxy tyres. You know why?"

"I guess they're pretty busy..."

"Busy fucking anything with a pulse. I had to go into town in the end. Seriously, Jodie, he should remember he's got a business to run down there, should try putting his dick back in his pants every now and again and getting some *real* work done."

I cleared my throat, ignored the paranoia in my belly. "They were doing real work earlier when I went down there. Plenty of cars booked in. Maybe you just caught him on a busy day?"

Real work apart from Porsche-bitch.

The thought of a string of women down there made me feel queasy.

She scoffed, pulled a face. "That's what he tells you, is it? Open your eyes, Jodie. The guy's a fucking loser."

"He doesn't tell me anything, that's just what I saw for myself."

279

"He's fucked at least twenty of our regulars, I've heard all the gory details. He's putting it about like he's some kind of fucking porn star, doesn't have any regard for safe sex either, from what I've heard. You know, Mandy Taylor says he..."

I really didn't want to hear what Mandy Taylor had to say about anything.

I held up a hand. "I appreciate your concern, Lorraine, really I do, but Darren and I have to sort through this crap for ourselves. I'd rather find out the score from him than worry about what big-mouth Mandy has to say. She's hardly reliable."

Her eyes were so angry. "And Trent is?"

I met her glare. "He's not a liar, Lorraine. If I ask him, he'll tell me."

She scoffed at me. "And you're going to ask him, are you?"

"We'll need to talk about it at some point."

"And then what?!"

"I don't know..." I said.

She grabbed a cloth, started wiping the counter vigorously. "I thought better of you than to consider getting back with a loser like him, Jodie, for the girls' sake if not for your own."

I had nothing to say, and it felt like shit. The whole thing felt terrible.

She didn't ease up with the torrent. "You may think it's noble to get back with the father of your children but believe me it's not. Not if their father is a total waste of space like Trent. He's fucking everyone in the village, Jodie, at least have a little respect for yourself."

"I'm not trying to be noble, Lorraine."

"Just as well, Jo, because you're falling way short."

I remembered all the times I'd cried on her shoulder when I first left him, how strong she'd been for me. I remembered all the times she'd told me to stand firm, for the girls and for myself, how we deserved better, how we deserved more...

"I know you don't like him, Lorraine, I know that." *But I do.* "I know things were bad before we split, I know you were there for me..."

"Doesn't seem to matter, though, does it? You're *still* chasing round after the waste of space all these years later."

"Lorraine... I just..." *I love him.*

The bell above the door tinged as a gaggle of school mums came in. I breathed in relief.

I willed them to order everything on the menu, just to keep us busy through to the end of my shift, but they wanted coffees and nothing else. I kept my distance from Lorraine, nursing my own frazzled spirit.

Up and down, up and down, up and down.

I was all churned up, sick to the stomach at the thought of him fucking someone else, yet still high at the sensation of him taking me, wanting me, staying last night when he would have usually run...

The high of loving him, the low of knowing he was giving out to anyone who was paying... the high of another chance at the love we lost, the low of knowing he'd loved another after me... more than me...

The ring still in the drawer.

The way he looked at me. The way he touched me. The way Darren Trent made me feel so alive.

The way he loved our girls. The way he'd defended Mia. The way he was there.

Mandy fucking Taylor.

I watched the clock. Only an hour until closing, but the minutes seemed to take hours. I scrubbed down tables to keep out of Lorraine's way, hoping she wouldn't try and pick up the cruddy conversation where we left off.

I was rearranging condiments when a car horn sounded outside. I stepped to the window and looked out at the street, expecting some kind of tractor-related traffic queue, but instead the big silver Audi swung into the carpark and stopped in front of the cafe doors. The horn sounded again, and I couldn't help but grin at the sight of my girls in the backseat, Nanna sitting between them with her pink silk headscarf knotted tight under her chin. This wasn't the weather for the roof down, not really, but they were clearly loving it. All of them.

Ruby saw me and pointed, said something to Darren, and they all waved. He beeped the horn again and beckoned me outside.

"What are you doing?" I called from the doorway.

"Taking the car for a spin," Darren shouted. "Room for one more." He patted the empty passenger seat.

"Come on, Mum!" Ruby shouted. "We're going to the mountains! Like on Top Gear!"

"I can't!" I laughed. "I have work!"

Darren beeped the horn again. "Come on!" he called.

I looked back inside the cafe, at the customers standing at the window. Lorraine was there, too, and she was scowling. *Oh hell.*

A car full of smiles and gestures, Nanna's face so happy. There were only a couple of customers, hardly anything, Lorraine could definitely cope.

I couldn't look at her as I rushed back to the counter and ditched my apron. "Can I go?" I said. "Please? I know it's early but I'll make up the time... I'll come in early tomorrow if you need me..."

She was glaring, I could feel it. I grabbed my bag and my coat, slipped it on as I made my way back out. I met Lorraine's eyes before I left, willing her to let me go.

She sighed. "If you must."

Yes. Yes, I must.

"Thanks," I said. "I'll make it up."

I raced out to the car and dropped into the passenger seat with a laugh. "Drive!" I said. "Before Lorraine changes her mind!"

Darren nodded, then indicated, pulled out onto the street. I fastened my seatbelt, cheeks burning at the memory of the car's cold bonnet against my naked tits, my palms against the windscreen as Darren pounded me. The smirk on his face told me he was remembering it too.

"Ooh, Jodie! We're going for a lovely drive!" Nanna said. She was so excited, giggling away as Darren picked up speed.

I loved him for making Nanna so happy. The girls, too. Loved him for coming for me.

He drove us out to the main Abergavenny road and put his foot down. The car growled and surged forward, and I laughed, lifted my hands in the air until the wind whipped them. The girls were laughing, and Nanna was, too, and in the spirit of the moment I reached out and squeezed Darren's knee.

He moved his hand from the wheel and gripped mine tight.

We were doing this. *Us.* Really doing it. At least, that's what it felt like.

The road through the Brecon Beacons was magical. Rugged mountains, moody under the grey sky. The wind whipping my hair as Darren pushed the car through the bends, driving hard enough that Ruby whooped in the backseat. *You're better than Clarkson, Dad!* she said.

I watched his chest puff up. Oh to be so idolised by our little girl. I felt his pride.

My hair was a mess by the time we pulled up at home, but I didn't even care. I sent the girls and Nanna on inside, said I'd be coming along right after them.

"Thanks for the ride," I said to Darren. "It was great."

"Which one?" He smirked.

"Both of them," I admitted.

"Any time." He looked right at me, and I wondered if he was going to kiss me, right there, right then, with the roof still down and the whole street in clear view.

He didn't.

"Girls are on half term break next week, remember?" I said. "I guess Ruby has already booked herself in at the garage."

He nodded. "You know it."

I cleared my throat, made myself broach the subject. "Will she be alright? I mean, if you have any... *services*... I don't want her to..."

"She'll be fine, Jo. She won't be seeing anything."

"Right," I said. "Ok, I guess I'll be seeing you."

"That you will," he said.

Come inside, have some dinner, stay with us... it was on the tip of my tongue, but he put the car back in gear.

"Best be getting this thing back to Lee. Said I'd have her back by six."

I smiled, and bailed out. I gave one last look at the bonnet, and my stomach did a flip. "Thanks again, Darren, for everything today."

"No bother," he said.

He beeped the horn long and loud before he disappeared out of view.

TRENT

Are you ignoring me? Don't ignore me, Darren. We need to talk.

Another pissing message from Lorraine. I'd been ignoring them for days, ever since I took Jo from work in the Audi. The stupid daft cow wouldn't give it a rest.

I shoved my phone back in my pocket and helped Ruby hold the screwdriver steady.

"Like this, Rubes," I said, adjusting her fingers around the handle. "Get a better grip."

It was only a little job, a brake light bulb change, but she may as well have been replacing an engine for the amount of pride she was taking in it.

I nodded to Sally Vickers, the owner of the motor Ruby was currently working on. "Our newest recruit," I said. "Best service you'll get."

She laughed. "She's really something."

I ruffled Ruby's hair. "Say that when you've got working lights."

"I know what I'm *doing*, Dad!" Ruby groaned.

She really fucking did as well, had them changed in no time.

I rang Mia once Sally was off, she answered in a flash. Good girl.

"Where are you?" I said.

She sighed. "Daisy's. Same as I was last time you called."

"Righto," I said. "Call you later."

Buck shook his head. "Leave the kid alone," he said. "Jesus,

Trent, you can't check up on her every bloody hour."

"Yes I fucking can," I said. "She's twelve."

"Nearly a teenager," he said. "You'll be cramping her style, man."

"Too damn right I'll be cramping her fucking style," I said. "That's my fucking job."

I slapped him on the back as I passed, and he rolled his pissing eyes at me.

I'd been wary of letting Mia off on her own this school holiday, even if she was joined at the hip to Daisy and a load of other kids whose names I'd never pissing heard before. Jodie said it was to be expected, that all her friends were doing it, that we had to trust her to live a little for herself. I can't say I liked the idea, though.

She may have looked older than her years, but she was still only twelve. *Thirteen,* Jodie kept saying. *Almost thirteen, Darren.* She should be playing tea parties with Mr Fluff and watching cartoons, not traipsing round the village without anyone to keep an eye on her.

Relax, Jodie kept saying. *It's only the village, Darren, she'll be fine.*

I was calling her on the hour, every hour, and I'd keep bloody doing it, too.

My phone pinged again. It was Lorraine a-fucking-gain.

Darren?! I wasn't joking. I need to talk to you.

I sent Ruby over to help Hugh, and lit up a cigarette.

I'm busy, I replied.

Busy fucking Jodie? Chasing her around like a sappy little spaniel? I get it, Trent. More fool you.

Another message. *You'll want to hear me out.*

I thought about deleting her number, sending her one final *fuck off* message and leaving it at that, but another message pinged before I could.

It's about Jodie.

I replied quickly. Probably too quickly. *What about Jodie?*

She stalled for a couple of minutes that felt like fucking hours.

In person only, Darren. This isn't for text.

Bitch.

A blot on an otherwise perfect fucking landscape.

A few days from the rally weekend and things were looking good. It was always hectic when the kids were off school, but Jodie had managed to slip out twice to mine already this week.

It was becoming a regular thing.

So regular that this *play it by ear* shit needed to come to a head one way or another. But I was nervous, like a stupid teenager, scared of blowing my chances by handling things too hard too soon.

I had a habit of doing that.

All I pissing needed was for Lorraine to put a spanner in the works. Rather she come to me than try to screw things up Jodie's end. Fuck knows what the bitch wanted from me.

Although I had an inkling.

Tonight, I said. *Come to mine. You'd best not be shitting me, Lorraine.*

I got back to work and didn't give the cow the courtesy of another fucking thought.

CHAPTER TWENTY TWO

TRENT

I swung the door open without any niceties, ignoring the fact that Lorraine was dressed in her finest with a bottle of wine in her hand. Like I ever fucking drank the stuff.

"What do you want?" I grunted.

She tutted, brushed past me and went to the kitchen like she owned the place. She took out two glasses and uncorked the bottle, pouring two hefty fucking measures. She held hers up.

"It's been a while, Darren. Cheers."

I pushed the second glass away from me, shunted it across the counter.

"What's this about?"

She smiled, pretended this was a regular thing. Like fuck it was. "It's about you. Me. *Us*..."

I couldn't hide my disgust. "There is no *us*, Lorraine. There's never been an *us*..."

"No," she said. "Because there's always been a *Jodie*, and I'm sick of it Darren, I'm sick of watching you chase after her like she's Mother fucking Mary, like she can do no fucking wrong."

I laughed. "Mother fucking Mary? I think she'd surprise you."

"*No*," she snapped. "I think she'd surprise *you*."

Her eyes twinkled, that smug grin plastered on her face as she sipped at her wine. She was a know it all, but I was done. I'd had enough of this shit.

I pulled my cigarettes from my jeans. "I'm gonna have a smoke. You've got a couple of minutes to either drink your wine and get out of my face, or tell me what the fuck you're really doing here."

"Don't be like that..."

I walked straight down the hall, practically launched the front door from its hinges. I was halfway through my cigarette when I heard her heels behind me. I didn't bother turning around.

"You want her, don't you?" she said, and there was that tone again, that condescending fucking tone she's always used around me. "You want to move back home, and get her to play little wifey, cooking and cleaning and looking pretty around the house while you go and bang half the fucking village and play a dirty bit of rough for anyone who's willing to pay for it."

"What I want with Jodie is none of your fucking business, Lorraine."

"Oh, but it is," she said. "I'm Jodie's boss, *practically* her best friend... and you and me... well, we're..." Her fingers trailed up my spine as she stepped around me.

I glared at her. "We're nothing. I offer a service, you paid for it. End of."

"*Offered*. Last I heard, you couldn't get it up."

I took a drag. "Yeah, like that sounds likely."

She bit her lip, raised an eyebrow. "Hope not, Trent. Hope you're not losing your touch. Maybe you need some more lessons..." Her hand shot to my crotch and squeezed. I grabbed her wrist, pushed her away. "Don't be coy," she said. "Not like I haven't seen it all before, baby. You're everything you are now because of me... Jodie's reaping the benefits and she doesn't even know it..."

"I'm done," I said. "With all of it. I'm done with you."

"Sure you are..."

"I am. Think what you fucking like, Lorraine. It's over."

"And that's it, is it? No more clients, no more *Bang Gang*, no more cash lump sums you can use to treat that cute little *family* of yours? Is my money not good enough for you all of a sudden? You've taken enough of it."

"Can't speak for the rest of the lads," I said. "Give Buck a call. I couldn't give a shit."

"I don't want a four-way, Trent, and you know it." Her eyes were full of spite. "But Jodie does... In fact, I don't think she'd care if you were there or not from the sounds of it..."

I looked right at her. "What the fuck are you talking about?"

She sighed, full of drama. "I didn't want to tell you, but I can't stand by and let you make a fool of yourself, even *I'm* not that cruel." I waited for it. "I know you may think this is about *you,* Darren, but she's using you. She doesn't see you as any more of a *keeper* than I do. You're just a piece of rough to her, same as you are for everyone else. She wants a gangbang just the same as every other cheap slut in this village, only she won't tell you that, will she? It's not as if she can afford one..."

I kept my gaze steady. "You think she's only with me because she wants to have a free fucking gangbang, Lorraine? That's seriously what you think?"

She grinned, triumphant. "That's what I *know.* She told me as much. She told me she'd never be with you, not properly, not with you being such a loser, such a liability, such a *player*."

"But she wants to fuck the rest of the guys? I'm just a free meal ticket?"

She nodded. "She's a woman finding herself again. It's only natural, Darren. She has needs and no means of paying for them, of *course* she's using you... It's clear she wants an *actual* relationship, just not with you. She needs someone who can be a proper role model to those girls, and she knows it... but in the meantime she's... out to have fun... at your expense, it would seem."

I flicked my cigarette away. "And when did she tell you all this?"

"Only the past few days, or I would have come sooner..."

"Let me get this straight. Jodie told you that she's only using me to get a shot at a gangbang with the guys, and she told you this a few days back?"

"I guess the gossip has finally reached her. Turned her head. Like I said, it's only natural she should want what other women are having." She smiled at me. "See how ridiculous you're being? How pathetic? Thinking she wants you when she only wants your cock, yours *and* your mates'..."

"Clear off," I said. "Now."

Her mouth dropped open. "What? Oh, come on, Darren! You can't seriously want to take this out on me. Don't shoot the pissing messenger!"

"Like hell you're a fucking messenger, Lorraine, you're nothing but a cheap liar."

She folded her arms. "I'm not lying, Trent. That's what she wants, you just can't accept it. Don't be a fool! She's using you! Laughing at you!"

I leaned in close, my mouth to her ear, and my voice was full of fucking malice. "The only person who's taking me for a fucking fool around here, Lorraine, is you." I brushed past her and stepped back inside, making it damn well clear she wasn't invited to follow me. "It's over, you and me," I said. "So stay out of my fucking face, and stay out of Jodie's too."

"Darren! Just hear me out! You're angry, I know, but you're making a big..."

I slammed the door before I could hear any more of her shit.

I nearly sent Jodie a message right there and then, nearly told her exactly what a conniving little cunt Lorraine really was, but to do that I'd have to tell all. I'd have to hash up all the sorry details of the long seedy history between me and that fucking woman, a woman I should never have touched with a fucking barge pole.

I'd have to tell her that I'd been fucking Lorraine in secret for years, that the majority of the cash in the box under my bed was from her seedy advances, that she'd been the one to orchestrate the whole fucking lot of it.

And Jodie thought they were friends.

They weren't fucking friends.

I tried to type it out, tried to say what I needed to say, but everything sounded shit. I've never been fucking good with words.

I changed my message to a general *we need to talk* that sounded so fucking ominous I didn't want to send it. And then what? If I did? I tell her about Lorraine and what? We weren't even together, not yet, not definitely. Something like this could put a spanner in the works before we'd even had a shot, before we'd even given ourselves a fair fucking chance of making something real again.

What if Jodie took Lorraine's side?

She wouldn't. Couldn't. Not with a bitch like her.

But would she believe me? Why would she believe me? She hadn't even trusted me with Mia's fucking bullying issues.

I hated to think what fucking shit Lorraine would whisper in her ear.

I smoked another cigarette when the cow had finally fucked off, and another after that. I needed to tell Jodie something, needed to warn her, but now wasn't the time.

We had the rally weekend coming up, in person would be better, talk her through it when I could see her face and she could see mine. Tell her it didn't mean anything, that Lorraine didn't mean anything, tell her that I wasn't even Bang Ganging anymore, hadn't been since she first came over.

I'd tell her everything. Lay it all out on the table.

Nothing like breaking the habit of a fucking lifetime.

JODIE

We were all packed up, my poor little Ford bursting to the seams with tents and sleeping bags and a million supplies we'd probably never need. I'd left Nanna with kind Maisie Harris, who came to do her toenails every month. She didn't mind house sitting, she'd said. No *need* to house sit, so Nanna said, but I wasn't convinced.

"I can't believe we're actually camping," Tonya said for the hundredth time. "We haven't been camping since that time we went out to the cider festival with Trent and Buck when we were kids. I still remember you puking behind the bandstand after too many vodkas."

"Urgh," Mia said from the back. "You got drunk, Mum?"

Daisy giggled, and Mia did, too. Two giggly peas in a very small pod, those two.

"It's an exaggeration," I lied. "I think I had a dodgy hotdog."

"Probably that, yeah," Tonya said, and flashed me a grin.

I wondered if Darren was there already. I guessed he was, and all the guys with him, at least that's what Ruby claimed. I imagined he was already hard at work, doing all the car stuff, whatever stuff needed to be done with these rally cars.

The event was signposted for miles, and we pulled up into open fields that had been segregated into camping areas. The attendant pointed us over to a spot in the corner, and Ruby squealed in excitement as we got out of the car. People were already setting up tents around us, so we grabbed ours from the car and marked out a spot. I still couldn't believe I was doing this.

Tonya opened a bottle of cheap fizz as I arranged the tent poles, handed me one in a crappy plastic tumbler. I couldn't stop laughing.

"Jesus, Tonya, it's not even ten a.m."

"Start as we mean to go on," she said and clinked my glass. "Cheers."

I took a courtesy sip and placed the tumbler on the car roof. "Let's get set up."

She downed hers. "Sure thing."

I was wrestling tarpaulin when Ruby's voice rang out. "It's Buck! Buckkkk! Over here!"

I couldn't help but notice how quickly Tonya pulled her head from under the canopy. Like a brother my arse.

Ruby was already hanging off his hip, yapping in his ear about her dad, and how brilliant this was going to be, and how many cars were there. He had infinite patience, answering her every question with a smile. I loved Buck for that. He'd always had so much time for the girls.

I watched him hitch her onto his shoulders and point into the distance.

"There he is!" Ruby shrieked. "Mum! Dad's over there!"

Those bloody butterflies started up again. "I'll catch up with your dad later, Ruby. We've got to get this bloody tent up, unless you want to sleep in the car."

Buck dropped Ruby at my side. "I'll give you a hand," he said.

He did, too. He had the tent up in no time, then blew up our airbeds with the foot pump without even breaking a sweat.

Mia and Daisy hovered, whispering into each other's ears before Mia found voice enough to ask if they could go *chill* amongst the crowds.

"Alright," I said. "But not far." I handed her a tenner for some drinks, and she put her hand on her hip like she was the coolest kid in town. The Daisy effect.

"Thanks, Mum. We'll stay off the hard stuff." Cue the laughter.

At least she was smiling again.

They checked their makeup in the rearview mirror before they left, and my heart gave a weird pang. My little girl, far too grown up for comfort. I waved them off.

Tonya sighed. "When did she get so bloody old?"

"I was just thinking the same thing," I said.

Ruby squeezed my hand. "Can I go with Buck? To find Dad?"

"Alright," I said. "Be good though, stay out of his way. He's working."

"Yeah yeah, I do *know*," she said.

I watched her leave, her little hand in Buck's big one, telling him all about the wonder of life the universe and all the cars in it.

I was a million miles away when Tonya nudged my ribs. She handed me my drink from the car roof and I relented, let myself smile.

"Cheers," I said, and downed the thing in one.

TRENT

I was busy as fuck, getting cars tuned up ready to go, but not too busy to hoist Rubes up on my shoulders and point out the track when she came running. She was a ball of energy, her voice higher than usual, squealing at this and that, cars and drivers, and stalls of merchandise.

"Be a good girl and give me a hand, will you?" I said, and her face lit up.

I got her passing me tools, and she took it proper seriously, eyebrows pitted in concentration as I barked out orders.

I sent her off with Buck and Hugh when the event started, told them to keep an eye on her. Off she went, swinging off their arms as she skipped between them. My heart swelled up, so proud I could burst, and there amongst it was Jodie. She was everywhere, right the way through me.

I kept an eye out for her, but I didn't spot her, not until I'd taken a break and slumped on the grass with a cold beer. I heard Tonya first, and her laugh told me she'd been drinking. My eyes followed the sound, and I caught a flash of cherry red amongst the crowd. My gut did that sappy flip.

They headed in my direction, talking and laughing, and didn't see me until they were almost on top of me. Tonya saw me before Jodie did, and nudged Jodie in the arm.

I loved the way Jodie lit up when she saw it was me. The smile that crept across her face said too much, and I suspected she'd had a couple with Tonya.

"Hey," she said.

"Alright," I said.

I got to my feet, wiped oily hands on my jeans. I wanted to pull her close, wrap my arms around her and kiss her like she was mine, but I didn't.

"Tent all set up?" I asked.

She nodded. "Yeah, Buck helped." She pointed to the field beyond. "We're in the corner, just over there."

I gestured to the opposite corner of the same field. "We're over that way."

"Great," she said. "Well, I guess we'll be... seeing you around..."

"Righto," I said, then cursed myself. I stumbled over words, so many of them. *Do you want a drink, Jo? A hotdog? Want to drink vodka with me until you're sick behind the bandstand and I have to hold your hair back? I kissed you after, do you remember? Do you remember me carrying you back to the tent and holding you all night long?*

She brushed her hair behind her ear. "We'll be... um... around later, I guess... if you're not too busy."

"I'll be around," I said. "I'd like that, Jo."

Tonya let out a laugh. "Jesus, you two. Maybe at this rate you'll get together sometime in the next ten bloody years."

Jodie's cheeks flushed pink, and I stared at the grass, ran my hand through my hair. Ridiculous, this was fucking ridiculous. I felt like a fucking kid again, trying to work out whether the fuck she liked me or not.

"The girls," Jodie said. "Have you seen them?"

"Rubes is with Buck and Hugh. Haven't seen Mia." I looked around the crowds. "Where is Mia?"

"Relax," she said. "She's with Daisy, I'm sure they're fine."

I couldn't help but scowl. "There's a lot of people here, Jo, a lot of people drinking, a lot of lads."

She rolled her eyes. "She'll be fine, Darren. She's nearly a teenager, I'm sure she can get some Cokes and hotdogs and wander around with Daisy."

I wasn't so fucking sure, but I bit my tongue. She saw my reservations a mile off.

"I'll find her," she said. "Make sure she's alright. Ok?"

"Alright," I said. "Thanks."

I spotted Jimmy O on the approach, Petey at his side. Jo saw them too. She waved to them, but made an exit, told me she'd see me later.

I watched her through the crowd until she disappeared out of sight.

JODIE

For a rally event, given that I don't know shit about cars, and struggle to be all that interested in them, the afternoon was a lot of fun. I had a couple of glasses of light fizz with Tonya, grabbed burgers for us and the girls, and checked in with Nanna who told me she was doing just fine.

It felt so strange to relax. It felt so strange to be me again, away from normal regular life. We sat on some fold up chairs and laughed about times gone by, and Ruby listened to every word, asked about her dad, asked about how we met, how we knew we loved each other.

I told her the truth.

That I'd known I'd loved her dad long before I reached out and took his hand on the way to get fish and chips. I'd known I'd loved him when he'd looked at me with eyes that said I meant something, with the same stare he'd been looking at me with ever since. I'd known I'd loved her father since he'd walked along the river with me and told me that nobody had ever made him laugh the way I made him laugh, and his face had lit up and I knew he meant it.

I always knew he meant it.

I knew Darren Trent inside out and back again.

And there he was, on the edge of the field, stood in a crowd with the other guys, trademark cigarette in his mouth as he laughed at some joke or other. I pulled my coat tighter around me, teeth chattering a little against the chill as the sun went down, and his eyes found me and held me, that same stare that made my tummy flutter.

I smiled and he smiled back, tipped his head.

I wanted him. Fuck, how I wanted him.

"Go to him," Tonya said.

I shook my head. "He's with the guys. Busy."

"I'm sure he's not gonna grumble." She laughed. "Go up and surprise him, grab him and stick your tongue down his throat."

Ruby pulled a face. "That's gross!"

Tonya ruffled her hair. "Sorry, Ruby. Adult speak. I've had too many wines."

Ruby nodded. "I get it, like garage talk. Still gross."

A gaggle of women joined the guys, and I felt my heart drop a little. They were dressed up like groupies, short skirts in October and a shit ton of makeup. How do you even look that good when you're supposed to be camping?

One of the blondes stepped close to Darren, looked at him every time he laughed. She was drinking beer from a can, her smile easy.

"She's nobody," Tonya whispered. "Just some dumb cow."

I shrugged. "Maybe she knows him."

"She wants to. That's all."

She leaned in and asked him a question and he dropped his head, smiled and laughed. I felt jealous and it was absurd. He was probably fucking other women every night of the week and some random blonde's drunken flirting was bothering me? Quite absurd.

"Can I go see Dad?" Ruby asked. "I've finished my burger." She showed me her empty polystyrene tray as evidence.

I nodded. "If he's busy with his friends, come back though, right?"

I watched her skip over to him, and the moment she arrived it was as though the blonde didn't exist. He scooped Ruby up and spun her around, and the world was only her. The blonde sidled away and he didn't even notice.

"You're going to have to talk to him," Tonya said.

"Sorry?"

"This thing, whatever it is, it's got to go one way or the other. You'll both end up insane at this rate."

I sighed. "I know, but it's got to be the right time."

"He wants to be with you, Jo, I can see that plain as day, even if you can't."

I wished I had her faith. "He's fucking half the village. He has Stacey's ring still in his bedside cabinet."

She raised her eyebrows. "He does?"

I nodded.

"Shit," she said.

"Tell me about it."

She took a swig of wine. "Doesn't add up, Jo. I didn't think he was all that bothered about Stacey. He never seemed it out at the pub, not like he was about you."

"He was engaged to her."

"Yeah, well, maybe she was rebound."

I laughed. "She wasn't rebound, Tonya. We'd been split up ages before he got with her."

"He wasn't *over it* ages before he got with her though, Jo, I'd put money on it. He was a mopey sod for a fucking long time before he hooked up with her."

"I wouldn't know," I said. "I was always home with the girls."

"It's true. I saw it. Back when I was dating Phil Evans and we were down the Drum every night. He wasn't over you, Jo. I don't think he ever has been."

The wine made me giggle. "Now you're really pushing it."

"No," she said. "I'm not. I'm just telling it how it is."

He was staring again, and not even hiding it. Ruby's hand was clutched in his, the guys caught up in some rowdy conversation or other, but his eyes were right on me.

Tonya poked me in the arm. "Go," she said. "Before I drag you over there. I'll powder my nose and I'll join you."

I sighed, finished the rest of my wine. "Alright," I said. "I'll go."

I was so ridiculously nervous as I crossed the field, weaving my way through groups of people as he watched me. I was smiling, just a few metres away from him, and he was smiling back, ready to make conversation when a godawful shriek cut out across the crowd.

"Dadddd! Dadddd! Help me!"

Mia.

My eyes widened and so did his. My heart thumped so hard I felt it right through me, terror reaching up and grabbing me by the throat.

I scanned the crowd, desperate for sight of her, wondering where the hell she was.

"Darren..." I said, but he was already moving, his direction hidden from me by moving bodies.

"Stay!" he called to Ruby. "Stay right where you are!"

I followed him with my heart in my throat, caring little for the people I shoved from my path as I fought my way towards our baby.

Buck was alongside me, Jimmy O, too, all of us pounding after Darren as he barged through the crowd.

And then I saw it, in the shadows at the edge of the park – the group of lads around our girl. The guy with his hand on Mia's arm, holding her tight as she tried to pull away.

"Daddd!" she shrieked, and he was there.

I saw him up ahead, saw him reach her and tug her free, and my stomach lurched as he pushed her behind him, lurched again as he grabbed Daisy from the crowd, too.

I didn't stop running, not even when Darren's fist landed on the guy's jaw. Not even when the other guy reeled and stumbled, not even when the crowd of lads squared up to Darren and he squared up to them right back.

I didn't stop running until my girl was in my arms, until Daisy was there, too.

"They wouldn't let us go!" Mia cried. "They wouldn't! They

wouldn't let us go!"

I looked at Darren and he was wired, red-misting with an anger I'd never seen before. The kind of anger that sent electric through my spine, adrenaline coursing right through me.

His fist landed again, connected with one of the lads facing up to him, and I felt it, I felt all of it.

The scene unfolded in slow motion, him standing strong and fierce even though he was vastly outnumbered. I saw the way he didn't even care.

I felt it in my stomach, in some strange part of me I never knew existed, something deep and primal and raw.

Buck and Jimmy O appeared at his shoulders, and he barely even noticed. He didn't care about that, either, didn't care if he had backup or not, didn't care if he was up against an insurmountable force.

The only thing he cared about was protecting our little girl, whatever the cost.

A couple of shoves and a whole load of expletives, and I told the girls to cover their ears, that it would be alright and not to worry.

A crack as Darren took another swing, and shunting bodies.

And then silence.

The lads backed away, and the crowd came closer, jostling in around the aftermath.

Darren looked at me and his eyes were so dark, so fierce. He shook out his knuckles, and headed over. My heart was like a train.

I didn't realise I was gripping the girls so tight until he crouched down and pulled Mia from me. He checked her over, his eyes searching hers.

"She's ok," I said, and my voice was shaky and weak. "She's ok,

Darren. They're both ok."

But I wasn't, I wasn't ok at all. My legs were jelly, my skin crawling, every part of me cranked up to fight or flee.

I've never been so relieved as the moment I felt his arm around my shoulders, ushering us back through the crowd and back towards our tent. I held on to the girls and he held on to me, flanked by Jimmy and Buck right the way back to Tonya and Ruby, who'd taken a seat at her side.

Darren sat himself down by our tent, and pulled our girls down alongside him, Daisy, too.

And that's where he stayed, all evening long, glued to those kids like he'd never let them out of his sight again.

And I knew.

I knew he was it. I knew he was everything.

I knew that there was nobody on earth who'd love my girls the way he did, who'd give everything for my girls the way he did, who'd do whatever it took to keep them safe, no matter what the cost, no matter what they needed.

I'd loved Darren Trent for a lifetime.

But never so much as now.

CHAPTER TWENTY THREE

TRENT

"We need to talk," she said. Her voice was just a whisper. I barely heard her above the chatter around us.

I nodded. "Where?"

She looked around us, at the campers huddled nearby and the thin tarpaulin between us and the girls. I doubted they were even asleep yet, I'd heard giggles from Mia and Daisy less than five minutes back.

She shrugged. "Your tent? Tonya's here with the girls. We could nip over there…"

I was still too tightly wound, the thought of leaving my stakeout hitting me right in the gut. She took my elbow. "They'll be fine, Darren. Those lads aren't even here anymore."

I didn't mean to glare at her, but I did. I'd known it was trouble. I knew Mia looked too old, was too made up, was too naive to be out in a crowd full of drunk lads. I should've fucking stopped it, should've known better.

"Darren," she prompted. "We'll be right over there."

"Alright," I relented. I drank down the rest of my beer and flashed

Buck a look. "You'll stay with the girls?"

"Aye," he said. "Won't be going anywhere."

From the way he was sitting with Tonya I doubted he would've been going anywhere regardless.

I led Jodie through the clusters of tents, her hand on my elbow as I picked out a route. Mine was in the far corner, in the shadow of the truck. I dipped down and unzipped the entrance and Jodie crawled inside. She sat herself down on my sleeping bag, pulled her knees up to her chest.

I zipped the door back up behind me, then flicked on the battery operated lamp at my side. The orange glow made her hair look darker, her eyes too.

I waited for her to speak.

"They told the lads they were older. Daisy apparently. Told them they were sixteen, and had a bit of beer with them. I really don't think they knew what they were playing with. They didn't mean any harm..."

"Why the fuck would she do that?"

Jodie shrugged. "I guess she wanted to seem cool. She's a teenage girl, Darren. I probably would've done the same myself at her age."

"She's twelve," I said. "She's not a fucking teenager, Jo."

"Daisy is. Daisy turned thirteen last month."

"This doesn't happen again, Jodie, I mean it. No wandering off on her own, no more pulling shit like this." I felt the fear again, the horrible fucking panic at hearing Mia scream. "What if I hadn't been there?"

Her eyes met mine. "You were there."

"Yeah, but what if..." My voice trailed off.

"You'll always be there, Darren. You're her dad."

The fear exploded, and words came with it. "But I'm not *there*, am I? I won't know where she is every night. I won't know when she's off with Daisy and what time she's gonna be back, I won't be waiting at home when she first takes the bus into town alone, I won't be waiting for her to get back in a taxi when she's gone out to a club when she's barely legal."

"But I'll... you'll know... I'll tell you..."

"How? Real-time fucking text updates? A nightly fucking phone call? How, Jo?"

She put her head in her hands. "If that's what you want, Darren. I'll call you ten times a day if that's what you want."

That's not what I want. I want to be THERE.

I unzipped the door enough to light up a cigarette, and caught her staring at my knuckles.

"How's your hand?"

I shrugged. "Alright."

"Doesn't look alright."

I held it under the light, swollen knuckles. I'd had worse. I told her as much.

She sighed. "This isn't how I wanted things to pan out."

"What do you mean?"

She wouldn't look at me. "I hoped we'd... talk... I had so much to say, but now..." She slapped her knees, dismissing the whole thing.

"Now what?"

"Now you're angry, and I don't know what to say anymore."

"I'm not angry," I said. "I'm just pissed off, Jo. Pissed off that those assholes had hold of our fucking daughter. Pissed off she lied, pissed off she was stupid, pissed off I didn't stop her going."

"And me? Are you pissed off at me, too? I said she could go,

307

Darren. Do you not think I feel like shit, too? Do you not think I know this is my fault?"

I stared at her. "I'm not pissed off at you. I get it, I get you have to let her do this shit, I get she has to be allowed to be her own person."

"So what now?"

I shrugged. "I don't fucking know. She's grounded for-fucking-ever, then there'll be no fucking lads trying their luck, will there? She can be a fucking nun, Jodie, we'll book her into the fucking convent when we're at work, just so no pricks can come calling when we're out."

She smiled and tried to hide it, covered her mouth with her hand.

"I'm not even joking," I said. "You think I'm fucking joking, don't you?"

Her smile turned into a laugh, that breathy giggle that comes when she's relieved.

"See if I'm fucking joking when I get the vicar round next week." I took a drag on my cigarette, and Jodie's giggle caught me. A laugh caught in my throat, and I struggled to keep a straight face. She saw it. Saw the flash of a smile on my face, and it set her off. She laughed so hard she fell back with her hands on her belly and I laughed, too.

"Stop it," I attempted, but it was pointless, I was on one myself, just the same as her.

"I'm sorry..."

"You're fucking not," I laughed.

She rolled on the sleeping bag, letting it all out, tension broken. I felt it too. That relief. That blissful fucking relief like a dam breaking.

The laughter eased off slowly, really fucking slowly, and it left something else in its place, a heaviness in the air, her eyes wide as she looked up at me, her pupils like big black pools.

"Thank you," she said. "I don't know what would've happened if you hadn't been there."

My chest pained. "It's alright, Jo. I *was* there."

She sighed. "But you're not... *we're* not..." She reached out for my hand, the swollen one. I flicked my cigarette through the door before she took it. She ran a thumb across my knuckles and it hurt like a bitch. I didn't say anything. "You were wild, Darren. I've never seen you fly so hard."

"They had our girl, Jo."

She nodded. "I know..."

"Don't try and tell me I shouldn't have gone in like that. I'll always go in like that if the girls need it, no matter what, Jo, whatever it takes. I'm not gonna say fucking sorry for it."

She took a breath. "What makes you think I'd want you to?"

My hand was still in hers, her fingers were cold. "You don't?"

She shook her head. "No. I don't." She pulled me towards her, ever so fucking slowly. "I love the way you love our girls, Darren. I love the way you look out for them. I love the way you're there. I love how you'd do anything it took to keep them safe." She paused. "Just like I would."

"I love those fucking girls, Jodie. You know I do."

And you. I fucking love you, too.

She nodded. "I know."

I shifted towards her, shunted myself so I was propped on my side, my hand still in hers. "What's going on here? We fucking talking or what? Where's this all going?"

"I want to talk..." she said. "But I... I just need..."

"What?"

She pulled my arm around her and wriggled in to my side, and it felt so good. It felt really fucking good. "Hold me," she said. "Please. Just for a minute."

As if she needed to fucking ask. I squeezed her tight, pulled her close, her head in the crook of my shoulder, my breath in her hair. "It's alright now, Jo. Everything's alright."

Her breathing slowed, fingers gliding up my arm and back again. Her leg shifted, hooked over mine.

Christ, it was the most natural fucking move in the world to pull her on top of me. Her legs fell so perfectly between mine, her tits to my chest, her face in my face. I brushed her hair back from her forehead and looked at her, really looked at her.

She looked absolutely fucking beautiful.

She smiled a shy smile. "What?"

"Just you," I said.

"Just what about me?"

Just that I love you, Jodie. I've always fucking loved you.

I brushed her cheeks with my thumbs, then held her there, pulled her face to mine. She tasted of wine and smelled of the smoke from the barbeque outside. She squirmed against me as we kissed, and I slipped my hands down her back, grabbed hold of that pretty ass of hers and shunted her tight against my cock. She moaned, ever so quietly, grinding her hips as I pushed against her. I helped her out of her jacket, pulled her top off over her head, and she raised herself enough to strip me of mine.

Skin to skin, just a flimsy bra between her tits and my chest. I had her out of it in a beat, and the cold hardened her nipples, they felt like bullets against my thumbs.

She loosened her jeans and wriggled them down, her knickers

with them, and she was naked, naked and fucking horny, guiding my fingers to her clit.

She straddled me, leaning back with her hands braced on my thighs. My thumb flicked at that tight little bud, and she rocked back and forth, her head tipped back as the sensations took her.

Her tits looked so fucking good in the lamplight, rippling as she moved, nipples dark and hard, just begging for my mouth.

I pinned her clit with my thumb and she moaned.

"*More*," she hissed. "*Like that...*"

I gave her more like that. I gave her enough that she shuddered, squirming around like a fucking cowgirl. She arched her back and I slipped two fingers inside her, curled them to find the spot.

"*Stay still*," she said. "*Don't move...*"

I didn't move, just stared up at her as she circled her hips, rode my fingers until she was squelching, her cunt sucking at my fingers and begging for fucking more. Her eyes were closed, her bottom lip between her teeth, her breath coming in short, sharp rasps.

She came hard, stifled by the back of her hand, her whole body tense, bouncing on my fingers.

I wriggled my way out of my jeans as she recovered, and she didn't miss a fucking beat, just took my cock in her hand and lowered herself straight on. I let out a grunt as her pussy took me right in, and she leaned forward, pressing her lips to mine as I thrust up at her.

"Stop," she whispered. "Don't move... let me..."

It was fucking bliss as she rode me, big slow circles of her hips, torturously fucking perfect. She pinned my wrists above my head and moved like a fucking wildcat, all feline and slinky, so fucking smooth I felt like I was floating in silk.

I let her lead, staring up in fucking wonder as she writhed and rocked, taking all of me. It took everything I had not to flip her over and pound the holy fuck out of her.

But I would've been cheating myself.

She lifted herself clear of my dick, and I braced myself, my body knowing her moves on instinct, memories I'd never forget. She gripped my cock and shifted forwards, and I felt the tight ring of her ass. Oh fuck, it felt so fucking divine as she lowered herself onto me, so fucking slowly, painfully fucking slowly.

Her ass was made to take my fucking dick, always had been. It was as good now as it'd ever been, so fucking good I could have shot my load before I was even all the way in.

I could hear the chatter outside, the laughter of people on the piss just a couple of feet away. I could feel the chill in the air, far too cold to be fucking naked in a tent, but nothing mattered. Nothing fucking mattered, just the way it felt to be inside her.

She kept her face a few inches from mine, her eyes staring straight down at me. Her hair tickled my cheeks, rippling as she lifted herself up and down.

She changed angle and let out a gasp, her pussy grinding against me, her movements frantic.

"That feels so good," she said. "Fuck, Darren... don't move... please don't move..."

I didn't. I didn't fucking move, just let her do her thing.

My balls tightened, my cock pulsing as she teased me to the brink. I held back, held it off, breathed my way through it until she shuddered, her breath sharp.

"God," she hissed. "Oh God, Darren... oh fuck..."

"That's it," I said. "That's it, Jo..."

Her pussy clenched as she came and her asshole tightened with it. It sent me over the edge, thrusting up at her like a man fucking possessed. I came deep and hard, pulling my hands free to grab her hips and force her down onto my cock and hold her there. I held her tight, held her still, unloading my balls right the way inside, and I never wanted to stop, never wanted to pull out, never wanted this to fucking end.

"Fuck," she murmured. "I can't even... that feels so..."

"I know," I said. "I fucking know it, Jo."

I pulled her forwards, skin to skin as our breathing calmed. I could feel her racing heart against mine. I wrapped her in my arms and held her tight.

I was breathing so loud I hardly heard her, hardly heard the whisper that came from her mouth.

"*I love you.*"

I couldn't quite believe it, my belly fucking lurching at the thought, in case I'd misheard, in case I'd got it wrong, in case I'd...

"I love you, Darren," she repeated. "I never stopped loving you."

My mouth was dry, eyes wide as I took her face in my hands and made her look at me.

She looked so shy, so unsure, hardly the minx that had ridden me senseless a few short minutes back.

I brushed her lip with my thumb, stared right into her eyes, willing myself to say the words, willing myself just to put it out there. I took a deep breath, and kissed her lips, held her there until the words would come.

"I love you, too," I said.

I hadn't realised how close people were outside. I could hear everything, every laugh, every drunk bit of banter, and the embarrassment flushed hard, knowing they'd probably heard me, too.

I was reeling a little, reeling that he'd told me he loved me, reeling that I'd said it first, that I'd been the one to raise the bar, to make this *something*. Worrying that he didn't mean it, that he'd only said it because I'd said it first.

But no. I'd seen it in his eyes.

I pulled on my clothes, and he pulled on his, and I said I should get back to the girls, and he agreed. He kissed my head before he unzipped the tent, and I crawled out into the open, burning up afresh as people turned to stare.

Yeah, they'd heard us alright.

Darren didn't even seem to notice, just clambered out after me and lit up a cigarette. We didn't speak as we made our way back across the field, smiles bright as we rejoined the others. We sat apart, like everything was just the same, even though it wasn't.

Nothing felt the same.

I couldn't drink any more wine, just poured myself a glass of water instead. My belly felt unsettled, and I felt so old because of it, too old to be drinking like I was a teenager anymore.

I called it a night soon after, my eyes lingering on Darren's as he held up a hand and said he'd see me in the morning.

Oh God, how I wanted him to stay with me.

I climbed into my sleeping bag and my toes were like ice. It took ages to warm up and as soon as I had I was blasted with cold air as

Tonya bumbled her way through the tent. She crawled into a sleeping bag at my side.

"Shit," she said. "I kissed Buck."

I laughed, and it felt so funny, so right that other boundaries were being blown open in this place.

"Was it like kissing your brother?"

"No," she said. "And if it was, then I'm an incest convert. It was pretty hot." She groaned. "I'm going to be hanging like shit in the morning, drank way too much."

I knew the feeling, even though I'd hardly had any. I felt so sick. Really sick.

Maybe this time really was a dodgy hotdog.

"What now?" I said. "Where's it going?"

She sighed. "Jeez, Jo, I dunno. He was probably drunk. *I'm* drunk."

"Would you want to do it again?"

"Wouldn't say no."

I couldn't stop smiling. "I told Darren I loved him," I whispered.

I heard her roll towards me. "No shit!"

"Yeah. I really did."

"And what did he say?"

"He said it back."

She gasped and hiccupped at the same time, threw her hand to her mouth, eyes like saucers. "You're fucking kidding me?"

I shook my head, my grin hurting my face. "Scout's honour," I said.

"Oh, Jo," she took hold of my hand. "And you smell of sex. Dirty mare."

I felt my cheeks burning in the dim light, felt Darren still inside me. Then we both burst into giggles. She hugged me and I hugged her back.

"Tell me," she said, "I'm all ears."

But my tummy rolled and I fought back the urge to puke. "I'm really pooped," I said. "Feel a bit sick. I need to sleep."

"Cop out."

"For real," I said. "I feel like shit."

"Yeah yeah," she said. "Goodnight then, lovergirl."

"Night night, brother-lover."

I laughed as she jabbed me in the arm.

Darren helped us pack up the tent, giving Ruby a running commentary on the results from yesterday's racing as he did it. I kept busy, but I was still hanging, the sickness in my belly was worse, and I'd actually thrown up first thing, managing to hold it back until I'd reached a hedge at safe distance.

No more drinking for me, ever.

Darren slapped the side of the car as we pulled away, and I beeped the horn as we drove out of sight. Ruby was in good spirits, but Mia and Daisy were sombre. I'd already told them I'd have to be reporting back to Daisy's mum. That had gone down like a lead balloon.

We dropped Tonya first, and she grabbed her case with a groan. Seems she was feeling as bad as I was.

I kept things brief with Daisy's mum, gave her the lowdown without too much drama. She tutted and scowled and told Daisy she should have known better than to be so stupid, and that her privileges of being *independent* were revoked well and truly.

It was gone lunchtime when we got home. I dumped the tent in the garage and dragged the bags indoors, but left them there, a chaotic pile in the hallway. I just couldn't face any more of it.

Nanna was happy enough, reading the Sunday paper like we'd never even gone. She'd had fun, she said. Fresh meat to watch *Question King* with. It seemed she'd had easily as good a time as we'd had.

I wasn't expecting the rumble of a truck outside, but Darren came round not long after we settled down for the afternoon.

He gave no explanation, and I didn't ask, just welcomed him in like this was an everyday occurrence. I put the kettle on and told him we were having chicken and chips for tea.

"Sounds good," he said.

I got on with it, leaving him chatting away to Nanna and the girls in the living room, but he joined me soon after. He took the peeler from me and got to work on the potatoes, making a messy job of it that was very much appreciated nonetheless.

"You alright?" he said. "You look washed out."

"Tonya snores," I said. "And I can't drink anymore."

"Thirty." He smirked. "It's the big birthday approaching. You'll have to be teetotal from now on."

"Seriously feels that way," I said.

I sipped at my water and took a seat at the kitchen table, and he carried on peeling, flashing me an occasional glance over his shoulder.

"About last night," he said. "Did you, um, did you mean it like?"

My cheeks prickled. "I... um..." *Yes, I meant it.* "Yeah... I guess I did..."

"Righto," he said.

I could have smacked him over the head with Nanna's newspaper if I had the energy.

I waited but he didn't say anything else.

"And you?" I prompted. "Did you, um… mean it?"

"Yeah," he said. He dropped the last of the potatoes in the bowl. "I guess I did." He sat down at the table alongside me. "We need to work this out, Jo. I don't know what the fuck's going on like."

I sighed. "Me neither."

"I just don't wanna get it wrong."

"Me neither."

"Alright," he said. "So we talk, yeah?"

I nodded. "Yeah, we talk." I looked into the hallway, it was clear. "When the kids are in bed."

He tipped his head. "Good, yeah."

It seemed to take fucking forever for the kids to go to bed.

Dinner time seemed more chaotic than usual, but it was probably just down to me feeling off. Mia had homework she'd mysteriously forgotten about through the half-term break, and Ruby was on a mission to watch a film instead of *Question King*. Nanna took some convincing. I told her she'd have to watch the re-run on *catch up*, and she relented enough to settle down to watch Ruby's choice with the rest of us.

Considering it was Ruby's choice she didn't last long into it. Too little sleep, for both girls, they were both flaked out on Darren's shoulders by halfway through.

When they were clearly out for the count, and Nanna was dozing in her chair, I flicked the TV to standby.

I nudged Mia gently and told her to make her way to bed. She moved on autopilot, giving us token hugs before she disappeared upstairs.

Darren lifted Ruby from the sofa and carried her up to bed. I followed and stood in the doorway to watch him, loving how tenderly he lowered her onto her mattress and tucked her in.

I was as pooped as they were, I told him so.

"I'll go then," he said. "We'll do it another time, no bother."

I reached out for his hand as he made his way towards the stairs. He stopped, stared at me, eyes widening as I led him along the landing to my bedroom door.

I'd have fucked him if I'd had the energy, but all I could do was ditch my clothes and slip into bed.

He undressed without words and climbed in beside me, and he was tense, nervous. It was unlike him.

"What is it?" I said.

"Just this..." he replied. "It's just... weird."

"Bad weird?"

He pulled me close, and I felt him shake his head. "No, not bad weird."

We lay there for ages, wrapped up together. His fingers stroked my hair, his shoulder so solid under my cheek. Just like old times.

I drifted in and out of sleep, but every time I moved he was right there, awake.

I guess he didn't sleep at all.

I heard Nanna climb upstairs and head into her room. I heard the neighbour's car pull up after her late night pub shift. I knew the time must be getting on by the time Darren nudged me from half-sleep.

"Am I staying, Jo?"

I mumbled something incoherent.

"I mean it," he said. "If I fall asleep then this is for keeps. The girls... if I stay, they'll..."

"They'll know," I said, suddenly wide awake.

He nodded. "This has to be for real, Jo. We have to be sure."

"I know," I said. "For the girls."

And for us.

He said nothing, just stroked my hair. The words were crammed in my head. *What about Bang Gangs? What about Stacey's ring in your drawer? Do you really love me, Darren, or are you saying it because you want to come home to your girls every night?*

"So?" he said. "Am I going or what?"

"We've so much to talk about..." I said. "There's so much to work out..."

He sighed. "Righto."

He kissed my head before he left me. I felt so horribly bereft that I pulled my knees to my chest, listening in horror to him pull his jeans on and buckle the belt. He sat on the bed, reached out and squeezed my arm. "Don't get up," he said. "I'll let myself out."

"This isn't a no, Darren, it's a we need to talk first."

He didn't say anything.

"Get some rest, Jodie, you look fucking spent."

I nodded, even though he probably couldn't see me. "Night, Darren," I said.

"Night, Jo."

It took me less than a minute to change my mind and rush onto the landing to call him back.

But he was already gone.

I listened to his truck pull away from the drive and knew I never wanted to hear that sound again.

Not the sound of him leaving us.

I wanted him back home for good.

CHAPTER TWENTY FOUR

JODIE

I spent Monday morning throwing up, thanking the hangover for the fact I had a legitimate reason to avoid *ladies who lunch*.

Tonya called on me afterwards. She said hello to Nanna who was engrossed in *Antiques Hunt*, then ushered me into the kitchen and informed me with glee that both Debbie Gibson and Mandy Taylor were *still in the queue*.

"I'm telling you now, Jo," she said. "He's not fucking them. I don't think he's got any intention of fucking them."

"Who knows," I said, "he might just be booked up."

"Yeah, right. Like fuck he is." She rolled her eyes. "You two are hopeless. Why don't you just ask him? No, *tell* him. Tell him to ditch this shit for good."

I avoided the question, because in truth I'd been avoiding it myself for long enough. The fear of rejection was always there, festering under the surface, the memory of losing him the first time around embedded so heavily in my heart that I wasn't sure I could go through that again. *That* was the truth of it. And it scared me.

The whole thing scared me. Icarus sailing way too close to Darren

Trent's sun for comfort.

I told her he'd nearly stayed last night and she clapped her hands. "I knew it!" she said. "It's just a matter of time. Tell him to come home, tell him to ditch this stupid Bang Gang nonsense and bring his stuff back round."

"And what if he won't..."

"Why wouldn't he?" she said. "It's not like he's busy fucking around every bloody night, you're seeing too much of him for that."

And that was another thing that was niggling me. We'd made no plans this week and I was still holding off on it. I was due any day, and although Darren really didn't give a shit whether I was on my monthlies or not, I did. The thought of the washing alone was exhausting, and what if this was just sex? What if he turned his nose up when he found it wasn't going to be rough and tumble all night long?

But he'd held me, last night, just held me.

"Lorraine collared me earlier," she said. "Told me she's having a party on Wednesday night. Some Halloween bash, *women's* interests."

The thought of Lorraine made me feel sicker than I was already. "*Women's* interests?"

She nodded. "Sex toys and that kind of shit, I guess." She grinned. "Better get that savings card of yours out, I'm sure there are plenty of *experiences of a lifetime* a couple of sex toys and Darren Trent could indulge you in."

"I think I'll give it a miss..." I said.

She pulled a face. "No way! We're totally going! I'd love to see what dodgy shit Lorraine gets up to behind that *Miss Prissy* facade. I bet she's pure filth."

"Lorraine?" I laughed. "She was married for a million years, told me her ex-husband was a terrible lay."

"Yeah, well, she's been *un*married for a million years, too. That woman's no stranger to a bit of bump and grind, I'm telling you."

"Guess we'll find out."

She smiled. "You'll come?"

I nodded. "Why not. I could do with building some bridges with Lorraine, things have been... tense..."

She raised an eyebrow. "Darren?"

"She doesn't think I should be going anywhere near him, made it clear she thinks I'm being an absolute fucking idiot."

She shrugged. "Gah, whatever. She'll get over it."

I hoped so. I really hoped so.

Tonya was waffling away about potential purchases when the hangover struck again. I raced to the kitchen sink and struggled to hold it back, retching up nothing and waving her to stay away.

"Shit," I said. "I really can't drink anymore. Seriously, that wine fucked me up. Pathetic, I know."

Her face was unreadable, and that's rarely the case with Tonya. "You hardly fucking drank any, Jo, not really. I polished off way more than you did, and I'm not throwing my guts up all over the place."

I shrugged. "I guess I'm not so used to it."

She was quiet for too long. "You and Trent have been careful, right?"

My cheeks burned, and my stomach did a horrible lurch that helped my queasiness none at all. "We... I have a period planner... I've been..."

"Jesus, Jodie! Condoms, yes or no?"

"Well, no... but I'm sure..."

"Christ All-fucking-mighty." She held out her hand. "Where's that pissing period planner, Jo. Have you looked at it?"

Oh the shame. No, no I hadn't. Not for a week or so, but I was sure. I definitely remembered the dates.

I wasn't such a reckless stupid idiot.

Except I was. I was and I knew it. Had no excuse for it. Nothing but a crazy hedonistic desire to have Darren come inside me.

Like that had been so successful first time round.

What a fucking idiot.

"I'm sure I'll be fine," I said. I grabbed my phone from the sideboard and handed it to her. My nerves were jangling as she tapped away at the screen.

"So, you've got your period, right?"

"Sorry?"

She turned the screen. "Saturday, you were due on Saturday, Jo."

I laughed. "*Tuesday*," I said. "I'm sure I should be due tomorrow."

She shook her head. "*Saturday*, Jo. You should be cramping all over the fucking place by now." I didn't want to look at it. She waved it in my face, and still I didn't look. "Jesus Christ, Jodie Symmonds, you fucking knew about this."

"No!" I said. "I didn't, I just... figured I did..." I stared at her and not at the phone. "First time was... *me*... I just, wanted to feel him."

"And the rest?"

I shrugged. "And the rest we just..."

"Fucking hell." She stared at my belly. "Baby Trent number three. Welcome to the world, little guy."

"Little guy?"

She smiled. "Odds. I reckon he'll get a little spanner-wielding son next go. Ruby will be stoked."

"Stop it," I said. "Seriously, I'm probably due on any minute."

"Alright then," she said. "Let's go get a test. You've got to get Nanna's pills anyway, right?"

My cheeks were on fire. I nodded.

She handed me my keys.

"This will be nothing," I said. "Just a waste of a tenner."

"And if it's not?"

Oh the sickness. "Then it's not... and we'll... I'll..."

"How are Mia and Ruby going to feel about twinning up? You'll need the extra room."

"Bit early for that..." I said. I rolled my eyes.

"Darren Trent only has to stare at you and you're bloody pregnant, Jo. Wine hangover my fucking arse."

And what about the rest of the village? Does he only have to stare at them, too?

No. He said he was careful. He told me so.

I cashed out with the test kit and Nanna's pills and Tonya wouldn't let up, insisted we head straight back to mine and get it done.

I tried to stall, tried to tell her morning was better, but she'd have none of it.

"Now!" she said. "You've been burying your head in the sand bloody long enough, Jodie." She sighed. "Christ, I sound like your mother."

I checked Nanna was still entertained by daytime TV before I went to shut myself in the bathroom. Tonya shoved her toe in the door.

"No way," she said. "I'm not missing the main event."

"Darren's normally here... when I do this..."

"Call him, then! We can have a pregnancy test party."

I retched at the thought. Shook my head. "I think you'll do plenty, you can be my test buddy this time round." I reached out and squeezed her arm, and she smiled. She unwrapped the packet, handed me the stick.

"Hope you need to pee."

I nodded, pulled down my jeans and sat myself down on the toilet. I shoved that test between my legs and pissed like a horse. *Probably nothing. This is probably nothing.*

My heart was pounding so fast I felt heady. I clicked the little cap on it and handed it to Tonya. She held it away from me.

"It's probably too early," I said. "Probably way too early to even know..." I rambled on about dates moving around on that period app and how it was probably nothing, how I'm sure the dates had been different last time I'd checked... probably a glitch... probably just an error on the app... and I'd definitely be careful next time, definitely... I'd buy some condoms myself, totally, a bumper pack...

"Two weeks," she said. "You're two weeks pregnant. Baby Trent number three is just a little tiny kidney bean."

My jaw dropped, and God fucking knows why. Of *course* I was fucking pregnant. Idiot. I was a fucking idiot.

I took the stick from her, and sure enough, it told me so. It told me in plain English as well. *2 weeks*, written across the little screen, not the blue line shit I'd been looking for last time around.

"That's so early," I said. "It's like…"

"Really early," she said. "You won't reach twelve weeks until the New Year. That'll be a nice midnight revelation for the family."

"Like I'd wait twelve weeks…"

She shrugged. "Wait as long as you want, or don't. Pregnant is pregnant, Jo."

"But it's early…" I said. "Dangerously early to go making crazy announcements."

"You are going to tell him, right?" Her eyes bored into me. "Like right now, today."

I put my head in my hands. "I'll tell him," I said. "But just… I just need a couple of days. Just to think."

"Think? Jo, you're having a fucking baby. He's gonna have to pull his shit together."

"And do what?"

She looked at me like I was mentally challenged. "And move the fuck in here, cancel this stupid bloody gigolo crap, and go get a big book of baby names…"

"I don't want him to move back in because I'm pregnant, Tonya." The stupidity of my actions hit hard, really bloody hard. "Not when I've just… found myself… not when we're just…"

"Just what?"

I tried to stop the tears, because I didn't deserve any self-sympathy, it was way too late for that. They welled anyway, prickling my eyes. "Not when we're just starting out… not when we stand a chance of fixing the crap we did wrong last time…"

She smiled, and it was kind. I was grateful. "Shit, Jo. You can still fix that stuff. A baby doesn't make any difference."

"But it does!" I said. "I'll be a mum all over again, he'll be under pressure all over again, working loads of hours all over again, we'll be busy, and we'll be stressed, and he'll be in the pub again, and this time I'll have three kids and Nanna to look after and I'll be frumpy Jodie again... I don't want to be frumpy Jodie again!" My throat was tight and hissy. "And this time he'll have everyone in a hundred mile radius out for a piece of his cock when I'm not looking... and what if he took it? What if I'm just a bore at home with crappy hair and baby sick all over me and Mandy Taylor's all over him like a rash?"

"This isn't how it's gonna be," she said. "Not at all! Seriously, Jo, this is just fear. It's just being scared."

But I shook my head. "You can't say that!"

"Yes, Jo, I bloody can. How long have I known you two? Give him a bit of credit, and if not him, then definitely give yourself some." She sighed. "You were a kid, Jo. It was hard. You had a million things to do, a million things to learn, years of growing up to do in hardly any fucking time at all. That isn't you *now*. You'll be fine this time! I won't let you turn into mum-zilla, I promise! I like having you back as your old self far too much for that."

I checked my phone, and I was running late. Again.

Fuck.

I wiped my eyes. "I've got to go, Tonya. Work."

"Shit," she said. "Can't you call in sick?"

I shook my head. "Lorraine's already pissed at me enough."

I flushed the toilet, and shoved the pregnancy test right at the back of the bathroom cabinet, behind the ear buds and pumice stone that never get used.

"You need to take it steady," she said. "Keep calm."

I nodded. "I'll be alright, just keep on keeping on."

"And Darren?"

"I'll tell him," I said. "Just let's get these next few days out of the way, hey? Ruby's got a play date party tomorrow evening and we've got Lorraine's thing on Wednesday. I'll call him over Thursday."

"Thursday?" her expression was stern. "Definitely Thursday, then, and not a day bloody later."

"Thursday. I'll invite him over."

"Alright," she said. "And make sure you get it clear, what you want. Don't just let him grunt his way through this shit, Jo. Find out what *he* wants, too. What he really wants. I'm sure it's you, he just needs to fucking say it for once."

I didn't fancy my chances of getting a gushing declaration of forever love from Darren Trent somehow, but I nodded anyway.

I took a breath, checked myself in the mirror and forced a smile. "Back to it," I said.

She squeezed my elbow. "I'll come along for a coffee."

TRENT

I got to work, shutting myself in the office through Eleanor Hartley's wailing fucking gangbang. My mind wouldn't stop harping on about Jodie, like it ever fucking stopped.

She'd told me she loved me, let me into her bedroom. That had to fucking mean something. Had to mean enough.

I'd tell her. I'd tell her fucking everything. Even about Lorraine. Lay it all out there and start over, make it clear this shit was all behind me. She'd have to listen, I'd make her listen. I'd have to find the words...

Bollocks.

I lit up a cigarette and tried to work through some invoices, but I couldn't think straight.

My phone pinged and my gut lurched. Jodie.

It wasn't fucking Jodie.

Lorraine.

Why the hell wouldn't she just piss off already.

I wasn't lying about Jodie. Sex party at mine on Wednesday night. She's coming. Will you be coming too? x

I laughed out loud. Like fuck Jo was going to a sex party at Lorraine's fucking house.

Nice try, I replied. *Just give it a fucking rest, Lorraine.*

Another ping a couple of seconds later.

Ask her if you don't believe me. Don't give her a hard time though, Trent. She's her own woman, last thing she needs is you being a damp fucking squib about this shit. At least be a man about it. x

I smoked through the initial burst of rage. Tried to keep a lid on it. Like hell Jodie would be going to that shit.

I called up Jodie's messages, typed one out, kept it casual. Just in case.

Just in case fucking what? In case Lorraine wasn't such a lying cunt after all? Of course she fucking was.

What's this about a dodgy sex party at Lorraine's house? You going?

She took ages to reply. Work. She was at work. No fucking need to panic.

I scrabbled for my phone as it pinged.

Ha! She told you?! Christ, word spreads. Yeah, I'll be there. Me and Tonya. I think she's invited quite a few!

I stared at it in shock. Just fucking stared.

Another ping.

Are you coming?!

Like fuck I was fucking coming.

Not quite my fucking scene, Jo. I couldn't stop the anger. *Have a good fucking time though.*

I waited. And waited.

I'm only going to let my hair down. Lorraine's been funny lately. You know what she's like about you. Thought it would be a good bonding experience.

I was fucking flabbergasted.

I fired off a text to Lorraine.

You can keep Jodie out of your seedy fucking shit. Just fuck off, Lorraine.

A reply in a heartbeat.

Aww, diddums. You're welcome to join us. I'm sure Jodie won't mind. xxx

I tried to clear my head. Tried to get my thoughts around this shit.

We said no fucking gangbangs. I told her that. I told her she wasn't on the fucking list.

I typed out a message.

What about us, Jo?

Sappy twat.

I pressed send anyway.

Her message didn't take long.

It's only one night, Darren. Ruby's at Lea Nicholl's house tomorrow evening, but Thursday works. Do you want to come over for tea? We need to talk. Good chance.

Another message. *I might have some fresh ideas after Lorraine's house. Should be fun, right? ;)*

A wink. She sent me a fucking wink.

I nearly launched the phone through the fucking window.

That's why you're going, is it? For us? For some fresh ideas? Thought we were fine as we fucking were, Jo.

She sent another message back and I couldn't believe it.

I thought you'd be pleased! Variety is the spice of life, Darren Trent, I thought you'd be well on board. x

Variety is the spice of fucking life?! I stormed on through to the garage, and the door flung on its hinges so hard everyone stopped working to look at me.

"A gig, Wednesday night, Lorraine's house. Is that yours?"

They looked at each other, then Buck shrugged. "Yeah. Didn't think you'd want in. She's paying a fucking fortune, says it's going to be quite a party."

I could've fucking killed them. Every single one of them.

"Touch Jodie, even fucking *look* at Jodie, and don't bother coming back to this fucking yard. Understand me?"

They didn't know anything about it. It was clear as fucking day.

Buck stepped closer. "Jodie's going? Why the fuck is Jodie going?"

"You tell me!" I barked. "This is Lorraine's fucking work. All of it."

"Christ," Hugh said. "Really didn't think that was on the cards..."

"You and me fucking both." I stormed past them, lit up a cigarette. Buck followed me.

"What you gonna do about it?"

I didn't answer.

"Shit, Trent, you've got to do fucking something. Tell her she's not to fucking go! Tell her it's fucking exclusive! Tell her Lorraine can get fucking stuffed!"

I shook my head. "I'm not fucking telling her what she can and can't fucking do like some sappy fucking twat, Buck. She wants to ride the fucking Bang Gang train, that's her business."

She said she loved me.

"Don't sit fucking right to me this," he said. "Something's well fucking off."

"Yeah, that cunt Lorraine. That's what's fucking *off* about this whole fucking thing."

"But Jodie doesn't seem..."

I glared at him. "Happy enough to hand over four-hundred fucking quid to have a go, wasn't she? Happy enough to hand it over a second time when I gave her a freebie, too. Of course she's fucking going, Buck."

"But you're..."

"We're what?!" I took a drag. "We're fucking nothing, Buck. That's perfectly fucking clear. I'm just a fucking cock to her, a cock who happens to be the father of her fucking kids."

He slapped my shoulder and I was tense as fuck.

"Talk to her, Trent. Just fucking talk to her. Set this shit straight before it rips you a-fucking-part, man."

Like fucking hell I'd talk to her.

I regretted every fucking thing I'd fucking said.

Soft fucking cunt. Sappy, naive fucking idiot.

Like she was gonna fucking have me back.

Of course she fucking wasn't.

I was just a piece of fucking rough. Just like always. She wanted a *Brian*, and a quinoa-munching fucking suit who'd drive a fucking

Aston Martin like a posh wanker.

Not me.

Of course she didn't want *me*.

I got back to fucking work.

CHAPTER TWENTY FIVE

JODIE

I got Ruby ready for her play date. Halloween. Christ, this year was zooming by. She wanted to go as one of the *Transformers* but I was hard pushed to find enough cardboard boxes to stand a chance of turning her into a truck-cum-robot. After a mini-tantrum we settled on a cat. She wore all black and I made her a little ear headband, stuffed a stocking with socks and pinned it to her leggings as a tail. It looked better than I'd expected.

A bit of makeup, some eyeliner whiskers and a pretty little pink nose and she looked cute as a button. I snapped some pictures and sent them off to Darren with a string of smiley faces.

He didn't even reply, but I didn't have time to worry about that. Too much to do, not enough time.

Mia was still subdued after her rally day drama, said she didn't want to do Halloween dress up at all this year.

Had enough horror this month already thanks, Mum.

Oh the drama. She was still grounded, moping around without her phone. As if Daisy would be on Skype even if Mia was. Her ass was as grounded as Mia's.

"Alright," I said. "Please yourself. Watch TV with Nanna and be good."

I was out of the door with about thirty seconds to spare, as per usual.

Ruby's play date was packed full of school mums, and out of the regular schoolyard context it made me feel uneasy.

How many of these women had taken Darren's cock and paid good money for it? I couldn't tell by looking at them, would never have been able to tell Debbie Gibson was game for it, probably not Mandy, either.

They could all be getting a piece for all I knew. They could have recurring diary appointments with the guy whose baby was growing in my belly, and I wouldn't have the faintest idea.

I'd been such a fool to think I could live with that. Such a fool to think I could carry on without giving it a thought.

I gritted my teeth and smiled through the party, made small talk as best I could, but it was a relief when it wrapped up for the evening and I could get home with Ruby. Bath and bedtime were earlier than usual, but I was still pooped. Insanely pooped.

I'm sure I was a million times more tired now I actually knew I was pregnant than I'd been before.

I crashed on the sofa to watch TV with Nanna, and she wasn't exactly coy with her conversation.

"No Darren this evening?"

"No, Nanna. He's probably busy."

Or ignoring me.

"We could do with a strong man around the house, Jo. Good for getting the cobwebs down from the landing."

"Yes, Nanna. I'll ask him to get up there with the feather duster next time he's over. He doesn't need to move in for that."

"Not for that," she said. "It's just a bit of icing on the cake, love."

I turned to face her. "You'd be happy with that? Darren moving in here?"

Like I needed to ask. Her smile was bright, creasing her cheeks with happiness. "Oh yes, love. The girls, too. Just think how happy the girls would be."

I was trying not to think about that. Trying not to ponder fantasies for their sake. The thought of crippling them with grief if it didn't work out again was too much to take.

I was yawning all the way through her crime programme, couldn't keep myself awake.

"I've got to go to bed, Nanna. I'm pooped."

I gave her a hug on the way past and she rubbed my back. "You get some sleep, my girl. You look exhausted."

I felt it.

I checked my phone again before lights out, but there were no messages.

Radio silence from Darren Trent. Maybe things weren't all that different this time around.

I tried not to think of all the people he might be with, tried not to consider that any of the women at Ruby's Halloween party could have made a move straight over to his after dropping the kids home.

My hand was on my belly, my thoughts were all with him. They'd always been with him.

I didn't want to cry, but I did.

I'd never been pregnant and alone before. Pregnant and scared, but never alone.

Christ, what a fucking mess.

I propped a load of pillows at the side of me and flung my arm over the lot of them, pretended there was someone there with me, pretended he was just busy, just busy with normal shit, pretended he wasn't a fucking gigolo and that things would be just fine.

TRENT

Halloween night. I could see the Drum through my window, packed to the rafters with people in daft fucking costumes. The urge for a nice cold pint was eating at me, but I didn't go out. I didn't want to see anyone, not one single fucking person in there.

I watched shit on TV and looked through the pics of Ruby that Jo had messaged through.

It broke my fucking heart.

I'd had a fair few cans before my phone pinged again, and again it was that fucking Lorraine bitch and not Jo.

Party starts at 7.30. I'd get there at 7.15 if I were you, make sure you're not late for the action, hey? Maybe you can take Jodie off for some one on one if she's game for it.

My text back was instant.

You're a bitter old fucking cunt, Lorraine. Stay the fuck out of my fucking face.

Another ping.

Oh, Darren! Don't be like that. You and I both know you'll be there. Sorry if I hurt your feelings, diddums, but I did try to warn you. xx

And another. *Don't let her get to you. I can't believe you ever thought she'd really have you back. x*

I threw my phone against the wall and the screen fizzled and went black. I threw my beer can after it. It caught the framed picture of Ruby and Mia on the roundabout up by my parents' house, and the whole thing swayed and then slipped from its hook. It landed with a crash of splintered glass. I pulled the photo from the wreckage and my girls smiled out at me.

I'd give anything to be with those girls. Any fucking thing.

But that wasn't it. Not even close. That didn't even come close to justifying how much I wanted to be back in Jodie's bed, back in her life, back in her arms at night.

Anger, so much anger, anger at that bitch Lorraine, anger at myself. Anger that I couldn't fucking say what I needed to say, couldn't put it out there enough to drive to Jodie's and tell her how it fucking was, tell her that I'd rather cut my fucking dick off than have her at some dirty fucking gangbang at Lorraine's house.

Tell her it was breaking my fucking heart.

That she was breaking my fucking heart.

That my heart had been fucking broken since the day she told me it was over. Since the day she'd finally packed up her things and left me on my fucking own.

It'd been a long fucking time since I'd cried actual tears over Jodie Symmonds.

The last time had been in Lorraine's seedy fucking arms, her greedy fucking cunt eating me up and making it all better.

Like Lorraine could ever fucking make it better.

Nothing would ever make it fucking better.

JODIE

Still nothing from Darren. I stared at my phone and scowled, shoving it back in my apron pocket before Lorraine caught wind of it.

"Excited for tonight?" she said.

I nodded. "Should be fun."

She came close. "You shopping for you and Darren?"

I didn't answer.

She nudged me in the arm. "Oh come on, Jodie. Don't think I'm not aware you two are back together. I know I was... concerned... but we're friends, aren't we?"

I smiled. "Yeah, we're friends."

"So," she prompted. "What are you going to be shopping for?"

I felt a blush brewing. "I don't know!" I kept my smile coy. "I'll have to keep an open mind, won't I? I'm sure something will take my fancy."

I didn't say that he was being a dick, that he was barely speaking to me, that I'd told him I loved him and he'd cooled off faster than a hotdog in the snow.

That still fucking hurt.

"Seven-thirty," she said. "Prompt. Make sure you're there on the dot, alright? We have some games planned."

I rolled my eyes. "Christ, Lorraine, I dread to think. Don't think I'm doing any of that *pass the vibrator between your knees* rubbish."

"Spoilsport," she scoffed. "Seven-thirty, right?"

I ditched my apron, shift done. "Seven-thirty," I said. "Don't worry, I'll be on time."

"Can't wait." She grinned.

My phone was trashed, wouldn't even start up.

I left it on the desk in the garage and tried to get on with the backlog of car services, tried to pretend I didn't give a shit about this gangbang at Lorraine's, that it didn't matter if Jodie was there or not, that it didn't matter if she really loved me.

I'll be alright, I told myself.

I'll get through it, just like last time.

The guys said virtually nothing all fucking day, banter well and truly dead to the bone.

"Did you talk to her?" Buck asked before they left for the day. "Please fucking tell me you talked to her?"

I shrugged. "Not my business, Buck."

He shook his head. "You're a fucking idiot, Trent."

"Yeah, well, better to be a fucking idiot than played for a fucking idiot."

He slapped my back. "Ain't none of us gonna be touching your missus, don't you be fucking worrying about that."

I nodded.

"I'll see you in the morning," he said. "Talk to her."

I tried to keep busy at the yard, but the clock kept fucking ticking. I couldn't stop fucking looking at it.

When the time neared seven I couldn't fucking take it, couldn't stay fucking still.

I tried to remember Jo's mobile number, to call her from the landline, but it'd been so fucking long since I'd dialled it manually that I couldn't fucking dredge it from my brain.

Shit.

I could make seven-fifteen, but only if I raced like a fucking idiot. I raced like a fucking idiot.

I pulled up outside Lorraine's with a big fucking screech. Bailed out of the truck without even locking it. I threw myself through the front door and along the hallway, swinging the living room door open wide as I called Jodie's name.

Jesus fucking wept.

Jodie wasn't anywhere to be seen, but she was about the only one.

Naked fucking bodies everywhere. I tried to keep my eyes on the faces and not the bouncing tits and gaping fucking pussy all over the place. Mandy Taylor, her cunt stretched around Buck's dick, Petey riding her fucking asshole at the same time. Debbie Gibson with Hugh's dick down her throat, makeup and spit all over her dirty fucking face.

Lorraine was riding Jimmy O, her big fucking tits bouncing around as he thrust up into her asshole. She had a vibe against her clit, and he was jamming his fingers in her cunt, stretching her over his knuckles.

Jesus fucking Christ.

A couple of other women I recognised from the garage. Mary Roberts, who'd dropped her car in three times this last month for stupid shit, and her neighbour Donna who kept flashing me slutty looks in the village shop. They giggled and spread their legs, pussies fucking glistening.

I knew before Lorraine said it. I just fucking knew.

"They're waiting for your gorgeous dick, Trent," she said. "Be a good boy and give it to them good and hard, won't you?"

I stepped backwards. "Where's Jodie?"

She pulled herself from Jimmy's cock with a squelch, and the prick looked at me like a fucking dullard, not the faintest fucking clue what was going down here.

I saw Buck look my way, but waved him to carry on, no point this shit turning into a bigger fucking mess than it was already.

Lorraine came over, swinging her naked hips like a wanton fucking whore.

"Jodie's not coming, Trent. Do you really think I'd let her come to a fucking *Bang Gang*? If she was here I wouldn't get a look in. I told her it was cancelled. You can relax now." She ran her hand up my chest. I took her wrist, held it still.

"No," I said. "I'm not fucking playing."

"I can pay well. I'll pay whatever you want. One final blowout. What harm would it do?"

"No," I said. "No fucking way. We're done."

She giggled, pretended to be drunk, and I saw all the empty bottles around the place. Seven-fifteen start my fucking ass.

Hugh shot his load all over Debbie's slutty face, and she groaned and grunted, flicked her clit as she licked it up.

Mandy was squealing like a pig. *Stretch me! Oh fucking stretch me! Make me fucking take it!*

I could hear the noise her cunt was making all the way across the fucking room.

Petey pulled from her ass and slid into her pussy alongside Buck, and I cringed. Lorraine hadn't been teaching him that fucking well.

She raised an eyebrow. "Lad's coming along, isn't he? Remember how wet behind the ears *you* were when you first came to my door?"

"Shut up," I said. "Just shut the fuck up, Lorraine."

She pulled a face. "Don't pretend you didn't love it, Trent. Remember when I made you eat my cunt all night long? Remember when I kept you on edge for five hours straight? Remember how hard you came?" She squeezed my dick through my jeans, grabbed hard. "You remember that, Darren, I know you do."

I stepped away from her but she followed. "Fuck off," I said. "I mean it. I was here for Jodie."

"Does she know how dirty I made you? Does she know all the filthy things we did together, you and me?" She laughed. "Does she know how you made me gush all over your cock, drench you and lick it all up again? Does she know how rough you got? Does she know you've still got scars from my nails, Darren? Has she seen them?"

I made my way to the door, my eyes burning hers, not fucking trusting her enough to turn my back.

She cupped her big tits, starting tweaking her nipples. "Does she know you let me tie you up? Does she know what I did to you?"

"Stop," I said. "I fucking mean it."

"Does she know how you loved my tongue up your ass? Does she, Trent?"

"Just shut the fuck up!"

"Does she know how you cried like a baby in my arms?"

"You're a bitch," I said. "A scheming fucking bitch."

She beckoned the girls up from the floor. "Take him." She laughed. "This is what you've been waiting for, ladies, he's only being coy."

Two giggling drunks leapt into action, and Lorraine rushed me before I could brush them off. She caught me off balance and jammed me into the wall, her hands on my belt before I could stop her.

I pushed Mary off me, but Donna was already laughing in my ear, her tits pressing against me. Her hands were under my t-shirt, she giggled as she tried to pull it off me.

I heard Buck's voice. "Eh, Lorraine. Knock it fucking off, yeah?"

I felt a flash of humiliation, like I needed the guys to get me out of this fucking shit. I pushed Donna away, but Mary was back, she took up what Donna started and her mouth was on my skin, licking up my belly. It made my skin crawl.

"Stop," I said. "Just fucking stop it."

I pushed her away, but Lorraine dug her nails into my wrist. My eyes were fucking fierce, it took everything I had not to give her a backhander right across her filthy fucking mouth.

She knew I wouldn't. She smirked as my jeans dropped, laughed as Mary's hand buried in my boxers and pulled my cock out before I could push her off me.

"You've got ten fucking seconds," I said, and my voice was low and vicious. "Ten fucking seconds to back the fuck off, or I promise you'll be fucking sorry. I'm not playing, Lorraine, I'm not fucking playing."

"Pack it in, Lorraine," Buck called. "He's not fucking game."

"Ten seconds," I repeated.

The whole room stank of sex, Mandy's cunt still fucking squelching as she rode Petey's dick. Jimmy O was in her face, slapping her mouth with his cock, opportunistic prick.

Debbie was looking my way, bouncing on Hugh's dick with a stupid grin on her face.

"Five fucking seconds," I growled.

I gripped Mary's wrist, pulled it from my cock.

"You want it." Lorraine smirked. "You're hard, Trent."

Three women laughed and grabbed me, and I was ready to lose my shit and shove those skanky bitches the fuck off me and get the fuck out of there, but I didn't get chance.

Footsteps in the hallway, and a laugh I recognised.

Lorraine's face was victorious as she registered the horror on mine.

She stepped away from me, turned naked to her latest guests.

I heard Jodie's voice and I could have fucking died. "Darren's truck is here. I can't believe he actually showed up!" She was laughing. She started as she saw Lorraine, and my heart fell. "What the hell? I thought this was a... girls' night... what the..."

Her eyes met mine, and it mattered little that I shoved those bitches flying and pulled my jeans up. Lorraine sidled up to me, tried to kiss me, and I shoved her away, too.

"Oh, Darren!" she said. "Don't be such a spoilsport. Look, Jodie's here now!"

Jo's face was a fucking picture. She stared at me, only me.

"Darren..?"

The fucking horror. Those bitches at the floor around my feet, stark bollock naked. The rest of the guys in the room, rutting away on people she fucking knew.

At her fucking friend's house.

Her *naked* friend's house.

Tonya's face looked like thunder. "What the fuck is this, Trent?"

"This isn't what it fucking looks like," I snapped.

Jodie's eyes were wide, her face like a fucking ghost.

"Jo," I said. "This isn't what it fucking looks like! I came here for you."

Her lip trembled, and the guys stopped rutting. Everyone stopped everything, apart from Petey who was grunting and spurting his cum over Many Taylor's tits.

Fucking hell.

Her voice was just a whisper. "You think I came here for this? You really think I'd come here for *this*? After what I said! After everything we said!" She shook her head in exasperation, and it was so obvious. So fucking obvious.

"Jo..." I said.

But she held up her hand.

"Sorry, Jodie," Lorraine said. She put her hand on Jodie's shoulder, pulled a sad face. "I needed to show you. It was the only way. The guy's a fucking loser, he's been fucking me for years. I should've told you sooner."

I could have ripped her fucking head off.

Buck was getting dressed. "Quit it, Lorraine!" he barked.

Hugh was pulling his jeans up, Jimmy too.

Jodie looked at the floor. "You set me up? Got me out here just to show me you were fucking him too?"

"Not just me! Everyone!" Lorraine sighed. "For your own good, Jodie. You don't need him... he's not worth it."

I watched Tonya lose her shit, her face a grimace as she made to land Lorraine a sharp one on the fucking jaw, but she didn't get a chance.

The attack came from Jodie, and it took my breath. Jo slapped her good and proper, right across Lorraine's stupid smug face. The crack of it sounded right through the fucking room, and Lorraine stumbled back, dumbstruck.

"Stay away from me!" Jodie hissed. "You're a bitch, Lorraine, nothing but a skanky fucking bitch!"

I took a step towards her. "Jo," I said. "This isn't what it looks like, I promise you."

Her eyes told me everything I needed to know, brimming with tears and burning with anger. "No!" she said. "I just can't... I can't believe you... you and... *her*..."

She turned on her heel and hurried away, and I went to follow her until Tonya landed me with the punch meant for Lorraine.

"You're a stupid fucking wanker," she snapped. "I thought you'd have better taste than that shrivelled up old fucking slut."

"This isn't what it fucking looks like!" I said again. "Tonya, just fucking listen to me."

But she wouldn't. She wouldn't even hear me out.

"Leave her alone," she said. "Just leave her the fuck alone, Trent."

I followed her out to the car, but it was already running. Jodie wouldn't even look at me. I knocked on her window, but she pulled away as soon as Tonya was in the passenger seat.

"Jodie!" I called. "Jodie, this isn't fucking right! I don't want Lorraine, I never fucking have! I fucking swear it!"

She pulled away so quickly that she showered me in gravel.

CHAPTER TWENTY SIX

JODIE

I was shaking. Really shaking.

I took a seat at the kitchen table and Tonya put the kettle on. I could've done with something much stronger.

The girls knew something was up, asked me a load of questions that I answered with a fake smile and a *nothing's wrong, girls.*

They gave it a rest after a while, and laptop wars resumed as normal. I let it slide for now, content that the voices were far enough through the house that they wouldn't hear us talking.

Tonya handed me a tea and sat down opposite. "I can't believe it. Lorraine! What an absolute skank."

"She hates him... she always has... I just can't..." I shook my head. "I cried on her shoulder so many times, Tonya. Told her everything. *Everything.*"

"Turns out she had her own fucking agenda, doesn't it?"

I kept breathing, kept calm for the sake of the girls and the plus-one in my belly. "I knew he was a gigolo. I knew the shit he does. I just... *Lorraine.*"

Tonya waggled her finger. "Uh, no way, Jo. No fucking way. Don't make excuses for him, this crap was well out of order. *Well* out of order. I mean that stupid cow Mandy was one thing, but Lorraine?! Your *boss* Lorraine, your *friend* Lorraine. He should have fessed up about this shit long before now."

I shrugged. "I didn't ask. I didn't push him."

"You shouldn't have had to *ask*, Jodie. He should fucking know better."

"She said years." I put my head in my hands. "It's been going on years and I didn't even know it."

"So *she* says."

I met her eyes. "I saw it in his face, Tonya. It's been going on years, believe me."

"Well, more fool him. More fool her, too. There's no doubt she was paying for it." She paused. "You do know that, right? He clearly hasn't got feelings for her. This is just a job to him."

I didn't know anything. Didn't even know where to begin working out what I did actually know. I shrugged.

She sighed. "He wants you, Jodie. He's a fucking idiot, but he wants you."

"I'm not so sure about that."

"He said he thought you'd be there... that's why *he* was there."

"I *told* him I'd be there." His messages flashed in my mind and I groaned. "Shit. He asked me if I was at Lorraine's seedy sex party. I thought he was just being funny."

"She planned this." Tonya scowled. "All of it. Everything. She knew he was gonna be there. She set you up... set *him* up."

The betrayal smarted. It really fucking hurt. "Why would she do that?"

"I guess she wants him. I guess he's not such a useless disgrace of a man after all."

The thought of her having him made me feel sick. The whole thing made me feel sick. "I trusted her."

"Yeah, well, maybe he did, too."

I shook my head. "If he's been seeing her for years it must mean something."

"Money under his bed, that's what it means."

"Maybe."

"Definitely." She took a sip of tea. "You gonna talk to him?"

I shook my head. "Not yet. I've got to think first."

"Think about what?"

I shrugged. "About me, the girls, the baby... about how we're going to cope without the cafe wage. About getting over him."

"Is that what you want?" She looked so horrified.

"No, of course not. But I can't... not now I've seen it... not now I know what this gigolo stuff actually means. I can't walk down the street and pretend it's ok. I can't turn a blind eye and pretend it doesn't matter to me if he's fucking for money every night of the week. I can't pretend that knowing he's been fucking Lorraine for years doesn't make a difference. It makes a difference. I don't think I can even look at her again, not ever."

She let out a sigh. "She's really fucked things up for you."

"Maybe they were fucked up anyway and I just didn't know it."

"Sounds like you think she's done you a fucking favour, Jodie."

I felt the venom, my hands shaking again. "Oh no, no. I don't think she's done me a fucking favour, Tonya. She's dead to me. She's no friend of mine."

"Good," she said.

I looked at the clock. "I'd better get those girls to bed." She squeezed my hand as I stood from the table.

The girls went about their bedtime routine without too much backchat, and I was grateful. I think any extra hassle would have sent me over the edge.

Nanna must have sensed something was wrong. She took herself off to bed early and gave me a nice big hug on the way.

I pottered around as usual, doing the girls' lunch boxes and feeding the cat.

"Just stop, Jo," Tonya said. "Give yourself a break."

"Life goes on," I said. "Just got to keep on keeping on."

"No," she said. "You fucking don't, Jodie. Just give yourself a bit of time, will you?"

I stopped wiping down the side and stood for a minute, and it hit me. It really hit me. Single, jobless, and pregnant.

Oh my fucking God.

"I can't believe this is happening..." I said, and felt the tears springing up. "I'm such an idiot for thinking we could make this work... for hoping we could start over..."

"You aren't an idiot." She let out a groan. "He is. He's the idiot."

"I really thought this could be something..."

She was about to speak when there was a knock on the front door. My heartrate rocketed, and I felt sick, dizzy at the thought of a showdown.

"I'll get it," Tonya said. She pointed at the table. "Sit. Relax. I'll deal with this, don't you fucking worry."

I didn't have the energy to argue with her.

Tonya stepped out onto the porch and closed the door behind her before I could say a word.

"You've got some fucking nerve, showing up here right now."

I took out my cigarettes and she held out her hand. I gave her the pack and she took one for herself, lit up with my lighter before she handed them back.

"I need to see her," I said. "This isn't as it fucking seems."

"Have you been fucking Lorraine, yes or no?"

"Yeah," I said. "But not..."

She shook her head. "Then it's as it fucking seems, Trent. You're fucking her friend, her fucking *boss*. That skank set her up, made a fucking idiot out of her. *You* let that happen."

"Like I had any fucking idea what that bitch was up to."

She shrugged. "How many years have you been fucking that skanky old cow?"

I took a drag. "What does that matter?"

"It matters a fucking lot, Trent. How long?"

I fought the urge to smash my fist into the brickwork. "I don't fucking know, wasn't keeping tabs. Three years maybe."

"Three fucking years?!"

"Since I did the fucking calendar," I said. "Since Jo got with Brian."

"Jesus Christ."

"Yeah, well, it was a fucking mistake, wasn't it?"

She glared at me. "No. The fucking mistake was keeping it from Jodie when you two got back involved. You should have fucking said something."

"Said what? I've been fucking your fucking boss and she's been paying for it? Hope that's fucking ok? Yeah right, Tonya. Get fucking real. She'd have run for the fucking hills."

"Like now you mean?"

The thought hit me in the gut. "That's how she feels, is it?"

She sighed. "Of *course* that's how she fucking feels, Trent! Can you blame her? She walked in on you getting your end away with a load of skanky bitches she knows! People she sees every fucking day at the cafe!"

"I wasn't getting my fucking end away with anyone, Tonya. I turned up there for Jo. Lorraine told me you two were going to her seedy fucking sex party, I could hardly fucking believe it myself."

"Not *that* kind of fucking sex party. Jo thought we were going to buy fucking sex toys, for you and her! I did, too!" She shook her head. "Well, it doesn't look too fucking good, does it? That sour old bitch was hanging off your fucking dick, Trent, plain as day."

"A set up," I snapped. "It was a fucking set up." I met her eyes. "Can I see her?"

"And what are you gonna say, huh? Sorry I fucked your friend, for three fucking years? I should have told you?"

I shrugged, and I had no answer. I didn't fucking know.

"She needs to stay calm," Tonya said. "For the girls and Nanna." She paused. "This is gonna fuck her up, she needs some fucking time."

"I should just fuck off then, should I?" My voice was so bitter. "Wait for a call from her that never fucking comes?"

Tonya's voice was more bitter than mine. "*Yes*, Trent, you should just fuck off and wait and see what she wants to fucking do, if fucking anything! Have a bit of fucking respect!"

I looked at the door behind her, contemplated just bursting in. But Tonya was right. Jo needed to stay calm, get her fucking bearings. Needed to decide if she ever wanted to see a stupid piece of shit like me ever again.

"Alright," I said. "I'll go. But tell her to call me, yeah? You will tell her?"

She glared at me. "I'll tell her what you said, but she's not gonna just roll over and play doormat, Darren, she's fucking hurt. Shocked and hurt."

"Tell her I'm fucking sorry, alright?"

"I'll pass it on."

"Righto," I said.

Fuck.

Fuck all this.

My throat burned with words I wanted to say. So many fucking words, but none of them would mean shit. Not now.

"I'll be off then," I said.

"Good," she said. "It's for the best."

Not for me it fucking wasn't.

JODIE

Lorraine called first thing in the morning, and again, and again, and again, over and over leaving messages about how she *hoped I was ok*, and how *she was sorry I found out like that*. She hoped I'd be in to work in the afternoon. Like I'd ever set foot in that fucking cafe again.

I had plenty to do to keep me busy around the house. I told Nanna

I had a stomach bug and had called in sick.

"Take it easy then!" she'd said, then tutted when I'd got the ironing board out.

A baby. I was having a baby.

The thought seemed so daunting yet so surreal all in one. I couldn't imagine being a new mum again. Couldn't imagine running around after the girls with a little one in my arms.

I'd been so stupid, caught up in some silly fairy tale of me and Darren Trent. I should've learned my lesson the first time round.

I got a call from the garage number at lunchtime. I ignored it.

I got a call from a random local number I didn't recognise, and I ignored that, too.

A voicemail played Darren's voice, and it was so typically him that I put my phone on silent and chucked it in the kitchen drawer.

Call me, Jo, yeah? I just want to fucking talk to you.

I figured that was as good as it was going to get from him.

I'd have to get through this shit on my own.

In the short term I could survive on Pops' money. So much for the *experience of a lifetime.* Paying the bills would have to be hedonistic enough for now. It would see me through for a while, and then maybe I could get another local job, just until the baby came, and then... then I could...

I didn't fucking know what would happen after that.

I stared at myself in the mirror as I passed by with a load of washing and could've cried at the sad woman staring back at me. I looked washed out again, drained again, stressed again. I looked like a frump again.

I dropped the washing on the floor and reached for my foundation. I couldn't let myself go, not now, not when I'd just learned to live again.

Things would be different this time, I'd make it so.

And in the meantime I'd just keep on keeping on.

Just like I'd always done before.

TRENT

A string of voicemails went unanswered. *Call me, Jo, please. Just fucking talk to me. Jo? Jo, just pick up the fucking phone please. This isn't how it fucking seems.*

I didn't go round there again, not with the girls and Nanna home.

It tore me apart to pretend life was normal, to shake customers' hands and show interest in their stupid fucking cars.

I didn't see the girls. Didn't dare interrupt their timetables, not this week.

It wouldn't have been so fucking weird once upon a time, but now it was fucking torture.

I'd felt so close to having them back, so fucking close. But I'd blown it. I'd really fucking blown it.

All because I'd believed Lorraine's fucking bullshit.

All because I hadn't said what I really fucking meant. All because I hadn't put myself out there.

All because I'm a fucking idiot.

Friday dragged like a sonofabitch. Buck slapped me on the back at close of play and I'd barely even noticed the day go by.

"You coming out tonight? Couple down the Drum?"

I'd been in the Drum last night until closing, stumbling across the street just to crash on the sofa until morning. What difference would a re-run make?

"Alright," I said.

"Gonna get yourself a beard like mine if you don't get a razor on it, Trent."

I answered with a grunt and he sighed.

"I'll see you down there," I said.

I staggered back to my place at closing and crashed on the sofa for the second time running. I woke up the next day and couldn't even be fucked to move. It wasn't my weekend with the girls. Wasn't my weekend to take them to the bonfire night celebration on the school playing field and buy them sparklers like I had the year before.

Wasn't my weekend to be there.

I flicked through the channels and a rerun of *Top Gear* put a lump in my throat. I went into the girls' room and made their beds, sat there for a while just thinking. Just fucking moping.

I tried Jodie's number and it went straight to voicemail. I left another message.

Please, Jodie. I'm really fucking sorry.

She didn't call back.

I forced myself to have a shave and a shower. Forced myself to chuck on some clean clothes and get out through the door.

I couldn't face the bonfire celebrations – families everywhere I fucking looked – so I headed back into the Drum and propped myself at the bar.

Buck joined me at seven, the others arriving soon after. I was already well on my way.

"Christ, Trent, you been in here all fucking night or something?" Buck looked worried, like a soft fucking idiot. "Can't you just go round and fucking see her?"

I shook my head. "Nah. She doesn't want to see a cunt like me, mate."

He slapped my shoulder. "Want me to have a word?"

I flashed him a glare. "What's that supposed to fucking mean?"

He raised his hands. "I *mean* have a fucking *word*, Trent. On your fucking behalf. Chill your fucking boots, will you? Pissing hell."

"No need," I said. "It's fucked, mate."

"If you say so."

I ordered another fucking beer.

JODIE

I put a face on it but I was shaking like a leaf. I could feel Tonya staring at me as I checked my makeup for the hundredth time.

"It's dark, Jodie, nobody is gonna bloody see you."

"*I* see me," I said. "I'm doing it for me."

Bonfire night was an event I couldn't get out of, not with two girls who go crazy for sparklers and rockets and fresh doughnuts. Nanna was determined she wasn't coming this year. She could see the fireworks from the garden well enough, she claimed. I didn't have the energy to argue with her.

"Coats!" I said to the girls. "Scarves! Boots, too! It'll be muddy!"

They were a whirlwind of groans and impatience, just wanted to get the hell out to the celebrations. Like there was anything to celebrate.

I chided myself. They were kids, they had everything to celebrate, they had *life* to celebrate. And so had I. New life. The very beginning of a brand new person in my belly.

I wrapped up warm, and Tonya linked arms with me on the way.

"She won't be there," she whispered. "Even she doesn't have that much fucking gall."

"And if she is?"

She smirked, pulled me close. "And if she is you can give her a slap again. I'll give her one right after you."

I rested my head on her shoulder. "Thanks, Tonya."

I ignored the nerves in my belly. Ignored the nerves everywhere. We'd have to pass Darren's place on the way, have to pass right by the Drum, too. The likelihood he wouldn't be in either was slim to nil.

Unless he was Bang Ganging.

The thought still made me feel sick.

I took a breath. He probably wouldn't even see us, probably wouldn't care if he did. I hadn't seen him since Lorraine's house. He hadn't been near since Tonya sent him packing. I'd stopped listening to his voicemails and he hadn't turned up in person.

No Casanova crying under my window at night.

Like he'd ever cared that much.

Keep on keeping on.

The kids rushed ahead as we reached the centre of the village. I had to call them back, tell them to stay at my side. *It'll be busy*, I said. *I'll lose you in the crowd!*

Mia had whinged that she wanted to find Daisy, but she was still bloody grounded so she could rock on with that idea.

I was alright until Ruby started up.

"Can we go call on Dad? He can come with us, right?"

I couldn't find the words through the stupid lump in my throat. Tonya came to my rescue.

"Your dad's probably busy, Ruby. See him another day, yeah?"

"But it's fireworks night! He always comes to fireworks night!"

"Not today," I managed. "He's just busy, Ruby. I'll drop you at his tomorrow maybe, alright?"

She scowled at me. "This is bullshit," she said.

I stopped in my tracks and pulled her to face me. "And that's a garage word, Ruby Trent. We don't say garage words, do we?"

"I don't care!" she snapped. "It's bullshit, Mum. It's just bullshit. Where's my dad?! I WANT MY DAD!"

I rubbed my temples. "Stop," I said. "Please, Ruby, just stop. We're supposed to be having a nice evening. Sparklers, yes? You want some sparklers and some doughnuts and to see the bonfire, don't you?"

"I want my dad!" She folded her arms. "Why isn't he coming round anymore?"

I looked from Ruby to Mia and back again. Mia was quiet as a mouse, hugging herself and chewing on her scarf.

"It's only been a couple of days," I said. "He's been working."

"He's always working! It's never stopped him before!"

I sighed. "Tomorrow," I said. "I'll drop you round there tomorrow. Are we going to these fireworks, or do you want to show off and go home to bed?"

It broke my heart to see the tears in her eyes. Her bottom lip trembled, but she nodded.

"Oh, Ruby." I pulled her in to my side, squeezed her shoulder as we walked along the street.

This was shit. The whole thing was shit.

Tonya took my arm on the other side and held out her hand to Mia. Mia sighed and took it.

I choked down the tears and kept on walking, breathing through the prospect of passing through Darren Trent-ville on our way.

Just had to keep on keeping on.

TRENT

I didn't care for banter. Didn't care for a game of fucking pool, nor darts neither. Didn't want a fucking bar snack. Didn't want to go and see the fucking fireworks.

I sat at the bar and drank my beer, grunted at everyone who said hello.

The guys surrounded me as the fireworks were due to start.

"What?" I said. "What's the fucking problem?"

"You," Buck said. "You need to get home, get to the fireworks, or loosen the fuck up."

"Like fuck I do," I snapped. "Just piss off, all of you."

"Come on, Trent," Hugh said. "This isn't doing any good now, is it? Drinking like this."

I swigged back some more of my pint. "Feels pretty fucking good from where I'm sitting."

Except it didn't. It felt fucking shit.

I heard Jimmy O groan behind me. "Leave the daft shit then. Just because you blew it with your fucking missus, mate, doesn't mean you have to take it out on the whole fucking village."

I spun on my stool. "What the fuck did you say?"

Jimmy O had had a few himself, his eyes were bloodshot and he was swaying, full of mouth.

He leaned in. "I *said*, you've blown it with your fucking missus, mate, so get a fucking grip of yourself and stop the fucking moping, yeah?"

"Leave it," Buck said. "Back off, Jimmy."

He held up his hands. "Just saying the fucking truth of it. He blew it. Not my fucking fault, is it?"

"Have a bit of respect, Jimmy," Hugh said. "Christ, man."

Petey didn't say a fucking word.

I glared at Jimmy. "Seem fucking pleased about it. Happy are you? Fancy a go on her yourself?"

Buck shook his head. "Leave it, guys," he said. "Just fucking leave it. This is bullshit."

Jimmy wouldn't leave it, and I fucking knew he wouldn't. He stood tall, put his glass down on the side. "One man's loss is another man's fucking gain, Trent. Stop being such a fucking prick about it and have a game of fucking darts, yeah?"

"Your gain, that what you're fucking saying?" I stood up, slapped my own pint on the bar.

Buck's hand was on my arm. "Easy, Trent, he's just fucking drunk."

Jimmy shrugged, laughed at me. "What if it was? She's a nice girl, Jodie. I liked the way she felt on my fucking dick." He stumbled forward a step, held up his fingers. "She's a good girl, Trent, I'll give you that. Horny, like. Think she'd take my whole fucking fist if I treated her right."

"Jimmy!" Buck barked. "Just shut the fuck up, you stupid asshole!"

"Just having a fucking laugh!" he said. "Chill the fuck out."

I met his eyes, saw the stupid drunk humour there, but it was too late. The rage sprung up from nowhere, burned right the way through my fucking body.

"A whole fucking fist, eh?" I laughed a stupid fake laugh. "How about I give you a whole fucking fist, you fucking cunt?"

He didn't even see it coming. I cracked my knuckles right into his jaw and he fell like a sack of shit. I stood over him while he scrambled to his feet, ignoring the shouts from Buck and Hugh, ignoring the shouts of the pub landlord, too.

Buck tried to hold me back and Hugh went for Jimmy, but I was too wired, I shoved past both of them and swung again, but Jimmy was ready this time, he landed his fist on my fucking jaw right back and hit fucking hard. I took a step to the side, shook my head, getting my fucking balance back, and then I flew for him again, screaming blue fucking murder.

Arms and hands, and raised voices, too many people to push aside, and I was out in the cold, kicked out on my ear, trying my best to swagger like I didn't give a fuck. I spat blood onto the pavement and everyone was staring. Loads of fucking people were staring at me.

"What?" I said. "Stare all you fucking want, I don't give a fucking shit. I don't give a shit what any of you fuckers think! None of you!"

But I was wrong.

I did fucking care.

Because amongst the crowd stood Jodie, and Tonya too. My girls were at their sides, and they were staring. Staring right at me, at my stupid drunken swagger and my swollen lip. Staring at the fucking state that was their father.

Ruby's eyes were like plates, her lip trembling.

Mia looked white as a sheet.

And Jodie looked mortified. She gripped Ruby's hand so tight.

Tonya shook her head at me, and Jodie raised a hand to her open mouth.

She may have looked surprised but she shouldn't have been, not really. She'd seen this all before.

"Dad!" Ruby called. "Dad, are you alright? What happened, Dad?"

I raised a hand to keep her back. "Stay with your mum," I said. "I'm fine, Rubes."

The air was cool, and it sobered me, made me feel queasy rather than fucking drunk.

"But Dad... Dad, you're bleeding!"

I shook my head. "Stay with your mum, Ruby. I'm alright."

I turned away and couldn't look back, couldn't face it. Couldn't face seeing their disappointment. Couldn't face knowing what a fucking wanker I was.

I stumbled across the road to my place, and I could hear Ruby crying, hear Jodie telling her I was fine, just drunk, just being silly after a long day, that's all.

Silly? It was more than I fucking deserved.

I opened the door to my place and only just made it inside before the tears came.

CHAPTER TWENTY SEVEN

JODIE

The poor girls. I hugged Ruby tight and forced a smile.

"He's alright," I said. "He's just had a few too many pints, that's all."

"He was bleeding!" she cried.

"He probably stumbled into the door, beer makes you silly like that."

"He was drunk," Mia said. "Really drunk."

"He wasn't *really* drunk," I lied. "He'd just had a few, he's probably skipped dinner like a silly fool."

"Whatever, Mum," she said. "He was wrecked."

I was figuring out what to say next when Buck arrived on the scene. I groaned inside, willed him not to say anything that would make things worse. He didn't.

"Can I have a word, Jo?" he said. "In private, like."

I looked at Tonya. "I'll get the girls a Coke," she said.

I nodded.

She rallied the girls and took them off towards the Drum. I sighed once they were out of earshot.

"What the hell happened, Buck?"

He shrugged. "Guess you saw enough for yourself. Jimmy was being a prick, Trent thumped him one, took one back. Not much more to it than that."

"Sounds about right."

"Nothing's about right, Jo, not with Trent at the minute."

I didn't know what to say, so I said nothing, just waited for him to carry on.

"Lorraine set him up," he said. "He wasn't supposed to be there, had no intention of being there, only she told him you were going, you and Tonya. Told him you were after another fucking gangbang."

I stared at him. "As if I'd go behind his back for another bloody orgy, Buck. For God's sake!"

"I know that, Jo, and you know that, but she's been whispering in his ear for fucking ages, telling him you think you're too good for him, telling him you're after other people, that he's just a bit of rough, a bit of fun."

Betrayal stabbed me all over again. "She really said that?"

He nodded. "Oh yeah, and a whole lot fucking worse, too. The woman's fucking poison."

I'd be damned if I was crying over that nasty cow. I choked back my upset. "I thought she was my friend."

"Yeah, well, she wasn't. She fooled a lot of people, Trent included."

"He's been seeing her a long time, hasn't he?"

He laughed, but it wasn't malicious. "Seeing her? Wouldn't call it that. She paid good money, he did what he had to. She was just a client, Jo, she didn't mean shit to him."

The thought made me feel sick. "See, that's the thing, Buck. I thought I could handle this shit, but I can't. I just can't. I can't cope with knowing he's off fucking half the village, people I know, people I see every day. I wanted to think it was alright, that it meant nothing, just another job, but it isn't alright. It's just not."

His eyes were wide. "You think he's fucking half the village?"

"Isn't he?" I scoffed. "I'm a big girl, Buck, I can take it."

"No," he said. "He's fucking not. He bailed out of Bang Gang, gave me the diary and called it quits. He's done, Jo. Has been for fucking weeks now. Ever since you turned back up on the scene."

My stomach lurched, turned right over. I felt the blood drain from my face. "You what?"

"I can't believe he didn't tell you this, dumb fucking idiot. He hasn't fucked anyone, Jo, not since... you know. Not since you and him..."

"Nobody? Not even for money? What about the blonde in the Porsche?"

He shook his head. "Nobody, especially not the blonde in the fucking Porsche, and believe me, they've offered, plenty good enough cash as well."

I felt unsteady, a bit lightheaded. "But why... why didn't he say anything?"

"Because he's Darren fucking Trent, I guess. He's a fucking fool like that, Jo, you know he is."

I did know. I knew it all too well.

"Jesus, Buck. I don't even..."

He sighed, squeezed my shoulder. "Go after him. I know he's a prize fucking tit, and he's brought this crap on himself, but seriously, if you want him then go after him. He's falling apart, Jo, breaking his fucking heart."

"He said that?"

"He doesn't need to say it, it's written all over him."

I was shaking all over again. "I didn't think he gave a shit."

"Yeah, well, he ain't fucking helped himself in that, has he?"

"But Lorraine... and her lies..."

"That bitch hasn't done either of you any favours, that's for sure." He smiled at me. "He fucking loves you, Jo, always has. Loves those girls, too."

I looked across the road, the lights were on upstairs.

"Go," he said. "He'll only be moping up there."

I took a breath, squeezed his hand. "Thanks," I said. "At least someone told me what the hell was going on."

"Tell him he can buy me a pint when he pulls his head out of his fucking ass."

I smiled. "I'll let him know."

My legs were wobbly as I climbed the steps up to Darren's place. I thought about knocking then decided against it, tried the door on the off chance. It was open.

The place stank of beer and cigarettes, the hallway dark. I fumbled around for the light switch, flicked it on.

"Darren?"

He came from the bathroom, his face dripping. He pulled a towel from the hook, wiped himself down. His lip was swollen, cut. His t-shirt was splattered with blood.

"Come to have a go at me?" he said. "Don't bother, I know I was a fucking prick."

He threw the towel aside and walked into the kitchen. I followed him, kept my distance.

"Are you going to tell me what happened?"

He shrugged. "Punched Jimmy O, he punched me back." He pointed to the kettle. "You want a cuppa?"

I shook my head. "Lorraine lied about me, I know that now."

"Lorraine fucking lied about a lot, Jodie."

"I wasn't there for an orgy, Darren, I can't believe you seriously thought I was."

"She said you were going to her sex party. I asked *you* if you were going to her sex party. You said yes."

"I was going to a girls' night! I was going to buy some stupid sex toys!"

"I know that now," he said. "Christ, Jo, she spouts some lies. I can't believe I was such a gullible fucking prick."

"Yeah, well, I guess that makes two of us."

He flicked the kettle on anyway, grabbed a couple of mugs from the drainer.

He stared right at me and it burned. "It wasn't how it looked. I wasn't there for that."

"It looked bad, Darren. It looked really fucking bad."

"I know how it looked, Jodie, but that's not... I wasn't about to fuck anyone. It was a pissing ambush."

"You never said you'd given it up, I never expected you had. It's just... *Lorraine*. She's my boss. *Was* my boss. *Was* my friend, too. How do you think that makes me feel?"

"I haven't been anywhere near Lorraine in months. Must've made her fucking crazy, like. Scheming fucking bitch."

He made me a tea and I took it. We stood drinking in the kitchen like this was normal.

"How long were you seeing her?" I didn't know why I was asking, since I already knew. I guess I just needed to hear it. Needed to hear a lot of things.

He shrugged. "Couple of years. She signed us up for the calendar, for some kids' charity she's on the board for. Came to me after, said she wanted a bit extra."

My heart was racing. "That was Lorraine?! *She* was your first client?"

"Yeah, the only client for fucking ages, too."

I thought back three years, to me still crying on her shoulder over Darren's engagement to Stacey. To the way she'd pushed me to online dating, told me to get over it once and for all.

He sighed. "You were getting with Brian. I'd just done the pissing calendar. The money sounded good."

"And it just went on and on? You didn't... fall for her..."

He pulled a face. "Hell no."

I nodded. "Alright. So she's a crazy twisted bitch. We know that now."

His eyes met mine. "I'm sorry, Jo. I fucked up. Should've said some things."

"We both fucked up, Darren. *I* should've said some things, too. I should've been firmer about this Bang Gang stuff, should have pushed to find out where we stood. I should've asked who you were fucking, should have found out what was going on."

He put his mug on the side. "No, Jo. *I* should've told *you* where we stood on the Bang Gang stuff, it was my gig."

A stupid rush of emotion bubbled up, I struggled to choke it back down. "Why didn't you? Why didn't you say anything?"

He didn't flinch. "Scared of being a fucking fool. Lorraine told me you weren't interested, said you were after an orgy and nothing else. She said you were chasing something better, *someone* better."

"And you believed her?!"

"Guess I half believed it myself and she put the nail in the coffin."

I sighed. "But why?! Why would you think that?"

"Because I'm no Brian, Jo. I'm just a bit of fucking rough, aren't I? I don't like fucking opera and strolls in the sunshine. I don't talk all posh like he did."

I shook my head. "Not this again! Jesus! I didn't even love Brian, Darren! I met Brian because I needed to move on, because you were engaged! Because I couldn't live my whole life alone while you married someone else!"

"I'd never have married someone else!" he snapped.

"You have a funny fucking way of showing it!" I snapped back.

"And here we are, back here again," he groaned. "Round and round in fucking circles."

"Seems that way."

I sipped my tea and felt sick. I willed it to ease off.

He touched his lip and it bled again.

"You need to clean that up," I said.

"Already done it."

I sighed. "Properly. Do you have any antiseptic cream?"

He smirked. "Yeah, right."

I tutted, starting rooting in my bag. "You have two girls, Darren, antiseptic cream isn't some kind of crazy novelty." I pulled out a couple of Ruby's sweets and some plasters. The antiseptic cream was right at the bottom. I pulled out an antibacterial wipe and closed the distance between us. "Can I?"

He grunted, nodded his head.

I wiped his lip and he didn't even flinch, just stared at me. I put some cream onto my finger and dabbed it on. It made my tummy flutter.

"I'm not a baby," he said. "Thanks, though."

A baby. My legs felt wobbly.

He checked his t-shirt, saw the blood splatter. "Jimmy made quite a fucking mess of me." He slipped past me and headed down the hall. I followed him to his bedroom doorway, stared at him as he sat on his bed, pulled his t-shirt off over his head and found a fresh one.

Now or never.

I took a breath.

"I'm pregnant," I said.

He stopped moving, stopped doing anything. Stopped even breathing, I think.

A long silence, and we just looked at each other.

"Well?" I said. "Are you going to say something?"

He looked at the floor. "Is it, um. Is it mine?"

My cheeks burned, horror washing over me. I put my hands on my belly, fought the urge to cry. He looked up and saw my face, and his eyes widened.

"Of course it's yours!" I spat. "Jesus, Darren, how could you even think it wouldn't be?!"

I shook my head, reeling. I turned away and propped myself against the doorframe.

"I didn't know!" he said. "For fuck's sake, Jo, I've had that bitch Lorraine in my head, spouting fucking all sorts. You came to me for a fucking gangbang, that's what you wanted! Another one, too! How am I supposed to know what to think? All this new hair and clothes and fancy makeup, how am I supposed to know what you're doing? What you want? Who you're fucking seeing?"

"I told you I loved you!" I said. I couldn't even look at him. "I can't believe you'd think that of me after all these years. I wanted *you*, Darren! I always wanted *you*!" The tears came, welled up. I sniffed them back but he heard me.

"Fucking hell, Jo, I'm sorry. I'm sorry, alright!" He kicked the bedside table. "I'm such a fucking prick, I never know what to fucking say. Always putting my fucking foot in it."

I wiped my eyes, turned back around. "Stop," I said. "I'm ok. We just need to talk... need to plan... I don't work at the cafe anymore and I'm scared... I need to know you'll help me... *if* you'll help me..."

He looked like I'd slapped him. "Of course I'll fucking help you."

I choked a sob of relief. "Thanks," I said. "I'm happy, I think. I mean it's crazy, and it was stupid, and I'm scared, and it's all messed up, but I'm happy."

He nodded. "That's good."

"That's all you've got to say, is it? *That's good*?" I shrugged. "Say something, Darren! For once in your life just fucking say something, will you? Tell me how you feel! Tell me anything! Just give me *something*! I'm out on a limb here and I'm all alone!"

"You're never alone, Jo," he said. "I'm always right fucking here."

I brushed stupid tears away, and he fumbled in his bedside drawer.

My heart raced as he shoved his hand to the back, rustled around in the paperwork.

No.

Please God no.

He pulled out the ring box and my heart turned cold. So cold.

He dropped to one knee, and opened the box, just like that, on his bedroom carpet amongst his dirty clothes.

I couldn't breathe. Couldn't fucking think.

"Will you marry me, Jo? Say you'll fucking marry me." His eyes were so intense.

I pulled a face, a horrible face. "Good God, no!" I said.

TRENT

I stumbled to my feet, reeling. Feeling like a stupid fucking idiot.

"But I thought... you said you..."

Her eyes were so cold. "You want me to wear someone else's ring?! Some other woman's ring? Like being second choice isn't bad enough without having Stacey's fucking engagement ring on my finger, Darren!" She put her hand to her forehead, paced back and forth. "I can't believe you'd ask me that, with *her* ring!"

I stared at the box, mute. Just fucking mute.

It took me a second to find my tongue.

"This was never Stacey's fucking ring, Jo! Jesus Christ, what do you fucking take me for?" I rooted in the bedside drawer, threw out papers until I found the receipt. I handed it to her and she took it, eyes wide. "It was *your* fucking ring! It was always *your* ring! She found it, thought it was for her, like I'd have ever fucking proposed to her! I never loved *her*, Jo! I loved *you*, I always loved *you*!" I stared at her as she read the recept. "She ditched me when she found out the truth, and I was glad. I was fucking glad!"

"Carmarthen..." she said, and her voice was so low, so faint. "When Ruby was just a baby... that year we went... stayed in the caravan with Mum and Dad..."

"Yes!" I said. "Mia won that crappy pink plastic ring in the arcade and it was too big for her. You wore it on your ring finger all day, and it fit, can you remember? You flashed it in my face and gave me a smile and I knew you'd say yes. I hoped you'd say yes! I went out the next morning for bacon and eggs, and I drove back into town, went to the jewellers in the market square, the posh one. You thought I'd been to the slot machines, but I hadn't! I took the plastic ring from the draining board. You'd left it there when you were washing up. Mia asked where it was and you looked for it, said you'd have to win another one, but it was in my pocket, Jo! It was in my pocket the whole time, I took it to them and they measured it, used it for size!" I reached up into the wardrobe, pulled out an old shoebox. I threw the contents on the bed, old pictures and letters and postcards, all of them from Jo, all of them about Jo. I found the plastic ring and held it up. "See? It was *your* ring, Jodie! I wanted to propose to *you*!"

I stared at her and she stared back.

I sighed, ran my fingers through my hair. "We came home and I got that big taxi job in at the garage, long fucking hours. It was shit, I was knackered, and I lost you! We fell apart those couple of months, I watched it happen, and I had that fucking ring in that fucking drawer the whole fucking time! We were going to go back on holiday! To stay in that same caravan again! I wanted to propose on the beach! I wanted to make it all fucking romantic, like, but it was too late. We were long fucking done by then, you went on your own!"

"I didn't think you were happy... I didn't think you wanted me..." She let out a sob, and I felt it in my gut.

"Jesus, Jodie, I always fucking wanted you. I never fucking

377

wanted anything else!"

She read the receipt again as though she couldn't quite believe it. "You never said anything, never tried to get me back..."

"I wanted to," I said. "But you were moving in with Nanna and busy at the cafe. You seemed so fucking sure!"

"I wasn't sure!" she said. "I was never sure! I cried every fucking night for a year, Darren! Over a year!"

"Well, we're both fucking hopeless then, aren't we?" I sat on the bed, completely fucking spent, twisting that pink plastic ring in my fingers.

She came and sat beside me, so near and yet so fucking far. "I always hoped you'd come back, I really did. I always hoped maybe one day we'd make it. And then there was Stacey... and it broke my heart... I couldn't even..." She took a breath. "I thought you were going to marry her, I thought our girls would be bridesmaids..."

"Never," I said. "I'd never have married her."

"And then you split up... but you never said... you never..."

"You were with Brian," I said. "By the time I'd got my act together enough to take the risk, you were already with Brian. And there was Lorraine... she said you didn't want me, said you were long over it..."

"That fucking bitch."

"Don't I fucking know it." I'd never needed a cigarette so bad. My leg was tapping. "I haven't fucked anyone," I said. "Not since the night you came here."

"I know," she said. "Buck told me."

I smiled. "Interfering prick."

She laughed, a quiet laugh. "Good job he is."

"Yeah, I'll have to buy him a pint."

"He said that..."

378

"I bet he fucking did." I dared to reach out, took her hand, praying she didn't fucking pull away.

She didn't.

She took the plastic ring from me and slipped it on her ring finger. "Still fits," she said.

My breath caught in my throat. "I fucking love you, Jodie. I always loved you."

"Can I see it?" she said. She gestured to the ring box. "Since it was mine and all..."

"It's *still* yours," I said. I passed her the box.

She flipped it open and her eyes welled up. I stared at her staring at that ring and my heart was pounding so hard I could hear it in my ears.

"Ask me again," she said. "Unless you're too drunk to mean it."

"I'm not fucking drunk," I said. "Not anymore, and even if I was I'd still fucking mean it."

I dropped down to the floor at the side of the bed, took the box from her and held it up, making myself say it for the second fucking time, even though my throat was dry and my heart was going fucking crazy. "Marry me, Jodie. Will you marry me? Please say you'll fucking marry me, I'm out on a fucking limb here."

She looked into my eyes. "This isn't for the girls, right? It's not for the baby, either?"

"No," I said. "Christ, Jo, I love those girls more than I love life itself, and I'll love the new one just as fucking much, but this is about you. It's always been about you." I closed my eyes. Made myself say it. "I'm not so good with words, Jodie. Fuck knows, I'm not. But I know what I want. I want to come home, I want to be where you are. I can't fucking stand being here without you. Please, Jo, just let me come home. I'd give anything to come home."

I heard a little choke, felt her shaking. I dared to open my eyes and hers were wet.

"Yes," she said.

"Yes?" I had fucking shivers. "You serious? You'll marry me?"

"Yes, I'll marry you!" She was smiling. "My God, Darren, it's what I always wanted. Always."

"And I can come home?" I took a deep breath. "I can come home with you? For good?"

She wrapped her arms around my neck and it was the greatest thing I've ever felt.

"You better fucking had do," she said.

JODIE

The ring fit. It fit.

It sparkled under Darren's bedroom light like the most beautiful star I'd ever seen. Only it wasn't Darren's bedroom light, not anymore.

He finished up packing some stuff into a suitcase. Dropped it by the bedroom door.

"That should do for now," he said.

I smiled. "We'll come back for the rest."

He nodded.

I pulled him close, brushed my thumb so gently against his sore lip. "We've got two girls out there itching to catch the rest of the fireworks. I promised them doughnuts and sparklers."

He raised his eyebrows. "Then they shall have doughnuts and sparklers, I'll pop back for the case after." He pressed his hand to my belly. "How far gone?"

"A couple of weeks," I said. "It's early."

"Too early to tell the girls."

I nodded. "We'll tell them at Christmas. An extra surprise."

"Sounds good to me."

"Sounds good to me, too."

He sighed. "We'll do things different this time round, Jo. I'll be home for dinner, I'll help with the baby, make sure things are better this time."

"I know," I said. "We're different people now, Darren. Different but the same, maybe a little older and wiser, hey?"

He laughed. "Not so sure about that. I don't feel so fucking wise, Jodie. Older, that's true enough."

I wrapped my arms around his neck, and his thumbs brushed my cheeks, held me there. When he kissed me he tasted of beer and blood. He smelled like Darren Trent, too. Of oil and cigarettes and that cool blue shower gel he's been using forever.

"I love you, Jo," he said. "I'll always fucking love you."

"And I love you," I said. "I'm glad I'm having another of your babies. We make such beautiful children, Darren."

He grinned and his eyes were beautiful. "Good job," he said. "Because chances are you'll be having another, too."

I pulled away and took his hand, walked past his suitcase into the hallway. Fireworks were calling. Fireworks and our beautiful girls.

"*Another*?" I asked. "Jeez, Darren, how many kids do you want?!"

He laughed. "Ain't about that, Jo. Can't seem to fucking look at you without getting you pregnant. We'll end up with a whole fucking network of garages at this fucking rate."

"Trent and sons." I grinned.

He grinned right back. "Trent and fucking daughters, more like it."

Tonya had already got the girls their doughnuts. They were covered in icing sugar, licking their sticky fingers.

I squeezed Darren's hand as we approached, careful to keep my ring from view.

Ruby saw us first. "Daddd!" she squealed.

She bounded over and launched herself into his arms, full of questions about his face and whether he butt-hurt someone in the pub again.

"Think I might have done," he said. "Sorry, Rubes, sometimes your dad can be a bit of a prick." He dropped her to the ground and took her hand, took Mia's too. He crouched down, at Ruby's height and looked up at me. "Can I tell them?"

I nodded. "I think you best had."

Ruby's eyes were wide. "Tell us what, Dad?"

"Me and your mum. We're getting married. I'm moving in with you, if you'll have me. If that's alright?" He looked between them, one to the other, but they didn't speak, didn't say a word. "I'd really like that," he said. "We can be a proper family again, I'll be there every day, every night... if that's ok? Is that ok, girls?"

I looked at Tonya and her mouth was open wide. She fanned her face, and she was welling up, I saw it.

Ruby bit her lip, and her face crumpled. It made my breath catch in my throat.

"Yeah," she said. "That's ok!" She clung onto his neck and she was crying. "You're really coming home, Dad? Really really?"

"Really really," he said, and I'm sure his voice was thick. He looked up at Mia. "How do you feel about that, Mia? Can I come home? You alright with that?"

She nodded and her lip was going too. "Yeah, that's ok... that's really ok..." Her cool facade burst open and she wrapped her arms around my waist. "Thanks, Mum."

"Don't thank me," I said, and my voice was wobbly. "Your dad was the one who proposed."

I showed them the ring, and Tonya crammed in, too.

"Beautiful." Ruby grinned. "Like a princess ring!"

"That's really beautiful, Mum," Mia said.

"Wow, Jo, that's really something," Tonya said.

I took a breath, smiled at Darren. "Yes, it really is."

I reached for his hand and he squeezed right back. Took hold of Ruby's with his other and I took hold of Mia's. She took hold of Tonya's and I laughed, started the walk over to the fireworks.

Ruby started waffling on and it made my heart soar.

We can watch Top Gear, Dad! And you'll have to watch Question King with Nanna, too. We all watch it! You'll read me a bedtime story, won't you? Can I come to the garage with you before school? Will Mum be Mrs Trent now? Can I be a bridesmaid? We have fish and chips on a Thursday, you can have them too if you like!

I was enjoying the monologue when a flash of expensive highlights appeared in the crowd in front of us.

Darren saw them too. His fingers crushed mine.

"Shall we turn back?" he whispered.

I shook my head. "When have you ever turned away from a confrontation in your life, Darren Trent?" I smirked and kept on walking.

Lorraine's jaw dropped right open when she saw us, she turned to face me, and plastered a huge fake grin on her face.

"Jodie!" she said. "I've been trying to get hold of you, I just wanted to say..."

I flashed her a smile, one of my finest, and then I gave the bitch the fucking finger.

"Stay away from my family you skanky arsed hoe," I said. "You can go fuck yourself."

I brushed past her as she gawped and Darren was laughing. He dropped my hand long enough to light up a cigarette, and Ruby was right there staring up at me, her mouth was open as we watched Lorraine make an exit.

"Mum! You just used garage talk! I think you went and butt-hurt her! You butt-hurt Lorraine! Real bad, too!"

I ruffled her hair and smiled at Darren, and then I sighed.

"Sometimes people get butt-hurt," I said. "And that's ok. Sometimes in life you've just got to give people the finger and tell them they can go fuck themselves." I smiled at her. "Just not too bloody often, Ruby, and not at school. Deal?"

She grinned her freckly face off.

"Deal!" she said.

The fireworks were the best I'd ever fucking seen.

EPILOGUE

JODIE

It was still dark when the door creaked open. The patter of Ruby feet sounded across the carpet, and then I felt her, her bony knees clambering up the bed, digging into my legs through the covers. She flung herself onto her back between Darren and me. I pretended to be asleep when I felt him move, just to hear their conversation.

I love listening to those two.

"Dadddd!" she whispered. "I think Father Christmas has been!"

"You think, Rubes?"

"Yessss!" She giggled. "I crept downstairs and there's presents *everywhere*. Shhh! Don't tell Mum. She said no sneaking! Said to stay in bed in the morning until the sun comes up or the shit will fly!"

"She said that, did she?"

"No, but that's what she meant..."

I tried to hold back a laugh.

"I think your mum can hear you well enough, Rubes. I think you're well and truly busted." He tickled her until she squealed.

"Little Ruby Sneaky-pants," I groaned. I pulled her close and her hair was a bird's nest, crazy curls against my cheek. I reached out for Darren, gave his arm a squeeze. "What time is it?"

He turned the alarm clock to face me. "Not even six."

"Bloody hell, Ruby. The sun's not even close to coming up." I yawned and flicked on the lamp.

"But he's beeeeeeen!" Ruby protested. "I heard him!"

Darren raised an eyebrow, brushed a curl from her forehead. "You heard him, did you? That right?"

She nodded. "And his reindeers. I heard them, too!"

"Good job you didn't catch him," I said. I flashed Darren a cheeky smile. "He'd have been embarrassed if you'd have caught him drinking your dad's beer."

Her eyes widened. "He drank your beer, Dad?!"

He nodded, pulled a fake scowl. "He did, liberty-taking asshole. He drank it all last night and left me none. Gonna tell that chubby prick what I think of him if he comes back round here again."

I couldn't stop smiling. "He had quite a party, I think. Made quite a racket."

"I think he bloody well did," Darren said. He reached out and brushed a thumb across my cheek. I took his hand, kissed his knuckles.

Christmas.

Family Christmas. All of us.

I'd dreamed of this for so long.

"So?" Ruby demanded. "Can I go get my presents now? Mia's awake too, she's just pretending to be all grown up and asleep, just because she's a *teenager* now."

"What about Nanna?" I said. "You'll have to go and see if she's awake. She might be flat out though, so don't be too..."

Ruby was off like a cannon before I'd even finished, announcing it was Christmas morning with enough volume to wake the whole fucking street, not just Nanna.

"...loud," I finished.

I listened to her yelling at Nanna to get her butt out of bed and I giggled, pulled a pillow over my face, but Darren was right there. He took it off me and kissed my neck until I squirmed.

He slipped his hands under the covers, over the little bump of my belly, and lower. I tingled all over, my breaths coming shorter. "Steady there," I whispered. "I don't think we're going to get away with a lie in somehow..."

"Appears fucking not," he growled. "That means an early night's on the cards then, doesn't it?"

I reached for him, pulled his mouth to mine. "I guess it does."

I dragged myself out of Darren's arms and out of bed. He tugged on a pair of jeans as I wrapped up in a dressing gown.

"Christmas morning," he said. "This'll be the best yet, Jo."

I knew it. My smile told him so.

The kids were already poised for action. We'd barely taken a seat on the sofa as they started tearing into their presents. Nanna was on the edge of her chair, her eyes twinkling as she giggled along with the girls. I linked Darren's fingers in mine and slipped them inside my dressing gown to rest on my swollen belly. The girls were too engrossed to notice.

Darren made all the right noises.

That's sweet, that is, Mia. Well tidy, like.

Father Christmas has done you bloody proud, Rubes. That's well cool.

Let's have a look at that. Pretty damn awesome.

Might have to forgive him for drinking my beer at this rate.

It was all him. He'd gone crazy this year, no expense spared. I'd told him off, told him he'd turn them into spoiled little brats at this rate, but he'd had none of it.

I just wanna see their faces, Jo. I just wanna see them smile.

I watched him watching them, and I think he was even more excited than they were. I told him so.

Ruby tore open a *Top Gear* box set and I took that back.

Nanna started on the brandy at breakfast time with a little nod Darren.

It's Christmastime, Nanna, get it down your neck.

He put the stupid Christmas songs album on in the kitchen and Ruby made us all wear ridiculous Santa hats. The pom-pom kept falling in my face as I prepared the veg with Darren, but the hell would she let me take it off.

"When are your parents getting here?" Darren asked.

"Midday, same as yours," I said.

I was nervous. I felt the jitters. *Good jitters.*

"And we're gonna tell them, right? Today? Everyone?"

I nodded. Smiled. "Today, yeah."

"Righto," he said, and he couldn't stop grinning.

We fucked up dinner a little but Darren dished out enough Christmas wine that nobody really cared. Who even likes turkey anyway? The sprout bowl remained filled to the brim, and the pigs in blankets disappeared like liquid gold. Standard.

Except nothing was standard about today.

The whole thing felt magical. Amazing. Just... right.

Darren and his dad made toasts to our health, our good fucking fortune, and the wedding we were having in March.

It was all booked, everything. Everything signed, sealed and put on order. The local church, the vicar, the after party in a heated marquee at the back of the Drum – Darren's idea, not mine.

I'd wanted to keep it small. Special, but reasonably priced, nothing too extravagant, not with the baby on the way. The pomp and circumstance didn't matter anyway, so long as Darren and the girls were there.

That's all that mattered.

I'd made the decision to use Pops' money for it. Darren had protested, said *no fucking way* in typical Darren Trent style, but I'd argued it. Stood my ground.

The experience of a lifetime, I'd said. *The experience of my lifetime. I can't think of a better way to spend it. I want to spend it this way, Darren. It's what Pops' would have wanted.*

It's what I want.

The experience of my lifetime would definitely be walking up that aisle and seeing Darren Trent waiting for me, that was sure enough.

So that's what we'd done, put the whole lot into the wedding – including the four hundred in cash stuffed in that bloody gangbang envelope. I'd giggled like a girl when Darren handed that back over.

He started fidgeting after pudding, kept flashing me glances amongst the conversation.

I met his eyes and nodded as my dad finished up the story about the couple who'd robbed the TV from their guesthouse.

My tummy fluttered as Darren cleared his throat and told everyone we had another Christmas present to spill the beans about. Something that *wouldn't be here until the summer but was definitely on order.*

He stood at my side with his hand on my shoulder, and I felt so stupidly proud, so happy, I couldn't help the tears spilling down my cheeks.

"Oh, Jodie, what is it, love?" Nanna said and all eyes were on me. Worried eyes.

I took a breath, wiped the tears with the back of my hand. "I'm just happy," I said, "happier than I've ever been." I whipped out the envelope from my pocket and gave it to Darren. He opened it up and pulled out the scan, held it up for the whole table to see.

I focused on the the girls, desperate for their reaction. Ruby's jaw dropped open wide, Mia's too.

"A baby?!" Ruby squealed. "Do I get a brother? A *real* brother?"

My heart melted and I reached out for her hand. "Not sure about a brother, Ruby, but a baby, yes. We're having a baby!"

Mia smiled, then frowned, folded her arms. "Does this mean I have to share my room with Ruby monster?"

Darren answered before I could. "Not when I've finished the extension, Mia. Nanna's having a nice downstairs bedroom, all kitted out flash, aren't you, Nanna? Will be just the job, like."

Nanna grinned. "For my knees," she said to Darren's mum and dad.

My mum took my hand and pulled me in for a hug, and the whole table was full of congratulations. It felt amazing. *I* felt amazing.

My dad had to wipe his eyes on a napkin, and Darren rolled his eyes, slapped him on the back and told him to *man up, Pops*. They shook hands and my dad congratulated Darren on the *good work*.

I flushed as Darren met my eyes, that stare of his so bloody intense as he told my dad it had been a *fucking pleasure*.

"Baby number three!" my mum said. "You'll end up with a whole load of garages at this rate, Darren, just to fit them all in the family business!"

I laughed. "Trent and daughters," I said. "It's already been decided."

"Now all we need is to make Jodie a bloody Trent, too," Darren said. "About bloody time as well."

But I'd *always* been Jodie Trent, right from those days at the bus stop all that time ago when he'd let me bum his cigarettes and I'd told him my name.

THE END

ACKNOWLEDGEMENTS

Johnny, my incredible editor, here we are again! Another book completed, another fantastic experience working with you. Thank you so much for everything, I couldn't do this without you. <3

Letitia, for the awesome cover. You are amazing! Thank you so much for the brilliant design.

Leigh, for the beautiful formatting. Excellent work, thank you so much!

Tracy, my awesome and tireless PA, I totally love your face. Thank you for all the hard work and enthusiasm, I'm so honoured to have you on my team.

To my amazing beta readers, thank you so much for the incredible feedback! Particular thanks to Siobhan and Louise, you ladies really helped me with this one. Thank you!

Michelle and Lesley, your support is incredible, thank you so much!

To my amazing reader group, you ladies (and gents) make me smile so hard! Thank you so much for your support and enthusiasm, it really does mean the world to me!

Blogger, authors, reviewers – I'm so lucky to have the support of so many people in this awesome community. Thank you all so very much for your faith, your enthusiasm, and for spreading the word about my books. <3

To my incredible friend Maria, this one is for you. Jodie has so much of you in her – the way you work so hard, the way you give so much, the way you care so brilliantly for your girls. They are a credit to you, and you are an inspiration to me. Love you loads. x

Richard, thank you so much for taking the time to teach me the finer details of being a mechanic, it was seriously appreciated. You're someone I've come to count on, and inspired so much of Darren Trent – I guess that's where the biggest thanks of all is due. (RW Services in Ewyas Harold, everyone – I cannot recommend them enough. They've been taking care of our cars for over four years now and have always done us proud.) ☺

To regulars of the Dog and the Temple – I've enjoyed hanging out with you all in the name of village research, thank you for the stories. ☺

Huge thanks to my lovely cousin Laura for Ruby and Mia - you pick such beautiful names for your kids, and have such beautiful kids to match up to them. Your Facebook stories entertain me no end. <3

So many friends to thank! Lisa, Dom, Jo, Sue, Marie, Lauren, Tom, Kate, Hanni, Kristeen, Marie... I'm so honoured to know you all. Thank you all for putting up with my incessant book-speak!

Jon, your support means everything. I love the life we have together and wouldn't want to do this with anyone else. Your encouragement and love are always felt and always appreciated. I love you. X

My amazing family, who are the best cheerleaders I could ever wish for. Mum, Dad, Nan and Brad – I love you all very much. The only good thing about finishing a novel (which always requires leaving a little bit of my soul behind) is that I get to spend more time with you. X

And of course, to my readers! Thank you for taking the time to read Bang Gang, I hope so much that you enjoyed Darren and Jodie's story. It's because of you that I get to spend my days writing, and there are simply no words to describe my gratitude. X

ABOUT JADE

Jade has increasingly little to say about herself as time goes on, other than the fact she is an author, but she's plenty happy with this. Living in imaginary realities and having a legitimate excuse for it is really all she's ever wanted.

Jade is as dirty as you'd expect from her novels, and talking smut makes her smile.

She lives in the Herefordshire countryside with a couple of hounds and a guy who's able to cope with her inherent weirdness.

She has a red living room, decorated with far more zebra print than most people could bear, and fights a constant battle with her addiction to Coca-Cola.

Find Jade (or stalk her – she loves it) at:
http://www.facebook.com/jadewestauthor
http://www.twitter.com/jadewestauthor
http://www.jadewestauthor.com

Sign up to her newsletter via the website, she won't spam you and you may win some goodies. :)

Made in the USA
Middletown, DE
11 October 2024

62440433R00221